THE GANGSTER

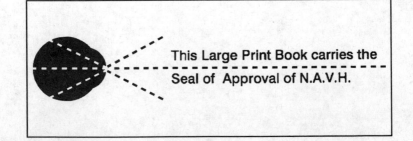

This Large Print Book carries the
Seal of Approval of N.A.V.H.

AN ISAAC BELL ADVENTURE

THE GANGSTER

CLIVE CUSSLER
AND JUSTIN SCOTT

WHEELER PUBLISHING
A part of Gale, Cengage Learning

GALE
CENGAGE Learning®

Farmington Hills, Mich • San Francisco • New York • Waterville, Maine
Meriden, Conn • Mason, Ohio • Chicago

GALE
CENGAGE Learning®

Copyright © 2016 by Sandecker, RLLLP.
Interior illustrations by Roland Dahlquist.
Wheeler Publishing, a part of Gale, Cengage Learning.

Wheeler Publishing Large Print Hardcover.
The text of this Large Print edition is unabridged.
Other aspects of the book may vary from the original edition.
Set in 16 pt. Plantin.

LIBRARY OF CONGRESS CIP DATA ON FILE.
CATALOGUING IN PUBLICATION FOR THIS BOOK
IS AVAILABLE FROM THE LIBRARY OF CONGRESS

ISBN-13: 978-1-4104-8486-4 (hardcover)
ISBN-10: 1-4104-8486-6 (hardcover)

Published in 2016 by arrangement with G. P. Putnam's Sons, an imprint of Penguin Publishing Group, a division of Penguin Random House LLC

Printed in the United States of America
1 2 3 4 5 6 7 20 19 18 17 16

CAST OF CHARACTERS

1895

Antonio Branco Immigrant Sicilian "pick and shovel man."

The padrone Labor contractor, Antonio Branco's boss.

Isaac Bell, Doug, Andy, Larry, Jack, Ron College freshman classmates.

Mary Clark Student at Miss Porter's School.

Eddie "Kansas City" Edwards Van Dorn detective.

1906

White Hand

Maria Vella Giuseppe Vella's twelve-year-old daughter.

Giuseppe Vella New York excavation contractor.

David LaCava Little Italy banker, proprietor of Banco LaCava.

Sante Russo Giuseppe Vella's foreman and blaster.

Black Hand

Antonio Branco Wealthy wholesale grocer, Catskill Aqueduct purveyor.

Charlie Salata Italian street gang leader; Black Hand extortionist.

Vito Rizzo Salata Gang lieutenant.

Ernesto Leone A counterfeiter.

Roberto Ferri A smuggler.

Sicilian groom

Francesca Kennedy A killer.

Irish Gangsters

Ed Hunt, Tommy McBean Cousins, Gopher Gang graduates, founders of the West Side Wallopers.

Van Dorn Agency Private Detectives

Joseph Van Dorn Founder and Chief Investigator, "The Boss," the "old man."

Isaac Bell Van Dorn's top man, founder of Black Hand Squad.

Wally Kisley, Mack Fulton Explosives expert and safecracking expert, respectively; partners known as "Weber & Fields."

Harry Warren Born Salvatore Guaragna, head of New York Gang Squad.

Archibald Angell Abbott IV Blue-blood New Yorker, a "Princeton man," former actor, boxer, Bell's best friend.

Aloysius "Wish" Clarke A drinking man.

Eddie "Kansas City" Edwards Rail yard specialist.

Bronson San Francisco field office.

Grady Forrer Head of Research, New York field office.

Scudder Smith Former newspaper reporter experienced in vice.

Eddie Tobin Apprentice detective.

Richie Cirillo Underage apprentice detective.

Helen Mills Van Dorn intern, Isaac Bell's protégée, Bryn Mawr College student, daughter of U.S. Army brigadier general Gary Tannenbaum Mills.

Friends of Isaac Bell

Marion Morgan His fiancée.

Enrico Caruso World-renowned opera tenor.

Luisa Tetrazzini Coloratura soprano, the "Florentine Nightingale," a rising star.

Tammany Hall

Boss Fryer "Honest Jim" Fryer, political kingpin of New York City.

Brandon Finn Boss Fryer's henchman.

"Rose Bloom" Brandon Finn's paramour.

Alderman James Martin Member of the "Boodle Board."

"Kid Kelly" Ghiottone Former bantam-

7

weight prizefighter, saloon keeper, Tammany Hall's man in Little Italy.

Plutocrats

J. B. Culp Wall Street magnate, Hudson Valley aristocrat, inheritor of steamboat and railroad fortunes, founder of the Cherry Grove Gentlemen's Society.

Daphne Culp J. B. Culp's wife.

Brewster Claypool J. B. Culp's lawyer.

Warren D. Nichols Banker, philanthropist, member of Cherry Grove Society.

Lee, Barry Prizefighters, J. B. Culp's bodyguards and sparring partners.

Cops

Captain Mike Coligney Head of the NYPD's Tenderloin Precinct.

Lieutenant Joe Petrosino Founder of the NYPD's Italian Squad.

Chris Lynch Secret Service Counterfeit Squad.

Rob Rosenwald New York District Attorney sleuth.

Commissioner Bingham New NYPD official shaking up the department.

Sheriff of Orange County

Cherry Grove Bordello
Nick Sayers The proprietor.
Jenny A resident.

The White House
Theodore Roosevelt "Teddy," "TR," President of the United States, Spanish-American War hero, former Governor of New York State, former Police Commissioner of New York City.
Chief of the President's Secret Service protection corps

The Catskill Aqueduct
Dave Davidson Contractors' Protective Association, superintendent of labor camps.
Contractors
Irish foreman

Freshmen Borrow a Locomotive

Prologue:
Murder and High Jinks

New Haven, 1895

Chest-deep in a ditch, an Italian pick and shovel man looked up at a rush of custom-made shoes and broadcloth trousers inches from his face. Rich American students were scooping handfuls from the earth pile and sifting the sandy red soil through their fingers.

The Irish foreman, seated in the shade of an umbrella, shook a fist at him.

"Back to work, you lazy dago!"

The students took no notice. Set loose from geology class for impromptu field study, they were examining the fresh-dug outwash for traces of Triassic rock that glaciers had ground from the highlands above the New Haven valley. They were happy to be out of doors this first warm day of spring, and Italians digging holes in the ground were as ordinary a sight as red-faced Irish foremen in derby hats.

11

But the Italians' padrone, the labor contractor the immigrants paid a stiff commission for the day's work, did notice. The padrone was an extravagantly clad and perfumed Neopolitan with a sharp eye for profit. He beckoned the laborer who had stopped work to gape at his betters — a young Sicilian who called himself Antonio Branco.

Antonio Branco vaulted effortlessly up onto the grass. His clothes reeked of sweat, and little distinguished him from the others toiling in the ditch. Just another peasant in a dirty cap, a little finer-featured than most, taller, and bigger in the shoulders. And yet, something about this one seemed off. He was too sure of himself, the padrone concluded.

"You make me look bad in front of the foreman."

"What do you care about a mick?"

"I'm docking half your pay. Get back to work."

Branco's face hardened. But when he did nothing but jump back in the ditch and pick up his shovel, the padrone knew he had read his man correctly. Back in Italy, the Carabinieri kept a tight rein on criminals. A fugitive who had escaped to free and easy America, Antonio Branco could not protest being robbed of half his pay.

Five freshmen closed the door, muffling the uproar of pianos, banjos, and horseplay shouts and crashes elsewhere in Vanderbilt Hall. Then they gathered around a tall, rail-thin classmate and listened spellbound to his scheme to visit the girls at Miss Porter's School in Farmington, forty miles across the state. Tonight.

They knew little about him. He was from Boston, his family bankers and Harvard men. The fact that he had come down to Yale indicated a rebellious streak. He had a quick grin and a steady gaze, and he seemed to have thought of everything — a map, a Waltham train conductor's watch, accurate to thirty seconds in a day, and a special employees' timetable that contained schedules and running directions for every train on the line, both passenger and freight.

"What if the girls won't see us?" asked Jack, always a doubting Thomas.

"How could they resist Yale men on a special train?" asked Andy.

"A stolen special," said Ron.

"A *borrowed* special," Larry corrected him. "It's not like we're keeping it. Besides, it's not a whole train, only a locomotive."

Doug asked the big question on every

13

mind. "Are you sure you know how to operate a locomotive, Isaac?"

"One way to find out!"

Isaac Bell stuffed his map, watch, and timetable into a satchel that held several pairs of heavy gloves, a bull's-eye lantern, and a fat copy of Grimshaw's *Locomotive Catechism.* Doug, Ron, Andy, Jack, and Larry crowded after him when he bounded out the door.

New Haven's Little Italy had sprung up close to the rail yards. Locomotive whistles and switch engine bells were moaning and clanging their nightly serenade, and coal smoke sweetened the stench that the rubber factory wafted over the neighborhood, when the padrone stepped out of his favorite restaurant.

Belly full, head singing with wine, he stood a moment, cleaning his teeth with a gold pick. He strolled homeward along Wooster Street, acknowledging people's deferential *Buona sera, Padrone* with haughty nods. He was almost to his rooming house when he saw Antonio Branco in the shadows of a burned-out lamppost. The Sicilian was sharpening a pencil with a pocket knife.

The padrone laughed. "What does a peas-

14

ant who can't read need with a pencil?"

"I learn."

"Stupidaggine!"

Branco's eyes glittered left and right. There was a cop. To give him time to pass, he drew an American newspaper from his coat and read a headline aloud: "Water Tunnel Accident. Foreman Killed."

The padrone snickered. "Read the fine print."

Branco made a show of tracing the lines with his pencil. He pretended to struggle with long words and skipped the short ones. "Foreman Jake . . . Stratton . . . injured fatal when Bridgeport water tunnel caved. He leaves wife Katherine and children Paul and Abigail. Four Italians also died."

The cop disappeared around the corner. The earlier crowds had thinned, and the few people hurrying home would mind their own business. Branco drove the pencil through the padrone's cheek.

The padrone's hands flew to his face, exposing his ribs.

Branco thrust. His pocket knife had a short blade, well under the four inches allowed by law. But the handle from which it hinged was almost as thin as the blade itself. As steel slid between bones, Branco shifted his palm behind the knife and pushed hard.

15

The thin handle forced the blade into the wound and shoved the needle-sharp sliver as deep in the padrone's heart as a stiletto.

Branco took the padrone's money purse, his rings, and his toothpick and ran to the trains.

Locomotive 106 sighed and snorted like a sleeping mastiff. It was an American Standard 4-4-0 with four pilot wheels in front and four tall drive wheels as high as Isaac Bell's shoulder. Looming above the gravel embankment where the college boys huddled, silhouetted against a smoky sky set aglow by city lights, it looked enormous.

Bell had watched every night this week. Every night, it was trundled to the coal pocket and water tank to replenish its tender. Then the railroad workers removed ash from its furnace, banked the fire to raise steam quickly in the morning, and parked it on a siding at the extreme north end of the yard. Tonight, as usual, 106 was pointed in the right direction, north toward the Canal Line, which ran straight to Farmington.

Bell told Doug to run ahead of the engine and throw the switch. Doug was a football player, strong, levelheaded, and quick on his feet, the best candidate to switch the siding tracks to the main line. "Soon as we're through, open the switch again."

"Why?"

"So if they notice it missing, they won't know which way we went."

"You'd make a fine criminal, Isaac."

"Beats getting caught. Soon as you open it, run like heck to catch up . . . Andy, you're lighting the lights . . . O.K., guys. On the jump!"

Bell led the way, loping long-leggedly over rails, crossties, and gravel. The other boys followed, ducking their heads. The railroad police were famously brutal, yet not likely to beat up the sons of American magnates. But if they got caught at this stunt, the Yale Chaplin would have them "rusticated," which meant kicked out of school and sent home to their parents.

Doug sprinted ahead of the locomotive and crouched with his hands on the switch rod. Andy, whose father had put him to work backstage operating lights in his vaudeville theaters, climbed on the cow-catcher and ignited the acetylene headlamp, which cast a dull glow on the rails. Then he jumped down, ran to the back of the tender, and lighted a red lantern.

Isaac Bell vaulted up the ladder into the cab. He pulled on gloves from his satchel, passed a second pair to Ron, and pointed at

17

the furnace door. "Open that and shovel on some coal."

Heat blasted out.

"Scatter it so you don't smother the fire."

By the orange glare of the furnace, Bell compared the controls to illustrations he had memorized. Then he counted heads. All had crowded into the cab except Doug at the switch.

Bell pushed the Johnson bar forward, released the air brakes, and opened the throttle to feed steam to the cylinders. The steel behemoth shuddered alive in his hands. He remembered just in time to ease off on the throttle so it wouldn't jump like a jackrabbit.

The guys cheered and slapped him on the back. It was rolling.

"Stop!"

The railroad cop was a mountain of a man with a bull's-eye lantern on his belt and a yard-long billy club in his fist. He moved with startling speed to pin Antonio Branco against the boxcar he had been climbing under when the cinder dick surprised him. Branco squinted one eye to a slit and shut the other completely against the blinding light.

"How many wop arms do I got to bust

18

before youse get the message?" the cinder dick roared. "No stealing rides. Get out of my yard, and here's something to remember me by."

The club flew down at his arm with a force intended to shatter bone.

Branco twisted inside the arc of the attack and ducked, saving his arm at the expense of an agonizing blow to his left knee. Doubled over, he pulled his pocket knife, opened the blade with the speed of ceaseless practice, and whipped it high, slashing the rail cop from chin to hairline.

The man screamed as blood poured into his eyes, dropped his club, and clutched his ruined face. Branco stumbled into the dark. His knee burned, as if plunged in molten lead. Battling for every step, he limped toward the empty north end of the yard, away from the lights and the cops that the screams would draw. He saw an engine moving. Not a switch engine, but a big locomotive with a red signal lantern on the back of its tender. It was rolling toward the main line. It didn't matter where it was going — Hartford, Springfield, Boston — it was leaving New Haven. Retching with pain, he staggered after it as fast as he could, caught up, and threw himself onto the coupler on the back of the tender. He felt the wheels rumble through a switch, and the locomotive began to pick up speed.

In America, Branco had learned, freight trains erased boundaries. The country was huge — thirty times bigger than Italy — but thousands of miles of interlacing railroads melted distance. A man who rode the rails could vanish in "Little Italy" city slums and "Shantyville" labor camps. The police never noticed. Unlike the Carabinieri, who were national police, American cops knew what happened only in their own territory.

Suddenly, brakes hissed. The wheels shrieked and the engine stopped.

Branco heard someone running in the dark. He dropped to the crossties, slithered under the tender, and drew his knife. A man ran past and climbed up to the cab, shoes ringing on iron rungs. The brakes hissed release and the locomotive lurched to motion again. By then, Antonio Branco had wedged himself into a niche in the undercarriage, and New Haven was falling behind.

"More coal, Ron! Doug, pass Ron coal from the tender. Larry, Jack, help Doug."

"There aren't any more shovels, Isaac."

"Use your hands."

Speed was all. If Isaac Bell was reading the night timetable correctly, all trains had stopped running for the night after ten thirty. But the timetable warned of maintenance trains and gravel trains that might be on the tracks. The shorter time he was on the single track line, the better. Sixty miles per hour would get him to Farmington in forty minutes. He checked his watch. He had lost five full minutes stopping the train for Doug. The speed indicator read forty.

"More coal!"

The boys passed coal. Ron scooped it onto the fire. It seemed to take forever, but slowly, gradually, the steam pressure increased and the speed indicator crept up and up and up until finally she was rumbling along at sixty miles per hour. Once the train was up to sixty, and running light with no cars to haul, Bell was able to pull the Johnson bar back to an easy cruising position and let his weary, blistered, black and greasy firemen take a break.

"What's that ahead?"

Andy had stuck his head out the side window to watch the tracks. Bell leaned out with him and saw a single dim light. He checked his watch and his map. "Mount Carmel Station." Eight and a half miles from New Haven. Thirty-two to go. Best of all, the station house was dark. The dispatcher, who would have telegraphed that

21

an engine was running "wild," was asleep in his bed.

Andy begged permission to blow the whistle. Bell vetoed it. Screaming like banshees was not in the interest of crossing Connecticut as stealthily as a ghost.

His luck held as 106 highballed past small-town stations at Cheshire, Plantsville, and Southington — all three lights-out and fast asleep. But the next station was Plainville. Boldface print in the timetable indicated it was a big depot, and, indeed, as 106 rounded a curve into the town, Bell saw the station house and platform ablaze in light.

Trainmen were on the platform, and he feared there would be workmen on the tracks. He reached for the air brakes. Then he saw that the signal post showed a clear white light — the proceed signal, according to the *Locomotive Catechism.*

"Pull the whistle, Andy."

Andy yanked the cord looped from the roof of the cab. Steam coursed through the whistle with a deafening shriek. Men on the platform jumped back and watched, slack-jawed, as 106 tore into and out of Plainville at sixty miles an hour.

Bell raised his voice so all could hear above the roar.

"The jig is up."

The boys groaned. "What are we going to do, Isaac?"

"We'll turn off into the Farmington yards and head for Miss Porter's cross-country."

Bell showed them the way on his map. Then he handed out train tickets, one-ways from Plainville to New Haven. "Head back to school in the morning."

"Lights ahead!" called Andy, who was watching from the window. Bell eased back on the throttle, the speeding locomotive lost way, and he braked it to a smooth stop.

"Doug, there's your switch. On the jump, they know we're coming. Andy, douse our lights."

Andy extinguished the headlamp, and Doug ran to the switch and shunted them into the yard, which stretched toward the lights of Farmington. Quiet descended, the silence eerie after the thunder of the pistons.

"Wait," Bell whispered. He had heard the rustle of boots on gravel. Now he sensed motion in the starlight.

"Someone's coming!" Ron and Larry chorused.

"Wait," Bell repeated, listening hard. "He's going the other way." He glimpsed a figure running away from the locomotive. "Only some poor hobo."

23

"Cops!" A lantern was bobbing toward them.

Bell saw a single cop stumbling through a pool of lamplight. A nightshirt was half tucked into his trousers, and he was struggling to tug his suspenders over his shoulders while he ran. "Stop! Halt!"

A figure ran through the same pool of light where Bell had seen the rail cop.

The bobbing lantern veered in pursuit.

"He's chasing the hobo."

"Run, guys, now's our chance."

The boys bolted for the dark. Bell looked back. The hobo had an odd running gait. His right foot flew out with each step at a sideways angle, reminding Bell of how a trotting horse with a flawed gait would "wing."

A second watchman ran from the station house, blowing a whistle, and charged after Bell's classmates. With a sinking heart, Bell knew that it was his fault they were here. He ran after them as fast as he could, got between them and the watchman, and when the watchman saw him, bolted in the opposite direction. The trick worked. The cop galloped after him, and the rest of the boys disappeared toward the town.

Bell headed toward a cluster of freight houses and coal pockets, timing his pace to gradually pull ahead, veered through the buildings, and used them for cover to sprint into a clump of trees. There, he hid and waited. This early in spring, branches hadn't yet leafed out and the stars penetrated so brightly they gleamed on his hands. He dropped the satchel at his feet, pulled his collar around his face, and hid his hands in his pockets.

He heard footsteps. Then labored breathing. The hobo limped into the trees. He saw Bell, plunged a hand into his coat, and whipped out a knife in a blur of starlight on steel. Run? thought Bell. Not and turn his back on the knife. He grabbed the heavy satchel to block the knife and formed a fist.

Ten feet apart, the two eyed each other silently. The hobo's face was dark, barely visible under the brim of his cap. His eyes glittered like a hunted animal's. His arms and legs and entire body were coiled to spring. Isaac Bell grew aware of his own body; every muscle was cocked.

The watchmen blew their whistles. They had teamed up, far in the distance, hunting in the wrong direction. The hobo was breathing hard, eyes flickering between him and the whistles.

Bell lowered the satchel and opened his fist. The instinct was correct. The hobo

25

returned the knife to his coat and sagged against a tree.

Bell whispered, "Me first."

He slipped silently from the trees.

When he looked back at the rail yard from the shelter of a farm wall, he saw a shadow pass under a light. The hobo was wing-footing the other way.

Doubting Thomas had called it wrong.

When Bell's classmates tossed pebbles at the Old Girls' house on Main Street, the girls flung open their windows and leaned out, whispering and giggling. Who are you boys? Where did you come from? How did you get here in the middle of the night?

They had decided, while stumbling across the countryside, that it would be best for everyone's future not to admit that they had stolen a train. They stuck to a story that they had chartered a special, and Miss Porter's girls seemed impressed. "Just to see us?"

"Worth every penny," chorused Larry and Doug.

Suddenly, from around the corner, a pretty blond girl appeared on the grass in a flowing white robe.

"You boys better run. The housemother telephoned Miller."

"Who's Miller?"

"The constable."

The Yale men scattered, all but Isaac Bell, who stepped into a shaft of light and swept off his hat. "Good evening, Mary Clark. I'm awfully glad to see you again."

"Isaac!"

They had met last month at a chaperoned tea.

"What are you doing here?"

"You are even blonder and more beautiful than I remember."

"Here comes Miller. Run, you idiot!"

Isaac Bell bowed over her hand and ran for the dark. The unforgettable Miss Mary Clark called after him, "I'll tell Miller you came from Harvard."

Two days later, he marched into the New Haven yard master's office and announced, "I'm Isaac Bell. I'm a first year student at Yale. There's a rumor on campus that detectives are inquiring about Locomotive 106."

"What about it?"

"I'm the guy who borrowed it."

"Sit there! Don't move. Wait for the police."

The yard master snatched up a telephone and reported Bell's confession.

An hour passed. A prematurely white-haired detective in a pin-striped suit arrived. He was leading an enormous man whose head was swathed in bandages that covered his entire face but for one glaring eye. The eye fixed on Isaac Bell.

"That's no wop," he mumbled through the bandage. "I told youse he was a wop."

"He says he stole 106."

"I don't care if he stole a whole damned train. He ain't the dago Eye-talian wop guinea what sliced me."

The white-haired detective walked the big man out. He returned in twenty minutes. He sat with Bell and introduced himself as Detective Eddie Edwards. Then he took out a memo book and wrote in a neat hand as he listened to Bell's story. Three times, he asked Bell to repeat it. Finally, he asked, "Did you happen to see the wop who slashed that yard bull's face?"

"Not at New Haven, but there was someone at the Farmington yards." Bell told him about encountering the hobo with the wing-footed gait. "He could have ridden under the tender."

"I'll pass it on to the railroad dicks. But he'll have worked his way to Boston by now." Edwards made another note and closed his book.

Bell said, "I hate to think I helped a

criminal escape."

"Any man who could whip that yard bull didn't need your help escaping. Come on, kid. I'll walk you back to school."

"You're letting me go?"

"By a miracle, your harebrained stunt did not lead to death, injury, or destruction of property. Therefore, it is not in the interest of the New Haven Railroad to prosecute the son of a Boston banker from whom they one day might want to borrow money."

"How did you know my father is a banker?"

"Wired a fellow in Boston."

They walked up Chapel Street, with Bell answering Detective Eddie Edwards' questions about landmarks they passed. At the Green, Edwards said, "Say, just between us, how many pals did you need to pull it off?"

"I did it alone," said Bell.

Eddie Edwards looked the young student over speculatively.

Bell returned the speculative look. Edwards fascinated him. The detective was a snappy dresser compared to the poor railroad detective who'd had his face slashed. And he was a chameleon, with an easygoing manner that disguised a sharp gaze and a sharper mind. He was considerably younger than his shock of white hair made him look.

Bell wondered where he carried his gun. A shoulder holster, he guessed. But nothing showed.

"Tall order, all by yourself," Edwards mused. "Frankly, I admire a man who stands up for his friends."

"Frankly," said Bell, "even if friends had come along, it would still have been entirely my idea." He showed the detective his maps, Waltham, and timetable. "Are you familiar with Grimshaw's *Locomotive Catechism*?"

"Good answer, kid. Backed by evidence. While changing the subject with a question. You have the makings of a savvy crook."

"Or a savvy detective?"

A smile tugged Edwards' mouth even as he said, firmly, "Detectives help people, they don't steal their property."

"Mr. Edwards, did you imply, earlier, that you don't work for the railroad?"

"The roads bring us in when a job calls for finessing."

"Who do you work for?"

Edwards squared his shoulders and stood a little taller.

"I'm a Van Dorn detective."

■ ■ ■ ■

BOOK I
CAPTAIN COLIGNEY'S
PINK TEA

■ ■ ■ ■

Eleven Years Later
1906

She Whispered Hail Marys for Courage

1

Little Sicily, New York City
Elizabeth Street, between Prince and
  Houston,
the "Black Hand block"

The Black Hand locked twelve-year-old Maria Vella in a pigeon coop on the roof of an Elizabeth Street tenement. They untied the gag so she wouldn't suffocate. Not even a building contractor as rich as her father would ransom a dead girl, they laughed. But if she screamed, they said, they would beat her. A vicious jerk of one of her glossy braids brought tears to her eyes.

She tried to slow her pounding heart by concentrating on the calmness of the birds. The pigeons murmured softly among themselves, oblivious to the racket from the slum, undisturbed by a thousand shouts, a piping street organ, and the thump and whirr of sewing machines. She could see through a wall of wooden slats admitting light and air that the coop stood beside the high parapet that rimmed the roof. Was there someone who would help her on the other side? She whispered Hail Marys to build her courage.

". . . Santa Maria, Madre di Dio,
prega per noi peccatori,
adesso e nell'ora della nostra morte . . ."

Coaxing a bird out of the way, she climbed up on its nesting box, and up onto another, until she glimpsed a tenement across the street draped with laundry. Climbing higher, pressing her head to the ceiling, she could see all the way down to a stretch of sidewalk four stories below. It was jammed with immigrants. Peddlers, street urchins, women shopping — not one of them could help her. They were Sicilians, transplanted workers and peasants, poor as dirt, and as frightened of the authorities as she was of her kidnappers.

She clung to the comforting sight of people going about their lives, a housewife carrying a chicken from the butcher, workmen drinking wine and beer on the steps of the Kips Bay Saloon. A Branco's Grocery wagon clattered by, painted gleaming red and green enamel with the owner's name in gold leaf. Antonio Branco had hired her father's business to excavate a cellar for his warehouse on Prince Street. So near, so far, the wagon squeezed past the pushcarts and out of sight.

Suddenly, the people scattered. A helmeted, blue-coated, brass-buttoned Irish policeman lumbered into view. He was gripping a baton, and Maria's hopes soared. But if she screamed through the wooden slats, would anyone hear before the kidnappers burst in and beat her? She lost her courage. The policeman passed. The immigrants pressed back into the space he had filled.

A tall man glided from the Kips Bay Saloon.

Lean as a whip, he wore workman's garb, a shabby coat, and a flat cap. He glanced across the street and up the tenement. His gaze fixed on the parapet. For a second, she thought he was looking at her, straight into her eyes. But how could he know she was locked inside the coop? He swept his hat off his head as if signaling someone. At that moment, the sun cleared a rooftop, and a shaft of light struck his crown of golden hair.

He stepped into the street and disappeared from view.

The thick-necked Sicilian stationed just inside the front door blocked the tenement hall. A blackjack flew at his face. He side-stepped it, straight into the path of a fist in his gut that doubled him over in silent anguish. The blackjack — a leather sack of lead shot — smacked the bone behind his ear, and he dropped to the floor.

At the top of four flights of dark, narrow stairs, another Sicilian guarded the ladder to the roof. He pawed a pistol from his belt. A blade flickered. He froze in openmouthed pain and astonishment, gaping at the throwing knife that split his hand. The blackjack finished the job before he could yell.

The kidnapper on the roof heard the ladder creak. He was already flinging open the pigeon coop door when the blackjack flew with the speed and power of a strikeout pitcher's best ball and smashed into the back of his head. Strong and hard as a wild boar, he shrugged off the blow, pushed into the coop, and grabbed the little girl. His stiletto glittered. He shoved the needle tip against her throat. "I kill."

The tall, golden-haired man stood stock-still with empty hands. Terrified, all Maria could think was that he had a thick mustache that she had not seen when he glided out of the saloon. It was trimmed as wonderfully as if he had just stepped from the barbershop.

36

He spoke her name in a deep baritone voice.

Then he said, "Close your eyes very tight."

She trusted him and squeezed them shut. She heard the man who was crushing her shout again, "I kill." She felt the knife sting her skin. A gun boomed. Hot liquid splashed her face. The kidnapper fell away. She was scooped inside a strong arm and carried out of the pigeon coop.

"You were very brave to keep your eyes closed, little lady. You can open them now." She could feel the man's heart pounding, thundering, as if he had run very far or had been as frightened as she. "You can open them," he repeated softly. "Everything's O.K."

They were standing on the open roof. He was wiping her face with a handkerchief, and the pigeons were soaring into a sky that would never, ever be as blue as his eyes.

"Who are you?"

"Isaac Bell. Van Dorn Detective Agency."

2

"Greatest engineering feat in history. Any idea what it's going to cost, Branco?"

"I read in-a newspaper one hundred million doll-a, Mr. Davidson."

Davidson, the Contractors' Protective Association superintendent of labor camps, laughed. "The Water Supply Board'll spend *one hundred seventy-five* million, before it's done. Twenty million more than the Panama Canal."

A cold wind and a crisp sky promised an early winter in the Catskill Mountains. But the morning sun was strong, and the city men stood with coats open, side by side, on a scaffold atop the first stage of a gigantic dam high above a creek. Laborers swarmed the site, but roaring steam shovels and power hoists guaranteed that no one would overhear their private bargains.

The superintendent stuck his thumbs in his vest. "Wholesome water for seven million people." He puffed his chest and belly and beamed in the direction of far-off New York City as if he were tunneling a hundred miles of Catskill Aqueduct with his own hands. "Catskills water will shoot out a tap in a fifth floor kitchen — just by gravity."

"A mighty enterprise," said Branco.

"We gotta build it before the water famine. Immigrants are packing the city, drinking dry the Croton."

The valley behind them was a swirling dust bowl, mile after mile of flattened farms and villages, churches, barns, houses, and uprooted trees that when dammed and filled would become the Ashokan Reservoir, the biggest in the world. Below, Esopus Creek rushed through eight-foot conduits, allowed to run free until the dam was finished. Ahead lay the route of the Catskill Aqueduct — one hundred miles of tunnels bigger around than train tunnels — that they would bury in trenches, drive under rivers, and blast through mountains.

"Twice as long as the great aqueducts of the Roman Empire."

Antonio Branco had mastered English as a child. But he could pretend to be imperfect when it served him. "Big-a hole in ground," he answered in the vaudeville-comic Italian accent the American expected from a stupid immigrant to be fleeced.

He had already paid a hefty bribe for the privilege of traveling up here to meet the superintendent. Having paid, again, in dignity, he pictured slitting the cloth half an inch above the man's watch chain. Glide in, glide out. The body falls sixty feet and is tumbled in rapids, too mangled for a country undertaker to notice a microscopic puncture. Heart attack.

But not this morning. The stakes were high, the opportunity not to be wasted. Slaves had built Rome's aqueducts. New Yorkers used steam shovels, dynamite, and compressed air — and thousands of Italian laborers. Thousands of bellies to feed.

"You gotta understand, Branco, you bid too late. The contracts to provision the company stores were already awarded."

"I hear there was difficulty, last minute."

"Difficulty? I'll say there was difficulty! Damned fool got his throat slit in a whorehouse."

Branco made the sign of the cross. "I offer my services, again, to feed Italian laborers their kind-a food."

"If you was to land the contract, how would you deliver? New York's a long way off."

"I ship-a by Hudson River. Albany Night

40

Line steamer to Kingston. Ulster & Delaware Railroad at Kingston to Brown's Station labor camp."

"Hmm . . . Yup, I suppose that's a way you could try. But why not ship it on a freighter direct from New York straight to the Ulster & Delaware dock?"

"A freighter is possible," Branco said noncommittally.

"That's how the guy who got killed was going to do it. He figured a freighter could stop at Storm King on the way and drop macaroni for the siphon squads. Plenty Eyetalian pick and shovel men digging under the river. Plenty more digging the siphon on the other side. At night, you can hear 'em playing their mandolins and accordions."

"Stop-a, too, for Breakneck Mountain," said Branco. "Is-a good idea."

"I know a fellow with a freighter," Davidson said casually.

Antonio Branco's pulse quickened. Their negotiation to provision the biggest construction job in America had begun.

A cobblestone crashed through the window and scattered glass on Maria Vella's bedspread. Her mother burst into her room, screaming. Her father was right behind her,

41

whisking her out of the bed and trying to calm her mother. Maria joined eyes with him. Then she pointed, mute and trembling, at the stone on the carpet wrapped in a piece of paper tied with string. Giuseppe Vella untied it and smoothed the paper. On it was a crude drawing of a dagger in a skull and the silhouette of a black hand.

He read it, trembling as much with anger as fear. The pigs dared address his poor child:

"Dear you will tell father ransom must be paid. You are home safe like promised. Tell father be man of honor."

The rest of the threat was aimed at him:

"Beware Father of Dear. Do not think we are dead. We mean business. Under Brooklyn Bridge by South Street. Ten thousand. PLUS extra one thousand for trouble you make us suffer. Keep your mouth shut. Your Dear is home safe. If you fail to bring money we ruin work you build."

"They still want the ransom," he told his wife.

"Pay it," she sobbed. "Pay or they will never stop."

"No!"

42

His wife became hysterical. Giuseppe Vella looked helplessly at his daughter.

The girl said, "Go back to Signore Bell."

"*Mr.* Bell," he shouted. He felt powerless and it made him angry. He wanted to hire the Van Dorn Detective Agency for protection. But there was risk in turning to outsiders. "You're American. Speak American. *Mr.* Bell. Not *Signore.*"

The child flinched at his tone. He recalled his own father, a tyrant in the house, and he hung his head. He was too modern, too American, to frighten a child. "I'm sorry, Maria. Don't worry. I will go to Mr. Bell."

3

The Knickerbocker Hotel was a hit from the day John Jacob Astor IV opened the fifteen-story Beaux Arts building on the corner of 42nd and Broadway. The great Caruso took up permanent residence, three short blocks from the Metropolitan Opera House, as did coloratura soprano Luisa Tetrazzini, the "Florentine Nightingale," who inspired the Knickerbocker's chef to invent a new macaroni dish, *Pollo Tetrazzini.*

Ahead of both events, months before the official opening, Joseph Van Dorn had moved his private detective agency's New York field office into a sumptuous second floor suite at the top of the grand staircase. He negotiated a break on the rent by furnishing house detectives. Van Dorn had a theory, played out successfully at his national headquarters in Chicago's Palmer House and at his Washington, D.C., field office in the New Willard Hotel, that lavish surroundings paid for themselves by per-suading his clientele that high fees meant quality work. A rear entrance, accessible by a kitchen alley and back stairs, was available for clients loath to traverse the most popular hotel lobby in the city to discuss private affairs, for informants shopping information, and for investigators in disguise.

Isaac Bell directed Giuseppe Vella to that entrance.

The tall detective greeted the Italian contractor warmly in the reception room. He inquired about Maria and her mother, and refused, again, an offer of a monetary reward beyond the Van Dorn fee, saying, good-naturedly but firmly, "You've already paid your bill on time, a sterling quality in a client."

Bell led the Italian into the working heart of the office, the detectives' bull pen, which resembled a modern Wall Street operation, with candlestick telephones, voice tubes, clattering typewriters, a commercial grapho-phone, and a stenographer's transcribing device. A rapid-fire telegraph key linked the outfit by private wire to Chicago, to field offices across the continent, and to Washington, where the Boss spent much of his time wrangling government contracts.

Bell commandeered an empty desk and a

chair for Vella and examined the Black Hand extortion letter. Half-literate threats were illustrated with crude drawings on a sheet of top quality stationery.

Vella said, "It was tied with string around the stone they threw in the window."

"Do you have the string?"

Vella pulled a strand of butcher's twine from his pocket.

Bell said, "I'll look into this, immediately, and discuss it with Mr. Van Dorn."

"I am afraid for my family."

"When you telephoned, I sent men to 13th Street to guard your home."

Bell promised to call on Vella that afternoon at Vella's current construction site, an excavation for the new Church of the Annunciation at 128th Street in Harlem. "By the way, if you notice you are being followed, it will only be that detective . . . there." He directed Vella's gaze across the bull pen. "Archie Abbott will look out for you."

The elegantly dressed, redheaded Detective Abbott looked to Vella like a Fifth Avenue dandy until he slid automatic pistols into twin shoulder holsters, stuffed his pockets with extra bullet clips, sheathed a blackjack, and loaded a shotgun shell into his gold-headed walking stick.

■ ■ ■ ■

Isaac Bell took the Black Hand letter to Joseph Van Dorn's private office. It was a corner room with an Art Nouveau rosewood desk, comfortable leather armchairs, views of the sidewalks leading to the hotel entrances, and a spy hole for inspecting visitors in the reception room.

Van Dorn was a balding Irishman in his forties, full in the chest and fuller in the belly, with a thick beard of bright red whiskers and the gruffly amiable charm of a wealthy business man who had prospered early in life. Enormously ambitious, he possessed the ability, rare in Bell's experience, to enjoy his good fortune. He also had a gift for making friends, which worked to the great advantage of his detective agency. His cordial manner concealed a bear-trap-swift brain and a prodigious memory for the faces and habits of criminals, whose existence he took as a personal affront.

"I'm glad for any business," said Van Dorn. "But why doesn't Mr. Vella take his troubles to Joe Petrosino's Italian Squad?"

New York Police Detective Joseph Petrosino, a tough, twenty-year veteran with an arrest and conviction record that was the envy of the department, had recently received the go-ahead from Commissioner Bingham to form a special squad of Italian-speaking investigators to fight crime in the Sicilian, Neopolitan, and Calabrese neighborhoods.

"Maybe Mr. Vella knows there are only fifteen Italians in the entire New York Police Department."

"Petrosino's got his work cut out for him," Van Dorn agreed. "This 'Black Hand' plague is getting out of control." He gestured at a heap of newspaper clippings that Isaac Bell had asked Research to gather for the Boss. "Bombing fruit stands and burning pushcarts, terrorizing poor ignorant immigrants, is the least of it. Now they're tackling Italian bankers and business men. We'll never know how many wealthy parents quietly ransomed their children, but I'll bet enough to make it a booming business."

Bell passed Van Dorn the Black Hand letter.

Van Dorn's cheeks reddened with anger. "They actually address the little girl! What scum would frighten a child like this?"

"Feel the paper."

"Top quality. Rag, not pulp."

"Remind you of anything?"

"Same as the original ransom note, if I recall."

"Anything else?"

"First class stationery." He held it to the light. "Wonder where they got it. Why don't you look into the watermark?"

"I already put Research on it."

"So now they're threatening his business."

"It's easy to make an 'accident' at a construction site."

"Unless it's a feint while they take another shot at his daughter."

"If they do," said Bell, "they'll run head-on into Harry Warren's Gang Squad. Harry's blanketed 13th Street."

Van Dorn showed his teeth in a semblance of a smile. "Good . . . But how long can I afford to take Harry's boys off the gangs? 'Gophers' and 'Wallopers' are running riot, and the Italians are getting bolder every day."

"A dedicated Van Dorn Black Hand Squad," said Bell, "would free your top gang investigators to concentrate on the street gangs."

"I'll think about it," said Van Dorn.

"We would be better fixed to attack the Black Hand."

"I said I'd think about it."

■ ■ ■ ■

Isaac Bell strode uptown from the 125th Street subway station through a neighborhood rapidly urbanizing as new-built sanitariums, apartment blocks, tenements, theaters, schools, and parish houses uprooted Harlem's barnyards and shanties. He was a block from 128th Street, nearing a jagged hill of rock that Giuseppe Vella was excavating for the Church of the Annunciation, when the ground shook beneath his feet.

He heard a tremendous explosion. The sidewalk rippled. A parish steeple swayed. Panicked nuns ran from the building, and Convent Avenue, which was surfaced with vitrified brick, started to roll like the ocean.

Bell had survived the Great Earthquake in San Francisco only last spring, awakening suddenly in the middle of the night to see his fiancée's living room and piano fall into the street. Now, here in Manhattan, he felt his second earthquake in months. A hundred feet of the avenue disintegrated in front of him. Then bricks flew, propelled to the building tops by gigantic jets of water.

It was no earthquake, but a flood.

A river filled Convent Avenue in an instant.

There could be only one source of the raging water. The Croton Reservoir system up north in Westchester supplied New York City's Central Park Reservoir via underground mains. The explosion in Giuseppe Vella's excavation — an enormous dynamite "overcharge," whether by miscalculation or sabotage — had smashed them open. In an instant, the "water famine" predicted by Catskill Aqueduct champions seemed unbelievable.

A liquid wall roared out of Convent Ave and raced down it, tearing at first-story windows and sweeping men, women, and horses around the corners and into the side streets. Its speed was startling, faster than a crack passenger train. One second, Isaac Bell was pulling the driver from a wagon caught in the ice-cold torrent; the next, he himself was picked up and flung into 127th Street. He battled to the surface and swam on a foaming crest that swept away shanties the full block to Amsterdam Avenue.

There the water careened downhill, following the slope of the land south. Bell fought out of the stream and dragged himself upright on a lamppost. Firemen from a nearby station were wading in to pull people out.

Bell shouted, "Where are the water gates?"

"Up Amsterdam at 135th."

Bell charged up Amsterdam Avenue at a dead run.

A third of a mile north of the water main break, he found a sturdy Romanesque Revival brick and granite castle. The lintel above its iron doors was engraved WATER DEPARTMENT. A structure this big had to be the main distributing point for the Westchester reservoirs. He pushed inside. Tons and tons of Croton water were surging up from a deep receiving chamber into four-foot-diameter cast-iron pipes. The pipes were fitted with huge valve wheels to control the outflow to the mains breached seven blocks away by the explosion.

Bell spotted a man struggling with them. He hurtled down a steel ladder and found an exhausted middle-aged engineer desperately trying to close all four valves at once. He was gasping for breath and looked on the verge of a heart attack. "I don't know what happened to my helper. He's never late, never misses a day."

"Show me how to help!"

"I can't budge the gates alone. It's a two-man job."

With the dynamite explosion no accident,

thought Bell, but a coordinated Black Hand attack to blame Giuseppe Vella for flooding an entire neighborhood, the extortionists must have left the helper bloodied in an alley.

"This one's frozen."

Isaac Bell threw his weight and muscle against the wheel and pulled with all his might. The old engineer clapped hands on it, too, and they fought it together, quarter inch by quarter inch, until the gate wheel finally began to turn with a metallic screech.

"Godforsaken Italians. I warned them again and again not to use too much dynamite. I knew this would happen."

As soon as they closed the last gate, Isaac Bell raced back to Vella's excavation.

The streets were littered with the corpses of drowned dogs and chickens. A dead horse was still tied in a wrecked stable. Trolleys had stalled on their tracks, shorted out by the water. The cellars of houses and businesses were flooded. A hillside had washed away and fallen into a brewery, and the people who had lived in the upended shacks were poking in the mud for the remains of their possessions.

An angry crowd was gathering at the excavation site.

Bell shouldered through it and found Giuseppe Vella barricaded in the board shack that housed his field office.

"Russo ran away."

"Who is Russo?"

"Sante Russo. My foreman. The blaster. He was afraid those people would blame him." Bell exchanged a quick glance with Archie Abbott, the Van Dorn shadow he had assigned to protect Vella. Abbott had managed to station himself near the door, but he was only one man and the crowd was growing loud.

"But it wasn't Russo's fault."

"How do you know?"

"Russo ran to me a second after the explosion. He said he found extra dynamite in the charge. He disconnected the detonator. But while he was coming to tell me, it exploded. The Black Hand reconnected the wires."

Policemen pushed through the crowd.

Bell said, "Soon as the cops calm them down, I'll escort you home."

The cops pounded on the door. Bell let them in.

They had come for Vella. Accompanying them was an angry official from the city's Combustibles Department. He revoked Vella's explosives license for the job on the spot and swore that Vella would be fined thousands by the city. "Not only that, you reckless wop, you'll lose the bond you had posted in case of damage. Look what you did to the neighborhood! 125th Street is almost washed away and you flooded every cellar from here to 110th!"

Isaac Bell issued quick orders to Archie Abbott before he accompanied Giuseppe Vella downtown. When they got to 13th Street, he confirmed that Harry Warren's detectives were keeping an eye on the man's home. Then he went to his room at the Yale Club, where he changed into dry clothes and oiled his firearms. He was retrieving the soaked contents of his pockets and smoothing a damp two-dollar bill, which would dry no worse for wear, when it occurred to him what the high quality paper that the Black Hand letter had been written on reminded him of.

"Mr. Bell," the hall porter called through his door. "Message from your office."

Bell slit the envelope and read a one-word sentence written in the Boss's hand.

"Report."

Bell got there just as New York Police Department Captain Coligney was leaving Van Dorn's office. They shook hands hello

55

and Coligney said, "Take care in Washington, Joe. Good seeing you again."

"Always a pleasure," said Van Dorn. "I'll walk you out."

Back in sixty seconds, he said, "Good man, Coligney. The only captain Bingham didn't transfer when he took over — presumably recalling that President Roosevelt boomed his career back when he was Police Commissioner."

Van Dorn threw papers in a satchel and cast it over his shoulder. "A flood, Isaac. Set off by an overcharge explosion of dynamite on the premises of our client Mr. Vella, who hired the Van Dorn Detective Agency to protect him. By any chance could we call it a horribly timed coincidental accident?"

"Sabotage," said Bell.

"Are you sure?"

"If a Water Department assistant engineer had not failed to show up for work at the main distribution gates, they could have stopped the water almost immediately. Archie Abbott found the poor devil in the hospital, beaten half dead. That makes two 'horribly timed' coincidences."

"Then how do we convince clients that the Van Dorn Detective Agency can protect them from the Black Hand?"

"Same way you had Eddie Edwards drive

56

gangs from the rail yards. Form a special squad and hit 'em hard."

"We've already discussed your Black Hand Squad. I'm not about to commit the manpower, and, frankly, I don't see the profit in it."

"Very little profit," Bell agreed freely. The fact was, ambition aside, Joseph Van Dorn cared far more about protecting the innocent than making a profit. All Bell had to do was remind him of it. "The Black Hand terrorize only their own countrymen. The poor folk can't speak English, much less read it. Who can they turn to? The Irish cop who calls every man 'Pasquale'?"

"Forgetting," growled Van Dorn, "that it wasn't that long ago Yankee cops called us Irish Paddy . . . But Mr. Vella and his fellow business men speak near-perfect English and read just fine."

"Those are the Italians we have to persuade not to forever link the Van Dorn Detective Agency to the Great Harlem Flood of 1906."

"I am not in a joking mood, Isaac."

"Neither am I, sir. Giuseppe Vella's a decent man. He deserves better. So do his countrymen."

"We'll talk next week." Van Dorn started out the door. "Oh, one more thing. How

57

would you feel about taking over the New York field office? Lampack's getting old."

"I would not like that one bit, sir."

"Why not?"

"I'm a field detective, not a manager."

"The heck you're not. You've ramrodded plenty of squads."

"Squads in the field. Frankly, sir, if you won't give me a Black Hand Squad, I would rather you appoint me Chief Investigator."

"*I'm* Chief Investigator," said Van Dorn. "And I intend to remain Chief Investigator until I can appoint a valuable man who is sufficiently seasoned to take over . . . Have you made any headway with that paper?"

"I have an agent on Park Row, canvassing the printers, stationers, and ink shops."

4

Before he opened the morning mail, David LaCava filled his show window with stacks of ten-dollar bills and heaps of gold coins. Banco LaCava was a neighborhood bank that offered many services. His depositors trusted him to telegraph money to relatives elsewhere in America and even cable it back to Sicily; they trusted him to keep their wills and passports in his safe; and when they bought insurance and steamship tickets from LaCava, they knew the insurance would be paid up and the tickets weren't forged. As the old country saying went, La-Cava was "as honest as the Lottery." But the plain, simple immigrants who had landed on Elizabeth Street direct from the countryside, or fled city slums that made Elizabeth Street tenements palaces by comparison, looked for proof in his show window that when they needed to withdraw cash Banco LaCava could cover them.

He opened his mail with trembling fingers. As he feared, more demands from the Black Hand. Under their "letterhead," if silhouettes of a black hand and a skull pierced by a dagger could be dignified as such, his tormentors had scrawled another threat in crude English:

Patients we lost. Sick and tired of writing. We ask man of honor for ten thousand. He spurs us.

A bitter smile twisted his face. "Patients" for "patience." "Spur" for "spurn." Illiterate brigands. Like his depositors, LaCava, too, had come from nowhere and nothing. The way to success was to embrace all things American — first and foremost, learning to speak, read, and write the English language.

We say be man of honor. We say, meet at bridge. He come not. Here we give last chance. Ten thousand dollar. We know you have in bank. Thursday night. We tell where later.

At the bottom of the page they had added a cartoon drawing of a stick of dynamite with a burning fuse. Like in the funny papers.

LaCava opened a drawer in his desk,

which faced the street door of his storefront bank, and laid his hand on the cool steel of a .38 revolver. A lot of good it would do against dynamite. He shoved the gun and the letter in his coat and walked uptown to 13th Street, where he found Giuseppe Vella sitting at his kitchen table in his shirtsleeves. The contractor looked miserable, stuck in the house when a man should be at his business. LaCava showed him the letter, and Vella exploded to life in a burst of indignation.

"I've been thinking," Vella said, "how to deal with these scum." He yanked on his coat, adjusted his necktie, and slicked back his hair. "Come on, we'll go see Branco."

"I thought of going to him," said LaCava. "Branco happened to be making a deposit when I got the first letter. I almost asked his advice, but I hardly know him."

"Let me do the talking. I know him well. I dug his cellars."

Business was booming at Branco's Wholesale Grocery. Endless lines of enameled wagons crowded the curb, loading, clattering off, returning empty to be filled again by an army of clerks dashing from the store with boxes of macaroni, cans of olive oil, salt, peas, beans, and anchovies, wine, fish stock, and soap. Like Vella, like LaCava and other *prominente,* Antonio Branco had made a success in America — a bigger success than any of them, having won the Bureau of Water Supply contracts to feed ten thousand Italians working on the Catskill Aqueduct.

"Hello, my friends," Branco called from the doorway. Like Vella, Branco made the effort to stick to English, even among countrymen. Although Branco's accent was still strong, far more noticeable than Vella's, and his American phrases often tangled words in odd order.

"When you are free," Vella said, "could you come across the street for a coffee?"

"You will drink coffee in my own back room," said Branco. "I am free right now." He beckoned a clerk. "Take over. The front wagon is for special customer. Only the best . . . Come." He led Vella and LaCava through the store to his office, which smelled of coffee. A kettle simmered on a gas ring. The long table where his staff took their meals was covered with a red and white checked oilcloth. A map of America's railroads hung on the wall.

"Sit while I make."

Vella smiled in spite of his troubles. "I

thought rich men's servants make their coffee."

Branco looked up from the grinder with a conspiratorial grin. "I make better coffee than my servants. Besides, I am not rich."

LaCava's eyebrows rose in disbelief, and Vella greeted such modesty with the knowing smile of a fellow business man. "It is said that you turn your hand to many things."

"I don't count in one basket."

Vella watched him putter about the makeshift kitchen, warming cups with boiling water, grinding the beans fine as dust. Antonio Branco had been the biggest Italian grocery wholesaler in New York City even before he landed the aqueduct job. Now he had thousands of captive customers shopping in labor camp company stores. He was also a padrone who recruited the laborers and stone masons directly from Italy.

In theory, city law banned padrones from the job, as did the unions, which fought the padrone system tooth and nail. In practice, the contractors and subcontractors of the Contractors' Protective Association needed sewer, subway, street paving, and tunnel laborers precisely where and when events demanded. Branco worked both sides, hiring surrogate padrones to supply newly arrived immigrants for some sections of the aqueduct, while he ingratiated himself with the Rockmen and Excavators' Union by operating as a business agent to furnish union laborers for others.

"You could teach a wife to make coffee," said Vella.

"I don't have a wife."

"I know that. However, my wife's younger sister — ten years younger — is already a splendid cook . . . and very beautiful, wouldn't you agree, David?"

"Very, very beautiful," said LaCava. "A girl to take the breath away."

"Convent-schooled in the old country."

"She sounds like a man's dream," Branco replied respectfully. "But not yet for me. I have things to finish before I am ready for family life."

He curled wisps of cream onto the steaming cups and handed them over. "O.K.! Enough pussyfoot. I hear you have troubles uptown."

"They took my license. The city is suing me. But that's not why I've come. The Black Hand is after LaCava now. Show him the letter, David."

Branco read it. "Pigs!"

"This is the fourth letter. I fear —"

"I would," Branco said gravely. "They could be dangerous."

"What would you do?"

"If it were me?" He sipped his coffee while he considered. "I would pay."

"You would?" asked LaCava.

Vella was astonished. He had assumed that Branco's city contracts made him untouchable.

"What else could I do? A small grocery I supply suffered attack last year. Have you ever seen what a stick of dynamite does to a store?"

Vella said, "I hate the idea of knuckling under."

"Who doesn't?"

"Besides, what's to guarantee they won't come back for more?"

"What would you do instead?"

"I have an idea how to stop them," said Vella.

Branco cast a dubious glance at LaCava. LaCava said, "Listen to him. He has a good idea."

"I am listening. What will you do, Giuseppe Vella?"

"I will make a 'White Hand' to fight a 'Black Hand.' "

Branco switched to Italian. "A game of words? I don't understand."

Vella stuck to English. "We'll form a society. A protective society. Remember the old burial societies? We'll band together. Like-minded business men who might well be threatened next."

Branco stuck with Italian. "Give them knives and guns?"

"Of course not. We're not soldiers. We're not policemen. We will pool our money and hire protection."

"And who will protect you from the protectors?" Branco asked softly. "Guards have a way of turning on their masters. Guards are first to see that might triumphs."

"We will hire professionals. Private detectives. Men of integrity."

Antonio Branco looked Vella in the face. "Is the story true that it was detectives who got your daughter back from kidnappers?"

"From the Van Dorn Agency."

"But weren't those same Van Dorns guarding your excavation in Harlem?"

"I waited too long to go to them. The Black Hand struck before the detectives were ready to fight. Would you join us, Antonio?"

Branco took another deliberate sip from his cup, stared into it, then looked up at Giuseppe Vella. "It will be less trouble to pay."

"We are American," Vella insisted. "We have a right to make business in peace."

"No. I'm sorry."

Vella stood up. "Then I thank you for your coffee, and I thank you for listening. If you change your mind, I will welcome you." He looked at LaCava. The banker hesitated, then stood reluctantly.

They were just rounding the corner onto Elizabeth Street when Branco caught up and took their arms. "O.K. I help." He pressed a wad of bills into Vella's hand. "Here's one thousand dollars for my dues. Get the others to pony up and your White Hand Society will be on its way."

"Thank you, my friend. Thank you very much. What changed your mind?"

"If you're right and I'm wrong — if your *Mano Blanca* defeats *Mano Nera* — I will benefit. But if I have not sided with you against our enemy, then I would benefit from your victory without helping. That would not be honorable."

Giuseppe Vella grinned with relief. Even LaCava looked happy. They were on their way. With Branco on board with such a big contribution, the others would be quick to join. "I hope I'm right. But if I'm wrong and you're right, at least we'll both ex-plode."

"You make terrible joke," said Branco. His expression turned so bleak that Vella wished he had not said it.

In a surprise, Branco smiled as if abandoning forever every thought of any unhappiness. "We'll be blown to bits, everything except our honor." He shrugged, and, still smiling, added, "We are invisible men in this country. We are poor. We have nothing but honor."

"Italians won't be poor forever," said Giuseppe Vella. "Already I am not poor. David is not poor. You are not poor."

"But at the Central Federated Union meeting last night, when they debated whether to support excavators striking the subway jobs, the Electrical Workers unionist shouted that Italian pick and shovel men were unskilled scum of the earth."

"I was there, too," said Vella. "A typesetter shouted back that his ancestors started here with a pick and shovel, and if the electrician was looking down on his ancestors, he better put up his fists."

Branco smiled. "But we are still invisible . . . On the other hand" — an even bigger smile lit his mobile face — "invisible men aren't noticed, until it's too late."

"Too late for what?"

"Too late to stop them."

5

Van Dorn detective Harry Warren, dressed like the workmen drinking in the Kips Bay Saloon in shabby coats and flat caps, planted a worn boot on the brass rail, ordered a beer, and muttered to the tall guy next to him, "How'd you talk the Boss into a Black Hand Squad?"

"I didn't," said Isaac Bell without shifting his gaze from the mirror behind the bar, which reflected the view through the saloon's window of the Banco LaCava storefront across the street. He had tricked out his workman's costume with an electrician's cylindrical leather tool case slung over his shoulder. In it were extra manacles for bomb planters who surrendered and a sawed-off shotgun for those who didn't.

"A bunch of Italian business men did it for me. Marched in with a bag of money to hire the agency for protection, and Mr. Van Dorn decided it was about time."

Warren asked, "Would they happen to call themselves the White Hand Society?"

No one knew the streets of New York better than Harry Warren. He had probably heard of the new outfit ten minutes after its founding. Which meant, Bell was painfully aware, so had the Black Hand.

"Giuseppe Vella launched it. He's been getting Black Hand letters. David LaCava joined him. And some of their well-heeled friends. Banking, property, construction, a wine importer, and a wholesaler grocer."

"Branco?"

"Antonio."

"What did you think of him?"

"He wasn't there. But Vella told me he put up the seed money that got the others into it. The Boss authorizes up to ten men — if you count apprentices."

"How many speak Italian?"

"Just you, Harry."

The Van Dorn New York City street gang expert had changed his name from Salvatore Guaragna, following the example of New York Italian gangsters like Five Points Gang chief "Paul Kelly," who took Irish names. He said, "I got an apprentice candidate who's Italian. Little Eddie Tobin's father found him living on a hay barge. Orphan. The Tobins took him in. Richie Cirillo.

Sharp kid."

"Glad to have him," said Bell.

"Who's the rest of your lineup?"

"Weber and Fields are parked down the street on a coal wagon." Middle-aged Wally Kisley and Mack Fulton were the agency comedians. Nicknamed after the vaudevillians Weber and Fields, Kisley was Van Dorn's explosives expert, Fulton a walking encyclopedia of safecrackers and their modi operandi.

Harry Warren grinned. "Helluva disguise. I couldn't figure out if they were guarding the bank or fixing to rob it. Who else?"

"I've got Eddie Edwards coming in from Kansas City."

"Valuable man. Though I'm not sure what a rail yard specialist can do on Elizabeth Street."

"Archie Abbott is selling used clothes from that pushcart next to the bank."

"You're kidding!" Archibald Angell Abbott IV was the only Van Dorn listed in the New York Social Register. Warren wandered casually toward the free lunch, shot a glance out the window at a different angle, and came back with a sausage wrapped in a slice of bread. "I didn't make him."

"He didn't want you to."

"I've also got Wish Clarke and —"

"Forget Wish," Harry interrupted. "Mr. Van Dorn is one step from firing him."

"I know. We'll see how he's doing." Aloysius Clarke, the sharpest detective in the agency — and the partner from whom Isaac Bell had learned the most — was a drinking man, and it was beginning to get the better of him.

"Who else?"

"Your Eddie Tobin."

Harry nodded gloomily. Another apprentice. The Boss wasn't exactly going all out.

"And Helen Mills."

"The *college* girl?" Mills was a Bryn Mawr coed whom Bell had offered a summer job with the prospect of becoming a full-fledged apprentice when she graduated.

"Helen's plenty sharp."

"Is it true what the boys say? She decked Archie last year down in Washington?"

"Archie started it."

Harry Warren went back to the free lunch for another look at the street. Bell divided his attention between customers going into Banco LaCava and toughs in the saloon who might be preparing an attack. Harry came back with a hard-boiled egg. "Let me guess," he joked. "She's the fat lady selling artichokes?"

"I sent Helen down to Park Row to get a line on where the Black Hand buys their stationery . . . Harry, why did you ask what I think of Branco?"

"He's a strange one. Wholesale grocers tend to extort the smaller shops, force them to buy only from them and charge top dollar for cheap goods."

"How do they force them to buy?"

"Run the gamut from getting them deep in hock to bombing their store. But I've never heard a breath of any of that about Antonio Branco."

"Honest as the Lottery?" Bell asked with a thin smile.

"I wouldn't go that far," said Harry, "about anybody making a business in New York. And he's also a labor padrone. Stone masons and laborers for the Catskill Aqueduct."

"There's a business ripe for abuse."

"They tend not to be choirboys," Harry agreed. "On the other hand, he's worked his way into the union's good graces. Slick."

"But not the first," said Bell. "D'Allesandro, with the subway excavators, started out a padrone."

"And now that Branco's joined the White Hands, he's a Van Dorn client."

"Unless he steps out of line," said Bell,

73

eye still locked on Banco LaCava.

"They're remarkable," David LaCava told Antonio Branco over a glass of wine in Ghiottone's Café, a saloon across Prince Street from Branco's Grocery that served as one of Tammany Hall's outposts in the Italian colony. Ghiottone — "Kid Kelly" Ghiottone, a popular bantam-weight boxer in his youth — delivered voters, and Tammany paid off with city jobs in the Department of Street Cleaning and immunity from the police. Which allowed the saloon keeper to lord it over the neighborhood.

LaCava told Branco how Isaac Bell's Black Hand Squad was guarding his bank with men in disguise. "You would not look twice at them."

Branco said, "So our White Hand Society has chosen well."

"I'm convinced we've hired the best."

"But how long can they stand guard?"

LaCava looked around the café, leaned closer, and whispered, "Guarding is only the first stage. Meanwhile, they observe and collect information. When they attack, the Black Hand won't know what hit them." He lowered his voice further. "I was talking to a New York Police Department detective —"

74

"Petrosino?"

"How did you know?"

Branco shrugged. "Who else?"

"Of course," said LaCava, chastened by the subtle reminder that he was not the only business operator cultivating men with pull. "Petrosino says this is how the Van Dorns dismantled railroad gangs."

"What did Lieutenant Petrosino say about the White Hand hiring Van Dorns?"

LaCava hesitated. "He says he understands. He knows he's got plenty on his plate already. To be honest, I think he would have preferred we go to the police. But since we hired private detectives, he respects that we chose the Van Dorns."

"Valuable men," said Branco. "We're lucky to have them."

The next morning, Isaac Bell stationed all but two of his Black Hand shadows on Elizabeth Street before David LaCava filled his display window and opened his door for business. The exceptions were Wish Clarke, who still hadn't shown up from nearby Philadelphia, and Helen Mills, whom Bell had sent back downtown to the printing district.

She was a tall, slim brunette who looked older than her eighteen years, and despite

75

their rigorous schedules and merciless deadlines, every printer, typesetter, and paper supplier she spoke to found time to inspect her samples and offer advice. Several, old enough to be her father, discovered they were free for lunch. She turned them down — inventing a Van Dorn Detective Agency rule that forbade it — and kept moving from shop to shop, pausing between each to write notes in the memo book Isaac had given her. The sooner she learned all there was to know about the paper, the sooner she could convince Isaac to let her join the rest of the squad undercover in the field.

Then, out of the blue all of a sudden, after an ink salesman left her alone with a pimply office boy to answer a telephone call, the boy said, "Money."

"I beg your pardon?"

The boy was even younger than she and barely came to her shoulder.

"You could almost print two-dollar bills on that paper. If you had plates and ink."

"Have you seen this paper before?"

"Not that same paper. But I've seen the type when they come for ink. The Boss sends them packing."

"Who?"

"Fellows making green goods."

" 'Green goods'? What are you talking about?"

"Passing the queer."

"Queer what?" asked Helen.

The office boy stared at her like she was the biggest nincompoop in the city.

Richie Cirillo swore he was sixteen, but he looked twelve.

Isaac Bell tried to get a handle on how old the kid really was. "Why'd you leave school?"

"They stuck me in steamer class."

"What is 'steamer class'?"

"For the dummies."

Harry Warren interpreted. "The teachers put Italian kids in the slow class. Their mothers work at home, finishing garments. The kids have to help. Sewing buttons and felling seams to midnight, then up at six for school — they're not slow, they're sleepy."

"I was told you're an orphan, Richie."

"My mother got diphtheria. My father went back to Italy. But I really am sixteen, Mr. Bell."

"What is this disguise you came up with?" In the business districts, a youthful Van Dorn apprentice would masquerade, typically, as a newsboy. But there were no boys hawking the *Sun,* the *Times,* the *Herald,* or the *American* on Elizabeth Street, where those who were literate only read Italian. Instead of newspapers, Richie Cirillo had a sack of cloth slung over his skinny shoulder.

"I'm a runner. Like I'm delivering dresses to be finished in the tenements and bringing them back to the factory when they're done."

"O.K. You'll do."

"Wow! Thank you, Mr. Bell."

"Keep your eyes open. One eye on the bank, the other on one of us, so you know who to run to if you get in trouble."

6

"Forgive me, Father, for I have sinned."

Francesca Kennedy was a dark-haired, blue-eyed Irish-Italian beauty. Her pale white face shone like a splash of sunlight through the confessional lattice that hid the priest. She knelt in a good coat with a fur collar and a modest scarf to cover her head.

"How did you sin, my child?"

"I stabbed a man to death."

"Did anyone see you?"

"No, Father."

"Are you sure?"

"One hundred percent. It was just me and him in the bed."

"Well done!"

A rolled-up silver certificate passed through the lattice. Francesca Kennedy unrolled it and examined it closely.

"It is not counterfeit," the priest assured her.

"You want we should hit the Van Dorn captain?" whispered Charlie Salata.

Salata's gang ran Black Hand letters, kidnapping, and protection, and he hadn't gone to confession since he was a boy in Palermo, but kneeling in church still made him whisper. "Gold Head . . . Right? Show the Van Dorns who owns Elizabeth Street."

Silence. He ventured a glance at the lattice. It was dark inside the priest's booth. All he could see through the perforations in the crisscross wooden screen were Stiletto Man eyes, empty as night, clouds mobbing the stars. Still silent, but for a staccato *click-click-click-click-click.* Was he spooked or did he really hear the man behind the screen opening and shutting a knife again and again and again?

Salata tried again. "You prefer we hit the old dicks on the coal wagon? Spook their horse so he gallops into people and Van Dorns get blamed." Again, Salata waited for a reaction. Precisely how his men should attack the Van Dorns guarding Banco LaCava would not ordinarily be worth troubling the Boss, but Salata recognized a delicate situation. The trick was to distract the Van Dorns so they could bomb Banco LaCava *and* get away with the money and at the same time

80

scare the White Hand Society out of existence.

"Maybe we hit the red-haired one, show they can't trick us."

"Hit the kid."

"The mick?"

"Not the mick. The Italian."

"But he's —"

"He's *what*?"

"Nothing." Salata backpedaled instantly. The stiletto was not a pistol. You didn't wave it around, making threats. You only pulled it to kill. And to be sure to kill, you had to pull it without warning. The narrow blade could fit through the grid and right in his eye.

"Hit Richie Cirillo."

That the Boss had discovered, somehow, the Van Dorn apprentice's name was a stark reminder that Charlie Salata's weren't his only eyes and ears on the street. "The kid is Italian. He will be an example for the neighborhood. Teach them never go to police. Never go to Van Dorns."

"How hard?"

"So hard, people don't forget."

Salata jumped from the kneeler and hurried out of the church.

Ten minutes later, right on schedule, his place was taken by Ernesto Leone, a coun-

81

terfeiter.

"The plates are O.K.," Leone reported. "The ink is better than before, but still so-so. The paper is the big problem. Like always."

"Have you tried to pass any?"

"It's not ready. Not good enough."

"Tell Salata to send someone to Pennsylvania. Buy stuff in general stores."

"I don't think it will pass."

"And Ferri. Tell Ferri send someone upstate."

"It's not good enough."

"It is costing money and earning none."

Leone said, "If there is trouble, Salata and Ferri will blame me."

"My patience is not endless, Ernesto Leone."

Leone scuttled from the church.

Roberto Ferri, a smuggler, confessed next. "My men caught wind of a heroin shipment. The Irish."

"How big?"

"Very big, I am told. From Mexico."

"Which Irish?"

"West Side Wallopers. Hunt and McBean."

"Well done, Roberto!" Hunt and McBean were up and coming "graduates" of the Gopher Gang.

Ferri said, "I hear there is a market for cocaine on the aqueduct job. The Negroes use it. But no market for heroin . . . If you know anyone on the aqueduct, maybe we could trade heroin for cocaine."

"You just get your hands on it. I'll worry about the market."

"You know someone to sell it to?"

"Good-bye, Ferri."

Ferri lit his customary candle on his way out of the church.

Antonio Branco waited in the priest's side of the confessional, his fingers busy as a clockwork as he practiced opening and closing his pocket knife. His knee had stiffened up, cramped in the booth. After Ferri left, he limped to the poor box and stuffed fifty dollars into it, "confessional rent" for the priests he had tamed. A flight of stone steps led down to the catacomb. Before he hit the bottom step, he had worked out the kink.

A low-ceilinged passage ran between the mortuary vaults under the church. He used a key to enter the crypt at the end. He locked the heavy door behind him, squeezed between stacks of caskets, unlocked a door hidden in the back, and stepped through a massive masonry foundation wall into a damp tunnel. The tunnel led under the church's graveyard and through another door into the musty basement of a tenement. Repeatedly unlocking and relocking doors, he crossed under three similar buildings, cellar to cellar to cellar. The last door was concealed in the back of a walk-in safe, heaped with cash and weapons. Closing it behind him, he exited the safe into a clean, dry cellar, passed by a room with an empty iron cell that looked like a police lockup but for the soundproof walls and ceiling, unlocked a final oak door, and climbed the stairs into the kitchen in the back of his grocery.

"Where's Gold Head?"

"I don't see him."

The detective's spot at the Kips Bay bar was empty.

"Where's the coal dicks?"

Their wagon was gone. So was Red-haired's pushcart of old clothes.

"Who's that?" A drunk was sprawled beside the Kips Bay stoop.

Charlie Salata crossed the street and kicked him in the ribs. The drunk groaned and threw up, just missing Salata's shoes. Salata jumped back, and looked up and down the street for the twentieth time. Where in hell were the Van Dorns? Elizabeth between Houston and Prince was the most crowded block in the city. Five thousand people lived in the tenements and today it looked like most were on the sidewalk.

"No Van Dorns? Let's do it."

But still Salata hesitated. It felt like a setup.

"False money," Helen Mills reported to Isaac Bell.

The tall detective was combing black shoe polish through his hair in the back of a horse-drawn silver-vault van parked at Washington Square nine blocks from Elizabeth Street. Helen had helped him and Archie on the Assassin case last year, and Bell regarded both her and her father as friends. Raised as an Army child, she had a refined sense of rank and protocol and had concluded she would address him as "Mr. Bell" on the job.

"Counterfeiters passing the queer?"

Her eyes were bright with excitement, which Bell did not want to damp down even as he explained why it was unlikely. "Good job, Helen. If the extortionists are also counterfeiters, we'll have stumbled upon something rather unusual."

"Unusual?"

"There are certain kinds of crimes that don't usually mix. The criminal who would attempt to print money is not usually the sort who would threaten violence."

"Never?"

"I'm not saying never, which is why I want you to follow up on this very interesting lead. The Secret Service investigates counterfeiting. It takes a lot of doing to get them to talk to private detectives, but they might make an exception for you. Go find Agent Lynch. Chris Lynch. He's their man in New York. Show him the paper. Tell him what you learned on Printer's Row."

To Bell's surprise, Helen bridled.

"What's wrong?"

She sounded indignant. "Am I supposed to bat my eyes at Lynch?"

"Bat them if you want to. Feel out the situation and act accordingly."

"Because I must tell you, Mr. Bell, the printers think being a detective makes me fast. Two asked me to lunch, and one old geezer tried to take me to Atlantic City for the weekend."

"I've not run into that problem," said Isaac Bell. "But here's a suggestion. Instead of batting your eyes at Lynch, try dropping your father's name. The Secret Service might be inclined to talk to the daughter of a brigadier general."

"Isaa— Mr. Bell, I know I'm only an intern, but I was hoping you'd put me to work in the street on this Banco LaCava job."

"If you make that stationery nail a Black Hand extortionist, I will personally promote you to full-fledged apprentice."

"Even before I graduate?"

Bell hesitated, imagining grim-visaged Brigadier G. Tannenbaum Mills turning purple. "I suspect your father will express strong views on the subject of leaving college before you complete your degree."

Charlie Salata made his boys prowl Elizabeth Street for an hour.

"They're here," he kept saying, anxiously scanning the street, sidewalks, wagons, pushcarts, windows, rooftops, and fire escapes. "I can't see 'em, but I feel 'em. Like I can smell 'em — what's that kid doing?"

"Pasting playbills."

The gangsters watched the kid plaster posters to walls, the sides of wagons, and even shopwindows when the owners weren't looking. They advertised a performance of *Aida* at the nearby Mincarelli Opera House, which catered to immigrants. The bill poster crossed Houston and plastered his way uptown and out of sight.

An unusually tall Hebrew caught Salata's eye when he emerged from a tenement dressed head to toe in coat, trousers, shoes, and hat as black as his beard. Salata studied him suspiciously. The Hebrew dodged the organ grinder's monkey plucking pennies from the pavement, and hurried inside the next tenement. Only one of the many Jewish needlework contractors who recruited Italian housewives to sew piecework in their kitchens.

"Why don't we just bomb the bank?" an underling asked.

"Why don't you shut your mouth?" It was obvious to anyone but a *cafon* two hours off the boat. Blowing the windows out of Banco LaCava was the easy part. Pawing through the wreckage to get the money out of the safe would take time. They'd have a few minutes before the cops and firemen arrived, but no time at all if Van Dorns were close enough to mob them. Plus — a big plus not to be ignored — the Boss had given orders to make an example of the Van Dorn apprentice.

"*There!* Richie Cirillo."

The kid was trotting past Banco LaCava with a clothes sack almost bigger than he was. Salata grabbed the *cafon.* "Stick that skinny little rat."

Richie Cirillo saw the killer coming after him, running in a low half crouch like a barrel-chested dog. Fiery eyes bored into his as the man shoved through the dense crowds.

The boy panicked. He dropped his clothing sack and ran across the street toward the Kips Bay Saloon, forgetting that Mr. Bell was no longer watching from the bar. His vision contracted. All he could see through a path of moving obstacles, rushing people, carts, and wagons was safety inside the saloon. All he had to do was reach the front stoop, leap over the drunk sprawled on it, and get inside.

People saw the fear on his face, and the path opened wide. They scrambled out of his way. He burst past them — they couldn't help if they tried — skidded on the greasy cobblestones, and fell on his face. Before he was back on his feet, the killer had halved his lead. A stiletto gleamed in his fist.

Isaac Bell bolted from a tenement in black Hebrew garb and ran after the thug chasing the apprentice. The block was packed with innocents, too many people for gunplay. An empty delivery wagon blocked his path. As he vaulted over it, he saw Archie Abbott, his hair dyed dark like Bell's, drop the reins of a horse cart heaped with rags and jump from the driver's seat. Harry Warren leaped from a second-story fire escape, slid down a canvas shop awning, and hit the sidewalk running.

The killer caught up six feet from the front stoop of the Kips Bay Saloon.

Richie's senses were heightened by fear. For a second, he could see and feel and hear everything at once — the drunk blinking awake at his feet, the shadow of the man behind him, the stiletto hissing as it parted the air. He twisted frantically from its path. Aimed at the back of his neck, the blade slipped past and tore through his ear. The pain stopped him cold, and, in that instant, the killer thrust again.

Richie heard a startled grunt.

The stiletto fell on the sidewalk, ringing like a chime. The killer doubled over, clutching his groin. A fist rose from the sidewalk like a pile driver in reverse and smashed the killer's face. Richie heard bones snap. Blood spattered the drunk, who sagged back down on the stoop and closed his eyes.

The man who had tried to stab him reached to pick up his knife. Bell stepped on his hand, and Abbott clamped manacles on his wrists.

Isaac Bell seized Richie's shoulder and clapped a handkerchief over his ear. "O.K., boy?"

"I think so. Thanks to this guy."

Bell knelt beside the drunk. "Wish, where did you come from?"

"Philadelphia," said Aloysius Clarke. "Sorry I fell asleep."

"Heck of a disguise."

"I've been practicing my whole life."

A loud explosion showered them with glass.

7

"Mano Nera! Mano Nera!"

Gold coins, ten-dollar bills, and broken glass flew from Banco LaCava's show window and cascaded into Elizabeth Street. Dust and smoke gushed from the shattered bank and the front of the tenement in which it was housed.

"Mano Nera! Mano Nera!"

Within moments, hundreds of people crowded onto fire escapes, screaming, *"Mano Nera! Mano Nera!"* and thousands surged from their tenements. As the mad rush filled the sidewalks and spilled into the street, David LaCava stormed out with a pistol and a wastebasket and began picking up the money. His cheek was cut, and blood reddened his shirtfront.

"You two help him," Bell ordered Wally Kisley and Mack Fulton, and led Archie and Harry Warren into the building. They searched for trapped and injured. Inside the

92

front hall, broken plaster and splintered lath littered the floor. Through swirling dust, Bell saw that the bomb had blown a hole in a wall between the building and the bank and LaCava's apartment behind it. Two men hauling sacks of money from LaCava's safe jumped through the hole.

Isaac Bell and Archie Abbott knocked both to the floor in a flurry of fists and blackjacks. A third thug leaped through the hole, waving a gun. Harry Warren fired his pistol first and dragged the money back through the hole, while Bell and Archie Abbott carried Mrs. LaCava and her two children out of their wrecked parlor.

Cops and plainclothes detectives arrived on the run from their Mulberry Street Station House. White horses galloped through the crowds, dragging fire engines.

"What are you doing here?" asked a detective, taking charge of the prisoner Harry Warren handed over. The others had escaped.

"Guarding the bank."

"Made a hash of it."

"No kidding."

Wally Kisley hurried up to Bell with a rag collector's sack over his shoulder. Bell asked, "Where's Richie?"

"Doctor's sewing his ear. Don't look now,

but the Boss is here."

"He's in Washington."

"Was," said Harry. "He looks mad enough to bite the heads off nails. Or detectives."

"I'm afraid I know which one," said Bell.

Sure enough, Joseph Van Dorn was shouldering a beeline for the Kips Bay Saloon. Bell caught up with him as he knelt beside Wish Clarke, who had fallen back to sleep. Van Dorn seized his shoulder in his massive hand and shook him hard.

"Wake up, Aloysius!"

Wish Clarke opened his eyes, wiped his mouth with the back of his hand, and smiled. "Hello, Boss."

"You're fired."

Isaac Bell said, "He saved Richie Cirillo's life."

"I heard all about it. He's drunk. Dumb luck he woke up in time and dumb luck he didn't get the rest of you killed. Aloysius, you're the best detective I know. I'll welcome you back when you're stone-cold sober and dry for the rest of your life. Until then, I don't want to see your face."

He stood up, turned, and hurried away. Then he turned back, knelt again, and awkwardly patted Wish's shoulder. "Bejesus, man, I've known you almost as long as I've known Mack and Wally. I hope you can come back."

"Thanks, Joe."

Van Dorn stalked off.

Isaac Bell helped his old friend to his feet. Wish said, "Sorry I let you down, Isaac."

"You didn't let me down. I'd have lost an apprentice without you. I'm only sorry the Boss doesn't see it that way."

Wish looked immensely sad and fumbled for his hip flask. "Don't get on the wrong side of this, old son. The Boss is right."

"What were you doing in the bank?" a police detective roared at the gangster the Van Dorns had turned over to him.

"Buy steamship ticket."

"Where to?"

"Italia."

"You're lying, Pasquale. Your type don't go back to Italy, they'd throw you in the hoosegow. What were you doing in the bank?"

"Big-a boom. Head hurts."

"What is your business?"

"None."

"Who do you run with? Salata?"

"Salata? Never heard of him."

"Where do you live?"

"I've forgotten."

The cop shouted, "You think I'm the soft

95

mark, wiseacre? I'll give you to Detective Petrosino. His boys'll strip you down to your socks."

"Won't do no good," Harry Warren muttered to Isaac Bell. "Sicilians don't crack."

Across the street, the killer whose nose Wish Clarke had broken insisted to the cops that he had been running into the Kips Bay for a beer when a drunk attacked him.

"Was that before or after you dropped your stiletto?"

"Not mine."

"Pasquale, I got witnesses saw you stabbed a kid with it."

"Nobody remember in trial."

The cop winked at Harry Warren. "If they was Italians who saw you stick the kid, you'd probably be right, Pasquale. You've got the poor devils too scared to remember their own mothers. But my witnesses are Van Dorns. They got a saying. They never forget. Never . . . So let's start over. What's your name?"

"Pasquale."

"What's your name?"

"Pasquale."

"He's Vito Rizzo," Harry Warren interrupted. "One of Salata's boys, aren't you, Vito?"

"Gimme lawyer."

Warren said to Bell, "He'll jump bail tomorrow."

"We'll press charges."

"He'll still be out on bail. They got pull at Tammany Hall."

The cops and firemen restored order, and the neighborhood started to settle down. But even as they cleared the street of people gawking, a long line of depositors, clutching bankbooks, formed at the shattered front door of Banco LaCava.

Bell gave the cops on guard a look at his Van Dorn badge, and Harry Warren slipped each two dollars. They found LaCava stuffing his safe with the money he had scooped from the street and Bell's squad had rescued.

"My business is ruined. People are running to my bank to take their money."

"Why? You got your money back."

"They can't trust their money will be safe with me. They know the Black Hand will come again. I should have paid like my friend Branco told me."

When Bell and Harry Warren were alone, the gang detective said, "His 'friend' Branco could be the guy who sent the extortion letter. First they send it. Then they just happen to show up like a friend or fellow business man, advising you to pay."

Isaac Bell studied Antonio Branco from the café across Prince Street from Branco's Grocery. Leaning, half seated, half standing, against a tall stool, he cut a well-to-do figure, in a tailored blue suit of broadcloth fit more for the board of director's dining room than a bustling grocery. Ditto his custom-made shoes, polished to a mirror shine.

He was significantly taller than the clerks and drivers he was overseeing loading his wagons, an animated presence with flashing eyes, a trim mustache, and thick, curly hair black as anthracite. His face was constantly changing: a robust smile for a quick-moving employee, a harsh scowl for a laggard, a satisfied nod for a full wagon. An orange fell from a broken crate, he snapped it out of the air with a lightning grasp.

Bell crossed the street. Branco tracked him with alert eyes and a curious gaze as if instinctively aware that the tall detective weaving smoothly through the traffic had business with him. He stood up and crossed the sidewalk to intercept him, and Bell saw that he walked with a slight limp, with one foot kicking slightly to the side. It did nothing to diminish the impression of a coiled spring forged of the strongest alloy.

Bell extended his hand. "Isaac Bell, Mr. Branco. Van Dorn Detective Agency. I understand you told David LaCava to pay the Black Hand."

Branco looked away with a sad smile. "I told David LaCava and Giuseppe Vella. Apparently, they should have listened to me."

"But if you felt that way, why did you join their White Hand Society?"

"I was skeptical. But it was the right thing to help. Even if not wise."

"Skeptical? Or afraid?"

When an expression of contempt hardened Branco's face and steel glittered in his eyes, Bell was struck by an odd feeling that they had met earlier. Before he could pin the memory, Branco smiled, and the steely glitter softened to a good-humored sparkle. "There are forces it sometimes behooves us to accommodate."

"Were you born in America, Mr. Branco?"

"No. Why do you ask?"

"You have a native's command of the language."

Branco beamed. "Would that were so. My accent ever marks me a newcomer."

"It is barely noticeable," said Bell, "while you turn a fine phrase. When did you arrive?"

"I first came as a harp slave when I was eight years old and I have lived here on and off ever since . . . You look puzzled. A 'harp slave' is a boy made to play music in the streets and bring his padrone the coins that kind people toss to him."

"A slave implies a cruel master."

Branco shrugged. "I learned my English, I learned to read."

"All at eight? You're practically a native."

"I returned to Italy when my padrone died. In those days, a steerage ticket back was seven dollars. Even a boy could go home."

"I've heard that now *you* are a padrone."

"Not for children," Branco said sharply. "I help padrones find work for grown men."

"On the aqueduct?"

"I am privileged to help the Excavators' Union build this important feat. Now, since you've come on detective business, do you have any more questions before I continue conducting *my* business?"

"One more. Will your White Hand Society disband?"

"You mean will the society continue to pay Van Dorn?"

Now Bell's eyes flashed annoyance. "The Van Dorn Agency will work to put the gang that attacked Banco LaCava behind bars,

100

gratis. I meant precisely what I asked you — will your protective society disband?"

"If you are not worried about being paid, why do you care?"

"Your society will be a source of information. And give strength to the weak."

"I hope it does not disband," said Branco. "Good men should stand together. If we did disband, why would you still hunt the Black Hand? To avenge your boy they stabbed? Or because they made you look bad?"

Isaac Bell's vow to avenge the attack on his apprentice and restore faith in the agency by catching the dynamiters was none of Branco's business and he answered only the higher truth. "Because they are criminals who prey on the innocent."

"It is not my experience that Americans care about innocent Italians."

"It is my experience that the sooner we care about them, the sooner they'll turn into Americans."

"How long do you intend to pursue the bombers?"

"Until we catch them. Good day, Mr. Branco. Thank you for your time."

Branco said, "I, too, have one more question — is Van Dorn a national enterprise?"

"We have field offices across the continent."

"Do you combat 'national' criminals?"

"We pursue criminals across state lines, if that's what you mean."

"No, I mean are there criminal organizations that span the country?"

"They would have to master modern systems of national organization."

"Like railroads?" asked Branco.

"Or the telegraph. Or Standard Oil and U.S. Steel. But since most criminals have trouble organizing a clean shirt in the morning," Isaac Bell added with a smile, "it would require powerful adjustments of attitude."

Bell walked away.

Antonio Branco enjoyed a private moment of satisfaction. Despite the detective's flattering compliments about his English, to lull him into letting down his guard, he still formed thoughts in Italian. When, and if, you do catch them, Mr. Bell, who will you have caught? Peasants. *Contadini.* Of which Italy has an endless supply.

Most criminals have trouble organizing a clean shirt?

Mr. Bell, you and your Van Dorn Detective Agency will be amazed when a criminal organization spans your nation.

Suddenly, Bell was back, striding at Branco like a panther, his eyes aglow.

"Mr. Branco."

"Did you forget something, Mr. Bell?"

"Do you recall when we met before?"

"I doubt we've run in the same circles."

"Eleven years ago. I was a student."

"Eleven years ago, I was a laborer."

"In New Haven, Connecticut."

"Wherever there was work."

"I was at college in New Haven."

"As I said, we did not run in the same circles."

"We were running, all right. Both of us. Running from New Haven Railroad cinder dicks."

Branco smiled. He looked intrigued. "Not in New Haven. I ran from no railroad police in New Haven."

"North of New Haven. In the Farmington yard."

Antonio Branco stared at Isaac Bell. He moved near and inspected him very closely. Then he stepped back and looked him up and down, hat to boots. *"Incredibile!"* he breathed at last. *"Incredibile!"*

"You remember?"

"It is incredible. Yes, I do remember. I did not get much of a look at you in the dark, but your stance is the same."

"So is yours," said Bell. "And your limp. Do you still carry your knife?"

"What knife?"

"The one you pulled on me."

Branco smiled. "I recall no need to pull a knife on a college boy."

"You did," said Bell. "And you also pulled one on a rail cop in New Haven earlier that night."

"No."

"Right before you rode my train to Farmington."

"No, Mr. Bell. I did not pull a knife on a rail cop. I did steal a ride on your train . . . I didn't realize it was your train. I thought it belonged to the railroad."

Bell could not help but smile back. "I borrowed it. College high jinks."

"I guessed as much," said Branco.

"The rail cop was attacked that same night. Did you happen to witness it?"

Branco hesitated. Then he shrugged. "It was long ago."

"So you did see it."

"A tramp cut the rail cop and ran away. It did allow me to escape, but I am not the man who cut him. Was the cop badly injured?"

"He survived," said Bell.

"Then all is well that ends well."

104

"He was horribly scarred."

"Good. I am glad to hear that."

"I beg your pardon?"

"He 'scarred' me, too. Nearly broke my leg. You yourself see, I limp to this day. It aches when storms are coming. Which is not supposed to happen to young men like me and you."

"Who was the man with the knife?"

"The tramp? I never saw him before."

"The cop said he was Italian."

"Many hobos were Italian in those days. Still are. I didn't know him. But I owe him. Thanks to him, I escaped the railroad cop. You owe him, too."

"How do you reckon that?"

"Thanks to him, you weren't caught when you 'borrowed' your train, which you would have been if he hadn't slashed the cop. So we have that tramp in common. He saved us both for better things."

"What better things?"

"The laborer became a business man. The train thief became a detective."

Isaac Bell laughed. "Only in America."

The tall detective and the wealthy grocer exchanged a powerful handshake.

Branco returned to his business, and Bell caught the train uptown.

Harry Warren was waiting in the detective

105

bull pen. "Black Hand?"

"I can't read him yet. But whatever Antonio Branco wants, he's capable of getting. A formidable man. Angry man, too, though he covers it. Mostly" — Bell considered Branco's tale of the tramp and the railroad cop and added — "he's also a first class liar."

Wally Kisley came in the back entrance, still in the costume of a rag collector with dirty hands and face. "I got something for you."

From his rag sack he pulled a red tube that looked like a dynamite stick. Detectives nearby edged away. Kisley tossed it to them and they dove for cover. It bounced on the floor with a hollow *thunk.*

Kisley grinned. "I emptied the nitro."

Bell asked, "Where'd you find it?"

"Under LaCava's safe."

"Why blow the safe? It was open during the day."

"I think it was part of the bundle that blew the wall. But it misfired. Got blown through the wall and bounced under the safe."

"What does it do for us?"

"Read the name."

"Stevens."

"You can't buy the Stevens brand in New York City. It's made in New Jersey by a subsidiary of Dupont's Eastern Dynamite Company and distributed to small-town hardware stores. It's a short stick, shorter than what you'd find in mining or big excavation jobs. For farmers blowing stumps."

"Where'd the Black Hand get ahold of it?"

"Some hardware or feedstore in New Jersey or Pennsylvania, I'd guess. Point is, they didn't buy or steal it in New York City."

Bell remembered that Giuseppe Vella claimed that his foreman, Russo, had discovered the overcharge too late to stop the water main explosion. It was a long shot, but he wondered whether Russo had noticed in the confusion the type of dynamite in the overcharge?

Vella had no telephone since the Combustibles Department put him out of business. Bell hurried downtown and found him at his house on 13th Street. Vella greeted him warily, and Bell guessed that he had paid the ransom the Black Hand had demanded for the rescued Maria. He showed Vella the empty Stevens dynamite tube.

"Have you ever seen this brand?"

"In the countryside."

"Not in New York?"

"Not on my jobs."

"Did your foreman Russo happen to say

anything about the dynamite in the over-charge?"

"He was excited, yelling, 'Big-a bang! Big-a bang!' "

"But when he disconnected the detonating wires, would he have noticed what brand it was?"

Vella shrugged. "Who knows?"

Only Russo, thought Bell. "Is it possible, Mr. Vella, that Russo himself laid the overcharge for the Black Hand?"

Vella shrugged. "Who knows? Anything is possible."

"How likely?"

"Not likely. Sante Russo is a good man."

"Do you know where he is?"

Vella hesitated.

Bell said, "I am hunting the criminals who ruined your job. The criminals who kidnapped your daughter. Russo can help me find them."

"How?"

"It is important that I learn if this is the same dynamite that ruined your job."

Vella nodded. "O.K. I understand . . . Russo sent a telegram asking would I wire him the money he was owed for his last week of work. His salary."

"Where did you send the money?"

"What makes you think I paid him?"

"You're an honest man, Giuseppe Vella. It would never occur to you not to pay a man who worked for you. Even if he's on the run and can't collect it. Did he come for the money or did you send it?"

"He asked that I wire it to St. Louis."

Isaac Bell set his squad on a search for foreman Russo.

8

Brewster Claypool was a slim-as-a-wisp, graceful Southerner who reminded people of the witty and stylish Oscar Wilde. Slouching languidly from the Metropolitan Opera House in white tie and tails, drifting down Broadway like an elegant parenthesis, he peered into the darker cross streets with a connoisseur's appreciation of New York's Tenderloin. Brightly lighted Broadway was lined with fine hotels and restaurants, but the rest of the district was devoted to sin. If a vice could be imagined, the Tenderloin offered it in gambling dens, dance halls, saloons, and bordellos priced for every purse. The Progressives called it Satan's Circus. Brewster Claypool called it Heaven.

He mounted the steps to the Cherry Grove bordello, a lavishly furnished elite house known as the Ritz of the Tenderloin, and rang an electric bell. A three-hundred-pound door guard ushered him into the sturdy brick mansion with great respect. A dazzling young woman in a red evening gown greeted him warmly. "Upstairs, Mr. Claypool?"

"I think I'll pop into the club first."

A group of top Wall Street men had formed a private club inside the whorehouse. The Cherry Grove Gentlemen's Society membership requirements were: extreme wealth and no blue noses. The house rules: No conversation or event left the room. No women were allowed in wearing more than two garments — neither garment could exceed the surface area of a dinner plate; a measuring stick was kept handy to settle disputes.

Claypool found his brother members lounging in vast leather armchairs, drinking champagne and whiskey cocktails. John Butler Culp, a vigorous big-game hunter and yacht racer who maintained the physique of a college pugilist and football hero, was cursing President Roosevelt.

"This wild, arrogant man, who only became president when the radicals assassinated President McKinley, will inflict fatal injury on our nation."

Culp was a Wall Street titan — sometimes partner, often as not rival, of J. P. Morgan, Judge Congdon, Frick, Schwab, and

J. D. Rockefeller. He combined cunning financial strategies with strict management to spawn railroads, mines, and mills, to consolidate wealth into great wealth, and to sharpen great wealth into power. He had the ear of Supreme Court justices, United States senators in his pay, and the confidence of presidents, but not this one. Late at night, alone with fellow "Cherry Grovers," he allowed his animosity free rein in a cold voice brimming with righteous fury.

"President McKinley defended property rights. This Roosevelt is a socialist rabble-rouser snatching our property."

"Teddy claims he won't run again," a banker interrupted.

"He lies! America is *doomed* if this darling of the Progressives serves this full term. Men of means will have no place in this country if he hangs on long enough to get reelected in '08."

Culp delivered this last with a glance at Brewster Claypool, a flash of dark eyes under heavy brows, so swift that none of the others noticed.

Claypool waved languidly to a raven-haired beauty in no danger of violating the dress code. She hurried to him with a crystal Old Fashioned glass and a bottle of Bushmills. "Just a splash, my dear. I must be on my way."

"Aren't you coming upstairs?"

"Not tonight, I'm afraid. I would be too distracted to be amusing."

He took his drink into the small library off the main room, settled into an armchair, and prayed that Culp would join him.

Claypool was "Culp's man," and he had heard enough to know that he had just received his marching orders. Truth be told, he had seen this coming since Roosevelt was elected in '04. Culp was afraid. In fact, he was terrified, which made him very dangerous.

President Roosevelt was breathing down his neck. It wasn't only that TR was leading the Progressive reform attack against monopolies, oil and railroad trusts, and stock manipulation — all sources of Culp's booming fortune — but down in the Isthmus of Panama, Teddy was "making the dirt fly," digging the ship canal to connect the Atlantic and Pacific oceans. And he had vowed, as only Teddy could — loudly and publicly — to prosecute business men who profited illegally from his canal.

Which, of course, Culp had — having financed a revolution to secure the route from friendly natives, rigged the Panama Canal Treaty to keep the canal out of the

113

hands of those same natives, stolen millions from investors, and maneuvered Congress into paying millions more for canal rights that lined the pockets of Culp and his friends.

Claypool's lawyers and lobbyists were working round the clock to disarm the canal time bomb. But if the President ever discovered that J. B. Culp had also masterminded the notorious Ramapo Grab — a private water company swindle that had almost won out over then-Governor Roosevelt's Catskill Aqueduct project — Teddy would not rest until Culp was in prison.

So Claypool was not surprised that J. B. Culp wanted the President of the United States removed from office. Culp *needed* the President removed from office. Unfortunately, impeachment was not possible. TR might exasperate and TR might unsettle, but even voters who didn't love him were at least fascinated, and two-thirds of the Senate was not was about to rile them by kicking out the President they had elected fair and square.

All of which meant that J. B. Culp wanted the President dead. As Culp's behind-the-scenes fixer, it was Brewster Claypool's job to find someone to kill him, while separating them from the crime by layer upon layer of isolation.

Unless he could talk Culp out of it.

Claypool nursed the whiskey until the glass was bone-dry, and he had almost given up hope when, at last, Culp lumbered in and loomed over his chair. He was a big man who used his bulk to intimidate.

"What are you waiting for?"

"An opportunity to talk sense. Would you please sit down?"

"My mind is made up. The man must go."

Claypool rose to his feet. "May I point out that he's not just a man. He is the President of the United States."

"I don't care if he's the King of England. Or the bloody Pope. Or the Almighty Himself. He will destroy us if we don't get rid of him."

"Is there no other way?"

Culp repeated, "Theodore Roosevelt will destroy us if we don't get rid of him."

9

"Look out, Mr. Bell!" the Van Dorn front desk man telephoned Isaac Bell in the detective bull pen. "Opera singer coming at you! I had to release the electric lock before she broke down the door."

Coloratura soprano Luisa Tetrazzini, the "Florentine Nightingale," burst into the bull pen and embraced Bell. Despite the Knickerbocker's steam heat, she was bundled in a coat, and her throat was swathed in an immensely long red scarf that trailed behind her. Her eyes were wild.

"Isaac!" she cried in a voice trained to carry to the back of a five-hundred-seat house. "Where is Joseph?" Knickerbocker permanent residents like her and Caruso, several theater impresarios, and the Van Dorns, shared a sort of small-town neighborliness. People dropped in to visit, lingered in hallways, and addressed each other by first name.

She was thirty-five years old, a shapely, Rubenesque dark-haired beauty with an expressive face, a love of drama, and a will of iron. She had made her American debut last year in San Francisco, before the earthquake. Caruso himself praised her voice and her acting. "Not yet a star," he had told Bell when Bell described hearing her sing in San Francisco. "But soon! Mark my words. The world will kiss her feet."

"Joseph," Bell answered, "is in Washington."

"But I am desperate. Look what they do." She thrust a letter at him. "Open!"

Bell recognized the paper. He unfolded it and saw what he expected, the now-familiar skull and dagger and the black hand. Mano Nera was stepping up in the world, first the helpless, then the well-off, now the famous.

Bella Tetrazzini,
    Were our need not great, we never trouble such artist. But we have no choice. Four thousand dollars must fall in our hands and so we turn to you singing for great success at Hammerstein. Please, Bella Tetrazzini, prepare the money and wait for instruction. Must

117

have before Thursday.

With great respect,
Your friends in need

"Don't be afraid," said Bell, "we'll —"

"I'm not afraid! I'm angry."

"When did you get this?"

"Twenty minutes ago. In the afternoon mail."

"Is this the first you've received?"

"Two last week. I thought it make joke."

"Do you have them?"

"I burned them in the fire. Isaac, I need guard. I'm going to sing in San Francisco again. For the earthquake victims."

"When do you leave?"

"Tomorrow. I think maybe I should not be alone with only my maid. I need Van Dorn guard."

Bell thought fast. His Black Hand Squad was up and running, though with no clients, the White Hand Society having terminated their contract. The hunt for Russo, the blaster, had shifted west from St. Louis. The Van Dorn Denver field office was looking for him in the mining camps. Russo could well be heading for San Francisco, which had a large Italian colony.

He fingered the letter. Definitely the same paper.

"Helen?" he called out. "Where's Helen Mills? There you are. This is for the Secret Service. Take it to Agent Lynch. Wait a minute. Helen? . . . Excuse me, Luisa, I will be right back." He led his intern away from the desk, out of earshot. "What's that bulge?"

"What bulge?"

Bell pointed. "That."

In her family's Dupont Circle mansion, Bell had seen Helen wear the latest styles of one-color, single-piece shirtwaist suits. Here, she wore the traditional young office girl's separate shirtwaist tucked into a trumpet skirt.

"That bulge is me."

"Not that. That pocket pistol under the pleats. Hand it over." He opened a big hand and waited for her to put the gun in it. "You know that Van Dorn apprentices are not allowed to carry guns."

"It's my father's."

"I'll return it to him next time I'm in Washington."

She checked the hammer was on an empty chamber and handed Bell the pocket pistol, butt first.

"Just for the record," said Bell, "interns are not even permitted a nail file."

"What if I break a fingernail?"

"Rub it on a brick wall."

"Mr. Bell?"

"What?"

"Are you going to tell me that you never hid a gun when you were an apprentice?"

"I didn't get caught. Go! Show Lynch . . . And Helen?"

"What is it?"

"See if you can find out something that Lynch really wants."

"He wants to take me to Coney Island."

Bell grinned. "Something he wants from us. Some business Van Dorns can do for him. I have a funny feeling about this counterfeiting."

He returned to Tetrazzini.

"I will escort you personally to San Francisco on the train. When we get to San Francisco, our field office will take good care of you. Mr. Bronson, the detective in charge, is a top-notch man and happens to be a great fan of the opera. I'm told he took to his bed when you left San Francisco."

"*Mille o tante grazie,* Isaac. I'm not afraid, but who can say . . . Isaac? Don't you have a fiancée in San Francisco?"

"As a matter of fact, I do."

As soon as she left, Bell telephoned Enrico Caruso. "Would it be convenient for me to come up and see you?"

Ten minutes later, Caruso welcomed him into his suite. They had met recently in the hotel's lower lobby bar, where residents knew to find a quiet drink in the afternoon. The tenor was only a few years older than the detective, and they had hit it off when they discovered they both had survived the earthquake uninjured.

Caruso was wearing a woolen dressing gown and had his throat wrapped in three scarves to Tetrazzini's one. His drawing room housed an eight-foot Mason & Hamlin grand piano and a wheezing machine of tanks and nozzles that emitted clouds of steam to moisten the air. *"La Voce!"* he said, stroking his throat. "Do feel free to remove your coat."

Bell did so, gratefully. Panama jungles were cooler and drier than Caruso's suite.

The singer stubbed out his cigarette and lit a fresh one. "I missed you at my *Pagliacci*!"

"I was busy getting dynamited."

"All work and no play . . ."

"Tetrazzini got a Black Hand letter."

"I know. I told her to go to you."

"How about you? Did you get a letter?"

"No," the singer said. "Why do you ask?"

"If they are the same gang that kidnapped Maria Vella and are dynamiting businesses,

121

they might be stepping up, trying to see how high they can make threats pay. Luisa is not as famous as you by a long shot. What if they're experimenting with her to see how it works? Before they go after a really big fish."

Caruso beamed. He had a big cheerful face with a high brow and it lit up bright as an electric headlight. "So suddenly I am a fish."

"A big fish."

"But of course."

"A big fish makes a big meal," said Bell. "They demanded four thousand from Luisa. What would they ask from you. Forty?"

"At least."

"I will keep you posted. Archie will be standing by if you need help while I'm in San Francisco."

"San Francisco?" Caruso smiled. "Isn't your fiancée in San Francisco?"

"As a matter of fact, she is," said Bell, and Caruso broke into a new song not likely to be heard at the opera:

" 'Round your heart a feeling stealing
Comes to drive away regret,
When you know you're not forgotten
By the girl you can't forget.

"How will the beauteous Marion feel about you sharing a transcontinental railroad train with a fiery soprano?"

Bell joked back that Luisa's maid, the formidable Rosa Ferrara, took firm charge of the coloratura's virtue. But he was thinking that if the threat against Luisa Tetrazzini was a test of the Black Hand's power, then when she refused to pay, they would go all out to make an example of her. And, he realized with sudden icy clarity, that the timing of the Black Hand letter was no coincidence. They knew she was traveling to San Francisco.

The farther from New York they attacked, the more threatening they would appear to future victims.

Shepherding Tetrazzini and her maid Rosa aboard the 20th Century Limited for the first leg across the continent, Isaac Bell kept a sharp eye on the gangs of immigrant laborers. Grand Central was in tumult — tracks and platforms shifted, steam shovels shaking the ground — as the demolition of the old station proceeded simultaneously with construction of the new terminal. Wally Kisley stood watch at the 20th's gate, dressed like a drummer in a loud checkerboard suit and pretending to read a newspaper. Mack Fulton was wheeling a handcart of luggage about the platform. Archie

Abbott glowered officiously in the blue and gray uniform of a New York Central conductor.

At Chicago's LaSalle Station, where they arrived on time twenty hours later, Van Dorn operatives from the head office guarded their change of trains. They made it to Union Station and boarded the Overland Limited without threat or incident, though Bell was not happy to see newspaper headlines ballyhooing the singer's journey across the continent. Dinner that evening was the Overland chef's version of her famous dish, Turkey Tetrazzini, and, at Omaha, opera fans mobbed the platform and forced their way onto the train, shouting, *"Brava, Diva! Brava, Diva!"*

Tetrazzini held court in the club car, swathed in scarves and uncharacteristically silent. Rosa Ferrara pantomimed the explanation, patting her own throat and whispering, "*La Voce!* Signora is resting her voice."

Isaac Bell kept a hand inside his coat, gripping his Colt, and watched the fans' faces. How easy it would be for a man or even a woman to thrust a stiletto from the crowd. He paid attention to their eyes, looking out for a telltale flash of ice, or fire, until the conductors had shooed the last of them off the train.

Peace prevailed at Ogden, two days later, where a wire from the Denver office was waiting for Bell. The Denver Van Dorns had missed Russo by hours. They speculated that he was headed to San Francisco, but an Italian who fit his description might have bought a ticket in the opposite direction, east to Kansas City.

In other words, thought Bell, Russo could be anywhere — including right here in Ogden. Nine railroad lines converged in the junction city, which would appeal to a man on the run. The lone Van Dorn Ogden operative, an aging, retired sheriff, met the train. Bell authorized him to dispense cash to rail dicks to keep an eye out for Russo.

The Overland continued steaming west, over Great Salt Lake on the Lucin Cutoff Trestle, and across Nevada. At Reno, powerful pusher engines joined on, and the train commenced the steep climb into the Sierra Nevada. Ascending for forty miles, the tracks crested at the seven-thousand-foot elevation. The train entered the long, dark Summit Tunnel and suddenly stopped.

Moments before the clash of brakes, and startled cries of passengers thrown from their seats, Isaac Bell and Luisa Tetrazzini and Rosa Ferraro had been exclaiming at the spectacular views of mountains soaring to the sky and lakes sparkling below. Now, in the dark tunnel, all was confusion. It turned swiftly to chaos when a gun battle broke out at the front of the train, with the crack of pistols, the crash of rifles, and the roar of a 12-gauge as the Overland's express messenger shot back.

Bell bolted from Tetrazzini's state room. "Lock the door behind me."

10

"Gangway!"

Isaac Bell ran full tilt toward the sound of guns echoing in the tunnel.

Smoke darkened the corridor.

Whipping his pistol from his shoulder holster, shouting at passengers in his way, he stormed through the stateroom car and into the forward club car, which rode directly behind the express car. He pushed through the vestibule and pounded on the express car's fortified door.

"Jake! It's Isaac Bell. You O.K. in there?"

He had, as was Van Dorn custom, introduced himself to the express messengers who guarded registered mail, bearer bonds, cash, and gold. An extra, armed hand was always welcome, and favors were returned. Bell shouted, "I've got the back covered. No gunmen here."

"Not here, either," said Jake, unlocking the door. He had a double-barreled sawed-off in his hands and a puzzled expression on his face. "Fire on the tracks, barricade of rocks, and shooting like a war in the tunnel, but I don't see no —"

Bell turned and ran back to Tetrazzini's state room, tearing down the narrow corridors along the state rooms, shoving people from his path, praying he wasn't too late.

Her door was still locked.

Through it he heard glass break and a terrified scream.

Bell levered off the corridor wall, sprang with all his strength, and hurled his shoulder against the door. It flew open, and the tall detective exploded into the state room, gun in his right hand, left fist cocked. He saw Luisa and Rosa on the day couch, seated where he had left them, their backs pressed against the cushions, their faces white with shock.

Through the smoke pouring in, a man materialized. He would have looked like a Gilbert and Sullivan pirate, with a grimy face and a gleaming stiletto clenched in his teeth, except for the Bodeo Italian Army revolver he was using to clear the sash of broken glass. His eyes fixed on Bell. The octagonal barrel flickered toward him. Bell landed a punch on his forehead and he fell backwards. The tunnel was narrow, roughhewn through the mountain. The killer banged against the stone and slid down between the wall and the train. But as he fell, he managed to pull the trigger. The Bodeo's .41 caliber slug creased Bell's neck. It missed his jugular but plowed a fiery furrow in his skin, and the impact of the heavy bullet passing so close nearly knocked him over.

Luisa screamed.

Swaying on his feet, Bell pointed his pistol out the broken window and peered through thickening coal smoke down at the gravel ballast under the car. The man he had punched was struggling to stand. He was still holding his gun, and still had the knife in his teeth. Bell dove out the window, landed beside him, and slugged him with his automatic. This was one Black Hand gangster Isaac Bell had no intention of shooting. This one he would make talk.

The gunman staggered beside the train. Bell tackled him. Still, he tried to run. Bell clamped a hand on one ankle and swung at his knee with the heavy automatic. The man tripped and fell. Bell grabbed his shoulder, but the burning in his neck was draining his concentration. His quarry wriggled loose, over the rail, and under the train. Bell rolled over the rail and spotted him by the flickering of the fire burning ahead of the locomotive. He grabbed the intruder's foot, and they wrestled in the shallow trough under the car, scraping fists on the splintery crossties and ballast, banging their heads and backs on the chassis.

The locomotive whistled. Three short shrieks were amplified by the rock roof and walls, and Isaac Bell realized that the engineer had to back the train out of the tunnel before his passengers were asphyxiated by the engine smoke. The Black Hander Bell was fighting realized it, too. His eyes glittered on the nearest wheel, three yards from where they struggled. As the air brakes released with a deafening blast, he grabbed Bell's arm and threw his weight on it to wrench it across the rail.

The train started to roll, and Bell felt the rail and the ties vibrate with the heavy grinding of iron on steel. He fought to free his arm with the little strength he had left. The wheel flange — the iron lip that kept the train on the tracks — was inching down on him like a butcher's slicing machine. He pounded the man's kidneys. A heavy coat absorbed the blows, and the Black Hander did not budge. Bell bent his knee, dragged his ankle toward his free hand, and snatched his throwing knife out of his boot. He raised the knife. A protrusion from the moving chassis struck his hand, and the blade started to slip from his fingers. He squeezed hard and plunged it into his assailant's kidney.

The man convulsed. Bell threw him off, jerked his arm from the rail, and flattened himself in the trough between the tracks. The car passed over him, as did the next stateroom car, the club car, the express car, and the tender. When at last the locomotive rolled away in gusts of steam and smoke, Bell sat up and took stock. He had two working hands. His neck began to ache savagely, and he was breathing hard, gasping to fill his lungs with the thin, smoky mountain air. The man who had stopped the train to attack Luisa Tetrazzini was staring at him with grinning teeth and empty eyes. Oddly, he seemed to have grown taller, until Bell observed that the head glaring blankly at him was on the far side of the rail, severed from its torso.

His stiletto had fallen beside his head.

Bell searched his coat for the sheath, then pocketed the weapon, retrieved his throwing knife, and staggered out of the tunnel.

Marion Morgan, a young, willowy straw-blonde with a beautiful, fine-featured face and a level gaze, was waiting at the railroad ferry pier. Isaac Bell sprang from the boat, ahead of the crowds, and swept her into his arms. "I am so glad to see you."

They kissed warmly, oblivious to hundreds brushing past. After a while, Marion released him. "I cannot help but notice that you have an enormous bandage on your neck."

"Cut myself shaving."

"It looks like you're still bleeding."

"Just a scratch."

"You're white as a ghost."

"Excitement . . . And joy."

"Shouldn't you be in a hospital?"

"I should be in bed. What are you doing for the afternoon?"

"But where is your opera singer?"

"I had Bronson's boys meet the train at Oakland. They've got her covered."

"Then come with me."

"Where?" The last time he had seen her she was living in a tent, as were most in the earthquake-ravaged and fire-gutted city. From what he had seen from the ferry crossing the bay, not a lot had been rebuilt in the burned districts.

"I borrowed a sweet little cottage from my new boss."

"What new boss?"

"I just got a wonderful job on a news-paper. I'll tell you all about it. Later. After we change your bandage."

In the short time they had been engaged, Isaac Bell had come to trust Marion's judgment and insight totally. Experienced in business and trained as a lawyer at Stanford — graduating with the first class — she was the only person outside of his fellow detectives with whom he would discuss a case.

"The killer not only found Tetrazzini's car in a dark tunnel swirling with smoke, but her exact stateroom window. He was well informed. Once again, I feel this so-called Black Hand bunch are considerably more organized than illiterate immigrants straight off the boat."

"No doubt their leader is," Marion conceded. "Did the railroad police happen to recognize the killer?"

"No. Why would they?"

"He attacked three thousand miles from New York, and he, or his henchmen, piled stones on the tracks ahead of your train, both of which suggest he was a California man following orders from New York. And he was obviously familiar with the railroad, so I'm wondering whether they had ever arrested him for stealing rides."

She had changed into a silk robe that complemented her sea-coral green eyes, and Bell watched avidly as she prowled the tiny cottage, refilling their flutes with Billecart-Salmon Brut Rosé champagne and returning to their bed. "What do you think?" she asked.

"I think we should sleep on it."

A heavy hand pounded the front door.

Marion called, "Who is it?"

"Bronson," thundered through the wood. "You in there, Isaac?"

"What?"

"Russo's in Ogden. I'll slide the telegram under the door."

Marion said, very sadly, "After I bandage your neck, I'll ride the ferry with you to the train."

11

Brewster Claypool was headed for Tammany headquarters, above Tony Pastor's vaudeville house in an opulent three-story Italianate building on 14th Street, when he heard chorus girls singing Victor Herbert's latest hit, "I Want What I Want When I Want It."

He stepped into the theater.

They were rehearsing a spoof with a bandy-legged comedian, who was costumed in a yellow wig and short skirt. Claypool exchanged blown kisses with the girls and got a wave from the comedian, then climbed the stairs with a world-weary smile.

"I Want What I Want When I Want It" summed up with grim precision the job of pulling wires for J. B. Culp.

Boss Fryer — wan, potbellied "Honest Jim" Fryer — greeted Claypool expansively. He would have inquired about his family, if Claypool had one, so asked instead about mutual friends on Wall Street. Claypool reported on their successes and travails, and asked about Honest Jim's family, who were prospering.

Jim Fryer ran the Tammany Hall political machine that ran New York City. Strict administrator of a party pecking order — district leaders down to election district leaders to block captains to saloonkeepers and building captains — he got out the vote on Election Day in the majorities required to beat the Reformers and dominated a confederation of police, clergy, streetcar magnates, and construction contractors.

They clinked glasses of seltzer lemonade with the fond respect of friends at the top of their games — men who ran cities had not the luxury to drink like elected officials — and traded gossip that others would pay fortunes to hear. Eventually, Fryer, who had a reception room full of cops, contractors, priests, and franchise grabbers waiting to see him, asked Claypool, with only the merest hint of time's pressure, "To what do I owe the pleasure of your presence?"

"I would like to meet a fellow who can help arrange something unusual."

The word "unusual" caused Fryer's eyes to narrow fractionally.

"Brandon Finn's your man. Tell him I sent you."

"It could be too unusual for Finn," Claypool answered carefully.

Boss Fryer stood up. "Brandon will know who to send you to," he replied, and both men knew the Boss had washed his hands of work best left to henchmen and heelers.

"Run-a! Run-a, Pasquale!"

They were after him again, and Sante Russo ran for his life, wondering why tramps, who were growing thin as food ran out and the first waves of winter cold oozed down the Wasatch Mountains, would waste their strength tormenting a single soul as poor as themselves.

He wanted to turn around and say, I won't eat much. Just leave me alone.

"Run, you dago!"

The out-of-work miner leading the mob had a pick handle. If they caught him, he would die. An awful voice inside said it might hurt less than running. But he ran anyway, praying he didn't trip and fall on the rough ground, fleeing the hobo camp, fleeing the hobos and the woods and swamps where they hid from the police.

Russo veered toward a distant creek, hoping the bed was dry enough to cross. But it was deep, the water running hard. They had him trapped. He turned hopelessly to his fate. As if things couldn't get worse, an enormous automobile suddenly careened out of the gloom, headlights and searchlight blazing. Now it was a race. Who would get to him first? The miner with the pick handle? The second mob, scooping up rocks to throw at him? Or the auto, belching blue smoke as the driver accelerated to run him over? Russo, who had dreamed of someday earning enough money to buy an auto, recognized a fifty-horsepower Thomas Flyer. It was heaped with spare tires, outfitted for crossing rough country. Would they use its tow rope to lynch him from a tree?

Russo was turning to jump in the creek when the driver shouted, "Sante Russo!"

Russo gaped. How did he know his name?

The auto skidded alongside in a cloud of dust. "Get in! On the jump!"

The driver grabbed Russo's hand and yanked him into the seat beside him. A rock whizzed between them, just missing their heads.

A tall man stepped from the mob with another rock in his hand. He wound up like a professional baseball pitcher, slowly coiling strength in his arm, and began to throw. The driver pulled a pistol from his coat.

The gun roared. The pitcher fell backwards.

"Mister?" asked Russo. "Who are you?"

"Bell. Van Dorn Agency . . . Hang on!"

Isaac Bell depressed the Flyer's clutch, shifted the speed-changing lever, and stomped the accelerator pedal. Drive chains clattered, and the rear tires churned sand, fighting for a grip. The Flyer lurched into motion, and Bell zigzagged around brush, rocks, and yawning gullies. The bunch he had shot at was backing off. But the main mob, egged on by the guy with a pick handle, was blocking their escape. Bell raised his voice. "I'll shoot the first man who throws another rock."

"There's twenty of us," the leader bawled. "Gonna shoot us all?"

"Most. Fun's over. Go home!"

For a moment, Bell thought he had them cowed. Instead, both mobs edged closer. Rocks flew. One grazed his hat. Another bounced off the hood. A third hit the center-mounted searchlight, which exploded, scattering glass. Bell fired inches over their heads, spraying bullets as fast as he could pull the trigger.

Some ran. Others surged forward. He saw a flicker of motion and fired in that direction. A rusty pistol went flying. He sent two more quick shots whistling close to their ears, and his hammer clicked on an empty shell. The mobs were closer, twenty feet away. With no time to reload, Bell shouted for Russo to hold tight and shifted up to third gear.

Two and a half thousand pounds of Thomas Flyer thundered at the mob. All but one man ran. He threw himself at the auto and grabbed at the steering wheel. Isaac Bell flattened him with his gun barrel.

He pressed the accelerator, speeding over rough ground for a quarter mile, and turned onto a dirt track that led toward Ogden. Russo sagged with relief. But when the town hove into view, the Italian asked, "What you want from me?"

"Help with my investigation," Bell answered and said nothing more until he pulled up in front of a hotel on 25th Street that had a haberdashery on the ground floor. The fact was, he had no idea whether Russo had run from New York because the overcharge that blew up the water mains was an accident, or was sabotage by the Black Hand, or had been laid by Russo himself for the Black Hand.

He led him into the hotel.

The front desk clerk said, "We don't rent rooms to dagos."

Bell put a ten-dollar gold piece on the

counter and laid his Colt next to it. The gun reeked of burnt gunpowder. "This gentleman is not a dago. He is *Mr.* Sante Russo, a friend of the Van Dorn Detective Agency. Mister Russo will occupy a room with a bath. And you will send that haberdasher up with a suit of clothes, hose, drawers, and a shirt and necktie."

"I'm calling the house detective."

Winter stole into the tall detective's eyes. The violet shade that sometimes accompanied a smile or a pleasant thought had vanished, and the blue that remained was as dark and unforgiving as a mountain blizzard.

"Don't if you don't want him hurt."

The clerk pocketed the gold piece, the better part of a week's pay, and extended the register. Bell signed it.

MR. SANTE RUSSO C/O VAN DORN
DETECTIVE AGENCY
KNICKERBOCKER HOTEL, NEW YORK CITY

"Tell the haberdasher not to forget to bring a belt. And some shoes. And a handkerchief."

Bell sat in an armchair while Russo bathed. It had been a long day and night since he left Marion in San Francisco. His

141

wounded neck ached, as did his knees, elbows, shoulder, and hands, from the fight under the train. A knock at the door awakened him. The haberdasher had brought a tailor and a stock boy. They had Russo decked out in an hour.

The blaster marveled at the mirror.

"I am thank-a you very much, Signore Bell. I never look such."

"You can thank me by taking a close look at this."

Bell tossed the hollow red tube. Russo caught it on the fly, took one glance, and sat down hard on the bed. "Where you find this?"

"You tell me."

"Not atta church. Not possible. Nothing left."

"What do you mean?"

"Big-a bang. *Big-a* bang ever."

"Are you saying that this stick could not possibly have been blown clear of that explosion?"

"Not possible."

Which led Bell to the bigger question. "The sticks you disconnected . . . were they like this one?"

"Same stick. Where you get?"

"What do you mean the same? You just said it wasn't possible."

"Not same, same. Same-a . . . *marca. Marca!*" He pointed at the Stevens name printed on the tube. "Where you get?"

"Same brand?"

"Uhhh?"

"Label?"

Russo shrugged.

"Mark?"

"*Si. Marca.* Where you get?"

"*Mano Nero,*" said Isaac Bell.

"Same. Yes. *Si. Mano Nero* make-a over-charge. Like I say."

On his way to the Ogden train depot Isaac Bell stopped at Van Dorn's field office. A wire had come in for him on the private telegraph line, Helen Mills reporting triumphantly, in Van Dorn cipher,

ALMOST PROMOTABLE
LYNCH ARRESTS PENNSYLVANIA
GREEN GOODSER
SAME PAPER

Bell wired Mack Fulton and Wally Kisley,

FIND WHO BOUGHT PAPER AND INK
PRINTER'S ROW BRING HELEN
STAY OUT OF AGENT LYNCH WAY

and ran for his train.

He had three days to New York to ponder how the Black Hand case had grown both larger and oddly interconnected. Sante Russo identifying the same dynamite and the Black Handers' penchant for the same stationery had pretty much confirmed that four separate crimes — kidnapping little Maria Vella, the dynamite overcharge that wrecked her father's business, bombing Banco LaCava, and the Black Hand attack on Luisa Tetrazzini were engineered by the same gang. And now counterfeiting? A gang of all-rounders? he wondered.

Except that all-rounders did not exist. Criminals were inclined to repeat themselves. Like most people, they stuck with what they knew best and trusted that what had worked before would work again. Strong-arm men intimidated, confidence men tricked, safecrackers blew vaults, thieves stole, kidnappers snatched, bank robbers robbed banks.

Changing trains in Chicago, Bell found a wire from Harry Warren waiting for him on the 20th Century Limited. Harry, too, found all-rounders unusual and said as much in the telegram.

PENNSYLVANIA GREEN GOODSER
SALATA THUG

144

"Ernesto!" said Charlie Salata. "Where you running off to?"

Ernesto Leone's heart sank. Salata had two gorillas with him and they blocked any hope of escape.

"I'm not running. I'm going home. You know I got a room in this house."

"Invite me in."

The four men climbed a flight of stairs. The counterfeiter unlocked his door. The gorillas stayed in the hall. Leone lighted a sputtering gas jet. The broad-shouldered Salata filled the room. Last time he was here, he stole some expensive paper. This time, it seemed to Leone, that he was sucking out the air.

"Listen, Charlie. I told the Boss the money wasn't ready. He wouldn't listen."

"Don't blame the Boss."

"I'm not blaming him. I'm just saying . . . Oh, come on, Charlie. We knew each other since we was kids. You go your way, I go mine, but we're not enemies."

Salata slid his fingers inside a terrible set of brass knuckles. A blade jutted from the metal rings. Leone stared at the weapon. Maimed or stabbed? How would Salata do him up?

Salata raised his fist very slowly and pressed the knuckles to Leone's cheek. Leone could see the blade in the corner of his eye. Salata said, "I got a man in jail. Thousand dollars bail."

"I'll get the bail." Where? He could only wonder.

"What else?"

"What do you mean?"

"What else you going to do to make it up?"

"I'll do what I can. What do you want? I'm getting better paper. You want part of the new stuff?"

"That was the last time I ever pass false money."

"Then what?"

"Me and Ferri got something started."

"Ferri?" echoed Leone. Roberto Ferri was a smuggler. "Since when do you hang with Ferri?"

"Since the Boss said to . . . You come on this business, make it up to us."

"What can I do for your business?"

"My guy took a fall. I want you to take a fall."

"For what? I'm just a counterfeiter."

"You're a lousy counterfeiter. But you're still *prominente*. Guys know you're not *ca-*

146

fon. If this thing goes wrong, you'll take the blame."

"The cops won't buy that. They know I'm only a counterfeiter."

Salata pivoted his hand. The knuckles turned away from Leone's cheek. The blade lined up with his eye. "Not for cops."

"Van Dorns?"

Salata laughed. "You'll wish it was Van Dorns."

Harry Warren was waiting for Isaac Bell on the platform at Grand Central with news of another Secret Service arrest.

"Agent Lynch is having a banner week. Secret Service just pinched a guy passing the same queer upstate."

"Salata's?"

"Nope. A Ferri guy."

"Who's Ferri?"

"Runs a bunch of smugglers."

Bell led the way out of the chaotic terminal, dodging work gangs and skirting gaping holes in the concourse floor. "Why's a smuggler taking chances passing the queer?"

"Odd keeps piling up," said Warren. "Like I said about Charlie Salata's boy pinched in Pennsylvania."

"Same paper?"

"Same queer, same paper."

"What are the odds that Salata's turned counterfeiter?"

"Same odds as a grizzly bear hosting a church supper. Anyhow, Agent Lynch told Helen the stuff was lame. The paper. No surprise they got caught. But the engraving was top-notch. Lynch thinks it was done by a guy named Ernesto Leone. Learned his trade in Italy and has trained a bunch of apprentices here."

"Helen got a lot out of Lynch."

"She'd given Lynch a description of Leone shopping on Printer's Row, so I guess Lynch figured he owed her."

"Did Lynch happen to tell Helen what the prisoners admit to?"

"That smitten he ain't. Helen asked. He sent her packing."

"Permanently?"

" 'Fraid so. I don't think we'll get any more out of the Secret Service."

The long-legged Bell set a fast pace across town to the office. Harry Warren trotted to keep up.

"You ever hear of this Ferri teaming with Salata?" Bell asked.

"Nope."

Bell said, "I never heard of an outfit of all-rounders. Birds of a feather is more the rule, but these guys are combining extortion, bombing, counterfeiting, smuggling, kidnapping. Crimes of brute force and crimes of quick wit. Is it an alliance of gangs — a 'cartel' of criminals? Or is a single mastermind forcing a variety of gangsters to do his bidding?"

"Damned-near impossible to whip any bunch of crooks into line," said Warren. "Not to mention different kinds."

"Cartel or mastermind, they'd be bigger, tougher, and better organized than the small-timers who call themselves Black Hand to scare folks. Makes me wonder what they'll turn their hands to next."

"Anything that pays," said Harry Warren.

Bell said, "Or what they'll stop at."

An Invitation to Pink Tea

12

You are hereby invited to Pink Tea
With Captain Michael Coligney
19th Precinct Station House
West 30th Street
3 p.m.
Sharp

A New York Police Department officer wearing a blue coat with shiny brass buttons and a tall helmet strolled the Tenderloin, twirling a nightstick and knocking on brothel doors with printed invitations for the proprietors.

Nick Sayers, proud owner of the Cherry Grove bordello, showed up early at the station house, ahead of his competitors. They trooped in soon after, looking anxious. Sayers waited with a small smile on his face. Captain Coligney's Pink Teas routinely culminated in orders to "resort keepers" to shut down their "disorderly houses" within twenty-four hours. But unlike his competitors, Nick Sayers had an ace in the hole, information to sell that even "Honest Mike" would buy.

Someone had tipped off the newspapers, of course, and police reporters crammed into Coligney's office, which was already packed with his invited guests, who were dressed to the nines.

"Will this change anything, Captain Coligney?" demanded the man from the *Sun*. "Won't new owners switch names and open up again?"

The broad-shouldered, handsome Coligney was resplendent in dress uniform and amply prepared to deal with the press. "Shutting down the resorts is better and fairer than hauling poor, unfortunate women into the station house, holding them for the night in jail, and dragging them into court before they're turned loose."

Having quelled the press, he turned to his guests.

"Gentlemen, and ladies" — he nodded gallantly to several wealthy proprietresses — "we have tea, sandwiches, and cakes, but before we partake, please be aware that you are hereby enjoined to shut down your disorderly houses in twenty-four hours. I don't want to see an open door or a light in the window after three o'clock tomorrow afternoon."

Tea was downed, splashed liberally from flasks, sandwiches and sweets consumed, and soon everyone left except the owner of the Cherry Grove.

"Nick," said Captain Coligney. "Shouldn't you be off packing your bags?"

"Well, Captain, you would think so, wouldn't you?"

A note of supreme confidence in Nick's voice brought the captain up short. "Apparently, you don't agree, Nick. Care to tell me about it?"

"I would prefer to keep my house open."

"I would prefer to spend my summers in Newport, but I don't see it in the cards."

"I see it in *my* cards," said Nick. "And I'm going to play them right."

"An ace in the hole?" Coligney asked with a dangerous glint in his eye. The bejeweled and cologned Nick was a former "fancy man" who had developed a flair for business that turned a string of streetwalkers into the Ritz of the Tenderloin, and Mike Coligney had heard just about enough.

But Nick stood his ground. "*Four* aces."

Coligney formed a fist. "I'm warning you, boy-o, you're about to run into a straight flush."

153

"Captain Coligney, I'm offering you price-less information in return for being allowed to stay open."

"Priceless?"

"And vital."

Coligney pointed at the clock on the wall. "Thirty seconds."

"A secret club meets in my house. Wall Street men. So secret that even you didn't know about it."

"What do they do?"

"Drink, talk, carouse."

"Sounds like all your patrons. Minus the talking."

"It's the talking that you will let me stay open for."

Coligney saw that Nick was in deadly earnest. The brothel owner truly believed that the cops would make an exception for his house. "O.K., spill it. You've got thirty seconds."

"Their secret club. It's kind of like a joke, but it's not a joke. These gentlemen run Wall Street."

"This club have a name?"

"The Cherry Grove Gentlemen's Society."

"Original."

"But, like I say, it's a joke. Sort of."

"Your thirty seconds is running out."

"I listen in on 'em," said Nick.

"How?"

"There's a vent shaft for air. I can hear upstairs what they say in the library."

"A vent which just happened to be there?" asked Coligney. "Or you had built so you could eavesdrop?"

"The latter," Nick admitted with a grin.

"Why?"

"I listen for stock market tips. I mean, these men know everything before it happens. Twice I made a killing. Once with U.S. Steel, once with Pennsylvania Rail —"

Coligney exploded to his feet, both fists balled. "Are you trying to bribe me with stock tips?"

"*No, no, no, no, no!* No, Captain. That's not what I'm talking about. I'm just telling you how I happened to hear it."

"Hear what?"

Nick took a deep breath and blurted, "They're going to kill President Roosevelt."

The police captain rocked back on his heels. Nick looked triumphant that he had captured his attention. Coligney sat back down heavily and planted his elbows on his desk. "What exactly did you hear?"

Nick reported in detail.

"Give me their names."

"I don't know their names."

"They're your regular customers."

155

"I can tell you who was there. But I can't tell which ones were talking." Nick explained that he could make out what they were saying but could not distinguish one voice from another, as sounds were distorted by the shaft.

Coligney said, "You must have recognized his manner of speaking."

"It's not like there's only one blowhard in the club, Captain. They're Wall Street swells, what do you expect? They're all blowhards."

Coligney questioned Nick repeatedly. Nick stuck to his story, and eventually the policeman was convinced he did not know who in the "club" had threatened the President.

Coligney wrote down their names. Seven of the richest men on Wall Street.

"O.K.," said Coligney. "Here's the deal. You shut down now, like everyone else. You change the name on your deed. You reopen at the weekend."

Nick nodded. "That way no one knows about this, and it looks like Tammany stepped in and lent me a hand."

"But if this ends up blarney, you'll be selling women to blacksmiths in Joisey. Now get outta here."

Five minutes later, Mike Coligney headed

156

out, too, wearing a greatcoat over his uniform and a civilian's fedora low over his eyes.

"Back soon," he told his desk sergeant. "Just going to clear my head."

"O'Leary's or the Normandie?" asked the sergeant.

"O'Leary's."

But he walked straight by O'Leary's Saloon. Continuing up Broadway, Coligney passed the Normandie Bar, too, and cut over to Sixth Avenue, thinking hard on what he had learned. "Satan's Circus" percolated around him as he strode past brick tenements and frame houses, street muggers and stickup artists, dance halls and saloons. Downtown again in the shadow of the El, pondering possibilities and weighing the complications.

The captain had a gut feeling that the plot was real. But as earthshaking as it was, who in blazes could he trust to help him dismantle it? The department was in an uproar. The new Police Commissioner — a friend, ironically, of President Roosevelt — was turning the force on its ear. Worse, Bingham was a stickler for communicating through "proper channels." Proper channels in this case would be through a politically connected inspector whom Coligney would not trust to solve a candy store theft.

Besides, who knew how long Commissioner Bingham himself would last? Or what disruption he would perpetrate next? For the moment, Coligney was the only precinct captain Bingham hadn't transferred, but he had fined Coligney eight days' pay for a technical violation of department rules. What if, in the midst of pursuing Nick's allegation, he suddenly found himself banished to a sleepy precinct in the Bronx? The grim fact was that the Commissioner, a by-the-book former military man, was not equipped to investigate a plot against the President, much less muster the speed required to save his life.

Coligney stopped in a saloon on 24th Street and placed a call on the owner's telephone. Then he walked over to Broadway and, when he was sure no one recognized him, popped down the stairs at 23rd and rode the subway train to 42nd Street, where he slipped quietly into the subway-level lower lobby of the Knickerbocker Hotel.

He entered a small, dark cellar bar off the lobby. At a corner table, backs to the walls, were waiting his old friend Joseph Van Dorn and Van Dorn's top investigator, Isaac Bell.

13

"Let me get this straight," said Van Dorn when Coligney had laid out his dilemma. "A New York Police Department captain wants to hire my private detective agency to run down hearsay that an unnamed member of a secret tycoon club is threatening to kill the President of the United States."

"It may be nothing."

"But if it is not nothing, it is dynamite."

"I can't pay cash. You'll have to take it out in trade."

"The life of the President, and the well-being of the nation aside," Van Dorn said drily, "my agency can't go wrong in the detective business by helping out a high-ranking cop. Particularly one whose career was boomed by this same President back when Mr. Roosevelt was Police Commissioner."

Van Dorn turned to Isaac Bell.

"What do you think?"

Bell had listened intently, struck by Coligney's intelligence and clarity, as well as how inventively he was tackling the Bingham complications. "Are you sure," he asked Coligney, "that your informant did not recognize the man who made the threats by his voice?"

"I interrogated him severely on that subject. I believe that an echo conveyed by the air vent made it impossible to distinguish voices."

"And he gave you a list of the so-called members of the club?"

Coligney patted his pocket. "Seven of 'em who were there that night."

Bell was dying to see the names but knew that Coligney would not hand them over until they had come to a firm agreement. He turned to Van Dorn.

"My gut is inclined to agree with Captain Coligney's gut. The brothel proprietor is likely telling the truth — or at least as much as he knows. He would have to be a lunatic to make up the story out of whole cloth, knowing the police would come down on him with all four feet."

"He's no lunatic," said Coligney. "He's one smart cookie. It's no accident he's prospered uncommonly at his unsavory trade."

160

Isaac Bell and Joseph Van Dorn exchanged a glance.

Bell said, "In other words, it's possible that he did invent the story, reckoning to buy time, gambling you might get transferred like the other captains and a more easygoing fellow be given command of the Tenderloin."

"It's possible he's making it up," Coligney conceded.

Bell traded another look with Van Dorn. The Boss shook his head. Then he addressed Coligney. "I've come to know the President, slightly, while dealing with his Justice Department. He's sometimes a reckless fellow. But his heart is in the right place.

"The sad fact is, based on the blood-soaked record, the presidency of the United States is a dangerous job. Until proven otherwise, I have to assume the threat is real. Isaac will work up the case."

"Can't ask for better than that," said Coligney. "Good luck, Isaac." He gave Bell the list and shook his hand. Then he thanked Van Dorn and sauntered out of the cellar bar with a lighter step than he had entered with.

Isaac Bell knew he'd need good luck and then some. He was suddenly working up two cases. The Black Hand was growing bolder every day. And while this new case hinged on the word of a less-than-trustworthy brothel keeper, no one could forget that Theodore Roosevelt himself had been hurled into office less than five years ago, when President McKinley was gunned down by an assassin.

Nick Sayers fingered Isaac Bell's card suspiciously. "What brings a private detective to the Cherry Grove so early in the morning? Are you seeking a merry end to a long night?"

"A crime has taken place," said Bell with a significant glance about the extravagantly decorated library.

"Crime?"

"Someone stole Madame Récamier's dress."

"What?"

Bell indicated the oversize copy of Jacques-Louis David's oil painting that dominated the room. A skilled artist had reproduced the portrait of the lady reclining on her couch in every detail except that a thin black headband was the only article of clothing that remained of her original costume.

Bell's observation elicited an admiring smile from the brothel owner. "You know,

162

Mr. Bell, you're the first to notice."

"I imagine your regular guests don't come for the clothes."

"What can I do for you, sir?"

"Join me in a private conversation," said Bell. "Which is to say, not in this library."

"What?"

"We have a mutual friend in law enforcement."

Three minutes later, they were hunched over Coligney's list in Sayers' private office upstairs. Bell said, "Tell me exactly what you heard."

"I didn't pay much attention at first. They were ranting about the President, really tearing into him. But I'd heard it all before. They hate him."

"But what did you hear?"

"What caught my ear, first, was one of them said, 'Men of means will have no place in this country if he hangs on long enough to get reelected in '08.' "

"All right," said Bell. "Anything else?"

"Nothing for a while. Then some of them moved out of the main library into the little sitting room."

"How do you know?"

"The sound is louder. I can always tell when someone moves there. And that's where the good stuff happens. Just a few, trading secrets."

"Is that where you heard about the U.S. Steel bonds?" Bell guessed, sizing up his witness.

"That's right!" Sayers answered unabashedly, as if eavesdropping for stock tips was as legitimate a profession as medicine or the pulpit. "That's why I listen real close when they move in there."

"What did you hear?"

"Just chitchat, first. Like, 'Why are you waiting?' 'Please sit down.' Then all of a sudden I heard, 'My mind is made up. The man must go.' And someone else said, 'He's not just a man. He is the President of the United States.' Then someone — some other guy, I think — got louder. 'I don't care if he's the King of England. Or the bloody Pope. Or the Almighty Himself. He will destroy us if we don't get rid of him.' First guy asked, 'Is there no other way?' And then, loud and clear, 'Theodore Roosevelt will destroy us if we don't get rid of him.' "

Isaac Bell took Coligney's list to Grady Forrer, the head of Van Dorn Research. His department occupied back rooms, where a small army of younger scholars was snipping articles from newspapers and magazines, poring through books, and listening

164

intently on telephones.

Forrer read the list in a swift glance, then repeated the names aloud: "Arnold, Baldwin, Claypool, Culp, Manly, Nichols, and Pendergast. A high-flying flock of tycoons."

"Two or more could be conspiring to kill the President of the United States."

Forrer, a very large man, raised a skeptical eyebrow bigger than a mustache. "They can afford to hire expensive assassins."

"Tycoons," said Isaac Bell, "do not personally hire murderers. Can your boys find me the names of their fixers?"

"It will take some digging to run down who their 'men' are. Operatives who pull wires and grease the ways favor the strict Q.T. Double that when recruiting killers from the underworld."

"I'm stretched thin," said Bell. "I'll take all the help you can give me."

"How are you making out with your 'cartel of criminals'?"

"The Black Hand Squad is working at it overtime. Trying to link kidnappers, extortionists, bombers, and counterfeiters."

"I can see why you're stretched thin."

Forrer's face was suddenly aglow with admiration. The long-legged, dark-haired Helen Mills raced into Forrer's office like a whirlwind. "There you are, Mr. Bell. Hello,

165

Mr. Forrer. Mr. Bell, Mr. Kisley and Mr. Fulton told me to tell you we found Ernesto Leone."

"Where is he?"

"On the waterfront. 40th Street and Eleventh."

Bell was already moving through the door. "What's a counterfeiter doing on the waterfront?"

"Mr. Kisley said he hoped you could figure that out."

14

Isaac Bell rushed from the Knickerbocker Hotel, caught a crosstown trolley, stepped off when it got hung up in traffic at Tenth Avenue, and hurried down to Eleventh Avenue. Spying a seamen's shop, he draped his business suit with a secondhand watch coat and removed his derringer from his hat, which he traded for a canvas cap and longshoreman's loading hook. Three minutes after bursting into the shop, he was dashing down Eleventh Avenue.

Kisley and Fulton met him at 40th Street.

"We got a tip Leone's been holed up in that rooming house since yesterday. We saw him come down to eat breakfast in that lunchroom, then right back inside. Haven't seen him since."

Mack said, "He's a nervous wreck. He may have made us coming out of breakfast."

"What's he doing here?"

"Could be waiting for something to be

smuggled off a freighter. Engraving plates from Italy, maybe. There's a boat in from Naples at Pier 75."

"There he is!"

Bell saw a thin, dark man edge from the building like a rabbit sniffing the wind.

"I'll take him. You boys hang back."

Bell turned away and watched the man's reflection in a window. Leone hesitated. He looked on the verge of running back into the building. He jerked a watch from his pocket, stared at the time, pocketed the watch, looked around again. Shoulders hunched, he set off briskly toward the river.

The sidewalks were crowded with long-shoremen and sailors and streetwalkers. Bell had little trouble staying out of sight as he shadowed him. He followed Leone across 40th Street to where it ended at a basin just above the 37th Street Pennsylvania Railroad Freight Station. The counterfeiter worked his way down the bulkheaded shore back up to 39th Street and suddenly darted to the water's edge.

Bell saw a boat turn into the slip between the finger piers and arrow toward him. It was a fast steam lighter of the type that delivered provisions to the ships. From the freight pier, two men raced after Leone, their dark features at odds with the neighborhood of fair hair and blue eyes. Leone climbed awkwardly onto the timber apron at the water's edge. The two men followed him and helped him down to the lighter.

Wally Kisley and Mack Fulton caught up with Bell.

"Those are Charlie Salata gorillas."

Salata's gangsters jumped aboard with Leone. The lighter backed into the slip, turned around, and disappeared onto the smoky river.

"Now where's he going?" said Kisley.

Fulton said, "Out of here before the Irish mob 'em, if they've got any sense."

Bell pointed at the railroad pier. "Go get the dispatcher to telephone the Harbor Squad. Roundsman O'Riordan ought to be at Pier A. Then call the office. Tell 'em to run down Eddie Edwards; he's working with the New York Central. And warn Harry Warren to watch the Salata hangouts in case they're headed to Elizabeth Street."

A livestock boat with tall, slatted sides nosed out of the coal smoke that shrouded the Hudson River. Tugboats shoved it into a Pennsylvania Railroad freight slip. Beef cattle lowed anxiously as deckhands moored it to the pier.

Ed Hunt and Tommy McBean, cousins

who ruled the West Side Wallopers, a water-front gang that preyed on merchant ships and railroad cars, waited inside a delivery wagon for the cows to unload. Hunt and McBean were taking a shot at big-time drug smuggling. A gang brother who had fled the cops and surfaced in Texas had a scheme to smuggle Mexican heroin in hollowed cow horns. The cousins had fronted the dough. Now all they had to do was wait 'til the cows were under cover to take their horns.

They passed the time writing a Black Hand letter to an Italian shopkeeper who could afford to fork over a thousand bucks if sufficiently frightened. They were New York Irish through and through, but you didn't have to be Italian to send a Black Hand letter. Spreading paper on a barrel-head, they labored by the light of the van's roof hatch. McBean illustrated it with skulls, knives, guns, and a black hand. Hunt scrawled the threats. They bantered in vaudevillian Italian accents.

"You pay-a de mon-ee?"

"How mooch-a?"

Isaac Bell flashed his Van Dorn badge and slapped five dollars into the hand of a Pennsylvania Railroad detective who tried to stop him. He ran to the end of the railcar float pier that thrust hundreds of feet into the river and climbed the gantry that raised and lowered the dock to align the rails with the barges. Twenty feet up in the air, he scanned the smoky river for the steam lighter that Leone and the Salata gorillas had boarded. It was gone, lost in the heavy traffic of tugs and barges, steamers and sailing ships.

He started to climb back down when he suddenly realized he was looking in the wrong direction. The lighter was nearby, almost at his feet, tied to a cattle boat that was moored alongside the railroad pier. Apparently, it had steamed out of the slip, turned around in the river, and steamed back into the next. Just as he spotted it, a dozen men with bulging sacks slung over their shoulders squeezed through the slats of the cattle boat and jumped onto the lighter. Ernesto Leone was the last aboard. The lighter cast off and steamed into the river, leaving Bell in the same position he had been moments ago, stuck on the gantry while the counterfeiter escaped.

Not quite, he thought to himself. He could see in the distance a New York Police Harbor Squad launch churning up the river at twelve knots. Roundsman O'Riordan, full speed ahead! The Italians spotted the water

171

cops. They turned the lighter on a nickel and raced back into the slip. By the time the Harbor Squad churned into the mouth of the slip, the last of the gangsters were stumbling ashore.

Hunt and McBean's van driver rapped on the roof with the butt of his carter's whip.

McBean put down the Black Hand letter and peered through a spy hole. "Here come the cows."

Hunt watched from an adjacent spy hole. Their laughter died.

"Where's their horns?" asked McBean.

Of the beef cattle shambling down the gangway to the livestock pens, many had no horns. Some had only one.

"Somebody stole our horns."

The Irishmen jumped out of the van, faces reddening, fists clenched, and ran to the pens. Hunt vaulted the fence and threw a headlock on the nearest one-horned steer. It tried to buck him off. McBean piled on, too. He couldn't believe his eyes. Where its horn should have stuck out of its head was a neatly sawn base with a threaded hole in the middle.

"Sons of bitches unscrewed them."

Their wagon driver ran up.

"Guy says a bunch of Italians just jumped

172

off a lighter."

"Yeah? So?"

"One of 'em dropped his sack. It was full of cow horns."

"Where'd they go?"

"Across 36th Street."

Charlie Salata and his top gorillas found their escape blocked by a long, slow New York Central freight train creeping up Eleventh Avenue at the pace of the city-mandated railroad cop escorting it on a horse. Salata was beside himself. Anything that could go wrong had gone wrong: Harbor Squad cops where they weren't expected, one of his men gored by a cow, and the boat trapped. At least they had the dope, including the sack that the worthless Ernesto Leone had managed to drop in plain sight of half the waterfront. But they were stuck on foot in Walloper territory, and it was a long way home to Little Italy.

All of a sudden, pounding up 36th Street, came the Wallopers.

15

Isaac Bell stuck close to the Italians he had spotted scrambling off the lighter. Only twenty yards behind when the freight train stopped them, he pressed into a shallow doorway.

There were nine men carrying sacks. Leone had dropped his while jumping ashore, spilling what looked like the horns of cows, before the rest of the gang scooped them up. The counterfeiter was a hapless sight, shooting frightened glances over his shoulder, bumping into the other gangsters, and generally getting in the way. The rest were cool customers, spoiling for a fight.

Bell recognized their leader, Charlie Salata, who had failed to ferret out the disguised detectives on Elizabeth, then sicced a stiletto man on apprentice Richie Cirillo. Running with him was the thug himself, Vito Rizzo, sporting the flattened nose Wish Clarke had smashed on the steps of the Kips Bay Saloon.

Whatever the Italians had stolen or smuggled had caught the attention of the local Irish — West Side Wallopers, Bell surmised by their gaudy costumes, a poisonous outgrowth of the Gopher Gang. A glimpse of their leaders' scarred faces revealed that Tammany Hall had sprung Ed Hunt and Tommy McBean from prison again.

More Wallopers were joining the pursuit, streaming out of saloons and ten-cent lodging houses. The gang stopped several doorways behind where Bell had taken cover. A sharp, two-finger whistle split the air.

Elaborately coiffed and behatted women ran to them. Shapely as Lillian Russell, hard-eyed as statues, they stood still when the men groped into their bustles and bodices for the revolvers that would get the men arrested when cops patted them down.

The Italians pulled their own guns, all but counterfeiter Leone.

It seemed to Bell that the first shots were fired simultaneously from both sides. Whichever gang shot first, it triggered a fusillade, and the tall detective found himself in the middle of a shooting war. Bullets splintered the wooden jamb, shattered windows, and ricocheted off cobblestones.

Bell drew his pistol in the event a charging Walloper or a counterattacking Salata gangster ran for his doorway. He was reasonably sure he was better armed with his heavy automatic, but there were at least twenty of them, jerking triggers as fast they could, spraying lead like dueling Maxim machine guns. Best to let them get it out of their systems, or at least run out of ammunition. A quick glance down the street confirmed that the Irish were banging away like the Fourth of July, and would be for a while, as their women were tossing change purses filled with fresh bullets.

The tall detective threw another quick glance at the Italians. They were pawing through their sacks for boxes of ammunition and reloading with the speed of men who had been in gunfights before. Bell pressed into his doorway, which was beginning to feel very shallow.

When he heard a lull, he looked again. A glimpse of the Italians offered a sudden opportunity to get his hands on Ernesto Leone. The terrified counterfeiter was attempting to slither away on his belly, hugging the cobblestones and shielding his head with his hands while trying to pull himself along on his elbows. If ever a man was out of place, thought Bell, it was Leone. And if ever a man could shed light on the alliance of extortionists, bombers, kidnappers, smugglers, and counterfeiters, it was Leone.

Bell pivoted out of the doorway. Bullets plucked his sleeve. One burned close to his shoulder. Hugging the buildings, jumping stoops and ash cans, he ran toward Leone, covered the twenty yards in six long bounds, seized the counterfeiter by the scruff of the neck, and hauled him into the closest doorway.

"You're under arrest."

"No gun, no gun," cried Ernesto Leone.

The madman who had rescued him was pointing a pistol in his face and frisking his clothing for weapons. "False money. No gun. No gun."

For days, Leone had had awful forebodings that someone was following him. He had spotted the shadows. Assuming they were Secret Service agents, he would not make counterfeiting charges even worse by getting pinched with a gun.

"Start talking."

"What?" Leone could barely hear him over the roar of the battle.

"You owe me your life."

Leone hung his head. "I know."

"Who's your boss?"

"I don't know."

Charlie Salata charged into the doorway, gun in hand.

Isaac Bell shot first. Salata jerked his trigger as he fell. The gangster's bullet tore into Leone's throat, ripping an artery that fountained blood. Bell dove on him, ripped Leone's shirttails from his trousers and clamped the cloth around his throat in a stranglehold to try to staunch the bleeding. It was hopeless.

Shotguns boomed. Bell recognized the rapid thunder of humpback 12-gauge Browning Auto-5s and wondered where the gangsters had found such fine weapons. Shouts of fear and men stampeding in every direction meant a third party had joined the battle with a vengeance.

He felt Leone die in his hands.

"Isaac!"

The freight train blocking Eleventh Avenue had rolled away. Italians were running east, Irish and their women running west, and a gang of New York Central Railroad cops were charging up the street, pumping fire from the autoload scatterguns. Leading the cinder dicks was the source of the Brownings, white-haired Van Dorn rail yard specialist Eddie Edwards.

"Heard the gunplay. Figured you'd be in the middle of it."

178

"Where's Salata?" The gangster who had shot Leone was nowhere to be seen.

"Halfway to Little Italy by now."

"I winged him," said Bell. "Come on! Let's get him."

Elizabeth Street was packed like a festival. The evening was dry and cool, and thousands had streamed from their airless tenements to enjoy the last of autumn out of doors before winter turned nights bitter. A puppet show blocked most of the street with its tall stage. People gathered under its garland of colored lights and spilled off the sidewalks into the street. Traffic was at a standstill. Peddlers were hard-pressed to sell to customers crammed shoulder to shoulder.

Antonio Branco strolled among them wearing a blue suit, a red scarf, and a derby hat. A commotion drew his eye: Charlie Salata, arm in a sling, swaggering behind a gorilla pushing through the crowd. If Salata was expecting a reward for scoring the Wallopers' dope, he would learn at his next confession that the Boss held him fully at fault for the death of his counterfeiter.

Exchanging pleasantries with the many who recognized him, Branco worked his way toward the puppets. Nearly life-size, with brightly painted faces and colorful costumes, they were visible at a distance, though one had to get close enough to hear the narrator. On the other hand, everyone in the street had known the stories since they were children. He bumped into Giuseppe Vella, who exclaimed, "What a fine night."

"You look recovered from your troubles."

Vella shrugged good-humoredly. "A 'court cost' here, a 'contribution' there, my licenses are returned."

Branco nodded at the marionettes, arrayed in knights' costumes. "What is the show tonight?"

"Un'avventura di Orlando Furioso."

"Roland?" Branco laughed. "Like you and me, my friend. We hold them off while we retreat."

Vella's mood darkened. "Look at those gorillas, lording over everyone."

Rizzo had joined Salata. He had a bandage covering an ear, and his eyes were still blackened from the broken nose the Van Dorns had dealt him. They were shoving through the crowds, knocking people out of the way.

"They act like they own the street," said Vella.

"Well, in some ways they do, I suppose,"

said Branco.

"It shouldn't be this way."

"It won't be always. *Buona sera,* my friend. I see someone I must say hello to."

Isaac Bell relied on his height to search the crowd for Charlie Salata. He was still wearing the cap, watch coat, and loading hook he bought on Eleventh Avenue in hopes of blending in. Harry Warren watched fire escapes for signs of a Black Hand ambush. He also kept a close eye on Bell; he had never seen the tall detective so angry, and he knew him well enough to know that he was blaming himself for the loss of the counterfeiter Leone. Ahead stood an impromptu marionette theater, blocking the street. Brightly costumed knights flailed at each other with swords and shields manipulated by rods and strings controlled from a curtained bridge above the stage.

"What are they fighting about?" asked Bell.

"Honor, justice, faith, and women."

"Like private detectives."

"Better dressed," said Warren.

"I hope they're doing better than we are at the moment."

Then it struck him. Staring at the puppets, he said, "I believe Ernesto Leone was telling me the truth."

"About what?"

"He really didn't know who his boss was."

"Maybe he didn't have one."

"He had one, all right. That's why Salata killed him."

"Sicilians don't talk."

"I have a feeling Leone wanted to. He'd have told me if he knew."

"Maybe."

"Leone wasn't a killer. A counterfeiter, just a crook. He was grateful I saved his life. But he didn't know. If I'm right about there being a boss — an overall mastermind — he's a secret puppet master who knows which strings to pull."

"How you figure that?"

"Look at those puppets."

"Yeah?" Harry Warren said dubiously. "What about 'em?"

"Puppets can't see who's tugging the strings . . . Harry! There they are."

Thirty feet away, Charlie Salata, arm in a sling; Rizzo, too, ear bandaged. They spotted Bell the same instant Bell saw them and jerked pistols from their coats.

A hundred men, women, and children milled between them and the detectives. The crowd was so dense that the only people who could see the weapons were standing beside the gangsters. To pull their own guns would set off a bloodbath.

Charlie Salata knew that. He waved a mocking good-bye. He and Rizzo disappeared behind the puppet stage. Bell went after them. Harry Warren grabbed his arm. "Forget it. They'll shoot. They couldn't care less who gets hurt."

Bell stopped. Warren was right. "O.K. We'll call it a night."

Warren turned away. Bell grabbed his shoulder. "Careful, in case you run into them."

Harry Warren, née Salvatore Guaragna, said, "I know the neighborhood," and vanished into the crowd.

Bell pretended to watch the puppets, flailing with their swords, while he continued to scan for faces, hoping to recognize Salata's underlings. Suddenly, behind him, he heard, "Good evening, Detective."

Bell turned to face Antonio Branco, who asked with a mocking smile dancing across his mobile face, "What brings you to Little Italy in longshoreman's attire?"

"A Black Hand gangster named Charlie Salata."

"You just missed him," said Branco. "Heavyset man with his arm in a sling,

183

shoving people like he owns the street."

"I know what he looks like."

"He went behind the puppets."

"I saw," said Bell. "There are too many people. Too many could get hurt."

"Your innocent Italians," said Branco. "I'm beginning to believe that you really mean that."

"Mean what?"

"That you can turn *cafon* and *contadino* into Americans."

"What are *cafon* and *contadino*?"

"Barefoot peasants."

"We've done it before, we'll do it again. Meantime, what are *you* going to do for them?"

"I find them work. And I feed them."

"That's only a start," said Isaac Bell. "You're a man of substance, a *prominente*. What will you do when criminals prey on them?"

"I am not a cop. I am not even a detective."

"Why don't you get behind your White Hand Society?"

"That did not work out so well, did it?"

Bell said, "Do it in a bigger way. Put in more money, put in more effort, use your talents. You're a big business man; you know how to organize. You might even make it a national society."

"National?"

"Why not? Every city has its Italian colony."

"What an interesting idea," said Antonio Branco. "Good night, Detective Bell."

"Do you remember the knife you pulled on me in Farmington?"

"I remember the knife I opened to defend myself."

"Was it a switchblade? Or a flick-knife?"

Branco laughed.

"What's so funny?"

"You have the manner of a man born to privilege. Am I correct?"

"Assume you are," Bell said.

"I laugh because you think an immigrant laborer would dare carry an illegal weapon. Your government called us aliens — still does. A switchblade or a flick-knife would get us beaten up by the police and thrown in jail. It was a pocket knife."

"I never saw a pocket knife open that fast."

"It only seemed fast," said Branco. "You were young and afraid . . . So was I."

16

A voice in the dark shocked Tommy Mc-Bean out of his sleep.

"What?"

"Listen."

"Who the hell are you?" McBean reached for the gun under the pillow. It wasn't there. That's what he got for going to bed drunk in a strange hotel with a woman he never met before. She was gone like his gun. Big surprise. She had played him like a rube.

Boiling mad, ready to kill with his bare hands, if he could only see the guy, he sat up in bed and shouted, "What do you want?"

"We have cow horns."

"Oh yeah?" Tommy shot back. "You have my dope? Who the hell are you going to sell it to?"

"We have buyer who pay-a top doll-a."

The guy talked like an Eye-talian. Another damned guinea. More every day. "Who?"

"Top doll-a."

"*Who,* damn you?"

"You."

"Me? What are you talking about?"

"We no steal your heroin."

"You just said you did."

"We no steal it. We kidnap it."

McBean swung his feet to the floor. Cold steel pressed to his forehead. He ignored it and made to stand up. Then he felt a needle prick between his ribs, and the voice in the dark said, "I'm-a four inches from inside your heart."

McBean sagged back on the bed. "Ransom? You're holding our dope for ransom?"

"You make-a distributor system. You sell it."

"You 'make-a' war on us."

The Italian surprised him, saying, "You win-a the war."

"Better believe it."

"Not how you think. You make-a Fordham College. You make-a Boston University. Me? Steamer Class for stupid dago."

"What are you gassin' about?"

"I have more hungry men than you. Micks move up. Dagos just start. Ten years, you all be college men. Ten years, we own the docks."

"You'll never own the docks."

He laughed. "We make-a side bet. After you pay-a ransom."

"What if I don't?"

"We dump drugs in river."

"Geez . . . O.K. How much?"

"Half value."

"I gotta talk to my cousin."

"Ed Hunt said no deal."

"Ed already said no deal? Then no deal."

"Hunt died."

"Ed's dead?"

"Do we have deal?"

Tommy McBean could not imagine Ed Hunt dead. It was like the river stopped. And now the Wallopers was all on him.

"What killed him?"

"It looked like a heart attack."

Antonio Branco walked from the waterfront to Little Italy.

They would be bloody years, those ten or so years to take the New York docks. The Irish would not let the theft of their drugs and the killing of Hunt go by without striking back. Chaos loomed and pandemonium would reign.

At Prince Street, he went into Ghiottone's Café, as he often did. The saloon was going strong despite the hour. Ghiottone himself brought wine. "Welcome, Padrone Branco.

Your health . . . May I sit with you a moment?"

Branco nodded at a chair.

Ghiottone sat, covered his mouth with a hairy hand, and muttered, "Interesting word is around."

"What word?"

"They are shopping for a killer," said Ghiottone.

"The grocer" can't fool everyone. Especially a saloon keeper who works for Tammany Hall. Cold proof of the chaos that threatened every dream.

"Why do you tell me this?"

Ghiottone returned a benign smile. "A padrone recruits employees. Pick and shovel men. Stone masons. In your case, you even recruit padrones. Who knows what else?"

"I don't know why you tell me this." Did Ghiottone know how close he was walking to death?

"Are you familiar with the English word 'hypothetical'?" Ghiottone asked.

"What *ipotetico* are you talking about?"

Ghiottone spread his hands, a signal he meant no harm. "May we discuss *ipotetico*?"

Branco gave a curt nod. Perhaps the saloon keeper *did* know he was close to death. Perhaps he wished he hadn't started

189

what couldn't be stopped.

"The pay is enormous. Fifty thousand."

"Fifty thousand?" Branco couldn't believe his ears. "You could murder a regiment for fifty thousand."

"Only one man."

"Who?"

"They don't tell me. Obviously, an important figure."

"And well-guarded. Who is paying the fifty thousand?"

"Who knows?"

"Who is paying?" Branco asked again.

"Who cares?" asked Ghiottone. "It came to me from a man I trust."

"What is his name?"

"You know I can't tell you. I would never ask who brought the job to him. Just as he would never ask that man where it came from. In silence we are safe."

What blinders men wore. "Kid Kelly" Ghiottone seemed unable to imagine that he was linked — like a caboose at the end of a speeding train — to a *titan* who could pay fifty thousand dollars for one death. Branco pictured in his mind jumping from the roof of that caboose to the freight car in front of it, and to the next car, and the next, running over the swaying tops, one to another to another, all the way to the locomotive.

"They came to you," Branco mused. "Why do they come to an Italian?"

Ghiottone shrugged. Branco answered his own question. The conspirators wanted someone to take the blame, a killer who is completely different from the titan who wanted the victim dead. What better "fall guy" than a crazed Italian immigrant? Or an Italian anarchist.

"What do you say?" asked Ghiottone.

Branco sat silent a long time. He did not touch his glass. At last he said, "I will think."

"I can't wait long before I ask another."

Antonio Branco fixed the saloon keeper with the full force of his deadly gaze. "I don't believe you will ask another. You will wait while I think about the man you need."

"Fifty thousand is a fortune," Ghiottone persisted. "A third or a half as a finder's fee would still be a fortune."

Branco stood abruptly.

"What's wrong?" asked Ghiottone.

"This is no place to discuss such business. Wait ten minutes. Come to the side entrance to my store. Make sure no one sees you."

Branco made a show of thanking him for the wine and saying good night as he left the crowded saloon.

■ ■ ■ ■

"Kid Kelly" Ghiottone waited five minutes, then walked across Prince Street and down an alley. Looking about to see that no one was watching, he knocked at the grocery's side entrance.

Antonio Branco led him through storerooms that smelled of coffee, olive oil, good sausage, and garlic, and down a flight of stairs into a clean, dry cellar. He unlocked a door, said, "No one can hear us," and led Ghiottone into a room that held an iron cage that looked like the Mulberry Street Police Station lockup from which Ghiottone routinely bailed out fools in exchange for their everlasting loyalty.

"What is this? A jail?"

"If a man won't repay the cost of getting him to a job in America, he'll be held until someone pays for him."

"Ransom?"

"You could call it that. Or you could call it fair trade for his fare."

"But you hold him prisoner."

"It rarely comes to that. The sight of these bars alone focuses their mind on repaying their obligation."

Ghiottoni's eyes roved over the thick walls

192

and the soundproof ceiling.

Branco said, "But if I must hold him prisoner, no one will hear him yell."

He exploded into action and clamped Ghiottone's arm in a grip that startled the saloon keeper with its raw power. Ghiottone cocked a fist, but it was over in a second. Outweighed and outmaneuvered, the saloon keeper was shoved into the cell with a force that slammed him against the back wall. The door clanged shut. Branco locked it and pocketed the key.

"Who asked you to hire a killer?"

Ghiottone looked at him with contempt and spoke with great dignity. "I already told you, Antonio Branco, I can never betray him, as I would never betray you."

Branco stared.

Ghiottone gripped the bars. "It's fifty *thousand* dollars. Pay some gorilla to do the job for five — more than he'll ever see in his life — and keep the rest for yourself."

Antonio Branco laughed.

"Why do you laugh?" Ghiottone demanded.

"It is beyond your understanding," said Branco.

Fifty thousand was truly a fortune. But fifty thousand dollars was nothing compared to the golden opportunity that Ghiottone had unwittingly handed him. This was his chance to vault out of "pandemonium" into a permanent alliance with a titan — escape chaos and join a powerhouse American at the top of the heap.

"I ask you again, who brought this to you?"

Ghiottone crossed his arms. "He has my loyalty."

Branco walked out of the room. He came back with a basket of bread and sausage.

"What is this?"

"Food. I'll be back in a few days. I can't let you starve." He passed the loaf and the cured meat through the bars.

"Kind of you," Ghiottone said sarcastically. He tore off a piece of bread and bit into the sausage. "Too salty."

"Salt makes good sausage."

"Wait!"

Branco was swinging the door shut. "I will see you in a few days."

"Wait!"

"What is it?"

"I need water."

"I'll bring you water in a few days."

■ ■ ■ ■

BOOK II
PULL

■ ■ ■ ■

The Trophy Room at Raven's Eyrie

17

Isaac Bell paced the New York field office bull pen, driven by a strong feeling that he had misinterpreted the Cherry Grove conversation. The words were clear; he had no doubt the brothel owner had heard most, if not all, with his ear pressed to an air vent.

What are you waiting for?

An opportunity to talk sense. Would you please sit down?

My mind is made up. The man must go.

But Bell could swear that he had missed what they meant. Though he knew his notes by heart, he read them again.

Would you please sit down?

My mind is made up. The man must go.

He paced among file cases. Then paused at a varnished wooden case that held the field office's Commercial Graphophone — a machine for recording dictation.

A telephone rang. He reached over the duty officer's shoulder and snatched it off the desk. "It's Isaac, Mr. Van Dorn. How are you making out in Washington?"

"That depends entirely on how you're making out in New York."

Bell reported on the heroin holdup and the waterfront shoot-out. "Salata got away, Leone's dead. The only thing we know for sure is the Black Hand is out of the counterfeiting business."

"I am still waiting for the go-ahead to warn the President."

"I have nothing solid yet," said Bell.

Van Dorn hung up. Bell resumed pacing.

He stopped to regard a wall calendar, a promotional gift from the Commercial Graphophone salesman. 1906 was winding down fast, but what caught his eye was the advertisement that ballyhooed, "Tell it to the Graphophone."

Bell wound up the spring motor and read his notes aloud into the mica diaphragm.

"What are you waiting for?

"An opportunity to talk sense. Would you please sit down?

"My mind is made up. The man must go."

He shifted the recording cylinder to the stenographer's transcribing machine, which had hearing tubes instead of a concert horn, and fit the tubes to his ears. His own voice reading the words sounded like a stranger

in another room. Or two strangers downstairs in the library.

What are you waiting for?

*An opportunity to talk sense. Would you
please sit down?*

My mind is made up. The man must go.

Isaac Bell heard what he had missed.

He headed to Research.

Grady Forrer started apologizing. "Sorry,
Isaac. Slow going on the fixers. The tycoons
use different men for different tasks. Twenty,
at least, among them."

"Forget that, I've narrowed it down to
one-in-seven." He slapped his list on Forrer's desk. "The fixer who will hire the killer
to murder the President *is* one of the men
in the library."

"Impossible. These men hold seats on the
Stock Exchange and controlling interests in
railroads, mines, banks, and industries.
They're as close as we'll get to gods."

"One of them only runs errands for the
gods."

"It's not a conversation, not even a discus-
sion. They're not equal partners. The first
speaker is the boss, the second an employee.
I don't care if he shouted or whispered.
What are you waiting for? He is the boss.
The fixer is not a tycoon, even though he's

in the tycoons' club . . . I feel like an idiot, it took me so long."

"O.K." Forrer nodded. "I get it. I feel like an idiot, too. So how do we separate servants from gods?"

Bell said, "Start with where they live."

The Social Register turned up addresses for four — Arnold, Claypool, Culp, and Nichols. Cross-checking telephone directory numbers with company records revealed New York City addresses for the other three. The newspaper society pages turned up the names and locations of the country estates for six of the men. The same six had Newport summer residences. In both cases — country homes and seaside cottages — the one exception was Brewster Claypool.

"He's from the South," said Bell. "Attended law school in Virginia. Maybe he's got a plantation down there."

There were Claypools in Virginia, including Brewster's brothers, but Claypool himself owned no plantation.

"Not even a town house in New York. He lives in the Waldorf Hotel."

"Perhaps," said Forrer, "Claypool prefers the simple life."

"A bachelor's life," countered Bell. He himself lived at the Yale Club when in New

York, in what Marion called his monastic cell.

"What if he lives in a hotel because he isn't as rich as the others?"

Research came up with Claypool's connections to boards of directors in steel, telegraph, and streetcars, but mostly as an adviser. He was, in essence, a Wall Street lawyer who worked as a lobbyist. Like a stage manager, Claypool stayed behind the scenes and avoided the limelight, which fit the definition of a fixer at the highest level.

Interestingly, Research came up with no pictures of Claypool, none of the engravings of prominent men found in the Sunday supplements, and no up-to-date photographs. He was definitely an offstage operator.

Bell, who always dodged cameras in the interest of investigating incognito, knew full well the threat of the accidental photograph. "Find out where he vacations. Some camera fiend must have snapped him with a Kodak . . . Meantime, if Claypool is our fixer, who does he fix for?"

"Pull is an ancient elixir," Brewster Claypool drawled in a soft Virginia accent. "Pull sweeps aside obstacles. But this can't come as news to a Van Dorn detective."

201

"Wouldn't a Wall Street lawyer prefer to go *around* obstacles?"

Brewster Claypool laughed. He was a little wisp of a man, wearing an exquisitely tailored pearl-gray suit, bench-made English shoes, and a blasé smile that concealed an all-seeing eye and a brain as systematic as a battleship's centralized fire director.

"Excellent distinction, Detective."

From the windows of Brewster's office on the top floor of a building at Cortlandt and Broadway, Bell could see into the steel cage-work of the Singer skyscraper under construction. The new building would block Claypool's view of Trinity Church and the harbor long before it rose to become the tallest building in the world, but, at the moment, the view included a close look at ironworkers creeping like spiders on the raw steel.

Claypool said, "May I ask to what do I owe the pleasure of your presence? Your letter was intriguing, and I was impressed, if not flattered, when you quoted my notion that it is humiliating to confess ignorance of anything in Wall Street. Beyond that, I felt curiosity mingled with admiration, having caught wind of the Van Dorn success in retrieving a kidnapped child from the Black Hand. Extraordinary how your operatives found their way straight into the lion's den."

"That is not commonly known," said Bell.

"I do not make a business of common knowledge," said Claypool. "But tell me this. Have you noticed a sudden quiet in the Black Hand camp? Little activity other than small-potatoes attacks on hapless push-carts."

"Few peeps out of them lately," Bell agreed, wondering why Claypool was showing off for him by establishing credentials beyond the canyons of Wall Street. "The Salata Gang got its nose bloodied by the Irish, and things have quieted down since."

For a man who enjoyed boasting, Claypool appeared oddly immune to flattery. Suddenly blunt, he asked, "What can I do for you, Mr. Bell?"

"The Van Dorn Agency needs a man to provide inside information."

Claypool looked genuinely puzzled by the offer of employment. "I'm sure that private detectives are better up in gangsters than I. My interest in the underworld is peripheral to my other interests."

"This is not about gangsters."

"About what, then?"

Isaac Bell pointed out the window. He traced with his finger the route of a cross-town street that began at the East River and

203

ended at Broadway, hard against Trinity Church's graveyard.

"Wall Street?" Claypool gave him a broad wink and joked, "Tread cautiously, Detective. President Roosevelt will clap you in irons."

"What do you mean?" asked Bell. The slick Claypool did not strike him as recklessly bold. That he blithely dropped the name of Roosevelt suggested he was unaware of a plot against the President. If so, Bell's "fixer hunt" had just hit as dead an end as Wall Street's graveyard.

"The manipulation of insider information by Wall Street tycoons is among Teddy's most despised bugaboos . . . But surely you know that."

Bell said, "You don't have to be a tycoon to manipulate inside information . . . But surely you know that."

Still acting vaguely amused, Brewster Claypool geared up his Southern drawl. "Spoken as a private detective who believes he already has inside information — about *me*."

"I do have such information," said Bell. "We've learned a lot about you."

"Why did you look into me?"

"I just told you. The Van Dorn Agency is seeking the services of an inside man.

204

Diligent investigation into your 'interests' indicated that we would find that man in you."

Claypool regarded the tall detective speculatively. "Services rendered by inside men are expensive."

"But not as expensive as services performed by a tycoon."

"Don't rub it in, Detective. You've already made it clear that you know I am not a tycoon."

"But I am among the very few who know that," said Bell. "Most people, including people who should know better, assume that you are as great a magnate as your associates. They put you in the class of tycoons like Manfred Arnold, William Baldwin, John Butler Culp, Gore Manly, Warren D. Nichols, or even Jeremy Pendergast."

If Claypool recognized an alphabetical list of members of the Cherry Grove Gentlemen's Society in attendance the night the President's life was threatened, he gave nothing away, drawling only, "I am flattered to be regarded in such company. But as you've already deduced, I am only a hardworking lawyer. By keeping my ear to the ground, my finger on the pulse, and my eye on the ball, I cultivate clients a thousand times wealthier than I could even dream of becoming."

Bell said, "The fact that you are assumed to run with such company forces the Van Dorn Agency to offer a higher fee."

Claypool's reply was brisk and to the point. "Save your money. I'll take my fee in trade."

"Done," said Bell, extending his hand. If Claypool were innocent, then the Van Dorn Detective Agency had just gained a shrewd source inside the upper echelons of American business; if Claypool were guilty, the Van Dorns were inside the inside man.

They shook on it, and Brewster Claypool asked, "What can I tell you about Wall Street?"

Isaac Bell leveled a cold-eyed gaze at the window. "Who down there hates the President of the United States enough to kill him?"

18

John Butler Culp's grandfather built a Hudson River estate at Storm King Mountain. Culp's father hugely expanded it, and the mansion was currently being enlarged and modernized by the son. They called it Raven's Eyrie, after the *Raven* — the grandfather's first steamboat that spawned their river, railroad, mining, and financial empires. Brewster Claypool dubbed it, archly, affectionately, and extremely privately, the *Birdhouse.*

Claypool found Culp in the gymnasium sparring with Lee, one of the prizefighters he kept on the place. The gym was a physical culture temple brightly lighted by a wall of windows. The morning sun beamed on the men perspiring in the ring. The other prizefighter, a heavyweight named Barry, was exercising with full-size twenty-pound, twenty-eight-inch Indian clubs. Neither of the boxers was the broken-down pug type

207

that some rich men kept around as body-guards, but competitors in their prime. Nonetheless, Barry had a black eye.

Black eyes tended to happen sparring with Culp, and Claypool helped him inflict another by flourishing his gold-headed cane to reflect the sun. Momentarily distracted, Lee received a powerful jab that knocked him into the ropes. That ought to teach him never to let down his guard around Culp.

Culp dismissed his fighters with orders to go to the kitchen and tell the cook to give them beefsteaks for their black eyes. Then he vaulted over the ropes, landed beside Claypool with a crash that shook the floor, and demanded, "What happened with Isaac Bell?"

Claypool reported in detail.

Culp snatched up his Indian clubs. But he listened intently, even as he whirled the bulbous lengths of varnished wood around his head like the Wright brothers' propellers. He interrupted only when Claypool said, "Finally, Detective Bell asked, 'Who hates Roosevelt enough to kill him?' "

"What did you answer?"

"I handed him the membership directory of the New York Stock Exchange."

Culp dropped the clubs, slapped his thigh, and roared with laughter.

The master-servant indignities suffered by Claypool as "Culp's man" were vastly mitigated by the sheer pleasure of conspiring with him.

"What's he looking for?"

"He's fishing."

"Can we be connected?"

"Never."

"Why?"

"We are separated by a long chain of people who don't know each other, much less us."

"Then where did Bell get his list? Manfred, Bill, Gore, Warren, and Jeremy Pendergast were all at the club the night you and I discussed this."

"Here, I believe, Isaac Bell made a mistake. He gave up quite a clue with that list."

"Right he did! Now we know someone in that room told him who was there."

"So it would seem."

"I want to know who? And why? Who's going to try to use this against me?"

Claypool said, "It couldn't have been any Cherry Grovers; none heard a word that could lead to putting two and two together."

Culp, growing agitated, asked, "The girls?"

"Of course not. Unless you indulged in uncharacteristic pillow talk."

"That'll be the day. What about you?"

"I left early that night," said Claypool. "With much on my mind."

"Then who?"

"I was as baffled as you are. Until I had time to think about it on the train. Do you recall that the Cherry Grove reopened immediately under the new name? The very weekend after Coligney's Pink Tea?"

"Of course I recall. I was there. So were you until you hustled the twins upstairs. Tammany called in a marker; you can bet they now own a bigger slice of Nick."

"That's not what I've heard," said Claypool.

"What do you mean?"

"Tammany did not impose its will on Captain Coligney."

"Then how . . . Oh, I see what you mean . . . Nick."

"Nick Sayers must have given Coligney something to be allowed to reopen."

"But how would that weasel know?"

"That I don't know. Perhaps it had nothing to do with us. A coincidence."

"I'll have the fellows sweat it out of him."

"I don't recommend that."

"Who is a whorehouse owner going to complain to?"

"If Isaac Bell catches wind of Nick suffering a beating, it will put him wise and he will be on Nick like a tiger."

"The fellows can make it impossible for Nick to be found by Bell."

"Unnecessary complications could ensue. As things stand now, there's no connection to whoever will do the job. No reason to stop. You can press ahead. If you still insist."

"I still insist."

"Then we definitely don't want any more complications."

"What's Bell's next move?"

"Don't be surprised when he comes calling on you."

"Why me? You said it can't be traced."

"It can't be traced. Which means he has to call on every man who was in that room. Including you."

"Especially me. He's already called on you. It won't take a Sherlock Holmes to connect us."

"Point is, what you insist on doing can't be traced to us."

Culp pondered that a moment. "I hope he does call on me."

"Why?"

"Because he'll wish he hadn't. And that will be the end of it."

Brewster Claypool fell silent.

Culp glowered at him awhile. "O.K.

What's wrong?"

"I don't mean to ascribe to the Van Dorns powers they don't possess. But they have a motto and they stick to it."

"I read it in the *Police Gazette:* 'We never give up.' "

" 'Never' being the operative word."

"A dramatic slogan to raise business."

"Even melodramatic," said Claypool. "But . . ."

"But what?"

"The trouble is, they stick to it."

"I stick to things, too."

"That you do, sir. It is among your most admirable qualities."

Suddenly, Culp's expression darkened and he got the thundercloud on his face that made him dangerous. "Wait a minute! Even if we can't be connected, our man's going to have a hard time doing it when they warn Roosevelt someone's gunning for him."

Claypool smiled.

"What are you grinning about? The Secret Service will take precautions."

"I am not 'grinning,' " said Brewster Claypool, "I am smiling, because I am imagining Teddy's reaction when they tell him he must take precautions."

"How? What? What will he do?"

"He will suck in his belly, stick out his

chest, and declare that he is not afraid."

"So?"

"The funny thing is, he'll be telling the truth. Teddy won't be afraid. And he will refuse to take precautions."

19

Isaac Bell went back to the Cherry Grove. The name gold-leafed above the lintel had been changed to "Grove House." He asked Nick Sayers which of the women had worked in the library the night Sayers had overheard the plot.

Only Jenny, a raven-haired beauty. Bell took her upstairs and, when their door was closed, handed her one hundred dollars and said, "I have a simple request and whatever you answer I'll tell no one."

Jenny said, "Don't worry, I always say yes. What do you want?"

"On the Saturday night before the Pink Tea shut down the house, two of the men in the Cherry Grove club left the main club room for the small library."

Jenny looked alarmed. "How do you know about the club? Are you friends with them?"

"Not really. One of the men was Brewster

Claypool. Do you remember who went with him?"

"Does Mr. Sayers know you're asking this?"

"Would you like to ask him to confirm it?"

She looked Bell up and down and said, "Well, that explains that."

"Explains what?"

"I was wondering why you came to a sporting house."

Bell smiled back. "I'll take that as a compliment, thank you. And may I say that if I ever felt the need to come to one, I'd make sure you were in it . . . Do you recall who Mr. Claypool left the room with?"

"He left alone."

"All alone?"

"I looked in a couple of times. He was just sitting there sipping his whiskey until Mr. Culp joined him."

Isaac Bell armed himself with solid information from Research about the members' habits in order to put his Cherry Grove Society suspects at ease. Then he cornered them, one by one, while masquerading as a gentleman who shared their interests. Most were not the sort who would ask his line of business when meeting in a social situation. Those who did learned that Isaac Bell was

215

an executive in the insurance business.

He ran down the first at the Grolier, a club for bibliophiles. He borrowed a police horse to catch up with another cantering in Central Park. Allowing a close-fought victory in a late-autumn race for New York "Thirties," he and Archie Abbott accepted drinks at the Seawanhaka Corinthian Yacht Club. He lunched at the Union League, and he met with a banker at the Chase National headquarters on Cedar Street, who declined to lend Bell money to buy a two-hundred-foot steam yacht. Of the seven, only one proved elusive, and Bell found him back where everything started, at the brothel.

All were easily maneuvered into admitting knowing Claypool. Two praised him for doing them the favor of getting them out of "sticky situations." The Chase banker dropped, casually, "Everyone knows that 'Brew' Claypool is Culp's man." But he was the only one who made the connection. Of the bunch, two struck Bell as possible presidential assassins of the type who would hire a killer — J. B. Culp and Warren D. Nichols.

Culp made no secret of disliking Roosevelt. The affable Nichols had a wintery eye; a valuable quality in a banker, perhaps, but something about him made Bell wonder

216

whether the wintery eye might mask a hunter's heart.

"Thin, thin stuff," he reported to Joseph Van Dorn. "A tycoon who hates the President and a banker with a cold eye."

The Boss agreed. "We've said all along that the threats overheard could be nothing more than angry talk. Maybe that's all it is."

Two hours later, Bell sent to Van Dorn on the private wire.

RESEARCH LEARNED NICHOLS WILL DONATE HUNDRED THOUSAND ACRES PRIME TIMBER LAND ADIRONDACK FOREST PRESERVE IN THEODORE ROOSEVELT NAME.

Van Dorn wired back.

CONCENTRATE CULP.

Culp's industries and mines and timber operations were protected by brutal strike-breakers. Culp's stock holdings were enriched by the best manipulators on Wall Street. His Washington lobbyists had bribed legislators to change the site of the inter-ocean ship canal from Nicaragua to the Isthmus of Panama. His agents in France and Panama helped him gain control of lucrative canal stock.

Many fixers worked for Culp behind the scenes, but Bell developed the strong impression that Claypool hired the fixers. All of them. Except Claypool was not about to personally hire murderers, much less presidential assassins. He would hire an agent, who would hire another agent, and on down the line. When the job finally reached the man with the gun, Claypool and Culp would be miles away.

"Forgive me, Father, for I have sinned," said Francesca Kennedy.

Her scarf concealed her face, but the hunch of her shoulders and her fingers anxiously working her rosary and the stricken tone of her voice were a convincing image of a woman desperate to save her soul. Had life been kinder to her, thought Branco, she would have been a great actress on Broadway.

"What sin did you commit, my child?"

"I lured a man to his death."

Branco laughed. "Relax. Tommy McBean's as alive as you."

"Do I still get paid?"

A woman who was good for killing was a rare and valuable resource and should be treated as such. She loved money, so money she would have.

Branco shoved a rolled hundred-dollar bill through the grille. "Of course you get paid. You earned it. It took some doing to wake him up."

"You know something?" she whispered. She turned to face the grille. "I think I'd rather do it with them when I know I'm the one that's going to do them after — instead of just setting them up."

"It takes all kinds."

"And you know —"

"Enough confession," Branco interrupted before she got wound up in a talking spree.

Though she had never seen his face, Branco had known of her since she was an ordinary streetwalker the night of her first murder — a customer who brutalized her. Her cool deliberation had so impressed him that he ordered Charlie Salata to rescue her from the cops. Francesca was a survivor who could turn on a nickel and give you the change. The instant he interrupted her, she went straight back to business.

"What's my next job?"

Branco passed another fortune through the grille. "Confess here on schedule. You'll know it soon."

"I get antsy sitting around."

"Put your impatience into preparation." He pushed more money through the grid. "Buy clothes to drink tea at the Knickerbocker Hotel. A suitable outfit to get past the house dicks. You must look like you belong there."

"That's easy."

"For you it is. You are an unusual woman."

Branco returned to his store through the tunnels under the graveyard and the tenements.

He filled a pitcher with clean, cold water and brought it and a glass to the underground room where he had locked Ghiottone.

20

"Kid Kelly" Ghiottone heard a flood. A street main had burst, some hundreds-year-old pipe laid by the Dutchmen who used to run the city, rusting, rotting, thinner and thinner, and suddenly exploding from the pressure. Water was everywhere, spouting out of the cobblestones, flooding basements. He would drown, locked in the cell, deep in Branco's cellar. But before he drowned, he would drink.

"Wake up, my friend."

He woke to the same smell he had fallen asleep to — mouldering sausage and the stink of his own sweat and despair. There was no broken main, no flood. Not a drop of water. He was dreaming. But he *heard* water. Opening his eyes and looking about blearily, he saw Branco standing outside the cell again. He was pouring water from a pitcher into a glass. Again.

"It is time to drink."

Ghiottone tried to say "Please." His mouth and throat were dry as sand. His tongue was stiff, and he could barely make a noise, only a croak, like a consumptive old drunk crawling in the gutter.

"Who asked you to hire a killer?"

Ghiottone tried again to speak. His tongue filled his mouth. No sound could escape. It was buried in dust. Branco put the pitcher and the glass down on the floor. Ghiottone stared through the bars at the glass. He saw a drop hanging from the lip of the pitcher. The drop looked enormous. Branco handed him a pencil and a piece of paper.

"Write his name."

Ghiottone could not remember how many of Branco's pencils he had broken, nor how many sheets of paper he had ripped. He grabbed the pencil and paper and watched, astonished, as the pencil moved across the paper, scribbling, "He will not know any more than me."

"One thing at a time," said Branco. "His name. Then water."

Ghiottone wrote "Adam Quiller."

Antonio Branco read it. Adam Quiller, a fat, little middle-aged Irishman he'd seen scuttling about the district carrying messages from the alderman. Quiller did Ghiottone favors in exchange for the saloon keeper delivering Italian votes on Election Day.

"Of course. I could have guessed and saved us both such trouble. But I had to know. Here, my friend. Drink!"

He opened the bars and offered the glass.

"Kid Kelly" Ghiottone lifted it in both hands and threw back his head. The water splashed on his lips and ran down his chin. What entered his mouth and spilled down his throat was cold and delicious. He tipped the glass higher for the last drop.

Antonio Branco watched the saloon keeper's elbows rise until they were parallel with his shoulders. The movement caused his vest to slide above the waistband of his trousers. His shirt stretched tight over his ribs.

"Have another."

He took the glass and poured it full again. "Tell me," he said, still holding the glass, "how would the killer be told the target?"

Ghiottone, thoroughly beaten, could not meet his eye. He tried to speak and found he could whisper. "When you give me the killer's name, I pass it up to —"

"To Adam Quiller."

Ghiottone nodded.

Branco frowned. "Then the target is passed all the way back down the chain?

223

That sounds slow, cumbersome, and not private enough. I don't believe you are telling me all the truth."

"I am, padrone. They didn't say how, but it would not come down the chain. They have some other way of telling him the target."

"And the money? The fifty thousand? How does that come?"

Ghiottone straightened up. "Through me. They will send me the money when the job is done. My job is to give it to you."

Branco handed him the glass, saying, "That makes you a very valuable man."

Ghiottone lifted it in both hands and threw back his head. This time, most of the water entered his mouth. He swallowed, reveling in the coldness of it, and tipped the glass to finish it.

Branco stuffed the body in a sugar barrel and nailed it shut and went to his stable, where he woke up an old Sicilian groom and ordered him to hitch up a garbage cart and dump the barrel in the river. Then he went hunting for Adam Quiller.

21

Late in the afternoon, when the Van Dorn detective bull pen filled with operatives preparing for the night by perusing the day's newspapers and exchanging information, Isaac Bell sat alone, opening and closing a pocket knife, reviewing notes in the memo book open beside him, and listening.

"*Tribune* says the Harbor Squad found "Kid Kelly" Ghiottone floating in the river."

"Looks like the Wallopers got some back."

"Why would the Wallopers do Ghiottone? He didn't run with Salata."

"He was Italian, thereby permitting the Wallopers to demonstrate they, one, are enraged about their dope being lifted, and, two, have the guts to snatch him out of Little Italy. His body was a mess, according to the paper; looked like he was beat with hatchets."

"That is not what happened," said Isaac Bell.

"Thought you were napping, Isaac. What do you mean?"

"Ghiottone wasn't beat up. At least not when he was alive."

"What makes you think that?"

"Barrel staves were floating around the body."

Every detective in the bull pen lowered his newspaper and stared at Isaac Bell.

"Meaning, they dumped the body in a barrel," said Mack Fulton.

"And a ship hit the barrel," said Wally Kisley.

"The steel-hulled, five-mast nitrate bark *James P. Richards,*" said Bell. "Outbound for Chile. According to the Harbor Squad."

Bell continued practicing with the pocket knife. Mack Fulton voiced a question. "Can I ask you something, Isaac?"

"Shoot."

"Your criminal cartel theory is driving you around the bend, and the Boss is all over you about the President."

"I'm aware I'm busy," said Bell. "Which is why I depend on you boys' invaluable assistance. What do you want to know?"

"Being so engaged, what made you query Roundsman O'Riordan about an Eye-talian saloon keeper floating in the river?"

"What do you think?"

"Because," Kisley answered for Fulton, "Isaac thinks Ghiottone is Black Hand."

Bell shook his head. "That's not what I got from Research, and they got their info straight from Captain Coligney, who used to ramrod the Mulberry Street Precinct. Ghiottone was a Tammany man — so what strikes me is, somebody's got it in for Tammany Hall. Adam Quiller was tortured and murdered last Saturday; Harry Warren says he was Alderman King's heeler. And this guy Lehane, Alderman Henry's heeler, was also tortured."

"Those reformers are getting meaner every day," said Walter Kisley.

Bell joined the laughter. Then he said, "Both heelers were finally killed with a stiletto."

"I didn't see that in the paper."

"You'll see it tomorrow. Eddie Edwards just spoke with the coroner. The papers will go wild when they see all three victims connected by a stiletto."

"How about connected by a Tammany boss under investigation who's killing off witnesses?" asked Kisley.

"Not likely. Bribing witnesses and jurors is more a boss's strategy. But here's the thing that strikes me. Look at the order of when they were killed — each stiletto victim stood a rung higher on the ladder of political power — Ghiottone, at the bottom; then Quiller, a heeler and block captain, one step up; then Lehane, the district election leader's heeler. Makes me wonder who's next."

"District leader?"

"More likely his heeler."

Helen Mills rushed into the bull pen. Detectives straightened neckties, smoothed hair, and brushed crumbs from their vests. She spotted Bell and handed him a small envelope.

"What's this?"

"Claypool."

Bell slit it open with his knife. Out fell a photograph, so recently developed it smelled of fixer. The picture was slightly blurred, as Claypool was turning his face, but it was him for sure, and anyone who knew the camera-shy lawyer would recognize him.

"Where'd you get this?"

"I snapped it. Some girls from school came into town. We pretended we were tourists, and I snapped him while snapping them, when he left his office for lunch."

Bell slipped it into his memo book. "Nicely done, Helen. Take the girls to Rector's Lobster Palace. Tell Charlie it's on me and I said to give you the best table in the house."

Detectives watched her leave.

Fulton said, "Quiller four days ago. Then Sullivan, Lehane's heeler, yesterday."

"Working their way up to a full-fledged alderman," said Kisley.

Isaac Bell put down the knife and picked up his fountain pen. "Which of them are under investigation?"

"Which ain't?" asked Kisley, holding up the *Times* with a front page column headline that read

TWO ALDERMEN HELD IN BRIBERY SCANDAL

"Of the forty crooks on the Board of Aldermen, James Martin's in deepest at the moment. Alderman Martin was always looking for patronage. Ten years if convicted, and sure to be convicted. Word is, he won't make bail."

"Why can't an alderman make bail? The whole point of serving on the Boodle Board is to get rich."

"Broke," called Scudder Smith, who was nursing a flask in the corner. "Lost it all to a gal and poker."

Bell said, "Are you sure about that, Scudder?"

Scudder Smith, a crackersjack New York

reporter before Joseph Van Dorn persuaded him to become a detective, said, "You can take it to the bank."

"Hey, where you going, Isaac?" asked Kisley.

The tall detective was already on his feet, pocketing the knife and his memo book, clapping on his hat, and striding out the door. "Criminal Courts Building. See if the gal and the gamblers left Alderman Martin anything to trade for bail."

Midway through the door, he paused.

"Harry?"

"What's up?" asked Harry Warren.

"Would you go downtown and find a way to shake hands with Antonio Branco?"

Harry Warren exchanged mystified glances with Mack Fulton and Wally Kisley. "Sure thing, Isaac. Care to tell me *why* I'm going to shake hands with Antonio Branco?"

"Do it and I'll tell you why," said Isaac Bell. "Just make sure he's not wearing gloves."

Alderman James Martin shielded his face from the newspaper artists with a hand clutching a half-smoked cigar while an assistant district attorney told the magistrate that he should be jailed in the West 54th Street Police Court Prison unless he put up a bond of $15,000. The DA's sleuth who had arrested him on the Queensboro Bridge after he left the Long Island City stone mason's yard, where he had received the money, stood smirking in the doorway. Thankfully, thought Martin, the DA had set the bribe trap in a stone yard, where he had legitimate reason to be. He was a building contractor, after all, wasn't he, like many a New York City alderman. He prayed the magistrate would buy that defense at least enough to reduce his bail to an amount low enough to borrow.

"Twelve five-hundred-dollar bills," the assistant DA raved on. "One for each of his fellow aldermen he would pay off to shift their votes on an issue critical to the health and well-being of every man, woman, and child in New York."

Alderman Martin's lawyer asked that his client be admitted to a more reasonable bail. Martin waited to hear his fate. Home for supper or weeks in jail.

The magistrate fixed bond at $10,000. The DA's assistant protested that it was too low, that Martin would run away, but it was, in fact, far more than he could raise, and the alderman pleaded with the magistrate, with little hope.

"Your Honor, I'm not able to furnish a

bond of ten thousand."

"The charge constitutes a felony. If convicted, your sentence could be ten years and a five-thousand-dollar fine. Ten thousand dollars bail is reasonable. I can reduce it no further."

"I don't have ten thousand — I had six thousand, but the DA sleuths took it."

The magistrate's eyes flashed. "The District Attorney's detectives did not 'take' the money. They confiscated *evidence*, which happened to be in bills marked ahead of time to ascertain whether you would accept a bribe."

"That money was given to me in connection with a business deal."

"The nature of that business deal led to your arraignment."

"I'm a contractor. It was an ordinary business consideration involving the supply of stone. I am not in the bribe line of business."

"You will have opportunity to assert that at your trial. Bail is fixed at ten thousand dollars."

There was a sudden commotion at the back of the small courtroom and the alderman turned hopefully toward it. He had been telephoning friends all afternoon, begging for bail money. Maybe one of them had

had a change of heart.

A message was passed to Martin's attorney, who addressed the magistrate. "Your Honor, I have a bondsman present. He will offer properties at 31 and 32 Mulberry Street as security for Alderman Martin's ten-thousand-dollar bail."

Isaac Bell bounded up the stairs to the bond room in the Criminal Courts Building and told the clerk, "I presume the court will accept my check on the American States Bank as bond for Alderman Martin."

"We'll accept an American States Bank check. But Alderman Martin is already free on bond."

"Where'd he go?"

The clerk shrugged. "Somebody sprung 'im."

Bell palmed a ten-dollar bill and slipped it to the clerk. "I was informed that Alderman Martin was running out of the kind of friends who would put up ten thousand."

"You were informed correctly," said the clerk.

"Any idea who paid the bond?"

"Fellow put up a couple of houses on Mulberry Street."

"Mulberry? That's in the Italian colony, isn't it?"

"It is."

"Isn't Martin's district in Queens?"

"Until they lock him up in Sing Sing."

"He's really on the ropes, isn't he?"

"Word is he's in hock to his eyeballs and run out of favors. The man's got nothing left."

Bell palmed another ten. "You must see a lot of strange goings on."

"Oh yes."

"Who would risk two houses betting that Martin wouldn't jump bail?"

"Somebody with more money than sense."

"What do you suppose they'd get out of it?"

"Something the Alderman still has."

Bell felt someone watching him. He looked around. "Is that fellow leaning on the door jamb a DA's detective?" he asked the clerk.

"Detective Rosenwald. He nailed Martin."

Bell walked up to Rosenwald. "Let me save you some trouble. I'm Isaac Bell, Van Dorn Agency. And I was asking that court clerk what I'm about to ask you."

Rosenwald said, "I'll save *you* some trouble by telling you don't try to grease *my* palm."

"Wouldn't dream of it," said Bell. "But I would like to buy you a drink."

■ ■ ■ ■

"Out of the frying pan," thought Alderman Martin, with an awful feeling he was headed for the fire. At first, it all went smooth as silk. Court officers, who were grinning like some swell had stuffed enormous tips in their pockets, let him out of the building by a side entrance. Instead of having to duck his head from a pack of howling newspapermen, he was greeted by a silent escort who whisked him inside a town car before the reporters got wise. But now that his rescuers, whoever they were, had him in the closed and curtained auto, they were not treating him with the respect, much less the deference, expected by a member of the New York City Board of Aldermen, who had jobs, contracts, favors, and introductions to dispense.

They would not tell him where they were taking him. In fact, they never spoke a word. Relieved to dodge the reporters, he hadn't taken notice of the fact that his broad-shouldered protectors were swarthy Italians. Kidnapped, he thought, with a sudden stab of terror. Snatched by the Black Hand. Abducted for ransom by Italians too stupid to realize that he was in so much trouble already that no one would pay to get him back.

He tried to climb out when the car stopped in traffic. They gripped his arms from either side and sat him back down forcefully. He demanded an explanation. They told him to shut up.

He filled his lungs to bellow for help.

They stuffed a handkerchief into his mouth.

When the auto stopped at last and they opened the door, it was parked inside a storehouse. He could smell the river, or a sewer. They marched him down stone stairs into a cellar lit by a single bulb, glaring from the ceiling. He saw a table in a corner with something spread on it under a sheet. In the shadows of another corner, a man was standing still as stone. There was a heavy, straight-backed chair under the bulb. They pushed him into it and shackled him to the arms with handcuffs and yanked the handkerchief from his mouth.

The escorts left. The man in the shadows spoke. Alderman Martin could not see his face. He had an Italian accent.

"Alderman Martin, your heeler confess-a you order him to hire assassin."

His heart nearly stopped beating. He had been right about the fire. This was no

236

kidnapping for ransom. Suddenly, he was thinking clearly and knew that the entire terrible day, starting with the bribe trap, was unimportant. This was a situation he shouldn't have gotten involved in — would not have gotten into if Brandon Finn's people hadn't known he was desperate — and it had gone terribly wrong. He had no hope but to bluster his way out of it.

"He would never say such a thing."

"He didn't want to."

The man lifted the sheet.

James Martin would have given ten years of his life to be sitting in a cell at West 54th Street. The heeler was dead. His face was bloody as a beefsteak. The eye they had left in his head regarded Martin with a dumbfounded stare.

"What did you do to him?" Martin asked when he could draw enough breath to speak.

"We asked him a question. We asked, 'Who told you hire assassin?' We now ask you that same question, Alderman Martin. Who told you hire assassin?"

"You know the 'Chamber of Horrors'?" Captain Coligney asked Isaac Bell on the telephone.

"The one at Union Square?"

"Meet me there."

22

Isaac Bell climbed the subway steps at the Union Square Station three at a time. At 16th Street, a leather-lunged barker manned a megaphone:

"Do you want better schools and subways? Do you want green parks and breezy beaches? Want to find out why you don't have them? Then step right up to the Committee of One Hundred Citizens' Exhibit against Tammany Hall to see how Tammany gets away with its bunco game."

The barker seemed superfluous. The line to get in snaked the length and breadth of Union Square and disappeared down side streets. The extras newsboys were hawking claimed that twenty-two thousand people had visited the exhibition in only three days.

In the show window, a papier-mâché cow represented Tammany milking the city. "Don't cry over spilt milk," read the placards. "Get a new set of milkmaids."

A competing Tammany Hall exhibit several doors down boasted a live elephant — representing Republicans eating the city — but it looked to Bell like the anti-Tammany show was outdrawing the pachyderm four-to-one.

Coligney had stationed a cop to escort Bell inside, where he followed signs pointing to the Chamber of Horrors. On the way, he passed "The Municipal Joyride to the Catskill Mountains," a huge cartoon of "Honest Jim" Fryer running over a small taxpayer in a town car, a depiction of the "Story and Shame of the Queensboro Bridge" that accused Tammany Hall Democrats of wasting $8,000,000 to build "nothing but an automobile highway" that should have been spent on preventing tuberculosis.

Down the basement stairs was the chief attraction, the Chamber of Tammany Horrors, and it was stronger stuff. Silhouettes of men, women, and children encircled the room like the rings of Hell, dramatizing the price of graft: the thirteen thousand New Yorkers who had died this year of preventable diseases; the children condemned to the streets by the shortage of schools.

Captain Coligney was waiting next to an exhibit illustrated by a floor-to-ceiling billboard: "How Tammany Hands Catskill

239

Aqueduct Plums to its Favored Contractors."

"A DA dick told me you dropped my name on him," he greeted Bell.

"Only your name. I was trying to get a handle on Adlerman Martin."

"I reckoned as much," said Coligney. He jerked a thumb at the billboard. "Thought you'd like to see Part Two of this exhibit."

Alderman James Martin was behind the billboard, barely out of the regular visitors' sight. He was hanging by the neck. His face was blue, his tongue as thick and gray as a parrot's, his body stiff.

Coligney said, "He wasn't here when they closed last night. They found him this morning."

"What time do they close?"

"Closed at eleven. Opened this morning at nine."

"Are we supposed to believe he committed suicide from guilt?"

"Martin didn't have a guilty bone in his body. But, at any rate, he's been dead a lot longer than twelve hours. Which means he didn't hang himself here."

"Not likely he hanged himself elsewhere, either," Bell noted. He inspected the body closely. "But it doesn't look like he put up a struggle."

240

Coligney agreed. "On the other hand, his pockets were empty, except for one thing." He held up a business card, balancing the edges between his big fingers. Bell read it.

"Who is Davidson?"

"Onetime reformer. Saw where the money was made and woke up thoroughly Tammanized. Big wheel in the Contractors' Protective Association."

"What's his card doing in Martin's pocket?"

"I'd guess same reason Alderman Martin is hanging here: To make Tammany look even worse than the Chamber of Horrors."

"So Davidson locked horns with whoever hanged Martin."

Coligney nodded. "And they've just sent him a threat."

Bell asked, "How much time would I have to interview Davidson before you make it official?"

Coligney found sudden interest in the ceiling. "My cops are busy. I'd imagine you have a day."

"I'll need two," said Bell. Time for Research to scrutinize Davidson before he braced him.

The side-wheel river steamer *Rose C. Stambaugh* struggled to land at Storm King sixty

241

miles up the Hudson from New York. Smoke fountained from the stack behind her wheel-house, and her vertical beam engine, which stood like an oil derrick between her paddle wheels, belched steam that turned white in the cold air.

The pilot cussed a blue streak, under his breath, when a bitter gust — straight from the North Pole — stiffened the American flag flying from the stern and threatened to hammer his boat against the wharf. Winter could not shut down the river too soon for him.

Isaac Bell stood at the head of the gang-way, poised to disembark. He wore a blue greatcoat and a derby and carried an over-night satchel. Red and green Branco's Grocery wagons were lined up on the freight deck, stacked full of barrels and crates destined for the aqueduct crews at the heart of the great enterprise. The siphon that would shunt the Catskills water under the Hudson River would connect the Asho-kan Dam with New York City.

The mules were already in their traces. The instant the gangway hit the wharf, Bell strode down it and pulled ahead of the long-eared animals clumping after him. Officials scattered when they saw him coming.

If his coat and hat made him look like a

New York City police detective, or a high-ranking Water Supply Board cop, Isaac Bell was not about to say he wasn't. Two birds with one stone on this trip included a second visit with J. B. Culp. This time, it would be on his home turf, Raven's Eyrie, which Bell could see gleaming halfway up the mountain in the noonday sun. In his bag were evening clothes. First he would look like a police detective *under* the mountain.

He found the site where they were sinking a new access shaft to the siphon tunnel. The original shaft had been started too close to the mountain edge, where the granite proved too weak to withstand the aqueduct's water pressure.

"Can I help you, sir?" the gate man asked warily.

"Where's Davidson?"

"I'll send somebody for him."

"Just point me the way."

The gate man pointed up the hill.

Bell stepped close, cop close. "Precisely where?"

"There's a contractor's shed about a hundred feet from the new shaft."

Bell moved closer, his shoulder half an inch from the man's cheek. "If you use that telephone to warn him, I will come back for you when I'm done with him."

Davidson's official job was to provide expert advice on the labor situation. That was window dressing. His real job was collecting contract fees from the Contractors' Protective Society — or, as former newspaperman Detective Scudder Smith put it, "Tammany's on-site fleecer of contractors and taxpayers." Originally a Municipal Ownership League proponent of public utilities, Davidson had switched sides after the city's Ramapo Water Grab victory and become, as Captain Coligney had noted, thoroughly Tammanized.

Across the Hudson — where the Catskills water tunneled under and emerged from the uptake — a stretch of aqueduct was being bored by a company that had paid Davidson an "honorarium" of five percent of the contract fee for his expert advice. Or so reliable rumor unearthed by Van Dorn operators had it. Vaguer rumors had Davidson shaking down Antonio Branco for $20,000 for a provisioning contract. Trouble was, hearsay was not evidence, and graft charges would never make it to court before the statute of limitations expired.

But despite his apparent immunity, Davidson was scared. Rattled, it seemed to Bell, at least too rattled to question Bell's masquerade as a cop. "I got the telegraph" were the first words out of the heeler's mouth.

"What telegraph?" asked Bell.

"The message. They left him hanging there for me. Warning me off."

"From what?"

"None of your business."

Bell said, "If you want me to run you in, the boat's heading back to New York. Or we can take the train if you prefer trains."

"Go right ahead."

"What?"

"Arrest me. I'll be safer in your custody than I am standing here."

"Fine with me," Bell bluffed, "if you think you'll be safer in a city jail."

Davidson wet his lips. "I don't know what you're talking about. Go see Finn. He'll set you straight."

"Which Finn?"

Davidson looked at him sharply. "There is only one Finn, and if you don't know him, you're not who you say you are."

Bell tried to bull through it. "I'm asking politely one more time. Which Finn?"

Davidson turned on his heel and walked again, leaving the tall detective with a strong feeling he had egg on his face. He hurried into the village, found a telephone building next to the post office, and phoned Captain

Coligney. It took a while to connect to the long-distance wire, and he assumed that the local operator was listening in.

"Do you know a 'Finn' in connection with our hanging?"

"I'm afraid you're talking about Brandon Finn. Not beholden to the powers in the usual way. Informal, if you know what I mean."

"You mean he operates off the usual tracks?"

"And covers his tracks."

"Who does Brandon Finn report to?"

"The Boss. But only on a strictly informal basis. Why do you ask?"

"It might be smart to keep an eye on him."

"Too late," said Coligney. "He died."

"Of what?"

"They don't know yet."

Bell composed a telegram in Van Dorn cipher.

PROTECT CLAYPOOL HOME AND
OFFICE

If Brandon Finn was linked directly to Boss Fryer, then whoever was killing the Tammany men was nearing the top of the heap. If Claypool was the fixer who started

246

the ball rolling, then he could be next.

Archie Abbott took for granted that he delighted women the way catnip fired up cats. So when an attractive brunette taking tea in the Knickerbocker Hotel lobby not only failed to notice him but looked straight through him as if he didn't exist, Abbott took it as a radical challenge to the proper order of things.

"Good afternoon."

She had arresting blue eyes. They roved over Abbott's square chin, his aquiline nose, his piercing eyes, his high brow, his rich red hair, and his dazzling smile. She said, "I'm afraid we've not been introduced, sir," and returned her gaze to her magazine.

"Allow me to remedy that," said Abbott. "I am Archibald Angell Abbott IV. It would be an honor to make your acquaintance."

She did not invite him to sit beside her. At this point, were he not known to the Knickerbocker's house detectives as a fellow Van Dorn, two well-dressed burly men would have quietly materialized at his elbows and escorted him to the sidewalk while explaining that mashers were not permitted to molest ladies in their hotel — and don't come back!

"My friends call me Archie."

"What does your wife call you?"

"I hope she will call me whatever pleases her when we finally meet. May I ask your name?"

"Francesca."

"What a beautiful name."

"Thank you, Archibald."

"Just Archie is fine."

"It pleases me to call you Archibald."

Abbott's sharp eye had already fixed on her left hand, where a wedding ring made a slight bulge in her glove. "Are you married, Francesca?"

"I am a widow."

"I am terribly sorry," he lied.

"Thank you. It has been two years."

"I notice you still wear the ring."

"The ring keeps the wrong type from getting the wrong idea."

"May I sit down?"

"Why?"

Abbott grinned. "To see whether I'm the wrong type."

Francesca smiled a smile that lit her eyes like limelight. "Only the wrong type would get the wrong idea."

"Tell me about your accent, I don't quite recognize it. I studied accents as an actor. Before my current line of work."

"What is your line?"

"Insurance."

"Sit down, Archibald," said Francesca Kennedy. "I am pleased to make your acquaintance."

23

The gatehouse at Raven's Eyrie looked like it had been built to repel anarchists and labor agitators. Sturdy as an armory, the two-story granite redoubt was flanked by high walls. The gate had bars thick as railroad track, and the driveway it blocked was so steep that no vehicle could get up enough speed to batter through it. But what riveted Isaac Bell's attention were the shooting slits in the upper story, which would allow riflemen to pick off attackers at their leisure. J. B. Culp was not taking chances with anyone who had it in for the rich.

"Please inform Mr. Culp that Isaac Bell has come to accept the invitation he offered at Seawanhaka to view his ice yacht."

"Have you an appointment, sir?"

The gatekeeper wore an immaculate uniform. He had cropped iron-gray hair and a rugged frame. His sidearm was the old Model 1873 .45 Colt the United States

Marines had brought back into service for its stopping power in the Philippine Campaign.

Bell passed his card through the bars. "Mr. Culp invited me to drop by anytime."

Five minutes later, Culp himself tore down the driveway in a six-cylinder, air-cooled Franklin — the same six-cylinder model that had just made a coast to coast run across the continent in a record-breaking fifteen days. "Welcome, Bell! How do you happen to be up here?"

"We're underwriting some of the aqueduct contractors' insurers. Hartford asked me to have a look at our interests."

"Lucky you found me at home."

"I suspected that phones and wires cut you loose from the city," answered Bell, who had had an operative keeping tabs on Culp's comings and goings since eliminating the other Cherry Grove suspects.

"Hop in! I'll show you around."

"I came especially to see your iceboat."

Culp swung the auto onto a branch of the driveway that descended along the inside of the estate walls all the way down to the river, where crew barracks adjoined a boathouse. Yard workers were hauling sailboats up a marine railway. Inside the boathouse, his ice racer was suspended over the water, ready to be lowered when it froze. It had the broad stance of a waterspider, a lightweight contraption consisting of a strong triangular "hull" — two crossed spars of aluminum — with skate blades at the three corners.

"Entirely new, modern design," Culp boasted. "Got the idea for aluminum from my Franklin. Strong and light." It struck Bell that Culp sounded like a typical sportsman obsessed with making his yacht, or racehorse, or auto, or ice yacht a winner.

Bell marveled at the rig hanging from the rafters. "Monster sail."

"Lateen rig. Beats the tried and true Hudson River gaff main and clubfooted jib. I cracked ninety knots last winter."

"Ninety? You'll beat the 20th Century."

"I'll beat a hundred, this winter. Come on, I'll show you the house."

The house at Raven's Eyrie was a very large mansion with striking views through sheets of glass so big they could have been department store show windows in New York. Here, too, Culp struck him as more the proud homeowner than a killer. For the interior, Culp had gone shopping in Europe. Bell exclaimed politely at regular intervals, and stopped dead in his tracks to study an enormous silver, lapis lazuli, and ivory sculpture on the dining room table. Dominating the table, where it would tower over thirty guests, it depicted Saint George, on horseback, running his lance through a dragon. Bell had just figured out that the giant bowls at the dragon's head and tail made it a salt and pepper cellar when Mrs. Culp suddenly appeared, leading her cook and majordomo.

She looked to be a decade Culp's junior, closer to Bell's age. She would hardly be the first rich man's wife whose husband spent nights in the Cherry Grove bordello, but, thought Bell, Daphne Culp was such a looker it would not seem worth the trouble leaving home.

"Bell," Culp introduced him brusquely. "Met him racing at Seawanhaka."

Bell praised the ice yacht and her house, and she asked, "Do I hear the faintest trace of Boston in your voice, Mr. Bell?"

"Guilty, ma'am. I thought most of it rubbed off at New Haven."

"Butler went to Yale, too, didn't you, dear?"

"John Butler Culp was a legendary Old Blue when I arrived," said Bell.

"Not that old, for gosh sakes," said Culp.

Daphne soon established she and Bell had in common distant cousins by marriage, and she asked him to stay to dinner. "Did you come up from New York? You better stay the night."

"Let me show you the gymnasium," said Culp.

"Your own prize ring," said Bell.

"And my own prizefighters."

Culp introduced Lee and Barry. They were well-knit men, with firm, elastic steps. Lee was tall and lean, Barry slightly shorter and twice as wide, and Culp would reap the benefit of training with different types.

"Did I hear somewhere you boxed for Yale?" Culp asked.

"I believe I heard the same about you."

"Shall we go a couple?"

Bell took off his coat and shoulder holster.

Culp asked, "Do you have much occasion for artillery in the insurance business?"

"Violent swindlers are notable exceptions," Bell answered, hanging his coat and gun on a peg. He stripped off his tie and shirt, stepped up onto the ring, ducked through the tightly strung ropes, and crossed the canvas into the far corner. Culp removed his coat, tie, and shirt and climbed in after him. "Do you need gloves?"

"Not if you don't."

"Put 'em up."

Barry, who had been punching the heavy bag, and Lee, twirling the Indian clubs, watched with barely concealed smirks. Barry banged the bell with the little hammer that hung beside it. Culp and Bell advanced to the center of the ring, touched knuckles, backed up a step, and commenced sparring.

Bell saw immediately that Culp was very, very good, sporting a rare combination of bulk, speed, and agility. Though ten years Bell's senior, he was extremely fit. Bell was not surprised. At the yacht club, Culp had bounded about the decks of his New York "Thirty" like a born athlete. What was slightly surprising was how determined the Wall Street titan was to give him a black eye. In fact, he seemed bent on it, swinging repeatedly at his head, to the point where it made him reckless. Frustrated by Bell's footwork and impenetrable guard, he began unleashing punches that opened chinks in his own defense.

Lee rang the bell, ending the first round. They took a moment's rest and went another.

In the third round, Culp threw caution to the wind and charged, using his bulk in an attempt to startle Bell into dropping his ground and hurling at him a mighty right.

Had it connected, it would have knocked Bell through the ropes.

Culp tried the tactic again, and Bell decided to end it before things got further out of hand. He opened Culp with two swift feints of his left hand, then planted a light jab with the same left in Culp's eye.

Unpadded by gloves, Bell's knuckles took their toll, and Culp staggered backwards. His face darkened with anger, and he stepped through the ropes, holding his eye.

"Take over!"

The tall, lean Lee put down the Indian clubs and climbed into the ring.

Culp lumbered toward the door. "You'll excuse me, I have to dress for dinner. Enjoy the facility, *Detective* Bell."

"I wondered when you'd figure that out," said Bell.

"Long before I saw your gun."

"Thank you."

"For what?"

"Now I know for sure what you're up to."

Culp laughed. "You won't know your own name when these two get through with you. Go to it, boys."

He whipped Bell's holster off the peg and took it with him.

Lee put up his fists. "Shall we say fifteen rounds?"

"Or until you get tired," said Bell.

"When he gets tired," called Barry, "it's my turn."

At the end of five rounds, Lee said, "Something tells me you didn't learn that footwork at Yale."

"South Side," said Bell.

Lee was breathing hard. So was Bell. Barry was watching closely, learning his moves.

"South Side of what?"

"Chicago."

"Thought so."

Barry rang the bell.

Lee backed slowly out of the ring after ten rounds. "Finish him."

Barry swung through the ropes, feet light on the canvas floor, which was slick with Lee's blood. "O.K., Chicago. Time for lessons."

"You'll have to do a lot better than your pal."

"First lesson: A good big man will always beat a good little man." Barry glided at him, fast and hard.

Isaac Bell was tired. His arms were getting heavy. His feet felt like he had traded his boots for horseshoes. His ear was ringing where he had caught a right. His cheek was swollen. No serious damage to his torso yet. Barry moved in, feeling for how tired Bell was.

Bell locked eyes with the bigger man and threw some feints to send messages that he was still strong and dangerous. At the same time, he forced himself to override the desire to move fast, which would tire him even more. Barry kept coming, jabbing, feeling him out. Suddenly, he tricked Bell's hands up with his own feint and landed a left hand to the tall detective's chest. The slim, long-armed Lee had thrown stinging punches. Barry hit like a pile driver. Bell forced himself to stand tall and hide the damage.

"Lee!" he called. "Come back."

"What?"

"I'm getting bored. Why don't you both get in the ring; we'll make this quick."

"Your funeral."

Lee climbed in slowly, stiff, sore, and exhausted.

"Hey, Barry, give your pal a hand, he's moving like an old man."

Barry turned to help. Bell drove between them and somersaulted over the ropes.

"He's running for it," yelled Barry, and both scrambled after him.

Bell turned and faced them. "I'm not running, I'm evening the odds."

He had a twenty-pound Indian club in each hand.

"Put those down or you'll really get hurt."

"Teeth or knees, boys?"

He swung the clubs at their faces. They raised fast hands to block and grab them. Bell had already changed course. The clubs descended, angling down and sideways. The heavy bulging ends struck like blunt axes. Barry gasped. Lee groaned. Both dropped their guard to clutch their kneecaps. But they weren't down. Both were fighting men and both battered through their pain to lunge at Bell.

Bell had already swept the clubs up and back to a horizontal position at head height. Gathering his strength in one last effort, he carried them forward simultaneously.

Isaac Bell strolled into the Raven's Eyrie dining room dressed for dinner in a midnight blue tuxedo. John Butler Culp was seated at the head of the table, Daphne Culp at some distance to his right, and a place setting across from her to Culp's left. The Saint George, his horse, and dragon cellar had been moved close to curtain off the rest of the long, long mahogany table, creating a cozy space for their small party.

"Good evening, Mrs. Culp," he said to the beautiful Daphne. "I'm so sorry I'm late. Evening, J.B. Say, where'd you get the black eye?"

Culp glowered.

Mrs. Culp said, "Jenkins, don't just stand there. Bring Mr. Bell a plate . . . Mr. Bell, are you quite all right? Your face is bruised. Butler, did you do that to Mr. Bell?"

Bell leapt to defend his host. "Of course he didn't. He wouldn't, even if he could . . . Oh, I almost forgot, J.B. The gentlemen who work for you in the gymnasium asked would it be possible for the cook to send soup or broth to their room. Something they can eat through a straw."

"O.K.," said Culp. "You won this round."

"I have indeed," said Bell. But he knew, and so did Culp, that he had won a hollow victory. One look at the tycoon, angry as he was, showed a man still absolutely secure in his belief that regardless of Bell's suspicions, John Butler Culp was still insulated from the dirty work, still set so high above the law that he could plot the death of the President. The crime would proceed.

That thought chilled Bell to the marrow: wheels were in motion, gathering speed like a locomotive fresh from the roundhouse, oiled, coaled, and watered, switched to the main line, tracks cleared, and nothing could stop it, not even Culp himself . . . Not quite no one, he thought on reflection. The one aspect that even Culp couldn't control was that Bell knew. He couldn't prove it yet. But he knew and he could stop it or die trying.

"Detective Bell," Culp said, "you're smiling as if very pleased with yourself."

Bell put down his knife and fork and leveled his gaze at the statue of Saint George, his horse, and the dragon. "Please pass the salt."

Mrs. Culp laughed out loud. "Mr. Bell, you're the first guest who's had the nerve to say that to him — Butler, at least smile, for gosh sakes."

"I'm smiling," said Culp.

"It doesn't look that way."

"It will."

24

"You look like you've been pounding rivets with your face," Harry Warren greeted Isaac Bell at the office.

"Slipped in the bathtub . . . I read Finn's obituary on the train; hard to tell, between the lines, who he really was."

"A first-rate heeler. Old-school, hard-drinking, hail-fellow-well-met. But not one to cross. Strictly backroom, and connected direct to Boss Fryer. Except you won't find a witness in the world to testify to that."

"Probably our direct connection to Claypool. If he weren't dead."

"By the way, Claypool doesn't need our protection. The boys spotted a pack of off-duty police detectives camping at his office round the clock."

"That cinches it. Claypool knows he's next."

"With his pull, he'll have the best protection. O.K. I shook Branco's hand. Now what?"

"Right hand?"

"Of course."

"Notice anything about it?"

Warren thought a moment. "Yeah. He's got a couple of weird calluses on his fingers."

"You're sure?"

"Yeah, I'm sure. Inside his index and middle fingers. Nearly an inch long."

"That's what I noticed the other night in Little Italy. Sort of recalled them the first time we shook hands. What do you suppose they're from?"

Harry Warren shrugged. "You tell me."

Isaac Bell took out his pocket knife. "Watch my fingers."

"I'm watching."

He opened the blade. "These fingers, index and middle."

Harry's eyes gleamed. "From opening it again and again and again."

"Practice."

"Cute way around the weapon laws."

"Branco told me about them. Though he left out the practicing."

Warren stared. "Wait a minute. Wrong hand. That's your left hand pulling the blade. I shook his right hand."

"He's *left-handed.* I saw him catch an orange that went flying. Snapped it out of the air faster than a rattlesnake." Bell folded his knife closed, then opened it again. "Of course, no matter how fast you whip it out, you still only have a short blade."

"Not necessarily," said Harry Warren. "I've seen Sicilian pen knives with handles so thin, you could shove it into the slit the blade makes."

"A legal stiletto?"

"Until you stick it in somebody."

His friends at Tammany Hall took over Tony Pastor's vaudeville house for Brandon Finn's wake.

Isaac Bell brought Helen Mills with him. "Keep your eyes peeled for Brewster Claypool. Question is, is he next? Assuming Finn was at the top link of a chain down to 'Kid Kelly' Ghiottone, did Finn get his orders from Claypool?"

Bell's theory that doorkeepers and floor managers did not question the presence of a man with a good-looking young girl on his arm proved correct and they mingled in the crush of politicians, cops, contractors, priests, and swells, eavesdropping and asking questions carefully.

Two things were obvious: Brandon Finn

had been loved. And the rumors that he may have been murdered baffled his friends. Who, Bell heard asked again and again, would want to hurt him?

As the drinking went on, tongues loosened and — as at any good wake for a loved man — tales of Finn's exploits began to spawn heartfelt laughter that rippled and rolled around the theater. Helen, who had a gift for getting men to talk, reported twice to Bell that Finn — dubbed admiringly as the "last of the big spenders" — had been spending even more freely than usual the night before he died.

Bell himself heard the phrase "came into big money" several times.

He speculated that the money had come from outside the Tammany chain, which would pay him in patronage rather than cash. He told Helen that an outsider had tapped Finn to send a request down the line to "Kid Kelly."

"What," she asked, "did he want from Ghiottone?"

"Keep in mind he did not want it specifically from Ghiottone — the whole point was not to know any names — but wanted someone who could deliver like Ghiottone."

"A murderer."

"Only the guy who paid Finn knows for

sure. But since we know what was said at the Cherry Grove, we have to presume they want a murderer." Bell pointed. "There's Mike Coligney. I'll introduce you. He'll look out for you while I pay my respects to Mr. Finn's companion."

"I don't need looking out for."

"Mourners are eyeing you cheerfully."

Bell maneuvered close to Rose Bloom, Finn's paramour's stage name, and spoke loudly enough for her to hear over the roar of a thousand mourners. "Brandon Finn cuts a finer figure laid out in his coffin than the rest of us do standing up."

"Doesn't he?" she cried, whirling from a clutch of men vying for her ear to take in the speaker of the compliment.

Bell was not exaggerating. The dead man's checked suit was tailored like a glove. A diamond stickpin glittered in his necktie. Three perfectly aligned cigars thrust from his breast pocket like a battleship turret, and his derby was cocked triumphantly over one eye. Even the Mayor McClellan campaign button in his lapel proclaimed a winner.

Rose Bloom had red eyes from weeping and a big brassy voice. "He was always the handsomest devil."

"I am so sorry for your loss," Bell said, extending his hand and bowing over hers. It was not hard to imagine what a couple they had made, a "Diamond Jim" Brady and Lillian Russell pair having a ball, with New York at their feet.

"Thank you, sir."

"Bell. Isaac Bell. My deepest condolences."

"Oh, Mr. Bell. The things you don't plan for. Just gone. Suddenly gone."

"They say the Lord knows what's right, but it doesn't seem fair at the time, does it? Were you together at the end?"

"The very night before. We had the most splendid dinner. At Delmonico's. In a private booth." Her voice trailed off and her eyes teared up.

"A favorite of his, I presume?"

"Oh, yes, his absolute favorite — not that we went regular. Much too expensive to eat there regular."

"I'm sure he's smiling down on us, glad he took you to Delmonico's his last night. Certainly not a night to save money."

She brightened. "Brandon's luck held to the end. Didn't cost him a penny. A Wall Street swell poked his head in the booth and picked up the check."

Men were pressing from every direction

to catch her attention, and Bell knew he was running out of time. "Was this the swell?" He opened his hand to reveal Helen Mills' snapshot of Brewster Claypool and watched her face. She knew him.

Before he turned away, he looked directly into her eyes. "Again, Miss Bloom, my condolences. I grieve, too, that you lost your good man."

Outside on 14th Street, he sent Helen back to the office with orders for Harry Warren to dispatch operators to the Waldorf Hotel and the Cherry Grove. "Tell him I've gone to Claypool's office."

"It's after hours, Mr. Bell."

"Claypool knows he's next. He reckons he's safe at his office surrounded by cops."

"How does he know he's in trouble?"

"He's the last link alive between Culp on top and Ghiottone's choice of a Black Hand assassin."

To Isaac Bell's eye, Brewster Claypool's bodyguards looked like former detectives demoted when Commissioner Bingham overhauled the bureau. They were shabbily dressed, unkempt men, and had not been up to the job of protecting Claypool.

Bell found one in the elevator, one in the hall, and two inside Claypool's office, all unconscious or slumped on the floor, holding their heads. He smelled gun smoke. Pistol in hand, he crashed into Claypool's private office. There he found a detective, unconscious on the carpet with a Smith & Wesson in his hand, and the Black Hand gang leader, Charlie Salata, shot dead.

"Claypool!"

Bell looked to see if he was hiding in the closets and the washroom, but Claypool wasn't there. He went to the windows that faced the Singer Building. He opened one and looked down. The office was twelve stories above Cortlandt Street. There was no balcony Claypool could have escaped to, and nothing to climb up the side of the building to the roof.

Bare light bulbs sparkled across the street inside the cagework of the Singer Building. Work had ceased for the night, and the steel columns, which had risen several tiers since Bell had been here last, were deserted, the derricks still, the hoisting engines silent. He could hear trolleys, a noisy motor truck, and horseshoes clattering in the street. Movement caught his attention. Five stories above the sidewalk, he saw the silhouette of a man climbing open stairs in the Singer frame — a night watchman or fire watch.

Bell hurried back to the closets, recalling

that one had been mostly empty. He inspected it carefully this time and found a door concealed in the back, its knob hidden under a winter coat. The door opened on a stairwell.

"Claypool!"

Silence. No answer, no footsteps. It was possible that Claypool had escaped during the battle, his retreat covered, perhaps, by the wounded detective who had shot Salata.

Bell went back to the windows. The man climbing the Singer steelwork stopped and looked down. Immediately, he lunged toward a ladder and scrambled higher. Bell leaned against the glass to see. Two stories below, another man climbed after him. He was limping, slowed by his "winging" gait.

25

Brewster Claypool collapsed into a triangle of cold steel, formed by a column, a cross-beam, and a diagonal wind brace, where he could hide from the monster chasing him. It was hide and pray or simply fall to his death, he was so exhausted. Even a physical culture devotee like J. B. Culp would be hard-pressed to climb as many stairs and ladders as he had — five, before he lost count — and he could not recall the last time he had climbed stairs when an elevator was available.

He had heard the monster's footsteps when he wedged his trembling legs into the triangle, still climbing down there, some-where down in the dark. Now he'd lost track of him. Muffled by the wind? Or had he stopped? Was he standing stock-still, listen-ing for his prey? For Claypool was prey. He had no doubt of that, prey in a situation that all the pull on earth could not get him out of. He tried to drag air silently into his storming lungs.

Gradually he caught his breath, gradually he began to hope that the killer had given up. Could he somehow just stay inside this little steel crook in the corner of the sky-scraper until dawn filled it with workmen? Would he freeze to death? The wind had begun to gust and it was fierce up here. No wonder the engineers riddled the structure with wind braces.

"Mista Claypool."

The voice was inches from his ear, and he was so shocked and frightened that he shouted, "Who are you? What do you want from me?"

"Who told you to tell Finn to hire an as-sassin?"

"I don't know what you're talking about."

"Then why did you barricade yourself with bodyguards when Finn died?"

In the shrewd, conniving worlds that Brewster Claypool had dominated his entire career, there was no one smarter than a "railroad lawyer" — except a Wall Street lawyer. But when he heard that question in the dark, Brewster Claypool felt every brainstorm he had ever had drain from his head; every parry, every counterstroke, every rejoinder.

"Why?"

Then, all the gods be praised, his brain began to churn.

"Why bodyguards?" he replied smoothly, speaking into the dark wind as if they had settled into club chairs at the Union League. "Because I watched as men were killed, one after another, each at a higher station. Were these the crimes of a madman? Or a man with a brilliant scheme? But when Brandon Finn died, I knew that the 'why' of it didn't matter. What mattered was that the killing would continue, and I had better take precautions — *Ahhh!*"

A blade bit into his cheek and cut a line to his lip.

Isaac Bell felt warm, sticky liquid dripping on the ladder as he climbed to the seventh tier of the Singer Building cage and smelled the piercing metallic scent of blood. He looked up. Ten feet above his head, he saw the shadows of two men grappling, one tall and broad, the other a wisp of a spider. Claypool didn't have a chance.

"Branco!" Bell shouted as he jumped for the next ladder.

Branco went rigid with surprise at hearing his name and Claypool squirmed free, slipped through the scaffolds laid across the beams, and fell.

Bell caught his hand as Claypool plunged and tried to swing him onto solid footing.

The lawyer's hand was slick with blood. It slipped from Bell's grasp. But Bell had arrested his fall and Claypool landed at his feet, only to slide between boards again and fall to the next floor.

Bell heard Branco scrambling overhead, racing across his tier to find a way down. It was too dark for Bell to see him. Claypool was directly under him at the edge of a pool of light cast by a dim bulb. He went down the ladder to help.

Claypool was sprawled on his back. The man was dying. His face had been slashed repeatedly, and the fall had been brutal, but what would surely kill him was the knife in his chest. His hands moved feebly, pawing at the handle.

Bell restrained them. "Don't touch it. I'll get you to the hospital."

Claypool made a noise in his throat that sounded like laughter. "Only if their doctors have pull with God." He focused vaguely on Bell's face. "Thank you for trying to save me."

"Was it Antonio Branco, the grocer?"

"Big aqueduct contractor. Must be Black Hand."

"Did you tell Branco that Culp sent you to Brandon Finn?"

"Culp is my friend," gasped Claypool, and Isaac Bell watched him die with that typically enigmatic answer on his lips. *Culp is my friend* told no one whether Branco's savage interrogation had forced him to reveal that J. B. Culp was the boss he had been tracking.

Bell checked his pulse and pressed his ear to his chest, but the fixer was dead. He reached for the knife protruding from the body, pulled it free, took it under the nearest light bulb. It was a folding pocket knife with a legal-length blade. The handle was the narrow sort that Detective Warren had described, barely wider than the blade itself, and tapered even thinner at the hinge that transformed it, when open, into a stiletto.

Bell saw no maker's mark. It had been fabricated by a specialty cutler.

He slung Claypool's featherlight frame over his shoulder and carried him down six stories to the sidewalk and up Broadway to Cortlandt Street and into his building. There were no cops yet or police detectives. Back on the street, Bell met up with Warren, Kisley, and Fulton, who had caught up in a REO town car the agency had on promotional loan from the manufacturer.

"We're going to Prince Street," Bell told them. "Move over, I'll drive!"

"Branco?"

"He'll need escape money. I saw him. Claypool fingered him. And I have his knife."

Isaac Bell drove as fast as he could, straight up Broadway, toward Prince Street. Traffic was heavy even at this late hour, but not at the standstill of business hours. The REO's motor was fairly powerful and its horn was very loud. His Black Hand Squad, crowded in beside Bell and in the backseat, checked over their guns, and traded info about the case.

Bell's Black Hand and President Assassin cases had converged like a pair of ocean liners on a collision course. The saloon keeper Ghiottone had recruited a Black Hand man to kill President Roosevelt, and Antonio Branco had seized the opportunity to send the ultimate Black Hand letter.

"The scheme backfired when Ghiottone told Branco."

"Instead of killing the President, Branco killed his way back up the recruiting chain to blackmail the man on the top."

"Can you imagine what Culp would pay?"

"Branco could imagine," Mack Fulton

said to general laughter. Bell wondered, though. Would it be enough for Branco to risk his entire setup or did he have his eye on something more?

Ghiottone's saloon had been taken over by the dead man's cousins and was doing a roaring business again. Across the street, Branco's Grocery was dark and shuttered.

"Hang on," shouted Bell.

He wrenched the steering wheel. The REO jumped the curb. He drove onto the sidewalk and blasted through Antonio Branco's front door ten feet into the store. The Van Dorns leaped out, guns drawn. They fanned out into the maze of stock shelves, Bell in the lead.

"Find lights . . . Wait! I smell gas."

"Maybe Branco stuck his head in an oven."

"Stove in here is fine," Mack Fulton called. "No leak."

"Don't turn on the light. Get out. Get out now!"

The odor was suddenly so strong, it smelled as if a torrent of gas was gushing into the store straight from a city main. Bell felt light-headed. "Get out, boys! Get out before it blows."

The Van Dorn Black Hand Squad bolted

for the door they had smashed.

"Leave the auto."

Bell was counting heads, vaguely aware that he was having trouble keeping track, when he heard Harry Warren shout. He could barely make out what he was saying. Warren sounded blocks away.

"Come on, Isaac! We're all out."

Bell turned slowly to the door.

He saw a flash. The REO reared in the air like a spooked horse. Cans flew from the walls. Jars shattered and barrels split open, but the tall detective had the strangest impression of total silence. It was like watching a moving picture of a volcano.

Then the floor collapsed under his feet and the ceiling tumbled down on his head.

BOOK III
STORM KING

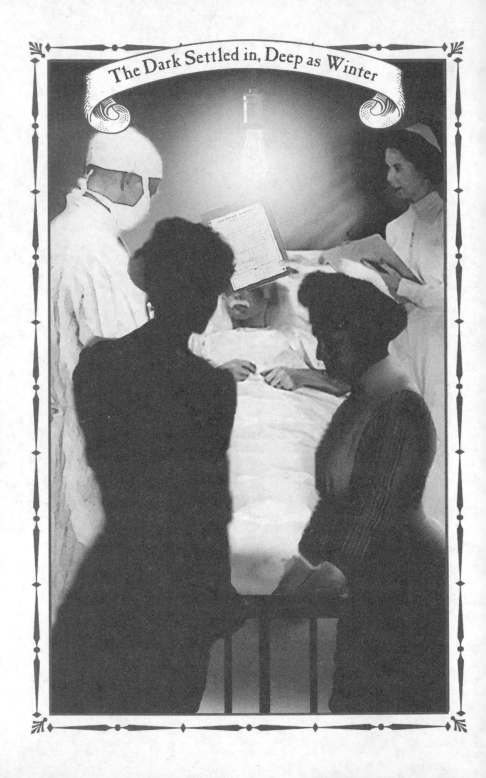

The Dark Settled in, Deep as Winter

26

The streets were crawling with cops and Van Dorns.

Antonio Branco stepped from a tenement doorway, hurried twenty feet to Banco La-Cava, and tapped his signet ring on the glass. David LaCava looked up from the gold he was stacking in his show window. Branco watched his expression and got ready to run. LaCava saw Branco. He gaped, shocked. Then relief spread across his face and he ran to unlock the door.

"You're alive!"

Branco pushed through and closed it behind him.

"They said you were missing in the explosion."

Branco made a joke to lull the banker. "Almost as bad. I was upstate in the Catskills." Then he turned fittingly grave. "I came back on the night boat. I only heard of the explosion this morning when we docked."

"How bad is it?"

"I couldn't see. The cops and firemen and sewer and building departments are squabbling over who commands the recovery. Fortunately, none of my people were in my building. But they say some poor souls are trapped in the tenements."

"There's a rumor Isaac Bell was in the building."

"I heard that, too — God knows what he was doing there. Here! Take these." He thrust a wad of paper into LaCava's hands.

"What is this?"

"Receipts and bills of lading for a pier house full of wine I stored on West 21st Street. You can see my situation. All my store stock is lost. I need to borrow cash to fill orders for the aqueduct."

"Is Prince Street insured?"

"It will take time to get the money and I need to buy new stock now. Total these up; you'll see the wine's worth fifty thousand. Can you advance me thirty?"

"I wish I could, my friend. I don't have that much on hand. My depositors are only trickling back."

"Whatever you can lend me right now . . . Immediately."

■ ■ ■ ■

Ten minutes after the grocer left with a satchel of cash, grim-faced detectives from the Van Dorn Black Hand Squad burst into the bank.

"Have you seen Antonio Branco?"

David LaCava said, "You just missed him. May I ask, is there any word on Mr. Bell?"

"No. Where did Branco go?"

"To buy stock. He has orders he must fill for the aqueduct."

Harry Warren and Eddie Edwards stared at the banker.

"Aqueduct?" Warren echoed.

"What are you talking about, Mr. LaCava? Branco's not filling orders; he's on the run."

"What do you mean?" asked LaCava.

"The thieving murderer blew up his own store," said Warren.

"We hoped he was buried in it," growled Eddie Edwards. "But someone saw him on the street headed this way."

LaCava turned paper white as the blood drained from his face. *"Basta!"*

Harry Warren gripped the banker's shoulder. "What's wrong?"

"I didn't know. Everybody said it was an accident."

283

" 'Everybody' was wrong. He blew it up, along with three buildings next door and half the graveyard."

"I just lent him twenty thousand dollars . . . But I have these! Don't you see? Collateral. You are mistaken. He is Antonio Branco. He has the Catskill Aqueduct contract."

"Honest as the Lottery?"

"But these bills of lading —"

The Van Dorn snatched them out of his hand.

Clad like a rich merchant, in a blue topcoat, a red scarf, and a derby hat, Antonio Branco tallied wine barrels on a Hudson River freight pier at 22nd Street. Stevedores were rolling them up the gangway onto a coaster about to sail for Philadelphia. The ship's captain stood beside Branco and they counted the barrels together. When the last were stowed in the hold, the captain gave Branco bills of lading attesting that the fifty-thousand-dollar cargo was aboard his ship.

Branco hurried two blocks to a wine broker who had already agreed to buy the bills of lading at a discount. Then he took the ferry across the river to Jersey City and walked to a laundry that served the working class neighborhood. The proprietor, a tiny old Chinaman with a misshapen face and a blinded eye, sorted through paper-wrapped packages of clothes never picked up and sold him a pair of rugged trousers, a short coat, and a warm watch cap that wouldn't blow off in the wind.

A thoroughly disgusted Harry Warren stared long and hard at the empty slip from where a coaster had departed an hour earlier. Eddie Edwards stomped out of the pier house, looking equally fed up.

"First the ice-blooded scum takes LaCava for twenty grand cash. Then he sashays across town, big as life, and leaves the pier here with fifty grand in bills of lading, according to the clerk in the pier house, for the *same* wine that he can turn to another quick thirty thousand cash — bills of lading being damned-near legal tender."

"On the lam with enough money to charter a private train."

"Or an ocean liner."

The detectives exchanged another black look, knowing that neither had exaggerated the value of Branco's haul. Fifty thousand dollars would buy a country estate, with servants, gardeners, gamekeepers, and a chauffeur to drive the lucky owner home from the railroad station.

"Now what?"

"Jersey City."

"What's there?"

"Fellow in there sent a boy after him. One of the bills had fallen off the pile. The kid spotted him on the ferry too late. It was pulling out of the slip."

Branco changed clothes in the Jersey Central Communipaw Terminal men's room and left those he had been wearing by a church, where some tramp would run off with them soon enough. He bought a surplus Spanish-American War rucksack to carry his cash and field glasses and ditched his fancy leather satchel. He gorged on a huge meal in a cheap lunchroom and rented a room in a ten-cent lodging house. He studied freight and passenger train schedules. Finally closing his eyes for the first time since he had killed Brewster Claypool, he slept soundly until dark. He ate again — forcing himself to cram his belly while he could — then followed his ears toward the clamor of steam pistons, switch engine bells, and locomotive whistles rising from the New Jersey Central train yards.

It was a cold, dark night, with a cutting wind under an overcast sky. Row upon row of parked trains sprawled under a swirling scrim of smoke and steam. Countless sidings merged from the freight car float piers and passenger terminal that rimmed the Hudson River into four separate sets of main lines leaving the city.

Branco tried to choose his train from a street that overlooked one of the lines. But there were hundreds of lines, and thousands of freight cars — an ocean of lanterns, sidelights, and headlamps — screened by electric and telegraph wires and poles. He noticed a disused switching tower in the middle of the dimly lit chaos that would give him a better perspective.

An empty lot behind a fence sloped down to the tracks. Skirting yard lights, dodging headlamps, watching for rail bulls, he climbed between cars at their couplings and worked his way across a score of sidings to the dark tower. A fixed ladder led to its roof, where he swept the yard with his field glasses.

Van Dorns were watching.

He spotted one slipping money to the regular yard bulls — recruiting man hunters. The detective gave himself away with an appearance that was a mighty cut above the regular rail cops and an expression of cold rage, mourning his precious Isaac Bell.

Branco was not surprised. Any detective

worth his salt carried the same railroad maps in his mind as he did and knew that for a man running to distant jurisdictions, Jersey City was the place to start. Scores of rail lines fanned south and west to Philadelphia, Baltimore, Pittsburgh, Chicago, St. Louis, San Francisco — each city home to a teeming Italian settlement.

The Van Dorns also knew that he couldn't risk riding as a paying passenger scrutinized by ticket clerks, platform guards, porters, and conductors. Trapped aboard a speeding flyer, no matter how fast, he could never beat a telegraph bulletin to the next station. So they would search all the places he would try to steal a ride: on the reinforcing rods underneath a car; or on top, clinging to a roof; or sheltered from the cold inside an unlocked boxcar; or riding "blind" platforms in front of baggage cars.

From the many trains that the switch engines were making up, he picked out a fast freight headed by a powerful camelback 2-6-0 locomotive. It consisted of flatcars carrying mining machines, empty coal hoppers, and reefers of fresh beef from the Jersey City slaughterhouses. Branco judged by the number of cars, some thirty that the busy switch engines had already shunted to it, that it would soon be highballing for

Pennsylvania's anthracite coalfields — first stop, Bethlehem Junction.

He edged toward the ladder, only to be distracted by a passenger train that emerged from the Communipaw Terminal and snaked slowly through the yards, its windows a warm russet glow in the bitter cold. The hour and the 4-4-2 locomotive towing twin baggage cars, four Pullmans, and a club car, said it was probably the crack Harrisburg flyer, "Queen of the Valley." Branco imagined the passengers settling into deep armchairs with cocktails in hand and every expectation of sleeping in their own beds by midnight. Motion of a different kind jolted him out of his reverie.

A man on foot was striding the crossties of a siding that curved beside the tower.

Switch yard brakeman? Rail cop? Hobo? Ignoring the locomotives steaming around him, he was coming Branco's way as purposefully as a lion stalking prey through a herd of elephants. No hobo walked like that; no brakeman, either. He had to be a rail cop or, worse, an alert Van Dorn who had spotted the empty switch tower for a fugitive's spy house.

A switch engine headlamp swept the siding. The beam blazed on a shock of white hair, and Antonio Branco recognized Isaac

Bell's Black Hand Squad detective Eddie Edwards, his face aflame with vengeance. Branco rolled off the roof, slid down the ladder, and sprinted after the Queen of the Valley.

The flyer was picking up speed even as it lumbered through countless switches that were shunting it from rail to rail out of the yard and toward the main line. He heard the detective give chase, boots ringing, running after him full tilt like a man who knew as well as Branco the treacherous footing of tracks, crossties, gravel, and ankle-snatching gaps beside switch rails.

Running as hard as he could, Branco pulled ahead of the lead baggage car, jumped for a handrail, and hauled himself onto the platform between the front of the car and the locomotive's tender. A brakeman was hiding there in the dark, his lantern unlit, lying in wait for hobos. He swung the lantern, threatening to brain Branco with it, and shouted, "Get off!"

When caught, a hobo was expected to jump off as ordered: Go try to steal a ride on some other brakeman's train. To resist was to bring down the wrath of the entire crew. But Branco was trapped. The Van Dorn detective was right behind him and catching up fast.

"Get off!"

The brakeman swung his lantern. Branco grabbed it, pulled hard, and used the man's momentum to yank him across the platform and off the blind.

The brakeman flew out of the dark, straight at Eddie Edwards in a blur of pinwheeling limbs. Edwards was not surprised. Brakemen often rode hobo patrol on baggage car platforms, rousting tramps, until their train was out of the yard, and Antonio Branco had proven repeatedly he was no ordinary tramp.

The detective dodged a boot and ducked under a heavy lantern that passed so close to his skull that it knocked his hat off. The train was accelerating, the engineer unaware of the drama behind him. Edwards put on a desperate burst of speed. He pounded alongside the blind. At his feet, a switch appeared out of nowhere. He cleared the yawning slot by a miracle and swung onto the blind, one hand on a grip, the other clenched in a fist for Branco.

The platform was empty.

He looked up. Branco had climbed onto the roof.

Grabbing ironwork, Edwards jumped onto a hand-brake wheel, muscled his way up between the front of the baggage car and the tender, and hauled himself onto the sloping end of the roof.

The roof was empty.

He whirled his head, thinking Branco was on the tender about to smash him with a lump of coal. But the tender was empty, too. He looked down at the empty blind. Where had the gangster gone? Only one place. Off the train. He must have jumped out the other side of the blind, back into a yard full of rail cops and angry detectives.

Antonio Branco climbed a slope out of the Jersey Central rail yards into a neighborhood condemned by the ever-expanding railroad and raced across town through dark streets of boarded-up tenements. Of the four lines he had seen leaving the city, there was one to the north of the Queen of the Valley's Harrisburg line. It was the Scranton line — the line he had wanted all along but did not want the Van Dorns to know he was riding. When he reached it — down an embankment and over a fence — he looked for the train he had chosen earlier.

Sorriso di Dio! Fortune smiled. There — the distinctive humped silhouette of the camelback center-cab 2-6-0 locomotive. The fast freight was made up and rolling, shunting out of the yard. He ran ahead, along the main line. The beam of its headlight threw shadows from his heels. He dove into the shallow trench beside the tracks and hid. The engine thundered past, straining to accelerate, in clouds of smoke and steam.

Branco sprang into the cloud and galloped beside the moving train. The reefer cars would be full, doors locked. Empty coal hoppers were deadly in the cold wind. Looking over his shoulder, he spied a flatcar on which a steam shovel was chained like a captive. He slowed to let the car overtake him and jumped aboard.

Nurses lingered.

"Handsome devil."

"What do you suppose he's thinking?"

"What makes you think he's thinking at all . . . ?"

Physicians argued.

"Coma —"

"I say stupor."

"Coma: laceration of the brain; capillary hemorrhage; lesion."

"The brain is a tissue. It has a capacity for healing."

"Lividity of the tongue and lips. Embarrassed respiration."

"Swallowing — impossible in coma . . . Toxemia?"

"Lesion."

A younger doctor weighed in, short on experience, long on science. "The patient's head is not turned. His eyes are not deflected to either side. If there was a lesion, the patient would look toward it. There is no lesion."

"Then what?"

"Asphyxia."

The moon hovered inside a silver halo. Full and perfectly round.

It was beautiful and distant, and then it slipped away.

The dark came back. It settled in heavily again, deep as winter.

27

Antonio Branco's fast freight to eastern Pennsylvania was sidelined to let the Lackawanna Railroad's "Phoebe Snow" passenger sleeper overtake. He jumped off the flatcar and climbed under it. Before the Phoebe Snow highballed past, he had found a safer and slightly warmer place on the rods.

He stuck with the train until the Bethlehem Junction yards, where he dodged a yard bull and climbed under a freight to Wilkes-Barre. At Wilkes-Barre, he caught a train to Scranton, riding on the roof, when he saw brakemen checking the rods. He clung to a ventilator and kept a close eye on the tracks ahead of the locomotive so he wouldn't be lurched off by a sharp curve, jumped when it slowed approaching the yards, found a barn a mile from the tracks, and slept in the hayloft. After dark, he climbed under a Delaware & Hudson coal train that turned slowly northeastward through Carbondale to Cadosia, where the coal hoppers were switched to the southeastwardly bearing New York, Ontario & Western Railway. He rode them at a glacial pace, night and day and night again, through Summitville, Middletown, and Maybrook.

After Meadowbrook, he smelled tidewater.

The first gray light of dawn revealed that the tracks squeezed between steep hills and the Hudson River, deep in mist. Estates appeared on the hillsides, Gothic, Greek Revival, and old American-style mansions set far apart on lawns as big as farms. An enormous summer tourist hotel loomed up unexpectedly, then a three-story icehouse with a wharf to barge the ice harvest to New York, then white boardinghouses, and, quite suddenly, redbrick factories.

He heard the locomotive back off and felt the heavy cars butt couplers. When he glimpsed a huge jetty surrounded by steamers, he flexed his stiff knee to get ready to run. The train slowed for its final stop, the Cornwall Landing coal docks at the foot of Storm King Mountain.

Filthy, hungry, and frozen to the bone, Antonio Branco had traveled five hundred miles in a circle that landed him — without a trace of where he had come from — just fifty miles north of where he had ditched the Van Dorns in Jersey City. No one knew he was there. No one knew where he came from — just another Italian pick and shovel man begging to work on the Catskill Aqueduct for a dollar seventy-five cents a day.

As the coal train entered the yards, the morning sun cleared a hill on the far side of the river and cast yellow light on a huge estate house that reminded Branco of Greek ruins in Sicily. He recognized John Butler Culp's famous Raven's Eyrie. He had seen it often from the Hudson River steamboats — long before he learned that Culp was his man.

But what riveted his attention was the sight of Culp's private train. It was waiting in the Cornwall Landing rail yards — splendid red coaches drawn by an ink-black Atlantic 4-4-2.

The locomotive had steam up.

Culp could leave at a moment's notice.

Branco had no time to lose.

He jumped from the rods before the train stopped rolling and ran to the aqueduct siphon shaft excavation, which he pinpointed by the sight of Negro men driving mule wagons across raw ground, and a vast cluster of locomotives, wagons, and steam shovels, emblazoned with the names of Irish contractors.

His immigrant laborer disguise worked perfectly. Moments after he was issued a pay number on a brass token, he was approached by a "key" — a Black Hand extortionist who pretended to be a terrified fellow laborer.

"Did you hear?" the key whispered. "The Black Hand says each man has to give a dollar on payday. They kill us if we don't pay up."

"Take me to your boss."

"What boss?"

Branco fixed him with a cold stare. "When your boss learns that you didn't take me to him, he will kill you."

Vito Rizzo, the Black Hand gangster dealt a broken nose and a ragged ear by the Van Dorns, had been told at "confession" to establish a labor extortion racket at Cornwall Landing and await orders. He operated out of a board-on-barrels saloon down the road from the siphon shaft.

When his gorillas marched a soot-blackened pick and shovel man into his back room, he addressed the laborer with utter contempt, failing to recognize a richly clad Little Italy *prominente* he had seen occasionally from a distance.

Antonio Branco handed him a brass token. It looked exactly like the payment number identification check he had been issued at the gate.

"Turn it over."

A simple asterisk had been punched into the metal.

Rizzo jumped to his feet. "Get out of here," he shouted at his gorillas. "All of ya." He slammed the door behind them. Then he tugged off his hat and stared at his boots, making a point of not looking at Branco's face — demonstrating that he could never identify this man who held over him the power of life and death.

He spoke humbly, and he made no effort to hide his fear.

"May I please help you, *Dominatore*?"

"I need a place to clean up and eat while you get me fresh clothes, a length of bell cord, a blasting cap, and a stick of dynamite."

The moon hovered inside a silver halo.

Full and perfectly round.

The dark returned.

The doctors had never met anyone like the extraordinarily beautiful young woman,

299

dressed in traveling tweeds and wearied by days on the train. She fixed them with a sharp, clear-eyed gaze that brooked no equivocation and no platitudes. Each found himself struggling to answer as straightforwardly as their professors had demanded at medical school.

"We are reasonably certain he suffered no lacerations of the brain. There are no indications of even slight capillary hemorrhage."

"Nor lesions in either hemisphere."

"The only marks on his head were old scars, long healed. There are no wounds to his torso or his limbs. It was quite miraculous — almost as if a giant hand had closed around him when the building caved in."

She said, "But still he sleeps."

"It is possible this confirms a diagnosis that his stupor, or coma, resulted from asphyxia caused by inhalation of poisonous gas."

"When will he awaken?"

"We don't know."

"*Will* he awaken?"

"Well . . . there is hope in that he was a strong man."

She rounded on them, fiercely. "He *is* a strong man."

28

In the immortal words of Brewster Claypool: *Money is made when the smart money acts on their smart ideas — bless their smart little hearts.*

Dead only five days, and already Culp missed him.

The conductor called, "Engineer's ready when you are, sir."

"One more," said Culp.

His man from eastern Pennsylvania was pacing the private train platform. Culp lowered his window. "Send in that bloody lawyer."

In came the bloody lawyer. He was one of a bunch that had reported to Claypool — sparing Culp the tedium — and he was everything that Culp's old "partner in crime" had not been: colorless, humorless, and duller than dishwater.

"The Department of Justice is widening

the investigation of the Ramapo Water Company."

Culp's face darkened. The Ramapo Grab — a dodge he and Claypool had cooked up to take over New York's water supply — would have milked the city of $5,000,000 a year every year for forty years.

"I thought you had spent a lot of my money encouraging them not to investigate."

"It would appear that the Progressives want to make an example."

"Why not make an example of J. P. Morgan? He stuck his big nose in the ship canal limelight. Why don't they shine it on him?"

The Washington lawyer answered blandly. "I'm afraid, sir, we must accept that it is what it is."

Lawyers loved that line of talk. "It is what it is" shifted the blame for their incompetence to the client.

"Roosevelt is behind this."

"It *is* President Roosevelt's Justice Department. In fact, sir, I would be remiss not to warn you that the impulse to prosecute appears to come straight from the White House."

"But why me, dammit? Why not Morgan's canal?"

Brewster Claypool would have mimicked

Roosevelt fulminating in a high-pitched falsetto: "Ramapo would levy a two-hundred-million-dollar rich-man tax against the parched citizens of the nation's greatest city."

Bloody, bloody hell!

"Did you say something, sir?"

This was much worse than Culp had feared. "I'm leaving Scranton," he said.

"Shall I ride back to New York with you, Mr. Culp? I can catch a Washington express from there."

Culp's conductor rousted the lawyer off his train.

His engineer blew the ahead signal.

His locomotive steamed from the private platform, maneuvered out of the yards onto a cleared track, and began to labor up the steep grade into the Pocono Mountains. Culp got to work, dictating mental notes into a graphophone. Suddenly, the front vestibule door flew open, admitting the full thunder of the straining locomotive. He looked up. As swarthy a complexioned Italian as ever had sneaked past immigration officials pushed into his car.

29

"Where the devil did you come from?"

Culp did not wait for the intruder to answer but instead grabbed his pistol from his desk drawer and leveled it at the swarthy man's head. The only reason not to put a bullet through it was that he might be a stupid track worker who had been somehow swept along when the train left Scranton, in which case sorting it out with the local authorities would end any hope of getting to the Cherry Grove in time for a late supper. But he wasn't a track worker; he was wearing a rucksack like a hobo.

"Do you understand English?" he roared. "Who the hell are you?"

The man did speak English, in a rolling manner that reminded Culp of Claypool at his most convoluted.

"I am a stranger with an irresistible offer to become well known to you."

"That'll be the day. Raise your hands."

The man raised his hands. Culp saw that he was holding a length of cord that stretched behind him and out the vestibule door. "What's that string?"

"The trigger."

"What? Trigger? What trigger?"

"To trigger the detonator."

"Deton—"

"I should lower my hand," the intruder interrupted. "I'm stretching the slack. If the train lurches, I might tug it by mistake. If that were to happen, a stick of dynamite would blow up the coupler that holds your private car to your private locomotive."

"Are you a lunatic? We'll roll back down into Scranton and both die."

"Chissà," said the man.

"Kiss-a? What the blazes is kiss-a dago for?"

"Chissà means 'who knows' if I live or die? Or should I say *we.*"

Culp cocked the .45. "You're dead anyhow, no 'kiss-a' about it."

"If you shoot me, you will die, too."

"No greasy immigrant is dictating to me."

Antonio Branco looked calmly down the gun barrel. "I am impressed, Mr. Culp. I was told that you are more interesting than a coddled child of the rich. Strong as stone."

"Who told you that?"

305

"Brewster Claypool."

"*What?* When?"

"When he died."

Culp turned red with rage. He stood up and extended the pistol with a hand that shook convulsively. "You're the one who killed Claypool."

"No, I did not kill him. I tried to save him."

"What are you talking about?"

"A fool I brought to help me acted like a fool."

"You were there. You killed him."

"No, I wanted him alive as much as you. I *needed* Claypool. He would be my go-between. Now I have no choice but to entreat you face-to-face. I've lost everything. My business ruined. My reputation. The Van Dorns are after me. And now, without Claypool to represent me, I stand alone with your pistol in my face."

"You killed Claypool."

"No, I did not kill him," Branco repeated. "He was my only hope."

"I don't understand . . . Lower your hands!"

Branco lowered his hands but stepped forward so the cord stayed taut. "Don't you know who I am?"

"I don't care who you are."

"The gas explosion."

"What gas explosion?"

"On Prince Street. It destroyed tenements. You must have read it in the paper."

"Why would I read about explosions in Italian colony tenements?"

"To know what happened to Isaac Bell."

The man had caught him flat-footed.

J. B. Culp could not hide his surprise. "Bell? Is that what put Bell in the hospital? What is Bell's condition?"

"Tu sogni accarezzévole."

"What's that dago for?"

"Sweet dreams."

Culp laughed. "O.K. So you lost everything. What do you want from me? Money?"

"I have plenty of money." Still holding the string, he shrugged the rucksack off his shoulder and lobbed it onto Culp's desk. "Look inside."

Culp unbuckled the flap. The canvas bulged with banded stacks of fifty- and hundred-dollar notes. "Looks like you robbed a bank."

"I lost only my 'public' business. I have my private business."

"What's your private business?"

"Mano Nero."

"Black Hand? . . . In other words, you used to hide your gangster business behind

307

a legitimate business and now you are nothing but a gangster."

"I am much more than a gangster."

"How do you reckon that?"

"I am a gangster with a friend in high places."

"Not me, sport." Culp tossed the rucksack at the man's feet. "Get off my train."

"A friend so high that he is higher than the President."

Culp had been enjoying crossing swords with the intruder, despite the very real threat of a dynamited coupler. But the conversation had taken a vicious twist. The man was acting as if he had him over a worse barrel than crashing down the mountain at eighty miles per hour.

"Where," he asked, "did you get that idea?"

"Claypool offered me the job."

"I don't know what you are talking about. What job?"

"Killing Roosevelt."

"Are you crazy? Claypool would never say such a thing."

"He had no choice," the gangster answered coldly.

30

The moon hovered inside a silver halo. Full and perfectly round.

It was beautiful and distant.

Cold rain sprinkled his lips, then a silken brush of warmth.

Suddenly, the sun filled the sky. It had a halo like the moon, but its halo was golden.

Isaac Bell opened his eyes. The sun was smiling inches from his face. His heart swelled, and he whispered, "Hello, Marion, weren't you in San Francisco?"

Marion Morgan blinked tears away. "I cannot believe you are actually smiling."

"I always smile at beautiful women."

Bell looked around, gradually aware that he was in a bed that smelled of strong soap. A kaleidoscope was whirling in slow motion. Through it, he saw grave doctors, in modern white coats, and a nurse, glowering at Marion, the only non-medico in the room. He said, "Something tells me we won't be enjoying the night in a hotel."

"Probably not tonight."

"We'll see about that." Bell moved his hands and feet, and stretched his arms and legs, and turned his head to face the doctors. "As far as I can feel, my brain is in working order, and I still have the same number of limbs I was originally issued. Can you tell me why I'm in your hospital?"

"This is the first you've sat up and spoken in eight days."

Bell felt the room shift a little bit, as if the bed was set on a creaky turntable. "I'd been feeling the need for a rest. Looks like I got it."

"Do you remember anything that happened before you lost consciousness? Any detail, no matter how small? Any —"

"The floor sank under me and the roof caved in."

"Do you remember why?"

"Are the boys O.K.?"

"Your squad dug you out."

Bell looked at Marion. She nodded. "They're all O.K."

The doctor said, "Do you remember why it happened?"

"Because Antonio Branco pulled another fast one — about the fastest fast one I've ever run into." He turned to Marion. "Did

310

the boys catch him?"

"He got away from Detective Edwards last week in the Jersey City yards."

"A week? He could steal rides anywhere in the country in a week."

"Or charter a special," said Marion. "Detective Edwards told me Branco swindled a banker and a wine broker out of fifty thousand before he left."

The bed shifted again. Bell had a feeling it would do this for a while, in fits and starts. The doctors were staring at him like a monkey in a bell jar.

"Events," Bell told them, "are coming back in a rush. I want you to move me to a quiet, semi-dark room where I can talk them out with my fiancée, Miss Morgan."

Marion leaned closer and whispered in his ear. "Are you really all right?"

Bell whispered back, "See if you can get them to send up a cold bird and a bottle of bubbly . . . *Wait!*"

"What is it, Isaac?"

"I just realized . . . *Marion, get me out of here!* Wire Joe Van Dorn. I don't care if he has to spring me at gunpoint . . . I just realized, Branco wouldn't have shoved a knife in Claypool's chest if Claypool hadn't already admitted his boss was Culp."

■ ■ ■ ■

Snow pelted the glass at Raven's Eyrie, where Antonio Branco luxuriated under a fur counterpane in a princely guest room attached to the gymnasium. It was far from the main house. Culp's wife had moved to their New York mansion for the winter season. The servants who had brought him supper the night they returned from Scranton, and breakfast the morning after, were a pair of bruised and battered prizefighters. Culp said they could be trusted.

"Mr. Culp is waiting for you in the trophy room," one of them told him after breakfast.

A nailhead-studded, Gothic-arched, medieval fortress door guarded the trophy room, which was as big as a barn — two stories high and windowless — and lighted by electric chandeliers. Mounted heads of elk, moose, and bison loomed from the walls. Life-size elephant, rhino, Cape buffalo, and a nine-foot grizzly bear crowded the floor. Tiger skins lay as carpet. Doors and alcoves were framed with ivory tusks.

J. B. Culp stood at a giant rosewood desk that was flanked by suits of medieval armor. Mounted on the wall behind him were hunting rifles and sidearms. He indicated a large, comfortable-looking leather armchair that faced his desk. Antonio Branco stayed on his feet.

"Sleep well?"

"I thank you for your hospitality."

"You didn't give me any choice."

"A dead president can't prosecute you."

"So you said on my train."

Branco said, "And the private aqueduct will be yours."

"The pot sweetener," Culp said sarcastically. But he was, in fact, deeply intrigued. The blackmailing Italian had a doozy of a scheme to take control of the Catskill Aqueduct — dams, reservoirs, tunnels, and all — that just might work. A second shot at the Ramapo Grab.

"You've had the night to think about your opportunity," said Branco. "What is your answer?"

"The same," Culp said coldly. "No one dictates terms to me."

"You can continue your wonderful life," said Branco. "And I can make it even more wonderful for you. The aqueduct will be only the beginning. I will help you in all your businesses."

Culp said, "You can count on the fingers of one hand the men in this country richer than I am, and none are as young. I don't

313

need your help."

Branco said, "I will eliminate labor problems. I will eliminate your rivals. I will eliminate your enemies. They will disappear as if you wave a fairy's wand. A coal strike in Colorado? Sabotage in Pittsburgh? Reformers in San Francisco? Radicals in Los Angeles? Anywhere you are plagued in the nation, I will *un*-plague you."

"Just out of curiosity, what will all this 'un-plaguing' cost me?"

"Half."

Culp pretended to consider it. "Half of everything you help me make? Not bad."

"Half of everything."

"*Everything?* Listen to me, you greasy little dago. I don't need you to get things I already own."

"You need me to *continue* enjoying the things you own."

Culp's face darkened. "You're offering to be partners *and* you are blackmailing me."

"You are correct."

Culp laughed.

"You laugh at me?" said Branco. "Why? In this arrangement, I take all the risks. The police can't walk into your mansion with guns blazing. They'll shoot the 'greasy dago.' They will never shoot Mr. John Butler Culp."

"I'm laughing at your nerve."

Branco stared at the man lounging behind his desk. Was Culp so insulated, so isolated from the world, that he was ignorant of the danger, the threat, Branco posed? A strange thought struck him: Or was Culp a man above ordinary men?

"Wouldn't you do exactly the same if our positions were turned upside down?"

"I sure as hell would," said Culp. "Exactly the same."

"Malvivente."

"What's that dago for?"

"Gangster."

J. B. Culp beamed. He suddenly felt as free as a hoodlum stepping out on Saturday night, with brilliantined hair, a dime cigar, and a pistol in his pocket. Anything could happen. He thrust out his hand.

"O.K., partner. Shake on it."

Branco said, "I would very much like to shake your hand. But I can't."

"Why not? I thought you wanted a partner."

"You put us at risk."

"What are you talking about?"

"Your prizefighters know too much."

Culp raised his voice. "Lee! Barry! Get in here."

They entered quickly. Too quickly.

315

"Were you listening at the door?"

They exchanged looks. Barry tried to bull through it. "Sure we was listening. You're alone in here with this guy. We gotta make sure you're O.K."

John Butler Culp reached back and took a Colt Bisley .32-20 target pistol from the wall of guns. He fired once at Barry. The heavyweight sagged to the floor with a hole the diameter of a cigarette between his eyes.

Lee gaped in disbelief.

Culp fired again.

Then he said to Branco, "Get rid of the bodies, partner."

31

Skeletons were scattered like pick-up sticks. The half of the graveyard nearest the church was still a timeless patch of headstones poking out of green grass, but the explosion had churned the rest into muddy earth and jumbled bones. Above it rose a mountain of bricks and timbers, all that remained of three five-story tenement buildings and Antonio Branco's grocery warehouse.

Isaac Bell surveyed the destruction from a roof across Prince Street. The Mayor had put the Health Department in charge of removing rubble to search for bodies. Scores of city workers were digging, shifting, and loading their finds into wagons.

"How," Bell asked, "did the gas penetrate three entire buildings before it exploded?"

The tall detective was flanked by explosives expert Wally Kisley and Gang Squad chief Harry Warren. They hovered at his elbows, braced to grab hold if he fell over.

317

Bell shrugged them off and took a long, hard look.

Branco's Grocery had occupied two lots, fifty feet of street frontage. Three side-by-side tenements, each twenty-five feet wide, measured another seventy-five feet. The explosion had leveled one hundred twenty-five feet of buildings and fifty feet of graveyard. As Kisley had put it when Bell walked out the hospital's back door, "One hell of a bang."

Now, looking down from the rooftop, Kisley did not sound entirely comfortable with his explanation about the scale of destruction. "Thing is, Isaac, they build tenements in rows, several at a time. The walls are made of brick, but they leave man passages so the workmen can move easily between them. When they're done building, they fill the holes with scrap material and lightly plaster them over. Not much to stop gas from seeping through."

"How did Branco set it off and escape with his life?"

"Could have left a timing device to spark it off. Could have laid a fuse."

Bell turned to Harry Warren. "I want you to investigate where and how Branco's legitimate businesses connected to the underworld."

318

"I've been looking at that ever since you first brought it up," said Warren. "I still can't find a single complaint about fraud or extortion. Branco ran his grocery business clean as a whistle."

Kisley interrupted. "It's like he was two entirely different people: a crook, and a choirboy."

"Then why didn't the crooked outfits attack him?"

"Only one thing would stop them," said Warren.

"Fear," said Bell.

Warren nodded emphatically. "Somehow, lowlifes knew better than to mess about with Branco."

"But if no one ever saw him with crooks, how did he give orders? He controlled gangs: Black Hand gorillas, drug smugglers, and counterfeiters. For that matter, how does he command them now while he's on the run?"

"I don't know, Isaac."

Another question puzzled Bell.

"Why did he blow up the building?"

"He ambushed us."

"No. He could not know precisely the moment we were going to break down his door. He just got lucky with us charging in, just like we got lucky not getting killed . . . And

319

if you guys don't let go of my elbows I'll break your arms! I'm fine . . . *Why* did he blow it up?"

"To hide evidence."

"What evidence? I already had him dead to rights at the Singer Building. He planned this ahead of time. He was ready to run when he had to."

Bell traced, again, the long line of destruction, the mound of rubble that had been Branco's store, to the taller heap of the tenements, down to the graveyard, and past the uprooted bones. The church itself was unscathed. Even its stained glass windows were intact. He still thought it remarkable how far the gas traveled.

"I want to know who owned those tenements . . . Keep greasing Health Department palms. Slip some of our boys onto their pick and shovel crews. Get a close look at everything they dig out. And call me the instant I can inspect what's left of Branco's cellar."

"Enrico," said Isaac Bell when he lured Caruso to the Knickerbocker's cellar bar for a glass of champagne, "you're Italian."

"Guilty," smiled the opera singer. "But, first, I am Neopolitan."

"Let me ask you something. What drives a

Sicilian?"

"A hundred invasions. Countless tyrants. They've triumphed by their wits for three thousand years. Why do you ask?"

"I'm reckoning how Antonio Branco thinks."

"Sicilians think for themselves — *only* themselves."

"When I asked Tetrazzini on our way to San Francisco, she called them 'bumpkins from down south.' Primitive peasants."

"Never!" Caruso roared, laughing. "Tetrazzini's from Florence, she can't help herself. Sicilians are the direct opposite of primitive. They are sophisticated. Strategic. Clear of eye, and unabashedly extravagant. They see, they understand, they act — all in a heartbeat. In other words —"

"Never underestimate them," said Bell.

"There isn't a law written they don't despise."

"Good," said Bell. "Thank you."

" 'Good'?"

"Now I know what he'll try next."

"What?" asked Caruso.

"Some unsuspecting bigwig is about to get a Black Hand letter. And it will be a Black Hand letter to end all Black Hand letters."

Archie hurried into the bar. Peering

through the gloom of Caruso's cigarette smoke, he spotted Bell, and whispered urgently, "Research says Branco owns the shell company that controls the shell company that owns the tenements next door to his grocery."

32

The Health Department laborers excavating the Branco's Grocery wreckage went home at night, leaving only a watchman in charge now that the bodies of all the missing had been removed. Wally Kisley and Harry Warren bribed him. They stood guard at the burned-out stairs that had descended from Branco's kitchen to the cellar.

Isaac Bell climbed down a ladder with an up-to-date tungsten filament flashlight powered by improved long-lasting, carbon-zinc dry cell batteries. He played its beam over a tangle of charred timbers and broken masonry and was surprised to discover a back section had somehow withstood the collapse of the building's upper tier.

The flashlight revealed the walls of a room that was still intact. It was a remarkable sight in the otherwise chaotic ruin. The mystery was solved when Bell saw a square of vertical iron bars that had supported the ceiling. The bars formed what looked like a prison cell. Then he saw a hinged door and lock and realized that it was indeed a jail cell or holding pen. Installed by labor padrone Branco to enforce contracts? Or by gangster Branco to show rivals who was boss?

He found another open space of about the same dimensions beyond a mound of debris. It had no bars, but the walls were solid steel, and the door, which was open, was massive, a full eight inches thick. A walk-in safe.

Bell stepped inside.

The cash boxes were empty. He saw no ash in them; the money hadn't burned but had left in Branco's pockets. Bell thought it curious that the gangster had fled well-heeled yet risked arrest by taking the time to defraud banker LaCava and the wine broker. A reminder that Branco was the coolest of customers.

The safe's walls were pockmarked. Twisted metal and charred wood littered the floor. Exploding ammunition had destroyed Branco's cache of shotguns and revolvers. Those explosions, or the original gas explosion, had buckled and shifted the back wall of the safe. It hung at a drunken angle, and when Bell looked closely, he saw another set of hinges. A door — an odd thing to find in what should be an impregnable wall.

His light began to fade. "New and improved" aside, it was still only a flashlight and couldn't last for long. He switched it off, to conserve the D cells, and felt the hinges with his hands. There was definitely a door at the back of the safe.

Bell gripped the edge with both hands and pulled it inward. Then he switched the light on again and peered behind it. All he could see was thickly packed debris, brick, wood, and plaster. Just as he doused the flashlight again to conserve the last of its power, he glimpsed a roughhewn stone wall rimming both sides of the door and he realized he was looking into what had been an entrance cut into the basement of the tenement building behind Antonio Branco's grocery.

"Now we know," Isaac Bell told Kisley and Warren, who were waiting at the top of the ladder, "how the gas traveled so far before it exploded. And also why Branco blew it up. It hid some kind of underground passage that ran from his place, beneath those tenements, and into the graveyard."

"What's in the graveyard?"

"Give the watchman more money and borrow three shovels."

The Van Dorns picked their way across

the fallen tenements, following narrow, twisting corridors burrowed by the Health Department, and emerged through a final shattered foundation. The graveyard was lit dimly by a few tenement kitchens that overlooked it and a stained glass clerestory at the back of the church.

Bell led the way over the rough earth that the explosion had plowed. The bones he had seen from the Prince Street roof had been gathered into an orderly row of coffins. The odor of fresh-sawn pine boards mingled with the pungent soil. The church and the surrounding tenements blocked street noise, and it was so quiet he could hear the whir of sewing machines in the apartments overhead.

Where the plowed ground met the grass, he said, "We'll start here."

Two feet down, their shovels rang on brick.

They moved back, off the grass, onto the raw earth, and dug some more.

"My shovel hit air!" said Wally Kisley. An instant later, he yelped out loud and disappeared. The ground had opened up. Bell leaped into the hole after him and landed on top of him in the dark.

"You O.K., Wally?" The explosives expert was getting too old for tumbling.

"Tip-top, when you get off me."

Harry Warren landed beside them. "What have we here?"

Bell switched on his flashlight. "It's another tunnel."

They followed it for twenty feet in the direction of the church and came to a door set in a massive masonry foundation. Bell, who had a way with locks, jimmied it open. His flashlight died. Kisley and Warren lit matches. They were in a crypt, stacked with caskets.

The crypt had another door, opposite the one they had entered. Bell jimmied it open and they found themselves in a narrow, low-ceilinged passage between mortuary vaults. A bare electric light bulb hung from the ceiling at the far end, illuminating a flight of stone steps.

Bell whispered, "Wally, you cover me here. Harry, go back out, around the corner, and watch the front of the church."

Bell mounted the steps.

He cracked open a door at the top and peered into the church. Despite the late hour, there was a scattering of worshippers kneeling in the pews. The front door was closed to the cold. The altar and choir seats were empty. Candles flickered in an alcove on the other side of the pews. There, an old woman in a head scarf waited her turn at a confessional booth, and nothing looked different than Bell would expect in an ordinary church in a city neighborhood.

He stepped back from the door and turned to start down the steps. Then he saw what looked like a cupboard door: a narrow slab of hinged wood. It was not locked. He turned sideways to fit his shoulders through the opening and stepped up into a cramped space that had a bench and grillwork that admitted light. He sat on the bench and looked through the grille into a similar booth. It had an open door through which he could see a black velvet rope that blocked the entrance from the pews.

Bell had already figured out that he was sitting inside a confessional booth. But it took a moment to orient himself. This was not the confessional where the old woman waited in the alcove across the pews but another in a corresponding alcove on his side. He sat there a few moments, pondering what it meant. The door to his side was closed. He was in the booth where the priest listened. Suddenly, a man scurried into the alcove and stepped over the rope.

With his broken nose and mangled ear, he could only be Vito Rizzo of the Salata Gang.

Rizzo hurried into the booth beside Bell's and closed the door, and Isaac Bell realized that Antonio Branco was an even a greater twisted genius than he had imagined. Branco commanded his gangsters from this booth at the end of the tunnel between his store and this church. They "confessed" in complete secrecy, and he offered "absolution" in complete secrecy. Best of all for the mastermind, the gangsters never saw their Boss's face.

Rizzo was trembling. He looked terrified. He spoke, suddenly, in Italian.

Isaac Bell drew his gun.

But why was the hard-as-nails gangster so scared? Because, Bell realized, Rizzo was new to this. This might be only his second "confession" since his boss Salata was killed. Only his second direct contact with a mysterious boss.

Bell pressed his handkerchief to his lips.

"Talk American," he muttered.

Through the grille, he saw Rizzo's eyes widen with surprise. But Bell had guessed right. Rizzo was too scared to question his boss. "O.K. I know good American. Forgive me, Father, I sinned . . . I'm sorry I missed confession last week. The cops were after me. So I didn't get your orders . . ."

"Go on."

"All I know is, Salata's dead. I don't know who takes over."

"You," said Bell.

"Thank you! Thank you, padrone — I mean, Father. Thank you, I'll do good, I promise . . . Can I ask ya something?"

"What?" said Bell.

"There's funny talk on the street about the Branco store blowing up. Does this have anything to do with us?"

"You tell me."

"I don't know. I hear maybe Branco is Black Hand. Is that so?"

"What if he is?" asked Bell.

"I don't know."

Bell let silence build between them. Rizzo started fidgeting, tugging his mangled ear. Bell spoke suddenly.

"Did you do what I told you last?"

"Yes."

"Tell me what you did."

"I did what you said."

"Tell me *exactly* what you did."

"I went to Storm King. I opened a saloon. I got my keys scaring the pick and shovel men. And all that time I waited for the guy to come with the sign."

"What sign?"

"The sign you said to look for."

"Which?"

"The one you said. The pay token with the mark."

"Did he come?"

"Yeah. I did everything he told me."

"Where is he now?"

"I don't know."

"What do you mean you don't know? I told you to stick close."

"No you didn't."

Bell let a silence build. Rizzo broke it.

"You told me to do what he said. I gave him what he wanted. I ain't seen him since."

"What did he want?"

"Clothes, food, stick of dynamite."

"You must know where he went."

"I don't know."

"When did he come?"

"Four days ago."

"And you haven't seen him since?"

"No. He left."

Bell sat silent. He had learned a lot, though hardly enough. But he doubted that Rizzo knew any more. The "guy with the sign" could be Branco or not, but even if he was Branco, Rizzo couldn't find him. Still, not a bad night's work, and Bell decided he had to act as if Branco was attempting to make contact with J. B. Culp. For if he was, President Roosevelt was still in danger.

It was time to shift his Black Hand Squad

up to Storm King.

"What do you want me to do, Boss?"

"I want you to raise your hands."

"What?"

"My son, twelve inches from your head is the muzzle of a .45 automatic."

"What?"

"Raise your hands."

"What did you say?"

"In your fondest prayers, it won't be a flesh wound. Elevate!"

"Who are you?"

"Bell. Van Dorn Agency."

The Black Hand gangster shouted a string of curses.

Bell sprang from his booth, threw open the confessor's door, and pressed his gun barrel inside Rizzo's good ear.

"Such language in church!"

33

"I hope you weren't seeking privacy, Mr. Bell, but there isn't a restaurant man in New York who would seat such a beautiful woman out of sight."

Rector's, the big, bright, loud Broadway lobster palace, was just around the corner from the Knickerbocker Hotel. The proprietor, an old friend of Joseph Van Dorn's from Chicago, had seated Marion Morgan at a highly visible banquet table ordinarily reserved for Broadway actresses.

Bell said, "Convey my apologies to any patrons whose view I block . . . We'll start with champagne. Billecart-Salmon Brut Rosé."

"I suspected as much, Mr. Bell. It's on its way to the table."

Bell and bottle arrived simultaneously.

"Billecart-Salmon Brut Rosé?" said Marion. "What are you celebrating?"

"Dinner with the prettiest girl in New

York. *And* the news that we nailed one of Branco's top lieutenants."

"Congratulations."

He took his seat opposite. "Marion, I've never seen you lovelier."

"Thank you, Isaac."

Bell heard an uncharacteristic constraint in her voice. "You sound anxious. Shall I have us moved to a less noticeable table?"

"If I didn't want to be noticed, I would not have bought a dress of cobalt blue."

"Something is troubling you."

She returned a tight smile. "You know me so well, don't you?"

"If you're worried about me, don't be. My memory's tip-top; I'm completely over the stupor, or coma, or whatever the devil the medicos call several solid nights' sleep."

Marion passed an envelope across the table. "I thought I should let you open this."

Bell recognized the stationery even before he read the address.

Signora Marion Morgan
The Fiancée of Isaac Bell
Knickerbocker Hotel

Flushed with fury, Bell plunged his hand into his boot.

"People," Marion warned with a significant glance at the full restaurant. She passed him an oyster fork, and with a grateful nod Bell used its wide tine to slit the envelope.

The silhouettes of a black hand, a revolver, and a skull pierced by a dagger were drawn with exceptional skill, the work of an artist. The wording of the threat was densely baroque, the threat itself, grotesque.

Dearest Signora Marion Morgan,
You have in your feminine power to persuade Isaac Bell to convince the highest authorities to act in accordance with listening to reason. Only you, beautiful lady, can make Bell entreat the powers that are to act for the goodness of all.

Bombing Catskill Aqueduct must be prevented.

This will require one million dollars to be gathered for necessary payments to prevent attack. Radicals and agitators and criminals are banded together. The City cannot protect the aqueduct. Water Supply Board helpless.

The Black Hand stands beside you. Together we stop tragedy before it befalls. Pay part day after next hundred thousand dollar at Storm King Siphon Shaft.

Fully aware that "Dearest Signora" and "in your feminine power" and "beautiful lady" were phrases deliberately calculated to set him off half cocked, Isaac Bell still had to fight hard to douse his rage. The intent of Antonio Branco's poisonous message was the same as a threat to bomb a Little Italy pushcart — sow panic. At least, thought Bell, it was exactly what he had predicted: a Black Hand letter to rival all Black Hand letters.

Did it mean that President Roosevelt was in the clear? Was the assassination plot that Brewster Claypool had set in motion for J. B. Culp no longer active? Just the opposite. Antonio Branco had landed on his feet. All four feet, as the saying went.

"Why are you smiling?" asked Marion.

"Am I?"

"Like a timber wolf. Why?"

"Only in America."

"What do you mean?"

"An immigrant gangster shakes hands with a blue-blood tycoon."

"Antonio Branco and J. B. Culp?"

Bell tossed the letter on the tablecloth. "This pretty much confirms what Vito Rizzo 'confessed.' The man he helped at Storm King was Branco himself. He's probably in Culp's mansion by now, warming his feet on the hearth."

"Why would a man as rich and powerful as Culp shelter a criminal?"

"Each offers what the other wants. Branco wants power. Culp wants the President dead."

Marion picked up the letter and read it.

"What is this about?" she asked, and quoted: " 'The City cannot protect the aqueduct.' "

"Branco is reminding us that it is nearly impossible to guard anything a hundred miles long."

"What about this? 'Water Supply Board helpless'?"

"Same thing . . . Except, funny you ask . . . Grady in Research said that initially there was a huge battle in New York whether to make the aqueduct a City-operated public project or a privately owned enterprise that charged the City for the water. The City won, but it was close-fought. You can bet the losers hate the Water Supply Board."

"Was Culp the loser?"

"It was fought by proxies. Shell companies. Could have been. Who knows?"

"I wonder why Branco wants the money delivered at the Storm King Shaft. Where is that?"

"Fifty miles up the river at Cornwall

337

Landing."

"Do you suppose that the 'powers that are' received their own letters like this?"

"I'm sure the Water Supply Board and the Mayor both got them. Ours was probably an afterthought to get my goat."

"Will they pay?"

"Not if I can help it."

"But Branco dynamited Giuseppe Vella's church job, and he bombed Banco LaCava. If he follows his pattern, he *will* attack."

"The only question is where," Bell agreed.

Marion said, "Storm King Shaft."

"How do you reckon that?"

"An explosion or sabotage anywhere else could be deemed an accident. But a bomb at the same place he names in the letter would leave no doubt that he means business."

Bell looked at his fiancée with deeper admiration than ever. "You'd be a crackersjack extortionist."

"It has the ring of truth, doesn't it?"

"It does indeed."

Bell signaled a waiter.

"Pack up our dinner in a picnic basket. And ask Mr. Rector if he would use his influence to book us a last-minute state room on the night boat to Storm King."

Marion put on her gloves and picked up

338

her bag. "Isn't there a Van Dorn Detective rule against bringing friends to gunfights?"

"This infernal letter makes you a candidate for round-the-clock Van Dorn protection — I guarantee no gunfights in our state room."

"How about fireworks?"

Drill heads battered the rock a thousand feet under the Hudson River. Boring into the circular heading, they scattered a pink powder of pulverized granite. Water seeping from minute seams in the vaulted ceiling turned the powder to a sticky grime that caked helmets, slickers, boots, and faces.

Isaac Bell, introduced by the siphon contractor as a newly hired foreman learning the ropes, was no stranger to digging underground, having masqueraded as a coal miner on the Striker case. Granite, however, was a lot harder than coal; the fourteen-foot-high pressure tunnel was of palatial dimensions compared to a mine shaft; and granite grime, unlike black coal dust, colored the hard-rock gang working the 8 p.m. to 4 a.m. shift as pink as marzipan pigs.

Bell had a Van Dorn detective operating the shaft hoist cage and picked men stationed around the shaft house. They were backed up by the contractor's own guards, while Water Supply Board Police roamed the perimeter. Archie Abbott had sped up on a morning train to escort Marion safely back to the Knickerbocker; Helen Mills was standing by with a newly issued sidearm that Bell knew the general's daughter was extremely capable of using; nor did he doubt that if the Black Hand tried anything, they would never run up against a more levelheaded duo in New York.

Marion Morgan and Archie Abbott's train to New York City hugged the riverbank at West Point. Rendered pewter by an overcast sky, the Hudson looked as cold as the stone fortifications. The sky threatened snow, and ice was hardening on still water in coves and creeks. Marion was thinking she had better buy a warm winter coat when Archie suddenly spoke up.

"I met a widow."

"How old a widow?"

"Twenty-two . . . She married young."

"Do you like her?"

"I'm besotted."

"That's a dangerous condition, Archie."

"Call it infatuated."

Marion laughed. "That's worse."

Archie looked at her, quite seriously. "It's never happened to me before."

Though younger than Archie, Marion felt that he was opening up to her like a big sister and she answered bluntly, "Besotted and infatuated imply a strong dose of foolishness."

"I know that."

"What's her name?"

"Francesca."

"Beautiful name."

"It fits her. She is intoxicatingly beautiful."

"Besotting, infatuating, and intoxicating? Francesca better look out for the Anti-Saloon League."

"She doesn't drink. Won't touch a drop. I've become a teetotaler around her." He grinned. "Drunk on love, instead."

Marion said, "Speaking from my own experience of meeting Isaac, I can only say one word: Congratulations! I look forward to meeting Francesca."

"Oh, you'll love her. She's really interesting. She can talk a blue streak about anything."

Helen Mills met them at the Jersey City Terminal. On the ferry, she explained that Mr. Van Dorn had arranged for the Knickerbocker to move Marion into a suite with two bedrooms, the second for Helen.

"I hope you don't mind a roommate."

"It will be like being back at school."

Archie escorted them to the hotel and rushed off to see Francesca.

At the end of the long shift, the hard-rock gang packed their round of bore holes with dynamite. They moved the short distance to the shaft, took cover, and shot the explosives with electric detonators. With a muffled rumble, the granite they had drilled all day was blown from the face and the siphon tunnel was put through another couple of yards. They boarded the shaft hoist cage for a lift to the surface, too tired, as one man put it, "even for drinking."

Isaac Bell stayed below to watch the mucking crew.

Before the smoke had cleared, the muckers raced with picks and shovels to the heading and started loading the dynamited rock into cars hauled by an electric locomotive. All but their hard-driving Irish foreman were Italian laborers. Any one of them could be Antonio Branco's saboteur. Or *each* could be exactly what he looked like: a hardworking immigrant shoveling his guts out for a dollar seventy-five a day.

The muckers were just finishing clearing rock when water suddenly gushed into the heading. A water-bearing seam had opened, disturbed, perhaps, by the last shift's blast.

"*Il fiume!*" cried a laborer.

The others laughed, and the Irishman explained to Bell. "Ignorant wop thinks the river's busting through the roof."

"Why are they laughing at him?"

"They're not as dumb as him. They know there's nine hundred feet of shale and a hundred feet of solid granite between the roof and the river. It ain't river water. It's just water that was in the rocks. How much you think it's running? Hundred gallons a minute?"

He gave Bell the broad wink of a know-it-all barfly. "Feller told me the company knew they'd hit water along this stretch, but kept it quiet. If you get my meaning . . ."

"I'm afraid I don't," said Bell. "I'm new here. If they knew they were going to hit water, why did they keep it quiet?"

"The way it works; they bid low to get the job, but they'll make it back with extras. They gotta grout the water-bearing seams. And that don't come cheap. Before they grout, they'll need more pumps, and pipes to divert the water. Might even have to build a reinforced concrete bulkhead to fill the entire heading to keep from flooding."

"You mean they get their cake and eat it, too."

"That's what the feller told me. Smart man . . ." The foreman's voice trailed off, and he frowned. The water was running harder. Some of the other muckers who had laughed at the Nervous Nellie moments ago were looking anxious.

"Calm down, you dumb guineas. Calm down. Back to work. Calm down. No worry."

But the laborers continued casting anxious looks at the face of the heading, where the seam gushed, and at water rising over the muck car tracks.

"Il fiume!"

Others repeated the cry. *"Il fiume!"*

"There's no 'fu-may,' dammit," yelled the foreman. "It's just rock water."

A laborer, who was older than the others, pointed with a trembling finger at the cleft in the stone where the water gushed.

"Mano Nero."

"Black Hand?" The foreman seized a young laborer he used as a translator. "What the hell's he talking about?"

"Mano Nero. Sabotage."

"That's nuts! Tell them it's nuts."

The translator tried, but they shouted him down. "They say someone didn't pay."

"Pay what?" asked Isaac Bell. It sounded like word of the Black Hand letter had trickled down to the workmen.

"The dollars we're supposed to give from our pay," said the translator.

"It's a Black Hand shakedown," said the foreman. "They make 'em fork over a buck on payday."

The lights flickered.

Every laborer in the mucking gang dropped their picks and shovels and fled down the tunnel. They ran in headlong confusion toward the shaft, splashing through the ankle-deep water, tripping on the muck car tracks, shoving and trampling each other in their panic. The foreman charged after them, bellowing to no avail.

Isaac Bell followed at his own pace. There would be a long wait for the hoist to come down the shaft and load all the men. Nor could he believe that the Hudson River had breeched a thousand feet of stone.

But when he got to the surface, rumor was rampaging through the labor camp, infecting not only the panicked Italian laborers but the Irish and German engineers, machine operators, foremen, and Board of Water Supply Police, and the Negro rock drillers and mule drivers. The Black Hand had sabotaged the siphon. The Hudson River had broken into the tunnel. Even the engineers, who should know better, were scratching their heads. Was the tunnel lost?

None of it was true, and it would be cleared up. The rock water would be pumped down, the cleft seam grouted, and the digging would continue. But, at the moment, newspaper scouts were wiring New York. On Manhattan and Brooklyn streets fifty miles away, newsboys would soon be hawking the baseless story.

"Extra! Extra!"

BLACK HAND SHUTS DOWN AQUEDUCT
WATER FAMINE THREATENS CITY

Bell cornered the pressure tunnel contractor who had welcomed the Van Dorn protection. He was a hearty, bluff, serious man with no nonsense about him. Like many of the contractors, he personally supervised his job. Was it true, Bell asked, that the likelihood of encountering water-bearing seams had been predicted?

"Between you, me, and the lamppost, diamond drill borings ahead indicated we'd run into water. Not so much it would stop excavation of the siphon tunnel, but enough to have to deal with. We knew we'd have to grout off the seam."

"How many people knew?"

346

"Just a handful, and all in the 'family' — engineers, me, fellows operating the diamond drill."

"Could any of them have told the Black Hand?"

"I don't follow you, Detective."

"I showed you the letter," Bell said. "I'm asking whether the Black Hand caught a lucky break that you hit water right after they threatened the tunnel? Or did the Black Hand know you would hit water and timed their threat to coincide with it?"

"The Black Hand extorts Italian labor, not American engineers. You can bet no one told them directly. But all it would take is one guinea a little smarter than the rest, cocking his ears for the inside word."

Bell said, "In other words, the Black Hand rode free."

"Truth will come out soon enough. The tunnel is doing fine."

But Antonio Branco's damage was done, thought Bell. The Black Hand looked powerful; the aqueduct looked vulnerable. He was hurrying from the contractor's shack when a long-distance telephone call came in from an anxious Joseph Van Dorn, who had just returned to New York.

"Were any of our boys drowned in the flood?"

"There is no flood."

"The newspapers say the Hudson River flooded the tunnel."

"Utterly untrue," said Bell. "Unfortunately, the Black Hand will take credit for sabotage."

"They just did. We got another letter."

"Was it addressed to Marion?"

"Like the last. He crows about the flood and threatens worse if the city doesn't pay."

Isaac Bell said, "We have to hit them before they attack."

"Agreed," said Van Dorn. "What do you propose?"

"Catch Branco with Culp."

"How do you intend to do that?"

"Raid Raven's Eyrie."

34

Twelve brawny, athletic Van Dorn detectives
studied the illustrated map of Raven's Eyrie
that Isaac Bell chalked on the bull pen
blackboard. He had left his undercover men
at Storm King when Van Dorn authorized
hauling in reinforcements from Philadelphia, Boston, and Baltimore. They listened,
commented, and queried while Bell pointed
out features of the estate the raiders would
hit upon.

"Main house. Gymnasium, including
guest quarters and Culp's trophy room.
Stable. Auto garage. Boathouse. Wall — two
miles around and, at a minimum, eight foot
high, enclosing one hundred sixty acres.
Front gate and gatehouse. Service gate.
Workers' barracks."

"How do you happen to know your way
around, Isaac?"

"I got myself invited and stayed for dinner. The front gatehouse is impregnable.

Steep approach and a gate that could stop locomotives. Culp even has rifle slits in the tower. The service gate's not much easier. But there's a high spot in the wall, here — out of sight of the service gate tower — where fit younger detectives can scramble over with grappling hooks, then drop rope ladders for the fellows who belly up to free lunches. We'll cut telephone wires, and the private telegraph, as we go over. They're a few yards farther along the wall."

"Why don't we cut the electricity while we're at it? Put 'em in the dark."

"Culp has his own power plant. It's here."

"You drew it like a church."

"The power plant looks like a church. The steeple masks the smokestack. Now we've confirmed that *Mrs.* Culp is here in New York in their mansion on 50th Street, which makes things easier."

"Screaming wives," said a grizzled veteran from the Boston field office, "take all the fun out of busting down a door."

"Worse than kids," said another.

"There are no kids. But there are plenty of staff. Mrs. Culp has taken her majordomo with her, but there is everything else, from footmen, to cooks, to housemaids, to groundskeepers."

"How about bodyguards?"

"Culp keeps a couple prizefighters in the gymnasium. They've got a room downstairs. So we'll need a couple of boys to get them into manacles."

"O.K. to shoot 'em in the leg if they resist?"

"Use your judgment."

"Where do we take Culp and Branco?"

"Culp's a big wheel in the Hudson Valley, so Mr. Van Dorn strongly suggests we avoid the local constabulary. We'll have a boat here" — Bell pointed at the boathouse pier — "to run us across the river. Then hightail it to a New York Central special standing by at Cold Spring and straight to Grand Central. NYPD Captain Mike Coligney will come aboard at Yonkers and make the arrests the second we cross the city line."

"What charge?"

"Harboring a fugitive for Culp. With more to come."

"How about trying to kill the President?"

"If we can pin it on him," said Bell. "The primary goal is to knock Culp out of commission so he can't kill him."

"What do we charge Branco with?"

"We'll start with the murder of Brewster Claypool. That should give the DA time to establish a Black Hand case. Same goal, though: Take him out of action before he can do more damage."

"How solid is the Claypool murder charge? Keeping in mind what the Italians do to witnesses."

"Solid," said Bell. "*I'm* the witness."

"I have an idea," said J. B. Culp.

The magnate was on his feet, looming over his desk in the trophy room, fists planted on the rosewood. Antonio Branco was pacing restlessly among the life-size kills. Culp waited for him to ask what his idea was, but the self-contained Italian never rose to the bait.

Culp tried again to engage him. "We kill two birds with one stone . . . Can you guess how, Branco?"

Branco stopped beside a suit of armor and ran his fingers across the chain mail. "We kill Roosevelt," he said, "when he makes his speech at the aqueduct."

Culp did not conceal his admiration. Branco was as sharp as Brew Claypool, as cynical, and as efficient. Lee's and Barry's corpses had disappeared as if they had never existed, along with their possessions and every sign they had ever occupied the rooms under the gym. The difference between Claypool and Branco was that Branco also had teeth, razor-sharp teeth.

"Good guess," said Culp.

"Easy guess," said Branco. "What better proof that the city can't manage its water system than to drown the President in the aqueduct?"

"Drown? Is that how you're going to do it?"

Branco said, "I promised not to saddle you with things you shouldn't know," and walked between the elephant tusks that framed the fortress door.

"Where are you going?"

"As I promised, you will not be saddled," said Branco and walked out.

Culp lumbered after him. "Hold on, Branco. I want to know when you're coming back."

"Later."

Branco followed a winding path through a forest of ancient fir trees and down the slope between the outside entrance to his rooms and the estate wall. Near the wall, he slid through a low break in a rock outcropping that opened into a small cave under the wall.

Only an experienced pick and shovel man would recognize the cave as a man-made construction of hidden mortar and uncut stone artfully laid to look like natural rubble cast off by a glacier. It had been built sixty years ago by Culp's grandfather, a "station master" on the Underground Railroad, helping escaped slaves flee to Canada.

"Why?" Branco had asked, mystified. He had studied the family; none were known to be what Americans called dogooders.

"He fell for a Quaker woman. She talked him into it."

"Your grandmother?"

"Not bloody likely."

Branco emerged outside the wall and hurried through another fir stand. The mule wagon full of barrels was waiting. The elderly Sicilian groom holding the reins obeyed Vito Rizzo's last orders before his arrest as unquestioningly as, back at Prince Street, he had obeyed Branco's to dump a sugar barrel in the river. The old man stared straight ahead and pretended he heard no one climb into a barrel behind him until Branco said, *"Muoversi!"*

Francesca Kennedy's "confession" two weeks ago in the Prince Street church had been her last. The Boss had ordered a complete change of their routine. From then on, she reported by telephone from a public booth in Grand Central Terminal at three o'clock in the afternoon on odd-numbered days. On even days, she checked a box at the nearby post office. The letters contained instructions and money. The instructions included the number she would tell the telephone operator to give her. But for two weeks, whatever number she asked for rang and rang but was not answered.

This afternoon, three on the dot, he answered. "What sins?"

"Adultery."

"I didn't know he was married."

"He's not. But I'm supposed to be a widow, so it's adultery until we marry, because, you see, the Church —"

"What have you learned from him?"

"You picked a good day to answer the phone. I just found out he's going on a big raid."

"Raid? What kind of raid?"

"A *detective* raid."

"Why would he tell you that?"

"He broke a date. He had to tell me why."

"Maybe he's seeing someone else?"

"Not on your life," she said flatly. "He's mine."

"Did he happen to say what he is raiding?"

"Some rich guy's estate."

"Where?"

"It's way up the river."

The Boss fell silent. The telephone booth

355

had a little window in the paneling. Francesca could see hundreds of people rushing for trains. She had a funny thought. The Boss could be right next to her, right beside her, in another booth. He knew where she was, but she could only guess where he was.

"Did Detective Abbott happen to mention the rich man's name?"

"Sure."

"Why sure?"

"I asked him. You told me find out everything the Van Dorns are doing, remember?"

"I am puzzled that a private detective would tell you so much about a case he was working up."

"I told you, he's mine."

"I find it hard to believe he would be that indiscreet, even with you."

"Listen, he's got no reason not to trust me. He's the one who started us. I set it up so he thinks he made the first move at the Knickerbocker. In fact, lately I've been wondering —"

"What's the rich man's name?"

"Culp."

Again the Boss fell silent.

"J. B. Culp, the Wall Street guy," she added, and pressed her cheek to the glass to look down the row of booths. The angle was too shallow. She couldn't see inside the other booths, only the operator's stand at the head of the row and the pay clerk at his desk.

Still not a peep out of the Boss.

"It's funny," she said. "Everybody reads about J. B. Culp in the papers — the swell's rich as Rockefeller. But only little old Francesca knows that a whole squad of detectives are going to bust his door like he's operating a low-down bookie joint."

"Did Detective Abbott tell you why the Van Dorns are raiding Culp's estate?"

"No."

"Did you ask?" the Boss said sharply.

"I nudged around it a little. He clammed up. I figured I better quit while I was ahead of the game."

"When is the raid?"

Francesca laughed.

"What is funny?"

"When you read about it in the morning paper, don't forget who told you first."

"Tonight?"

The grappling hooks whistled, cutting the air. Isaac Bell and Archie Abbott swung their ropes in ever-growing circles, building momentum, then simultaneously let fly at the wall that loomed slightly darker than the cloud-shrouded night sky. The hooks cleared the top, twelve feet above their heads, and clanked against the back side. Bell and Abbott drew in the slack and pulled hard. The iron claws held.

"Cut the wires!"

It went like clockwork. Up the knotted ropes, over thick folds of canvas to cover the broken glass, drop the rope ladders, then down the inside and running along a mowed inspection track that paralleled the wall. There were no lights in the gymnasium, the barracks, or the boathouse. The main house was dark upstairs, but the ground floor was lit up like Christmas.

"Dinner in the dining room," said Bell.

Bell sent two men to capture the prizefighters and another man down to the river to rendezvous with the boat. Then he and Archie Abbott led squads to the house. Bell took the back door, Archie the front.

"They're here," said Branco.

"This should be great fun," said Culp. "Too bad you can't observe in person. I'll fill you in later."

Branco was not convinced that it was a good idea, much less "great fun." But they were on Culp's home turf and it was up to Culp to call the shots. "Vamoose!" Culp

358

told him. "While the going's good."

Branco opened a servants' door hidden in the dining room paneling.

"Branco."

"What is it?"

"I'm impressed that you came back, knowing the raid was coming. You could have disappeared and left me to it."

"I need you," said Branco. "No less, no more, than you need me." He closed the door. A narrow, twisting staircase went down to the silver vault, which had been originally a slave hidey-hole. Branco unlocked it, let himself inside, and locked it again.

J. B. Culp snatched a heavy pistol from the sideboard, strode to his front door, and flung it open, shouting, "Mr. Bell, you are trespassing."

35

"Detective Bell is at your back door," said
Archie Abbott. "I'm Detective Abbott. Put
that gun down before you get hurt."

J. B. Culp lowered his pistol and backed
into his foyer, a large entryway flanked by
twin reception rooms. "Judging by your red
hair, I'd have recognized you anywhere,
Detective Abbott. Even on my private property."

Abbott said, "Judging by your ruddy
complexion, blond hair, and blue eyes, you
are not the fugitive Antonio Branco, but
John Butler Culp, the man who is harboring him. Put your gun on the table."

Culp said, "There are people here anxious
to meet you and your" — he looked over
the burly detectives crowding in behind
Abbott — "gang." Then he raised his voice.

"Sheriff!"

A big bruiser with an Orange County
sheriff's star on his coat stepped from one

of the reception rooms. "You're under arrest, Detective Abbott."

"I am not," said Archie Abbott.

"Boys," the Sheriff called.

Six deputies entered from the other reception room carrying shotguns.

The Sheriff said, "You're all under arrest."

"For what?"

"We'll start with trespassing."

"We are not trespassing."

"Drop your weapons and reach for the sky."

"We are not trespassing," Abbott repeated. "We are pursuing a fugitive Black Hand gangster named Antonio Branco."

The Sheriff turned to Culp, who had a small smile playing on his face.

"Mr. Culp, sir, have you seen any fugitives on your property?"

"No."

The Sheriff turned his attention back to Archie Abbott. "Do you have permits to carry those guns?"

"Of course. We're Van Dorns."

"Orange County permits?"

"Now, hold on, Sheriff."

"You're trespassing in Orange County. You're carrying illegal weapons in Orange County. You are endangering public safety in Orange County. And if you are the

Detective Abbott I heard Mr. Culp greet, the Orange County District Attorney has received reports about your radical tendencies."

"Are you nuts? I'm a Princeton man."

"Last chance: Raise your hands before we start shooting. My boys' twelve-gauges don't leave much for the surgeon."

Isaac Bell walked into the foyer with his hands in the air, trailed by his squad similarly elevated. He saw Culp smirking ear to ear. Archie looked poleaxed. But the out-of-town Van Dorns were tough customers, and Bell intervened quickly before it turned bloody.

"Guns down, gents. Hands up. We'll settle this later."

Archie said, "He says he's the Sheriff."

Bell said, "The men at the back door are New York Army National Guard officers. And there's a fellow eating a sandwich in the kitchen who represents the Governor. We're skunked."

"Sheriff!" said J. B. Culp.

"Yes, sir, Mr. Culp?"

"Get these trespassers off my property."

"Yes, sir, Mr. Culp."

"Lock 'em up. I'll send someone to the jailhouse to press charges in the morning."

■ ■ ■ ■

Nine arrested Van Dorns were crammed into a cell in the county lockup that smelled like it was reserved for drunks. The other three had escaped on the boat.

"I want to know how they knew we were coming," said Isaac Bell.

"They knew we were coming, didn't they?" said Archie.

"Unless by amazing coincidence the Sheriff, the Army Guard, and the Governor's man all dropped in on the same night," said Isaac Bell.

Bell was seething. The cost of the botched raid was almost incalculable. Culp was in the clear. Branco was still on the loose, deadly as ever and protected by Culp. Culp had demonstrated his power to bring in big guns to defend his secret alliance with the gangster. While they had somehow managed the near impossible — catching wind ahead of time about a secret Van Dorn raid.

Archie repeated, "This is awful. They knew we were coming."

"We will find out how," Bell repeated.

Bell was dozing on his feet, shoulder to shoulder with the rest of his squad, when he heard Joseph Van Dorn thunder in full voice. The Boss stood outside the cell in a derby hat and a voluminous overcoat.

"Sorriest bunch of miscreants I've ever seen in one lockup. They're an insult to the criminal classes. But hand them over anyway."

The Sheriff looked abruptly awakened and very anxious. "Mr. Culp is going to be mighty angry."

"Tell Mr. Culp to take it up with the United States Attorney for the Southern District of New York, which has federal jurisdiction over Orange County. Show him that letter the U.S. Attorney gave me to give to you. Open up, man! We have a train to catch. Come along, boys. Double-time . . . Lord, that jailhouse stink! Good thing I chartered a cattle car to take you home in."

A scathing nod in Bell's direction instructed him to join the Boss for a private word. They stood in the vestibule when the train left the station. Van Dorn's voice was cold, his eyes colder.

"The U.S. Attorney owed me an enormous favor. Springing your squad cleared the books, and he made it abundantly clear that next time we're on our own. So let *me* make it abundantly clear, Isaac: No Van Dorn detective will scale the Raven's Eyrie wall again without my express permission."

"Except, of course," said Bell, "if we're in hot pursuit of Antonio Branco."

Van Dorn's cheeks flared as red as his whiskers and the Boss was suddenly as angry as Bell had ever seen him. "If Antonio Branco is halfway over Culp's wall and you are hanging by his ankles, wire me on the private telegraph and wait for my specific go-ahead."

As the train neared the city, Archie Abbott whispered, "Isaac, I have to talk to you."

Bell led him into the vestibule where Van Dorn had expressed his displeasure. "What's up?"

"It was my fault, Isaac."

"Everyone did their job. We hit, front and back, right on the nose. It's not your fault they were waiting."

"I'm afraid it was," said Archie.

"What are you talking about?"

Abbott hung his head. He looked mortified, and it began to dawn on Isaac Bell that his old friend Archie Abbott was more deeply downcast than even the Raven's Eyrie fiasco would warrant.

"What are you saying, Archie?"

"I think I was played for a sucker."

"Who played you — the girl you've been

365

seeing?"

"Francesca."

"You told Marion you were 'besotted.' "

"Totally."

"What did you tell Francesca?"

"Only that I was going on a raid. I had to break a date. I said I'd be away overnight, up the river."

"Archie . . ." Bell felt his head swimming. Culp was in the clear. Culp protected Branco.

"I just didn't think."

"Did you tell her we were after Culp?"

"No! . . . Well, I mean, not really."

"What the devil does 'not really' mean?" Bell exploded. "You either told her it was Culp or you didn't."

"I said it was Culp's house. I didn't say we were after Culp. It could have been anyone on the estate. I was sure that was the impression I left. Until —"

"Until Culp had the Sheriff and the Army Guard ambush us . . . What the devil were you thinking, Archie? . . . Sounds like you weren't thinking."

"Not clearly. What do you want me to do, Isaac? Should I resign?"

Isaac Bell looked him in the face. Not only were they the closest friends but Bell felt responsible for him because he had talked

Archie into joining the Van Dorns. He said, "I have to think about it. And I have to talk to Mr. Van Dorn, of course."

"He'll fire me in a second."

"He's the Boss. I have no choice."

"I should save him the trouble and quit."

Archie should resign, thought Bell. He knew the Boss well enough to know that Van Dorn was in no mood to forgive. But he was getting the glimmer of an idea how he might turn the tables on Branco.

"You know, Archie, you're still not thinking clearly."

"What do you mean?"

"Pray this doesn't get in the papers. Because if it does and your Francesca reads it, she will put two and two together and realize that the boss she 'confessed' to in that church is Branco. And she will also know that when Branco reads it, he will know that she knows. Branco went to great lengths to ensure that the criminals who carried out his orders could never implicate him, much less testify against him."

"What are you saying?"

"How long will he let Francesca live?"

"I have to get to her first," said Archie.

"*We* have to get to her first. She'll know a lot about Branco's crimes and, with any luck, what he plans next."

"Wait a minute, Isaac. What does Branco care if Francesca exposes him? He's exposed already."

"When we catch him, he will stand trial, defended by the best lawyers money can buy. The prosecutor will need every break he can get. He will trade years off Francesca's prison sentence for her testimony."

"Prison?"

"Archie, you weren't the first job she did for him. Just the easiest."

36

"Where does Francesca live?"

"I don't know."

"You don't *know*? How could you not know where a woman you were seeing lives?"

"She never let me take her home. She was very proper."

" 'Proper'?" Isaac Bell echoed sharply. As good as this plan was, he was still angry enough to throw Archie Abbott off the speeding train.

"Ladylike. I mean . . . modest . . . Well, you know what I mean."

"Where would you meet up?"

"The Waldorf-Astoria."

"How'd you manage that?" Bell asked. Archie was a socially prominent New Yorker, welcome in any Blue Book drawing room, but the Abbotts had lost their money in the Panic of '93 and he had to live on his detective salary.

369

"Francesca's quite well-off, and her husband had business at the hotel, so she has a good arrangement with the management."

"You said you don't know where she lives. Now you're saying she lives at the Waldorf?"

"No, no, no. She just books us a room."

"When were you supposed to see her next?"

"Tomorrow afternoon, actually."

"Will she show up?"

"I have no idea."

"I think she will," said Bell.

"How do you know?"

"She will be curious about what you'll tell her next."

Again, Abbott hung his head. "How long are you going to rub salt in the wound?"

"Until I am absolutely sure that I can override a powerful impulse to knock your block off."

Archie was late.

Francesca Kennedy had already luxuriated with a hot soak in the porcelain tub. Now, wrapped in a Turkish robe, she curled up in an armchair and let her eyes feast on the beautiful hotel room. It had a fine bureau with an etched-glass mirror, a marquetry headboard that matched the bureau, and French wallpaper. She peeked through the drapes; it was snowing again. Warm and cosy, she settled in with the afternoon newspaper.

Standing in the rocky cavern 1,100 feet under the bed of the Hudson River a week after he returns from Panama, President Theodore Roosevelt will press a key and electrically fire the blast to "hole through" the Hudson River Siphon Tunnel of the Catskill Aqueduct . . .

Footsteps were muffled in the Waldorf's carpeted halls, and she lowered the paper repeatedly to glance at the crack under the door, waiting for Archie's shadow to fall across the sill.

"Are you an opera singer, sir?"

Antonio Branco gave the elevator runner a dazzling smile. "If I-a to sing-a, you will-a run holding ears. No, young fellow, I only look-a like one."

Americans scorned and despised Italian immigrants, but they were amused by well-off Italians who dressed with style. A cream-colored cape, a matching wide-brimmed Borsalino, an ivory walking stick, and a waxed mustache did the job. His masquerade wouldn't fool a Van Dorn detective, or

371

anyone who had met him face-to-face, but it drew salutes from the Waldorf-Astoria Hotel doormen and bows from house detectives. Across the lobby and into the gilded elevator, he was questioned only by the star-struck boy running it.

"Floor, sir?"

"*Sesto!* That means floor seeze. *Pronto!*"

Francesca had worked her way to the back pages, where features were tongue-in-cheek.

A far-flung correspondent reports that our country cousins upstate in rural Orange County awakened twice this week to outlandish rumors. First, as our readers in New York and Brooklyn learned, too, the Catskill Aqueduct tunnel under the Hudson River — the so-called Siphon, or Moodna-Hudson-Breakneck Pressure Tunnel and Gauging Chamber, as the waterworks engineers dub it — was breeched by the river, flooding the tunnel and destroying all hopes of completing the aqueduct ahead of the next water famine. Happily, this proved not the case. The plumber was summoned. The leak was small and has already been patched.

New rumors flew hot and heavy this morning. One had the Sheriff of Orange

County raiding Raven's Eyrie, the fabled estate of the Culps, whose many generations have accumulated great fortunes in river commerce, railroad enterprises, and Wall Street dexterity. Locked up were a dozen men found there. Speculation as to why the Sheriff raided Raven's Eyrie prompted new rumors, the most intriguing of which had the Sheriff hot on the heels of Italian immigrant Black Hand fugitive Antonio Branco.

It was unclear why a gangster (formerly purveyor to the city's Catskill Aqueduct) who is running from the law would choose to go to ground in a plutocrat's fortified retreat. It was equally unclear who the men arrested were. Hearsay ran the gamut of imaginings, from immigrant laborers, to private detectives, to Tammany contract grabbers.

The Sheriff of Orange County denies the event ever took place and displayed for our correspondent his empty jail.

Mr. J. B. Culp's offices in Wall Street report that the magnate is currently steaming across the continent on his private train and therefore unavailable to comment.

The Italian Branco left no forwarding address.

Francesca flung off the terry robe and pulled on her clothing. She *knew* Branco. Not as a gangster, but as a wealthy grocer who had set her up in a small apartment with a stipend that allowed her to get off the streets. He hadn't visited it in two years — not since, she realized now, she had been summoned to confession with the Boss. She had lived on tenterhooks, wondering when it would stop, but he had kept sending money and kept paying the rent.

She was stuffing her things into her bag when a shadow fell on the sill.

The lovely room was suddenly a trap. An interior door connected to an adjoining room. She gripped the knob with little hope. Locked, of course. She had only rented the one room, not the suite. She backed up to the window and pulled the drapes with even less hope. No fire escape; the Waldorf was a modern building with indoor fire stairs. No balcony, either. Only the pavement of 33rd Street, six stories down. She carried no knife on this job, no razor, no weapon that would warn Archie Abbott that she was trouble.

Antonio Branco opened the door with a key and swept into the room.

Francesca Kennedy backed against the window. "I was just reading about you."

"I imagined you were."

Though her mind was racing, nearly overwhelmed with fear, she was struck, as always, by how handsome a man he was. There was a sharpness to him she had not seen before, an alertness he had hidden, which made him even more vital. But when his expression hardened, he looked suddenly so familiar that she glanced at her own face in the bureau mirror, then back at his.

37

His eyes were as dead as hers when she did a job.

Branco's flickered at the window, and she realized instantly how he would do her. Francesca Kennedy wouldn't be the first young and beautiful suicide to jump to her death from an expensive hotel room. Fell for the wrong man?

He turned around to lock the door and was reaching for the latch, when it flew inward with explosive force, smashing into his face and hurling him across the room. The armchair in which Francesca had been reading stopped his fall and he kept his feet, blood pouring from his nose.

Archie Abbott burst through the door he had kicked open.

The tall, golden-haired Isaac Bell was right behind him.

The detectives bounded at Branco like wolves.

Branco had lightning reflexes. The Italian had retained his grip on his walking stick and managed to twist it around as Archie charged. He rammed the tip into Archie's gut. Archie doubled over. Isaac Bell knocked the stick out of Branco's hand. It flew into the drapes and dropped at Francesca's feet. When she picked it up, she was shocked by the heavy weight of its steel core.

Bell and Branco traded punches, grappled and fell against the chair with Bell on top. Branco clamped his arms around the tall detective in a crushing grip. He surged to his feet. His bloodied face contorted with herculean effort, he lifted Bell's hundred seventy-five pounds off the floor. Bell broke his grip and pounded Branco's ribs. They tumbled past the bed. Bell crashed into the bureau, shattering the mirror. Branco whirled to the door. But Archie was up again, throwing a hard, expert punch that drove the gangster to his knees.

Francesca held the walking stick in both her hands and swung it like a baseball bat. It connected with a loud thud, and she dropped the stick and ran into the hall. Antonio Branco's eyes opened wide in disbelief as Archie Abbott sagged to the floor.

Branco snatched up the stick. Isaac Bell

was back on his feet. Branco aimed for his head, but Bell was too fast for him and ducked the blow. Branco swung again, but, as he did, the half-conscious Archie Abbott kicked him. Thrown off balance, Branco missed Bell's head but caught him instead in the back of his knee. Bell's leg flew out from under him, and Branco was out the door.

He saw Francesca racing down the hall.

"Come with me," he called.

"You'll kill me."

She darted into a service stair. Branco ran past it to the end of the hall where, before going to her room, he had confirmed an escape route down a stair to the hotel kitchens.

Isaac Bell tore after them.

The hall was empty. He ran full tilt, spotted a service stair, and wrenched open its door, which emitted a scent of fresh linen. Then he saw blood farther along on the hall carpet. He ran to it, spotted another stain, and kept going until he found a second service stair.

It was dimly lit and smelled of cooking grease.

He cocked his ear to the sound of running feet and plunged after it. Three flights down, he passed a waiter, who was slumped, stunned, against the wall. Three more flights and he reached the kitchen at the bottom of the steps. Men were shouting. A woman screamed. Bell saw cooks in toques helping a white-jacketed sous-chef to his feet. They saw him coming and scattered.

"Where'd he go?" Bell shouted.

"Into the alley."

They pointed at the door. Bell shoved through it. The alley was empty but for a set of footprints in the snow. At the end of it, crowds were hurrying along 33rd. Bell ran to the street. The side-walks were packed and he couldn't see farther than fifty feet in the snow. Branco could have run either way. He hurried back into the kitchen.

"Did you see a woman with him?"

"No."

He asked directions to the laundry. A cook's boy took him there and he began to search for Francesca Kennedy. Frightened laundresses pointed mutely at a laundry cart. Bell seized it with both hands and turned it over.

Isaac Bell borrowed manacles from a house detective and marched Francesca Kennedy back to the wrecked hotel room. Angry Waldorf detectives paced in the hall, steering curious guests past the open door. Archie was slumped on the armchair, holding his head, attended by the hotel doctor.

"Why did you hit me?" he asked Francesca. "Why didn't you hit Branco? He was going to kill you."

Francesca asked matter-of-factly, "What's the difference? You were going to arrest me, and it'll kill me when they hang me."

Bell eased his grip on her arm and said quietly, "Why don't we discuss ways we can arrange things so they don't hang you?"

She raised her blue eyes to smile up at him and Bell forgave Archie for most of his stupidity. As he had told Marion, Francesca Kennedy was intoxicating — and then some.

"Shall we talk?" Bell prompted.

"I like talking," said Francesca.

"So I've heard."

She said, "Could we, by any chance, talk over dinner? I'm starving."

"Good idea," said Bell. "We'll have dinner at Captain Mike's."

"I don't know it."

"It's on West 30th in the Tenderloin."

Captain "Honest Mike" Coligney of the 19th Precinct Station House posted a police matron outside the room he had provided for Isaac Bell to interrogate his prisoner.

"I hope you know what you're doing,

380

Isaac," said Coligney. "That woman is poison."

"I don't know any one more familiar with Antonio Branco than she."

"Even though they never met face-to-face."

"He gave orders. She carried them out."

Bell stepped inside the room and closed the door.

"What would you like for dinner?" was his first question.

"Could I have a steak?"

"Of course."

"Could we possibly have a glass of wine?"

"I don't see why not." He stepped out of the room and handed Mike Coligney twenty bucks. "Best restaurant in the neighborhood — steaks, the fixings, a couple of glasses of wine, and plenty of dessert."

"You're wasting your dough," Coligney said. "What makes you think she'll turn on him? When she had a choice of braining Branco or Detective Abbott, she chose the detective."

"The lady likes to talk and the deck is stacked against her."

"As it damned well should be."

"She knows that. From what she told me on the way over, she would be the last to claim angelhood."

Bell went back inside. Francesca had remained where he had left her, seated at a small, rough wooden table that was bolted, like both chairs, to the concrete floor.

"You know, Isaac . . . It's O.K. if I call you Isaac, isn't it? I feel I've known you forever the way Archie talked about you . . . I've been thinking. I always knew it had to happen some time."

"What had to happen?"

"Getting nailed."

"Happens to the best," said Bell.

"And the worst," Francesca fired back. "You know something? Archie was my favorite job the Boss ever gave me."

"I'm not surprised," said Bell. "Archie is excellent company."

"I had to buy wonderful clothes to be with him. Archie's used to the best girls. I could spend like a drunken sailor and the Boss never complained."

"Do you remember the first job you did for Branco?"

"I didn't know it was Branco."

"Of course not. You got it from the 'priest,' so to speak. Do you remember it?"

"Sure. There was this guy who owned a bunch of groceries in Little Italy. The Boss said he had to go. But it had to look natural."

"How did you learn to make a murder look like natural causes?"

"Not that kind of natural. *Natural!* The grocery guy had a taste to do certain stuff to girls and he'd pay a lot for it. But everybody knows if a guy goes around houses doing that, one of these days some girl's going to get mad enough to stab him. So when he got stabbed, he got stabbed, naturally."

"Why did the Boss want him killed?"

"I never knew until now it was to get the guy's business. It's how Branco got to the big time, owning a string of shops. Big step on his way to the aqueduct job, right? Now he's on top . . . Or was."

"Could you tell me about the next job?"

Isaac Bell coaxed her along, story to story, and Antonio Branco emerged as a criminal as ruthless as Bell had expected. But the gangster was unerring in his ability to couple effective methods to precise goals.

Captain Coligney interrupted briefly when dinner arrived.

Francesca ate daintily and kept talking.

Bell asked, "How did you happen to meet the Boss?"

"I don't really know. I got in trouble once — big trouble — and out of nowhere some gorillas come to my rescue, paid off the cops. One second I think I'm going up the river, next I'm scot-free. Then I get my first message to go to confession." She cut another bite of porterhouse, chewed slowly, washed it down with a sip of wine, and reflected, "Sometimes things really work out great, don't they?"

"Did you help him get the aqueduct job?"

"I sure did! I mean, I didn't know then. But now . . . There was this guy, celebrating a big, big deal. Practically takes over a whorehouse for a weekend. Champagne, girls, the whole deck of cards. I went to confession. Next thing you know, the guy is dead. Before he died, he told me he won this huge city contract to provision the aqueduct. Guess who got the contract after he died?"

"Branco."

"You got it, Isaac."

"What was the last job you did for him?"

"Archie."

"Were you supposed to kill him?"

Francesca Kennedy looked across the table at Bell and cocked an eyebrow. "Is Archie dead?"

Bell gave her the laugh she expected and said, "O.K. So what did Branco tell you to do with Archie?"

"Listen."

"For anything in particular?"

"Anything to do with your Black Hand Squad."

"What did you hear?"

"Not one damned thing."

"But you learned about the raid?"

"Nothing until then. That was the first thing Archie spilled. And the last, I guess," she added, glancing about the windowless room.

Bell asked her how she had informed Branco, now that he wasn't a priest anymore, and she explained a system of mailboxes and public telephones.

"How about before Archie?"

"I did a double. A couple of cousins. You know what the Wallopers are?"

"Hunt and McBean?"

"Oh, of course you know. This was a strange one. Wait 'til you hear this, Isaac . . . Could I have a little more wine?"

"Take mine." Bell tipped his glass into hers, and cleared the plates and flatware and stacked them in the corner. "How was it strange?"

"I picked up Ed Hunt at a party the Boss sent me to and took him to the hotel where the Boss had booked me a room. What I didn't know was the Boss hid in the closet. All of a sudden, when Hunt fell asleep, he stepped out of the closet. I almost jumped out of my skin."

"You saw his face?"

"No. It was dark. I never saw his face until this afternoon. Anyhow, he shooed me out — sent me to the next job — and next I hear, Hunt had a heart attack. Well, I have to tell you, Isaac, if he was going to have a heart attack, it would have been while I was still there."

Bell said, "As I understand it, a stiletto played a role in the heart attack."

"Big surprise," said Francesca.

"You said you went on to the next job. What was that?"

"Hunt's cousin, McBean. The Boss gave me strict orders. Don't hurt him. Just put him to sleep and go home. Which I did. Just like with Hunt. Then I learned at confession that McBean's alive and kicking, not like Hunt. So I'm thinking they made a deal. You hear anything about that?"

"I heard heroin changed hands," said Bell.

"Which reminds me of a job I don't think I told you about yet . . ."

Bell listened. One story blended into another, which reminded her of another. Suddenly, he asked, "What did you say?"

"I was telling you how he confessed to me."

"Would you repeat that, please. What do you mean 'confessed'? Branco confessed to you?"

"I mean, one night he confessed to me. In the church. I was trying to figure out how to do this guy he wanted dead. All of a sudden, it was like I was the priest, and he started telling me about the first man he ever killed — when he was eight years old, if you think I'm bad. You know what he said? It was 'satisfying.' Isn't that a strange word to talk about murder. Satisfying? And when he was only eight?"

"I wouldn't know," said Bell. "What do you think?"

"I wouldn't call it satisfying. I'd call it, like, finishing. Completing. Like, 'That's over,' if you know what I mean. Anyway, then he told me how he killed a padrone who robbed him."

"How does he kill?"

"He plans and he hides."

"What do you mean?"

"He gets close to kill. To get close, you have to plan. Study the situation. Learn it cold. Then make a plan."

"He told you that?"

"He taught me: Plan what to pretend. Pretend you're reading a newspaper. Pretend you're busy working. Or pretend you need help. To throw 'em off. You know what I mean, Isaac? He makes an art of it."

"Of killing."

"Yes, if you want to call it that."

"So Branco was your teacher?"

"He taught me how to do it and not get killed. I owe him a lot, you could say. But what's the difference now?"

"What else did he tell you?"

"You're not listening, Isaac. He didn't *tell* me that; he *taught* me."

"Get so close that they can't be afraid?"

"*Plan* to get so close that they let their guard down."

"Thanks for the advice," said Bell.

"What advice?"

Bell whipped the automatic from his shoulder holster and pressed the muzzle to her forehead.

"What are doing?"

"Francesca, reach into your blouse with two fingers."

"What are you talking about, Isaac?"

"Lift out of your corset the steak knife you palmed at dinner."

"What if I don't?"

"I will blow your brains out," said Bell.

"You'd be doing me a favor. Quicker than hanging. And a lot quicker than being locked in the bug house."

Bell slid the muzzle down her nose and chin and neck and touched it to her shoulder. "This won't kill you, but wherever you end up — bug house, prison, even escape — you'll never use this arm again."

The knife rang on the concrete.

"You look like a wreck," said Archie Abbott when Isaac Bell finally stumbled into the Van Dorn field office.

Bell shook sleet off his coat and hat and warmed his hands over a radiator. "I feel like I've been up a week with that woman. She would not shut up."

"Did she tell you anything useful?"

"How Branco will attempt to kill TR."

"How does she know?"

"She was his apprentice. She knows how he operates. It won't be a sniper or a bomb. It will be up close."

38

They reported to the White House early in the morning. The President was exercising on a rowing machine. Van Dorn did the talking. When he had laid out the threat in succinct detail, he concluded, "For your own safety, Mr. President, and the good of the nation, I recommend curtailing your public appearances. And avoid altogether any in the vicinity of the Catskill Aqueduct."

"The aqueduct is the great enterprise of our age," said President Roosevelt, "and I worked like a nailer to start it up when I was Governor. The very least I can do as President is lend my name and presence to the good men who took over the job. They'll be at it for years, so celebrating the Storm King Siphon Tunnel is vital for morale."

"Would you have the history books forever link the Catskill Aqueduct to your assassination?"

"Better than the history books saying, 'TR

turned tail and ran.' "

"I seem to have failed," said Van Dorn, "in my effort to explain the danger."

President Roosevelt hopped off his machine. "I grant you that J. B. Culp's tendencies toward evil are indisputable. Culp is the greatest practitioner of rampant greed in the nation. His underhanded deals rend a terrible gulf between the wealthy few and the millions who struggle to put a meal on the table. Unchecked, his abuses will drive labor to revolution. He is as dangerous as the beast in the jungle and as sly as the serpent. But you have not a shred of evidence that he would attempt to assassinate me."

"Nor do I have any doubt," said Van Dorn.

"You have hearsay. The man is not a killer."

"Culp won't pull the trigger himself," said Isaac Bell.

The President glanced at Van Dorn, who confirmed it with a grave nod.

"Of course," said Roosevelt. "A hired hand. If any of this were true."

"Antonio Branco is no hired hand," said Bell. "He is personally committed to killing you. He'll call in a huge marker that Culp will be happy to pay."

"Poppycock!"

Van Dorn started to answer. Isaac Bell interrupted again.

"We would not be taking up your valuable time this morning if the threat were 'poppycock,' Mr. President. You say you worry about revolution? If the atmosphere is so volatile, couldn't a second presidential assassination, so soon after the last, trigger that revolution?"

"I repeat," Roosevelt barked. "Poppycock! I'm going to the Catskill Mountains. If your lurid fancies have any basis in truth, I'll be safe as can be on the Navy's newest battleship."

"May I ask, Mr. President, how do you happen to be traveling to the Catskill Mountains by battleship?"

"Up the Hudson River to Kingston, where we'll board an Ulster & Delaware special to inspect the reservoir, eventually take the special down to the siphon." He laughed and said to Van Dorn, "Shall I order the railroad to lay on an armored train?"

"I'll see to it," said Van Dorn.

"I'll bet you will and slap the government with a mighty bill."

Van Dorn's expression could have been a smile.

Isaac Bell said, "Sir, will you please agree to obey closely instructions your Secret

Service corps issue for your protection?"

"Of course," the President answered with a sly grin. "So long as I can make my speech . . . Listen here, young fellow, you run down those supposed criminals. I'll speechify the greatest aqueduct ever dug and" — he plunged a hand into his pocket and he pulled out a crumpled bill — "five bucks says my battleship and I finish first."

Isaac Bell slapped down a gold coin. "Double it."

"You're mighty sure of yourself."

"You'll have to trade your battleship for ice skates, Mr. President. Last time I looked, the Hudson River was freezing solid."

"*Connecticut*'s eleven-inch armor belt will smash ice."

Isaac Bell held off reminding the Commander-in-Chief that USS *Connecticut*'s armor tapered to only four inches in her bow, but he could not resist saying, "Far be it from me to advise a military man, Mr. President, but how do your admirals feel about the *Connecticut* smashing ice with her propeller blades?"

TR threw up his hands. "O.K., O.K. I'll take the train. That satisfy you?"

"Only canceling your public appearances until we nail Culp and Branco will satisfy me."

"Then you're bound for disappointment.

393

I'm going and that's all there is to it. Now get out of here. I have a country to run."

Bell and Van Dorn retreated reluctantly.

"Wait!" Roosevelt called after them, "Detective Bell. Is that true?"

"Is what true, Mr. President?"

"The Hudson River is freezing early."

"It's true."

"Bully!"

"Why 'bully,' sir?"

"They'll be racing when I'm there."

Van Dorn asked, "What kind of racing?"

"Fastest racing there is. Ice yacht racing."

"Do you race, sir?" asked Bell.

"Do I race? Cousin John founded the Hudson River Ice Yacht Club. His *Icicle* cracked one hundred miles per hour and won the Challenge Pennant. Ever been on an ice yacht, Detective?"

"I skippered *Helene* in the Shrewsbury regattas."

"So you're a professional?"

"I was Mr. Morrison's guest," said Bell, and added casually, "Culp races ice yachts, you know?"

"Daphne!" shouted the President. "Fast as greased lightning!" He flashed a toothy grin. "Just goes to show you, Bell, the Almighty puts some good in every man — even J. B. Culp."

The President's hearty ebullience offered an opening and Bell seized it. "May I ask you one favor, sir?"

"Shoot."

"Would you make your speech at the Hudson River Siphon your only speech?"

Roosevelt considered the tall detective's request for such an interim that Bell saw reason to hope that the President was finally thinking of the assassination that had flung him into office.

"O.K.," he answered abruptly. "Fair enough."

Joseph Van Dorn was staying on in Washington, but he rode with Isaac Bell on the trolley to the train station. "That was a complete bust," he said gloomily. "One speech, ten speeches, what's the difference? Everywhere he stops, the reckless fool will wade into the crowds — knowing full well that McKinley got shot while shaking hands."

"But his only *scheduled* appearance will be the speech. Branco will know precisely where and when to find him at the Hudson Siphon — the only place the President will be a sitting duck."

"That is something," Van Dorn conceded. "So how do we protect the sitting duck?"

Isaac Bell said, "Clamp a vise around

Branco. Squeeze him."

"To squeeze him, you've got to find him."

"He's holed up in Culp's estate."

"Still?" Van Dorn looked skeptical. "Where'd you get that idea?"

"Culp's private train," answered Bell. "I sent Eddie Edwards to nose around the crew. Eddie bribed a brakeman. It seems that ordinarily by November, Culp spends weekdays in town, but the last time he left the property, he took his train to Scranton and came back the same night."

"I wouldn't call that definitive proof that Branco's holed up with him."

"Eddie's brakeman is courting a housemaid at Raven's Eyrie. She tells him, and he tells Eddie, that Culp is sticking unusually close to home. She also says the boxers don't live there anymore. And we already knew that Culp's wife decamped for the city. Add it all up and it's highly likely that Branco's in the house."

"Yet Branco's been to town, and he's still bossing his gangsters."

Bell said, "I have your Black Hand Squad working round the clock to find how he gets out and back in."

The letter was waiting for Joseph Van Dorn when he got to the New Williard.

THE WHITE HOUSE
WASHINGTON, D.C.

December 1, 1906

Joseph Van Dorn
Van Dorn Detective Agency
Washington, D.C., Office
The New Williard Hotel

Dear Joe,
Your Isaac Bell has a given me a bully idea. I will deliver only one prepared speech whilst inspecting the Catskill Aqueduct. In so doing, I can concentrate all my efforts on a big splash to boom the waterworks enterprise.

So before I go down the Storm King Shaft to fire the hole-through blast, accompanied by the newspaper reporters, I will speak to assembled multitudes on the surface. To this course, I have asked the contractors to gather their workmen at the shaft house and build for me a raised platform so all may see and hear.

"May the angels preserve me," said Joseph Van Dorn.

Hearty Regards,
Theodore Roosevelt

P.S. Joe, could I prevail upon you to accompany my party on the tour?

Deeply relieved by the unexpected glimmer of common sense in the postscript, Van Dorn telephoned a civil servant, a former Chicagoan who now led the Secret Service protection corps. "The President has asked me to ride along on the Catskills trip. I don't want to get in your way, so I need your blessing before I accept."

His old friend gave an exasperated snort, loud enough to hear over the phone. "The Congress still questions who should protect the President and whether he even needs protection. Nor will they pay for it, so I'm juggling salaries from other budgets. And now they're yammering that one of my boys was arrested for assault for stopping a photographer from lunging at the President and Mrs. Roosevelt with a camera that could have concealed a gun or knife. In other words, thank you, Joe, I am short of qualified hands."

"I will see you on the train," said Van Dorn. And yet, in his heart of hearts he knew that when some bigwig persuaded the President to let him stand beside him, the founder of the Van Dorn Detective Agency would end up too far away to intercept an attacker.

Between the Raven's Eyrie wall and the foot of Storm King Mountain, the estate's telegraph and telephone wires passed through a stand of hemlock trees. Isaac Bell and a Van Dorn operative, who had been recently hired away from the Hudson River Bell Telephone Company, pitched a tent in the densest clump of the dark green conifers.

Bell strapped climbing spikes to his boots and mounted a telegraph pole. He scraped insulation from the telephone wires and attached two lengths of his own wire, which he let uncoil to the ground. He repeated this with the telegraph wires and climbed back down, where the operative had already hooked them up to a telephone receiver and a telegraph key.

An eight-mule team hauled a heavy freight wagon up to the Raven's Eyrie service gate. A burly teamster and his helper wrestled enormous barrels down a ramp and stood them at the shoulder of the driveway. They were interrupted by a gatekeeper who demanded to know what they thought they were doing.

"Unloading your barrels."

"We didn't order any barrels."

The teamster produced an invoice. "Says here you did."

"What's in 'em?"

"Big one is flour and the smaller one is sugar. Looks like you'll be baking cookies."

The gatekeeper called for the cook to come down from the kitchen. The cook, shivering in a cardigan pulled over her whites, looked over the flour barrel, which was as tall as she was. "This is a hogshead. There's enough in it to feed an army."

"Did you order it?"

"Why would I order a hogshead of flour and a full barrel of sugar at the end of the season?" she asked rhetorically. "Maybe they're meant to go to 50th Street. That's their winter palace in New York City," she added for the benefit of the teamster and hurried back to her kitchen.

"You heard her," said the gatekeeper. "Get 'em out of here."

The teamster climbed back on his rig.

"Hey, where you going?"

"To find a crane to lift 'em back on the wagon."

The gatekeeper called the estate manager. By the time he arrived, the wagon had disappeared down the road. The estate manager gave the hogshead an experimental tug.

It felt like it weighed six hundred pounds.

"Leave it there 'til he comes back with his crane."

THE WHITE HOUSE
WASHINGTON, D.C.

December 3, 1906

Joseph Van Dorn
Van Dorn Detective Agency
Washington, D.C., Office
The New Williard Hotel

Dear Joe,
Further the booming of the aqueduct enterprise, a White Steamer automobile will be carried on the special train to deliver me to the various inspection stops, and particularly the Hudson River Siphon Shaft, so the workmen at the shaft house may see me arrive.

"Good Lord," said Joseph Van Dorn.

Hearty Regards,
Theodore Roosevelt

PS: I'm back on my battleship, but only as far as the icebreaker can open a channel. The train can meet us there.

VAN DORN DETECTIVE AGENCY
KNICKERBOCKER HOTEL
NEW YORK CITY

Dear Mr. President,
I do hope I may accompany you in the auto. May I presume you will wear a topper?

Sincerely,
Joseph Van Dorn

Whether the President wore a top hat, a fedora, or even a Rough Rider slouch hat, Van Dorn would wear the same — and wire-framed spectacles — to confuse a sniper. He would even have to shave the splendiferous sideburns he had cultivated for twenty years.

Ten men and women dressed in shabby workers' clothes got off the day coach train from Jersey City and marched out of Cornwall Landing and up the steep road to Raven's Eyrie. When they were stopped at the front gate, they unfurled banners and began to walk in a noisy circle. The banners demanded:

**HONEST WAGES FOR AN
HONEST DAY'S WORK**

and accused the Philadelphia Streetcar Company, owned by the United Railways Trust, of unfair treatment of its track workers.

The workers chanted:

"Wall Street feasts. Workers starve."

The Sheriff was called. He arrived with a heavyset deputy, who climbed out of the auto armed with a pick handle. Two more autos pulled up, with newspaper reporters from Poughkeepsie, Albany, and New York City.

"How'd you boys get here so fast?" asked the Sheriff, who had a bad feeling that he was about to get caught between the Hudson Valley aristocracy and the voting public.

"Got a tip from the workers' lawyers," explained the man from the *Poughkeepsie Journal.*

"Did J. B. Culp instruct you to disperse this picket line?" asked the *Morning Times.*

The progressive *Evening Sun*'s reporter was beside himself with excitement. Ordinarily, the biggest news he covered in the Hudson Valley was the state of the winter ice harvest. He had already wired that the intense cold meant harvesting would start so early that the greedy Ice Trust would not be able to jack up prices when the city sweltered next August.

Now, outside the Wall Street tycoon's gates, he put the screws to privilege: "Sheriff, has J. B. Culp instructed you to permit or deny these American citizens to exercise their constitutional right to free assembly?"

"There's an inch of ice on the river, Isaac. They've hauled all their boats out of the water at Raven's Eyrie, and I just saw that the signboard at the passenger pier says the steamers are stopping service for the winter."

"I sent Archie to Poughkeepsie to buy an ice yacht."

"I'm amazed that Joe Van Dorn authorized such an expense."

"This one's on me," said Bell. "I want a special design. Fortunately, my kindly grandfather left me the means to pay for it."

Isaac Bell found New York Police Department Detective Sergeant Petrosino's Italian Squad in a small, dimly lit room over a saloon on Centre Street. Exhausted plainclothes operatives were slumped in chairs and sleeping on tables. Joe Petrosino, a tough, middle-aged cop built short and wide as a mooring bollard, was writing furiously at a makeshift desk.

"I've heard of you, Bell. Welcome to the highlife."

"Do you have time to talk?" said Bell with a glance at those detectives who were awake and watching curiously.

"My men and I have no secrets."

"Nor do I and mine," said Bell. "But I am sitting on dynamite and I'm obliged to keep it private."

"When a high class private investigator offers me dynamite, I have to ask why."

"Because Harry Warren thinks the world of you. So does Mike Coligney."

"Mike and I have Commissioner Bingham in common. He's been . . . helpful to us both."

Bell answered carefully. "I do not believe that Captain Coligney reckons that this particular dynamite is up the Commissioner's alley."

Petrosino clapped a derby to his head and led Bell downstairs.

They walked the narrow old streets of downtown. Bell laid out the threat.

"Have you informed the President?"

"Mr. Van Dorn and I went down to Washington and told him face-to-face."

"What did he say?"

"He refused to believe it."

405

Petrosino shook his head with a bitter chuckle. "Do you remember when King Umberto was assassinated by Gaetano Bresci?"

"Summer of 1900," said Bell. "Bresci was an anarchist."

"Since he had lived in New Jersey, the Secret Service asked me to infiltrate Italian anarchist cells to investigate whether they were plotting against President McKinley. It was soon clear to me they were. I warned McKinley they would shoot him first chance they got. McKinley wouldn't listen. He took no precautions — ignored Secret Service advice and let crowds of strangers close enough to shake his hand. Can you explain such nonsense to me?"

"They think they're bulletproof."

"After McKinley died, they said to me, 'You were wrong, Lieutenant Petrosino. The anarchist wasn't Italian. He was Polish.' "

"I know what you mean," Bell commiserated. "I'm pretty much in the same boat you were."

"How do these fools get elected?"

"People seem to want them."

Petrosino gave another weary chuckle. "That's cop work in a nutshell: Protect fools in spite of themselves."

Isaac Bell asked, "Who do you think

Antonio Branco will hire to kill the President?"

"If he doesn't do the job himself?"

"He may well," said Bell. "But for the sake of covering all bases, who would he hire?"

"He's got a choice of Black Hand gorillas or radical Italian anarchists," said Petrosino. "Pray it's gorillas."

"Why's that?"

"Criminals trip themselves up worrying about getting away. The crazy anarchists don't mind dying in the act. They don't even think about getting away, which makes them so dangerous."

"Do you have a line on Italian anarchists?" Bell asked.

"Most of them."

"Could you take them out of commission when the President goes to Storm King?"

"The lawyers will howl. The newspapers will howl. The Progressives will howl."

"How loudly?"

Petrosino grinned. "I been a cop so long, so many gunfights, my ears are deaf."

"Thank you," said Bell. "I hope the Van Dorn Agency can return the favor one day. What about the gorillas?"

"Too many. I'll never find them all. But like I say, they're not as dangerous as anarchists."

■ ■ ■

"Well done on the anarchists!" Joseph Van Dorn said when Bell reported. "But the assurance that 'gorillas' are not as dangerous as radicals doesn't exactly make me rest easy. Particularly as the President has decided to make your 'one speech only' open to all. He wired me this morning that he's going to lead the workmen in a parade."

"A parade," said Bell with a sinking heart. What if he was wrong about Branco killing in close? A parade was an invitation to a sniper, and a criminal as freewheeling as Branco could change tactics in an instant.

Van Dorn echoed his thoughts. "The parade is madness. He intends to lead it in the Steamer. I asked, would he at least put up the automobile's top? Look what he wired back."

Van Dorn thrust a telegram across his desk.

SNOW ON LABOR
SNOW ON PRESIDENT

Bell asked, "Who's marching in the parade?"

"Everyone."

"Even the Italians?"

"Especially the Italians. Last we spoke in Washington, he had a bee in his bonnet about immigrants learning English to facilitate fair dealings between classes of citizens. He was tickled pink when I told him that the Italian White Hand Society is our client and what fine English Vella and LaCava speak."

"Why don't you invite Vella and LaCava to the parade?"

"Excellent idea! I'll bet TR shakes their hands."

"Invite Caruso and Tetrazzini, while you're at it."

"I wouldn't call either sterling pronunciators of the King's English."

"Any hand the President shakes that is not a stranger's hand will make me happy," said Bell. "Along with a snowstorm to blind the snipers."

Van Dorn turned grave. "But in the event that a providential snowstorm doesn't blind a sniper, how else are you closing the vise around Branco?"

"My operators are watching Culp's gates and his boat landing round the clock."

"I thought you told the President the river was frozen."

"I put a man on an ice yacht."

"Where'd you get an ice yacht?"

"Bought myself one in Poughkeepsie."

"Who other than you knows how to sail it?"

"Archie Abbott."

"I wondered where that fool had gotten to. What else are you doing?"

"I have a tapper up a pole listening to the Raven's Eyrie telephone."

"*Outside* the walls?" asked Van Dorn.

"Yes, sir. Outside."

"What about telegraph?"

"It's all in cipher."

"I would lay off the telegraph wire. Culp conducts business from the estate. Tele-*phone* tapping is one thing; the law's so murky. But we don't want to be liable to charges of tele*graph* tapping for inside knowledge of Culp's stock market trades. What else?"

"What else would the Chief Investigator recommend?" Bell asked his old mentor.

Van Dorn sat behind his desk silently for a while. He gazed into the middle distance, then made a tent with his fingers and stared inside it. At last he spoke. "Go back to that woman."

"Francesca?"

"Find out what she didn't tell you."

Bell was itching to return to his detectives watching Raven's Eyrie and guarding the

410

siphon tunnel dig. "She already admitted to every crime in the book."

Van Dorn said, "She knew she was headed to prison, at best, and more likely the hangman. She may have talked your ear off, but she's drowning, Isaac. She had to hold on to something, something for herself."

Archie Abbott woke before dawn in a cold bed in a cold room. He pulled on heavy underclothing and over it a snug suit of linen. Then he donned thick woolen hose, trousers, and waistcoat. He encased his feet in high felt boots. Finally, he buttoned a fur jacket over the woolen waistcoat and a pea jacket over the fur. He covered his head and ears with a fur hat and pulled goggles over his eyes.

He stepped outside, crossed the New York Central Railroad tracks, and hurried down to the frozen river. His ice yacht waited in a boathouse at the edge of the cove. The runners were frozen to the ice. He kicked them loose and pushed the yacht outside.

The breeze in the shelter of the cove was barely enough to stir the pennant at the masthead. But Isaac Bell had commissioned an exotic doozy from J. B. Culp's own builder, with fifty extra feet of sail and lead ballast to try to keep from flipping upside

411

down in a squall, and that breath of air started it moving like a restless horse. Abbott climbed hastily onto the car — the cockpit at the back end — and grabbed the tiller just as the yacht bolted onto the open river.

A bitter breeze struck the rigid sail. Abbott sheeted it in tight and concentrated on the tiller to dodge oversize ice hummocks, rocks along the shore, and wind skaters flashing by with sails on their backs. She was a light-footed gazelle. She felt like she was making thirty miles an hour until they overtook a New York Central express. Judging by the locomotive's flattened smoke, Isaac Bell's ice yacht was cracking forty-five.

When the sun cleared Breakneck Mountain and cast thin, cold rays on Storm King on the other side of the river, Archie turned the boat toward Raven's Eyrie. Unlike the other Hudson River estates where lawns rose from the water's edge, Culp's place was easily recognized by the fir trees that screened its walls.

He crossed the frozen water in a flash and commenced the first of many cold, cold passes by Culp's dock. Some Van Dorn had to freeze half to death keeping vigil and Abbott was the one, atoning for his stupidity and staying out of sight of the Boss on the slim chance that Antonio Branco may suddenly embark by ice yacht. At least Isaac hadn't condemned him to be one of the operatives on hogshead duty — watching from inside the barrel left at the service entrance and spelling each other only in the dark — though he would have if Archie wasn't too tall to fit.

Other boats started skittering down the river, flying Poughkeepsie and Hudson River Ice Yacht Club burgees and speeding, like his, on the edge of a smashup. Archie joined in impromptu races with them and the sail skaters. Bell had issued strict orders not to draw attention by winning races, for word of a new fast boat would get back to J. B. Culp in a flash. But it was still a welcome change of pace and a natural cover for the Van Dorn watch.

The visiting room in the women's section of the Tombs was divided by a wall broken with a small mesh-covered window. Francesca Kennedy looked so gaunt that Isaac Bell suspected their steak dinner had been the last she had eaten. Her face was pale, her expression sullen.

"What are you doing here?"

"I came for what you didn't tell me," Bell said bluntly.

"Didn't I give you enough to send me to the gallows? Oh, what am I talking about? I keep forgetting."

"Forgetting what?"

"It's not the hangman anymore. It's the electric chair."

"I came —"

"Go away, Isaac. Anything I didn't tell you I didn't want to tell you."

She was seated on a stool. Bell indicated the stool on his side. "May I sit down?"

She ignored him.

Bell pulled up the stool and sat face-to-face with her, inches from the mesh. "I came to change your mind."

"Forget it."

"I've spoken with some men in the prosecutor's office. It is possible that I can persuade the District Attorney to offer you some kind of a break."

"You want to give me a break? Get me out of here."

"I can't."

"Let me go home."

"I can't."

"So I can't remember what I didn't tell you."

"I can't get you out of jail, Francesca. No one can. But maybe I can make it better."

She glanced about her. "Better than this

414

wouldn't be hard."

"I'm thinking of *much* better. If we can convince a judge that you should be in an asylum."

"I don't think the bug house is better."

"There are still some excellent private sanitariums."

"Really? How excellent?"

"For wealthy patients. Very wealthy patients."

"I'm not wealthy, Isaac. And I'm sure as heck not *very* wealthy."

"I can arrange it," said Bell.

"Pay out of your own pocket?"

"The agency will pay at first. At some point after we seize Branco's assets, we can tap into them."

"Won't the government keep them?"

"Not if the Van Dorn Agency deserves a bounty. And certainly not if we, in essence, pay you for your testimony against Branco with Branco's money."

"That would be ironic."

"How so?"

"Is this on the square?" she asked, and for the first time she let Bell see that she was scared.

"Yes."

"You'll really do it?"

"You have my word you will get a square deal."

Francesca Kennedy nodded. "I'll take your word . . . Shake on it." She slipped her fingers through the mesh. Bell squeezed them before the matron interrupted with a sharp "No hands!"

Francesca flashed her a pleasant smile and said, "Sorry." To Bell she whispered, "It's ironic, because Branco used to be a regular customer."

"You knew Branco? You said you didn't."

"Not as the Boss . . . I didn't lie to you, Isaac. I just didn't tell you everything."

"When was this?" asked Bell, thinking to himself, Bless Joseph Van Dorn for steering him back to her. The "old man" had invented the best tricks in the detective book.

Francesca took a deep breath. "Back when I was streetwalking. He set me up in an apartment. All I knew was, he was a rich grocer. Gave me this little apartment and a few bucks a week if I'd stay off the streets. I said to him, 'What are you, jealous of my other customers?' and he said, 'You'll get killed on the street and you're too valuable to get killed.' Fine with me. Nicest thing anyone ever said to me. Besides, he was right. You die on the street; it's just a matter of time. Anyhow, 'til he showed up at the

Waldorf, I hadn't seen him in ages — not since I started 'confessions' with the Boss. But he had kept sending the dough and paying the rent."

"Didn't you recognize his voice?"

"Not through the grille. And he talked different, too. Different words. I feel kind of dumb, but I never thought for a second he was the same man."

"Where was the apartment?" asked Bell.

"I still have it. Or did 'til now."

"Would he hide there?"

Francesca shrugged. "He never came to my place. When he wanted me, we'd meet at an apartment he kept on Prince Street."

"His home that blew up?"

"No, he didn't live there. I never saw his home. Our place was over near Broadway. He just kept it for me. And whoever else I guess he had."

"What was the address?"

Antonio Branco returned to Raven's Eyrie the way he had left, through the cave. His handsome face was battered from the fight with Bell and Abbott, both eyes blackened, his nose swollen.

"Detectives are watching my safe house."

"You've become a less valuable asset," J. B. Culp shot back.

"It means nothing."

"You are turning into a liability."

Culp was ready to pick up a gun and shoot him. End this whole thing before it got worse. He had his story ready: Italian fugitive snuck in here. I caught him trying to steal my guns. Thank God I got the drop on him. Reward? No thank you, give the money to charity.

He was about to turn around and pluck the Bisley off the wall when Branco surprised him by answering mildly, "I am moving my business to Canada."

"Canada?"

"I have padrone business in Montreal. The railroads are hungry for labor. The Italian colony grows larger every day, and many owe me their place in it. A good place to lay low."

"What about our deal?"

"I'll stay here until we've finished Roosevelt. After, I'll run my end from Canada. It's easy to travel back and forth. The border is wide open."

"What about your big idea to discredit the city aqueduct? How can you do that in Canada?"

Branco spoke mildly again, but his answer made no sense. "Would you look at your watch?"

"What?"

"Tell me the time."

"Time to make a new arrangement, like I've been telling you all morning."

What time is it?" Branco repeated coldly.

Culp tugged a thick gold chain. "Two minutes to eleven."

Branco raised two fingers. "Wait."

"What? Listen here, Branco —"

"Bring your field glasses."

Branco strode into an alcove framed with tusks and out a door onto a balcony. The day was cold and overcast. Snow dusted the hills. The frozen river was speckled with ice yachts and skate sailors skimming the glassy surface. He gazed expectantly at Breakneck Mountain, three-quarters of a mile opposite his vantage on Storm King.

Culp joined him with binoculars. "What the devil —"

The Italian stilled him with an imperious gesture. "Watch the uptake shaft."

A heavy fog of steam and coal smoke loomed over the lift machinery at the top of the shaft, the engine house, and the narrow-gauge muck train. Culp raised his field glasses and had just focused on the mouth of the siphon uptake when suddenly laborers scattered and engineers leapt from their machines.

"What's going on?"

Branco said, "Remember who I am."

A crimson bolt of fire pierced the smoke and steam and shot to the clouds. The sound of the explosion crossed the river seconds later and reverberated back and forth between Breakneck Mountain and Storm King.

Culp watched men running like ants, then focused on the wreckage of the elevator house. It appeared that the lift cage itself had fallen to the bottom of the thousand-foot shaft, which was gushing black smoke.

"What in blazes was that?"

"Four hundred pounds of dynamite to discredit the city."

A Sniper Loves a Parade

39

The New York newspapers arrived on the morning train.

OVERTURNED LANTERN SET OFF AQUEDUCT NITROGLYCERIN FUSE

The overturning of a lantern at the Catskill Aqueduct Hudson River Siphon at Storm King ignited a fuse that set off 400 pounds of dynamite destroying the east siphon uptake engine house and elevator.

"The papers got it wrong. As usual," Wally Kisley told Isaac Bell. "The contractor runs an up-to-date enterprise. There weren't any fuses to ignite. They fire the shots electrically."

"Are you certain it was sabotage?" asked Bell.

"Sabotage with a capital *S*. Very slick timing device. You gotta hand it to these Eye-talians, Isaac. They are masters of dynamite."

Kisley sat down abruptly. Bell reckoned that the long trek down to the tunnel and back up by makeshift bosun's chairs and rickety ladders had exhausted him. But to Bell's astonishment, the tough old bird covered his face with his hands.

"You O.K., Wally?"

Kisley took a breath. "I can't claim I'm a stranger to carnage."

Bell nodded. Kisley and Mack Fulton and Joe Van Dorn had worked on the Haymarket Massacre case to determine who had thrown the bomb, and, in the ensuing twenty years, scores more bombing cases. "Goes with the job," he said softly.

"The men were *hammered.* The tunnel looked like a reefer car leaving the slaughterhouse."

"The wooden framework of the engine house crumbled and beams crashed downward toward the machinery that operates the elevator. One beam struck a brake handle, releasing the heavy wooden cage, which crashed at full speed downward to the bottom of the shaft. Twisted into a mass of debris, it choked the passage and blotted out the air and light.

"The contractor assures the public that the shaft itself was not damaged."

J. B. Culp laughed. "No one will believe that."

"That they had to print the lie," Branco agreed, "tells us they are in terror."

"Asked whether the explosion confirmed speculation about Black Hand letters threatening to attack the water system, the contractor answered vehemently, 'No. This is the Catskill Water Supply, not some poor devil's pushcart.'

"The Mayor concurred, saying, 'The Water Supply Board Police have investigated thoroughly and find absolutely not one shred of evidence to support such speculation. It was an accident, pure and simple, a terrible accident, and the faster it is cleaned up and order restored, the sooner the city will receive fresh water from the Catskills.'

"Asked to comment on talk of a strike by terrorized Italian laborers fearing another Black Hand attack, the contractor said, 'They are paid well and treated well and have no intention of striking.'

"Tunnel work will continue as soon as

the ruins are lifted out by means of horses and a windlass. Besides three Americans killed, there were among the dead numerous Italians and Negroes."

"What were Negroes doing down in the tunnel?" asked Culp.

"Best rock drillers in the business. And the contractor keeps some around in case Italians get any ideas of striking for higher wages."

"What about this strike they're talking about? Labor striking would make the city look like they lost control of the job. Will they strike?"

"They'll strike when I tell them to strike," said Antonio Branco.

"What are you waiting for?"

"Would President Roosevelt come here to make a speech if they were on strike?"

"Good question," Culp conceded. "He might take a strike as a challenge . . . No, he's too damnedly unpredictable."

"That reminds me," said Branco. "Can you pull wires to have the Italian Consul General invited to the ceremony?"

"Of course. I can't promise you he'll accept."

"He'll accept. He's got his hands full with immigration complaints. He will make friends anywhere he can. And to be invited to hear the President's speech will be an honor for all Italians."

Signora Marion Morgan
The Fiancée of Isaac Bell
Knickerbocker Hotel

Why you no believe us? Catskill Aqueduct bomb could have been prevented.
City no protect aqueduct. Water Supply Board helpless.
Black Hand stands by you. Together we stop tragedy.
Pay.
Or.
Next attack break hearts.

"This is beginning to annoy me," said Marion Morgan.

She was feeling prison crazy, locked up in the Knickerbocker. Helen Mills was fine company, but she missed her job, the outdoors, the city streets, and, most of all, Isaac, who was working round the clock at Storm King. He had his detectives covering every base, but no matter how he tried, he could not find Antonio Branco.

"What do you want to do about them?" asked Helen.

426

"I wonder if Grady Forrer can help Isaac find how Branco gets in and out of Raven's Eyrie."

The women marched to the back of the Van Dorn offices, into the shabby rooms that housed Grady Forrer's Research section. Scholars looked up from heaped desks. Researchers poked heads from crammed library stacks. Interviewers whispered, "I'll call you back," and hastily cradled their telephones.

"Welcome, ladies," boomed Forrer, adding, sotto voce, over his shoulder, "Back to work, gents. I'll take care of this."

"Thank you, Grady," said Marion Morgan. "But, in fact, we're going to need *everyone* who has a few free moments to lend a hand."

"What do you need?"

"The architects' plans for Raven's Eyrie."

Twelve hours later, a deflated Grady Forrer apologized.

"The problem is the estate has been under almost continuous reconstruction for nearly a hundred years, starting shortly after Robert Fulton invented the steamboat and the first Culp destroyed his rivals in river commerce. The builders of J.B.'s New York mansion would have filed plans with various city

427

departments, but apparently that was not the practice in the wilds of the Hudson Valley, at least in the face of bred-in-the-bone Culp hatred of government interference."

Six hours later, when Grady had collapsed face-first on a cot and most of his young assistants had stumbled home, Marion suddenly whispered, "I'll be darned."

"What?" asked Helen.

Marion looked up from a folder of ancient yellowed newspapers. "Grandfather Culp had an affair with a Quaker woman from Poughkeepsie."

"They printed that in the newspaper?"

"Well, they don't come out and say it, but it's pretty clear reading between the lines . . ." She checked the date on the top of the page. "This didn't come out until after the Civil War. Raven's Eyrie was a 'station' on the Underground Railroad."

"The Culp's were *Abolitionists*? That doesn't sound like the Culp we know and love."

"Her name was Julia Reidhead. She was a member of the American Anti-Slavery Society. But according to this, the Hudson Valley was not Abolitionist. They still kept slaves into the early nineteenth century. Only a few Quaker strongholds were against slavery."

"Grandpa Culp must have been a brave man to be a station master."

"It doesn't quite say that. According to this, Julia Reidhead talked him into building a secret entrance through the wall so they could help runaway slaves on their way to Canada. Sounds to me like he did it for love."

"Was she J. B. Culp's grandmother?" Helen asked.

"No. She ended up marrying a missionary. They served in India."

Helen read the story over Marion's shoulder. "I hadn't realized the wall was that old."

"First thing they built. It seems the Culps have never liked other people."

Antonio Branco walked into J. B. Culp's trophy room and calmly announced, "The Italian Squad just arrested my assassin."

"*What?* Can you bail him out?"

"The Carabinieri confirmed he's an anarchist. He will stay locked up until your government deports him."

"How could they confirm it so fast?"

"The Italian Consul General keeps a Carabinieri officer on his staff for just such occasions," Branco answered drily.

"What a mess! . . . Wait a minute. How did the police know he was yours?"

"They don't. He was one of many caught in Petrosino's dragnet."

"Bloody Isaac Bell put Petrosino up to it."

"Of course he did," said Branco. "I would be surprised if he hadn't. Thanks to Bell, there isn't an Italian radical who isn't behind bars or in hiding this morning."

"We're running out of time. Roosevelt's going to be here in two days."

Branco tugged his watch chain. "Two days and six hours."

"Well, dammit, you'll just have to give the job to your 'gorillas.' "

"No."

"Why not? They're killers, aren't they? All your talk about 'un-plaguing' me. Strike-breaking, getting rid of reformers, making enemies disappear?"

"Gorillas are not the tool for this job."

"Why not?"

"They would bungle it."

"Then you'll have to kill him yourself."

Branco shrugged his broad shoulders as if monumentally unconcerned. "I suspected it would come to this."

Culp shook his head in disgust. "You sound mighty cool about it. How will you do it?"

"I've planned for it."

"You'll only get one chance. If you muddle

it, you'll force Roosevelt to hide, and we'll never get a second shot at him."

"I planned for it."

"Do you mean you planned to pull the trigger all along?"

"I never planned to pull a trigger" was Branco's enigmatic reply, and Culp knew him well enough by now to know he had heard all that Branco would spill on the subject. Instead, he said, "Did you get the Italian Consul General invited to the President's speech?"

Culp nodded. "Why do you want him there?"

"He will provide a distraction."

"You don't know yet how you're going to do the job."

"I have ideas," said Branco.

Marion Morgan and Helen Mills' report on the Underground Railroad entrance to Raven's Eyrie emphasized the strong pro-slavery sentiments in the pre–Civil War Hudson Valley. So while the Black Hand Squad watched gates and boat landings, and undercover operatives kept an eye on the siphon tunnel, Isaac Bell and Archie Abbott climbed down from the top of Storm King Mountain. In theory, the Abolitionists' passage for fugitive slaves would have been more safely hidden in the uphill side of the estate wall rather than in view of the busy river.

Slipping and sliding on a thin coat of ice-crusted snow, the Van Dorns descended within yards of the wall, then scrambled alongside, just above it, clinging from tree to tree on the steep wooded slope. Culp's estate workers had kept a mown path clear of brush, but the stones were laced with ancient vines of grape and bittersweet that in summertime would have blocked any hope of spotting a break in the eighty-year-old masonry. Now that the leaves had fallen, they had a marginal chance of spotting a long-abandoned opening put back in use by Antonio Branco.

"Cunningly *concealed*," Archie noted. "Seeing as how the neighbors would have loved to turn in Grandpa and his Quaker. Not to mention collecting the bounty on the poor slaves."

Isaac Bell was optimistic. "Nice thing about a wall — if we can't see in, they can't see us poking around outside." He was right. The two-mile wall lacked the regularly spaced turrets of a true fortress. And while the main gatehouse overlooked some of the front section — and the service entrance tower and some of the south side — neither was close enough to observe the back side.

"Are you forgetting that Mr. Van Dorn said don't set foot on Culp's estate?"

"As I recall," said Bell, less worried about getting fired and more about the President being murdered, "Mr. Van Dorn said, in effect, no Van Dorn detective is to scale the Raven's Eyrie wall again without his express permission. He didn't say I couldn't go through it. Or under it. Or lay a trap inside it to ambush Branco."

"We've still got to find it."

"We have two days," said Bell.

But his optimism proved futile. They probed the full half mile of the uphill wall before darkness closed in but found nothing. "The Culps could have cemented it shut after the Civil War," said Archie. "Or maybe the ladies turned up another quaint old Hudson Valley legend."

40

In Wallabout Basin, across the East River from Manhattan, battleship USS *Connecticut* raised steam for a maiden voyage unique in the history of the Brooklyn Navy Yard.

Shipbuilders and sailors swarmed over her guns, searchlights, superstructure, and decks, harassed by frantic officers exhorting them to paint, polish, and holystone faster. Put in commission only two months ago, and scheduled to head south for her shakedown cruise, *Connecticut* suddenly had new orders: Convey the Commander-in-Chief forty-five miles up the Hudson River.

To the great relief of her officers, icebreakers were clearing the channel only as far as West Point. So many things could go wrong on a brand-new ship that the sooner the Navy men landed President Roosevelt at the Military Academy pier, the fewer chances of a humiliating disaster. With luck, she would steam back to Brooklyn deemed worthier than her archrival USS *Louisiana* to be flagship of an American cruise around the world — while TR toured the Catskill Aqueduct by train and auto, shaking a thousand hands.

The south wall of Raven's Eyrie, which was closest to the main mansion, was divided midway by the service gate tower, which overlooked long sections in both directions. The Van Dorns who peered through a spy hole in the hogshead barrel had reported seeing no gatekeeper watching at night. But Bell was taking no chances. He and Archie Abbott made a thorough search of the sections in sight of the tower before dawn. They pressed farther along the wall in daylight but found no hidden passage and no indication that one had ever existed.

The Raven's Eyrie north wall was almost as remote as the hillside wall the Van Dorns had first searched, though here and there they could glimpse the rooftops and chimneys of a neighboring estate house. Someone watching with good field glasses might notice two men creeping through the trees along Culp's wall. But it seemed unlikely they would pick up the telephone to warn Culp when he and Archie could easily be stone masons making repairs or the estate foresters clearing brush. They traversed the full half mile of wall and again saw no relic of the Underground Railroad. All that remained unobserved was the long wall that faced the river, but they had lost the light.

Bell told Archie Abbott, "I'm worried he'll use a sniper. You're the only outdoorsman on the squad. The rest are city boys. Mark off a five-hundred-yard perimeter of the road to the siphon shaft and search every possible sniper hide. I'll take the ice yacht tomorrow."

"We will plan my escape," said Antonio Branco.

"Miles ahead of you," said Culp. "My train will have steam up and be designated a special on the Delaware & Hudson's main line to Albany. North of Albany, I'll have the tracks cleared straight across the Canadian border and through Lacolle."

"Are you sure the tracks will be cleared?"

Puzzlement creased Culp's face. Who could impede his private train? As if to a child, he explained, "The Delaware & Hudson Railroad *to* Canada owns the Napier Junction Railroad *in* Canada."

"Yes, but how can you be sure about the Delaware & Hudson?"

436

"I own the Delaware & Hudson."

"Will Customs board your train at the border?"

"My man at Lacolle handles Customs."

Branco nodded. "What is my other option?"

"With no radiator to freeze, my air-cooled Franklin is a superior winter auto. The chauffeur repaired her. I had trunks added for tools and food. And extra tanks of gasoline and oil. She's ready to roll."

"What is my third option?"

Culp was getting fed up with Branco grilling him. "Won't a train or an auto be enough?"

"I can't count on your train. What if the Van Dorns watch your train? I can't count on your auto. What if they watch your auto? So if your train and your Franklin become stalking horses to fool the detectives, what is my third option?"

Culp wondered what option Brewster Claypool would have come up with. Then realized that if Claypool were still around, he would be in way over his head. A wintery grin took hold of Culp's face, an expression that combined cold calculation, deep satisfaction, and deeper pride.

"Your third option is a beaut."

■ ■ ■ ■

Starting at dawn, Isaac Bell pinned his last hope of finding Branco's secret way in and out of Raven's Eyrie on the river side of the estate, having found nothing in back or at either end. All he had left to search was the wall that angled up from the boat landing, but the weather was not making it easy.

Squalls rampaged up from the narrows of West Point and down from the mountains. They were tight little storms, with several often in sight. The temperature plummeted moments before one struck, and visibility dropped from many miles to mere feet, warning Isaac Bell to hold on tight. Hard knots of wind-whipped snow banged his sail, threatening to stand the ice yacht up on one runner and dump him out of the car.

The latest squall raced off as suddenly as it hit. The morning sun glared on the snow-dusted hills.

Bell juggled the tiller and field glasses, keeping one eye on an enormous lateen-rigged Poughkeepsie Club boat tearing after him and the other probing the fir trees that spread from inside the wall up the slope toward the gigantic barnlike building that housed Culp's gymnasium. A thinner group of firs and leafless hardwoods speckled the slope outside the wall.

He cut upwind of the Poughkeepsie boat, challenging it to a race, which gave him cover for a closer look. He noticed a clump of rocks in the woods and swept them with the glasses. Intrigued, he nudged the tiller to steer too close to the wind. The sails shivered. The ice yacht slowed. The Poughkeepsie boat pulled ahead.

It was hard to tell through the trees, but the rocks appeared to be close to the wall almost as if the wall had been built on top of them. Bell glanced about. As luck would have it, a squall was dancing down the mountain. He waited for it to envelop Culp's mansion and outbuildings, and when they were curtained by the swirling snow, he steered for the shore.

Isaac Bell ran the ice yacht off the river, crunched the bowsprit into the frozen bank, threw a line around a driftwood log, and jumped off. The wall was set back a hundred yards from the shoreline. When he ran toward it, he discovered that the trees had obscured a rough road that looped down toward the town of Cornwall Landing. It had been traveled recently. Hoofprints, manure, and wagon tracks in the frozen snow.

Bell spotted a line of footprints. Boot marks came and went from the direction of the rock formation he had seen from the boat, blended with the wagon tracks, and disappeared. Two men, maybe three. He knelt down and looked more closely. *One* man. All the tracks had been imprinted by the same soles. One man walking from the wall and back again repeatedly. Here and there, they were deeper, as if he had carried a heavy load on one of the trips from the wall.

Wind shrieked suddenly.

The squall that had enveloped Culp's buildings had continued down the mountainside and struck like a runaway freight. Snow and sleet clattered through the trees. Blinding bursts of it filled in the footprints and covered the wagon tracks. Bell moved quickly beside the fading footmarks and traced them through the trees to the wall. It rested, as he had glimpsed earlier, on a rock outcropping.

A branch broke from a tree with a loud crack. The heavy widow-maker scythed down through the snow and crashed to the ground beside him. More cracking noises sent him diving for cover under an overhang in the rocks. Broken branches rained down on the space Bell had vacated. Moments later, the squall raced away, the wind abated, and the sun filtered down through the tree-tops.

Bell peered among the dark stones that had sheltered him. He lit a match. The orange flame penetrated the dark, and Bell saw that the overhang was the mouth of a cave. He opened his jacket to free up his pistol and crawled inside.

41

Isaac Bell's second match revealed a masonry ceiling that arched over a narrow passageway. He moved in deeper, and before he needed to strike a third, daylight illuminated an opening. He emerged to find himself among the hemlocks inside J. B. Culp's wall. A mere dusting of snow had penetrated the trees, and the footsteps were easy to trace up the slope.

The trees began to thin out. Lawns, lightly snow-covered, spread ahead and to the left for two hundred yards up to the pillared main mansion. The trees continued thinning to the right, toward the immense, barnlike building that housed the gymnasium. Bell saw the tracks veer toward it. Employing what little cover the remaining trees provided, he moved up the hill until he reached the ground floor side entrance to the servants' quarters, where the boxers Lee and Barry had lived when he was here last.

He tried the door. The knob turned freely.

Two narrow beds were draped with muslin dust cloths. The steam radiator was shut off, and it felt almost as cold inside the room as outdoors. A rank odor hung in the air. The scent puzzled Bell. It was not quite a gymnasium locker room aroma. Sharper than the stale stink of sweating boxers, it smelled more like a kennel than a locker room, but even ranker than a kennel. A decomposing body? he wondered fleetingly. But there was no body in the room. And, besides, it reeked of life, not death.

A recollection of something totally different flashed through his mind. It was so odd that he wondered was it a lingering effect of his long asphyxiation sleep. He did not smell shoe polish, but for some reason he suddenly had a vivid memory of blacking his hair to masquerade as a Hebrew needlework contractor in Little Italy.

Footsteps sounded directly overhead.

Out the interior door in an instant, Bell found stairs and vaulted up them silently.

He drew his pistol, held it at his side, muzzle pointed at the floor, and stepped through an open door. Another empty room, but considerably larger and more finely appointed, with a fur coverlet on an enormous bed, an easy chair, a carved writing desk, and a matching case full of books. A fire burned low in the hearth. A black kettle hung in the corner of the fireplace, and a pot for brewing coffee stood beside silver cream and sugar service. Pot, pitcher, and bowl were almost empty. If this was where Culp housed Antonio Branco, out of sight of the servants in the main house and near the Underground Railroad passage, the gangster had been here within the hour.

"Oh!"

A middle-aged housemaid had just stepped from the bathroom with an armload of towels. "You gave me a fright."

Bell holstered his weapon as she squinted nearsightedly across the room. "It's Mr. Bell, isn't it? I'm Rachel. You stayed at the main house when Mrs. Culp was still here."

"Who stayed in this room?"

"I have no idea, sir. They just sent me down this morning to clean up. Most everyone's gone to New York City."

"When did the man staying here leave?"

"I guess this morning. The fire's still burning."

"Where could I find Mr. Culp?"

"I don't know, sir . . . I've got to get back to the house. Is there anything else you need, sir?"

"Wait one moment, please. What is that

444

smell?" He smelled it here, too, but fainter.

Still holding the towels, she sniffed the air. "What smell? The coffee?"

"No. Something else. Like a zoo."

"There's a zoo next door."

"A zoo?"

"A dead zoo. Where he keeps the creatures he shoots."

"The trophy room?"

"Lions, tigers, and bears. Maybe you smell a new one, just stuffed."

She pointed Bell down the hall and rushed off.

Bell hurried past a secretarial cubby hole, which was equipped with a typewriter, telephone, and telegraph key. A fortress door blocked the end of the hall, studded with hand-forged nailheads and secured high and low by iron bolts. Bell slid them open and pulled the door toward him. It swung heavily on concealed hinges, and the tall detective walked under an arch of elephant tusks into a two-story, windowless room lighted brightly by electricity.

Culp's big game kills were preserved, stuffed, and mounted as if they were alive.

Lions roamed the floor. Panthers crouched on tree limbs and boulders. An elephant charged, ears spread wide, trunk upraised. Horned heads loomed from three walls. A taxidermied grizzly bear reared.

Suits of armor gleamed on either side of Culp's desk. Arrayed behind it were express rifles and sidearms, bird guns, daggers, cutlasses, and swords. Bell spotted an empty space where a pistol was missing, and another, longer telltale space in a section of rifles with telescope sights. He sniffed the air but smelled no odor of the zoo, only leather, gun oil, and cigars.

When suddenly he felt a presence, he glided behind a panther and drew his pistol.

"Bell," called J. B. Culp. "You keep turning up like a bad penny."

The magnate was in the hall, one hand on the nailheaded door. In the other, he held a revolver. Bell recognized the highly accurate Colt Bisley Target Model by its flat top strap.

He braced his own gun barrel between the big cat's ears. "Drop the gun and raise your hands."

Culp turned sideways like a duelist and took deliberate aim.

Isaac Bell fired one shot at the only man who could tell him how Branco would attack the President. He hit the gun squarely. The Bisley glittered in the lights as it spun through the air. J. B. Culp clutched his hand

and bellowed in pain.

Bell bounded toward him, commanding, *"Elevate!"*

Culp slammed the door in Bell's face and drove the bolts home.

Bell raced the length of the room, weaving through the trophies. The only other door he had seen was in an alcove. It was smaller than the fortress door and was secured by a single bolt. He slid the bolt open. But the door was still locked, bolted like the fortress door, from outside as well. He threw his shoulder against it. It stood firm as masonry.

He ran to the telephone on the rosewood desk to call the Van Dorn detective who was tapping the line. It rang before he reached it. He picked it up and said, "Stop this while you still can, Culp."

"Sit tight," said Culp. "I'll send the Sheriff when he's done guarding the President's speech and he'll arrest you for trespassing again, stealing my 1903 Springfield rifle, and for shooting me when I caught you sneaking in to steal another."

"Antonio Branco will squeal on you the second he's arrested."

"He won't be arrested," said Culp.

"The Van Dorn Agency won't give up until he is. Never."

"He won't be arrested," Culp repeated.

"Guaranteed."

The line went dead.

Bell's eyes roamed the trophy room for a way out and fixed on the wall of weapons.

The suits of armor caught his eye.

One of them held a long jousting lance and it gave him an idea. He went back to the alcove door and inspected it closely. It was made of oak. A cold draft under it indicated it opened to the outside. All the better. He rapped it with his fist. Layers of oak, laminated crosswise to give the wood the strength of iron.

The alcove, like the main entry, was framed by eight-foot elephant tusks.

Bell took a broadsword from a suit of armor, chopped the brackets that held the bigger tusk, crouched down, and heaved the ivory onto his shoulder. It felt like it weighed a hundred and fifty pounds. He carried it across the trophy room, staggering around the taxidermied animals, and leaned it on the grizzly bear. He walked back, shoving stuffed lions and antelope and a warthog out of his way to clear a path. He used the broadsword to score a large X in the middle of the door.

Heading back to the grizzly, he kicked the zebra rugs out of the way.

He tipped the tusk toward the horizontal, clamped both hands under the massive weight, and held it tight to his side with the heavier root end aimed ahead. He filled his lungs with a deep breath and started across the trophy room, walking at first, then picking up speed.

He neared the door and fixed his eyes on the X.

He broke into a run.

Isaac Bell tore through the alcove and rammed one hundred fifty pounds of ivory into the oak. It struck with a thunderous impact that smashed the door two inches out of its jamb. Cold air poured in the sliver of space he had opened. Bell threw his shoulder against it, but it wouldn't budge. He dragged the tusk back across the trophy room, picked it up, and charged again.

The fourth try was the charm. The tusk blasted the door entirely out of its jamb and over the railing of a narrow balcony.

Bell dropped the tusk and clapped a hand on the railing to vault off the balcony. There he hesitated, thinking hard on what Francesca Kennedy had told him about Antonio Branco's modus operandi. *To get close to kill, you have to plan. Study the situation. Then make a plan.*

Instead of jumping to the ground, Isaac Bell hurried back indoors.

Ten minutes later, he jumped from the balcony and raced through the hemlocks to the Underground Railroad cave. Outside the wall, he ran to the riverbank, kicked his runners loose from the grip of the ice, shoved the yacht around, and caught the wind.

There was not a squall in sight on the frozen river. The sky was a hard-edged blue, the visibility sharp, perfect for a sniper.

42

A nameless, faceless Italian dug a hole in the ground.

The Irish foreman patrolling the edge of the ditch stopped and stared. The laborer was older than most. He still had a thick head of hair, but it was grayer than his mustache. He was shoveling fast enough, but the orders today were to report on anything off-base . . . what, with the President coming.

"Who you?"

The Italian kept shoveling.

"Old guinea! Who you?"

An immigrant who knew a little English nudged the new man and said in Italian, "Give him your number."

Eyes cast down, Antonio Branco handed over his pay token.

The foreman read the numeral stamped in the brass. "O.K. Get back to work!"

A thousand feet under the river, Wally Kisley prowled the pressure tunnel looking for where in the high-ceilinged passage hewn through granite he would hide a lethal charge if he were an anarchist or a criminal. The circular roof and sides were remarkably clean and smooth, there being no need to timber the strong rock. But the muck car rails on the floor provided numerous indentations that would hide a stick of dynamite. The contractor's men had searched hourly, accompanied by a Secret Service operative, but Kisley had been hunting clues of sabotage since they were in short pants and trusted only his own experience. He inspected what remained of the face — the last barrier of natural rock between the western and eastern halves of the boring — where the final charges had been set, awaiting only the ceremonial pressing of an electric detonator by the President.

He knelt suddenly, switched on his flashlight, and froze.

The dynamite was virtually invisible, the stick having been inserted in a hole drilled in a wooden crosstie. The blasting cap, too, was neatly camouflaged and looked like a knot in the chestnut. The trigger was the giveaway. It had been fashioned to look like the head of one of the railroad spikes that

452

held the track to the crosstie. But whereas the heads of the other spikes nearby were shiny, having been only recently pounded into the wood with a steel maul, the one that had caught his eye was rusty.

Down on all fours, resting his cheek on the splintery tie inches from the spike, Kisley saw a space under the head. There was no nail, merely a detached head waiting to be driven into the blasting cap by the weight of the first person who stepped on it. The result would be simple physics. TNT was so stable you could run it over with a wagon and nothing would happen, but a blasting cap would go off if you looked at it cross-eyed. Jarred by the spike-head trigger, the cap would explode with the force to detonate the dynamite.

Kisley laid out his pocket tools to disarm the booby trap. He thought it was a miracle that no one had stumbled on it already.

Archie Abbott marked four possible sniper hides in the wooded slopes around the siphon shaft house, and Isaac Bell dispatched a man with a shotgun to cover each. Another man was guarding the roof of a redbrick warehouse that overlooked the road.

Abbott followed a hunch he had had all

453

morning about an empty summer boarding-house. It was a full seven hundred yards from the raised platform where the President would speak — an extremely long shot — but Abbott had had a feeling every time he caught the white clapboard building in the corner of his eye.

The house was as deserted inside as it looked from the outside, with dust cloths thrown over furniture and curtains folded in closets, but he prowled room by room, just to be sure, and even climbed into the attic to look for loopholes. He was making one last pass through the second floor when he noticed a table in a window. It seemed an odd place to put a table. Unless it was a rifle rest.

He found the rifle in the closet.

Eddie Edwards watched J. B. Culp's train crew coal and water the tender. The locomotive had steam up. The cook received deliveries from a butcher wagon and a bakery.

"He's ready to go somewhere," he reported to Isaac Bell. "I've got fellows at the Delaware & Hudson and the New York Central checking whether Culp's ordered clearance for a special. But I can't count on them since Culp owns most of the lines around here."

Bell asked, "Is Culp's auto still in his garage?"

Edwards nodded. "Harry's got little Richie up a tree with field glasses."

USS *Connecticut*'s great white hull turned majestically in midstream, hauled around by tugs at her bow and stern, and before she followed her icebreaker back down the Hudson River, the battleship bid the President godspeed with a twenty-one-gun salute. The final retort was still reverberating from the hilltops when a grinning Theodore Roosevelt jumped from the 20-foot gasoline dory that had sped him ashore.

As if propelled through the air by the warship's thunder, thought Joseph Van Dorn.

Roosevelt landed nimbly on the Military Academy pier. He shook hands with the commandant. He waved to the citizens crowding the ferry wharf and the West Shore Railroad Station. He saluted the ramparts of the stone fort on the bluff, which were gray with cadets in their full-dress coats. Then, surprising no one, especially Van Dorn, he gave a speech.

He thanked the Army grandly for its welcome, the citizens of West Point for turning out to greet him in such a bitter cold, and the United States Navy for its "hearty salute, which reminds all Americans gathered here that we look forward to the day when disputes between nations are settled by arbitration, but, until then, *Connecticut*'s mighty twelves will do our arbitrating for us."

It fell to the chief of the President's Secret Service corps to spoil the mood with an abrupt change of plans. "We will not board the train — with your permission, Mr. President — but embark directly from here in the White Steamer."

"Why? Storm King expects me on the train, not in an auto."

"That is precisely why, sir. To confuse any enemy counting on you to arrive as scheduled at the station. The drive is only five miles and the road isn't bad."

"Whose idea was this?"

"It was Joseph Van Dorn's idea."

"I should have guessed."

"When I told him that you might not be one hundred percent pleased, he said that a war hero like yourself would recall the power of surprise."

"I am in the hands of the professionals," President Roosevelt intoned, but a dangerous glint in his eye informed the chief of his protection corps not to take any more liberties.

Joseph Van Dorn waited beside the big White Steamer, wearing a slouch hat, a polka-dot bandanna, and wire-framed spectacles. He held the automobile door for the President and said, "I would appreciate it if we would raise the top."

Roosevelt looked him over sharply.

"What happened to your face?"

"I shaved my sideburns."

"What are you up to, Joe? You don't wear specs, but you're wearing specs — without glass in them. And what's that hat doing on your head? You weren't a Rough Rider; you were a United States Marine."

"Confusing the enemy," said Van Dorn.

"Has it occurred to you that if you confuse them too successfully, you'll be the one shot?"

Van Dorn answered with a straight face. "The voters spoke loud and clear, Mr. President. Not one of them voted for me."

"The top stays down."

Van Dorn said, "Would you read this wire from Detective Bell?"

LOST BRANCO
CULP'S 1903 SPRINGFIELD GONE

"The 1903 Springfield is —"

"A deadly sniper rifle," the President completed Van Dorn's warning. "O.K. You win! Raise the top."

Van Dorn and the chief quickly unfolded the canvas and locked its framework. The chief got behind the wheel. Van Dorn climbed in next to him.

"That make you happy?" the President called from the backseat. "You don't look happy. Now what's wrong?"

"If you'd agreed earlier, you would have saved my whiskers."

Roosevelt poked the canvas with his finger. "This top is going right back down at Storm King."

"Leave your shovels," the Irish foreman bellowed at the pick and shovel gang grading a drainage ditch. "All a youse." He pointed at the road to the shaft house. "Get up there with the rest of 'em."

A thousand Italian laborers already lined the road, six deep on either side, a festive crowd celebrating the unheard-of luxury of paid time off. The contractor had handed out bread and sausages. Wine bottles hidden under coats washed it down. Accordions wheezed, drowned out by an organ grinder's jaunty tunes that carried in the clear, cold air like a miniature steam calliope. Rumors flew that the great Caruso would appear with the beauteous Tetrazzini. Best of all, the President of the United States — *Il Presidente* himself — the famous Spanish-American War hero Colonel TR — was coming all the way to Storm King to thank them for digging a "bully" aqueduct.

"Get up there! He's on his way."

They scrambled out of the ditch and raced to the road. Head still bowed, hat brim shadowing his face, eyes fixed on his boots, and slouching to disguise his height, Antonio Branco struggled to keep up, limping like an old man.

The foreman urged them into line, then swaggered into the road and cupped his hands to his mouth.

"Listen, all a youse," he bawled, beckoning the young laborer he used to translate orders on the job. "Tell 'em, when the President comes by, take off your hats and cheer real loud."

The translator rendered the order into Italian.

"If, God forbid, the President was to take it in his head to stop and talk to you, hold your hat over your heart and nod your head and give him a big smile."

The translator repeated that.

459

"When he speechifies, tell 'em watch me. When I clap, they clap hands like it's an Eye-talian opera."

The Irishman pantomimed applause.

"And the second after the President goes down the shaft, I want to see a stampede of guineas running back to work."

Antonio Branco wedged his way toward the front of the crowd on a path surreptitiously cleared by Black Hand gorillas. They were dressed convincingly as laborers, but the legitimate pick and shovel men instinctively steered clear of them. Branco stationed himself in the second row, where the crowd was thickest, just behind the organ grinder.

The organ grinder reached inside the instrument and shifted the barrel sideways to change the tune. Then he resumed turning the crank that made the barrel move the keys and the bellows blow air in the pipes. His monkey, costumed for the occasion like a Roosevelt Rough Rider in a polka-dot bandanna and blue shirt, went back to work catching pennies in a miniature slouch hat.

The immigrants lining the road exchanged puzzled looks. Instead of the familiar romantic strains of "Celeste Aida" or a rollicking tarantella, the street organ piped out a lively American march.

Only laborers who had been in America long enough to have worked digging the New York Interborough Rapid Transit subway back in '04, recognized a Republican campaign song bellowed by Roosevelt voters.

"Il Presidente!" they explained to later arrivals. *"Il Presidente canto."*

The translator shouted the title of the song.

" 'You're all right, Teddy!' "

43

Isaac Bell strode up and down the road leading to the siphon tunnel shaft.

They had built a reviewing stand near the shaft house and hung it with bunting that flapped cheerfully in the bitter wind. The stand was packed with contractors and city officials in overcoats and top hats. Luisa Tetrazzini and Enrico Caruso huddled there, both barely visible wrapped in woolen mufflers. Italy's elegant white-haired Consul General for New York City sat between the opera stars, beaming like he had won the Lottery.

Wally Kisley hurried after Bell to report on the booby trap he had defused. He thought that the hard-driving young detective looked as if he were hoping he could somehow search out the intentions in every one of the thousand faces before the President arrived.

"Isaac!"

Bell cut Kisley off before he could say another word.

"Look inside that street organ. It's big enough to hold a bomb, and the auto's going to pass right in front of it."

"On my way . . . Then I got to talk to you."

"Take Harry Warren to talk Italian to the organ grinder. If the old guy's scared we're stealing his livelihood, it'll start a riot."

Warren engaged the organ grinder in conversation and finally persuaded him to stop cranking for a moment. Kisley looked it over, inside and out. He felt under it and leaned down to inspect the leg that propped up the heavy instrument. When he was satisfied, he nodded his O.K. and stuffed a dollar into the monkey's hat. Then he hurried back to Bell and paced alongside him while he described the booby trap in the pressure tunnel.

"How'd you spot it?" Bell's eyes were flickering like metronomes.

"I'd seen it before . . . But here's the funny thing, Isaac. It was sloppy work."

Bell looked at him, sharply. "What do you mean?"

"It could have gone off at any moment. Before the President even got down in the tunnel."

"But you told me they were masters of

463

dynamite."

"Either these ones weren't or they got lazy."

"Or," said Bell, "they're blowing smoke to lull us. Archie found a Springfield rifle in a sniper hide."

"Just sitting there?" asked Kisley.

"In a closet."

"I don't mean to take away from Archie's investigative talents, but that sounds a little too easy."

"Archie thought so, too. He didn't believe the rifle. You don't believe the booby trap. I don't believe either. So far all we see is what Branco wants us to see."

Walter Kisley said, "So what does he *not* want us to see?"

"I still say he's going to do it in close. But I still don't know how."

"And here comes Teddy."

Isaac Bell had already spotted the White Steamer creeping through the throng. The auto was wide open, its top down, with President Roosevelt clearly visible in the backseat. The chief of his Secret Service corps was driving. Joe Van Dorn was up front with him, riding shotgun.

Bell broke into a long-legged stride.

■ ■ ■

"Slow down," ordered the President. "They've been standing hours in the cold waiting to see me. Let them see me."

The chief exchanged wary glances with Van Dorn.

"Slower, I say!"

The chief shifted the speed lever to low. The White slacked to a walking pace.

Van Dorn loosened the firearm in his shoulder holster for the fourth time since they arrived at Cornwall Landing and the President ordered the top lowered. The only good news — other than knowing he had his top detectives in the case — was the height of the Steamer. The auto rode as high off the ground as a stage coach, which meant that criminals and anarchists intending to jump into the open auto had some climbing to do. Otherwise, the attacker held every advantage: surprise; a mob of people to spring from and melt back into; the automobile's glacial pace; and the victim's open heart.

The President was grinning from ear to ear. The car rolled slowly between applauding rows of engineers and contractors' clerks and machine operators, who poured into the road behind the automobile and followed in the parade the President had demanded. Next were Negro rock drillers, cheering mightily.

"Honk the horn for them, Joe!" TR shouted. "The Spaniards called our colored regiments 'Smoked Yankees,' but the Rough Riders found them to be an excellent breed of Yankees covering our flanks."

Van Dorn stomped on the rubber bulb and the White let loose a gay *Auuuugha!*

The rock drillers peeled out of their rows and joined the march.

Ahead waited legions of mustachioed, swarthy Italian laborers in brimmed hats. They were quiet, lining the road six deep on either side. But they smiled like they meant it, and Van Dorn had the funny thought that by the time the celebrity President got through with them, he'd convert them all to the Republican Party.

When Roosevelt heard their street organ, his grin doubled and redoubled.

"Do you recognize the tune that organ grinder's playing?"

" 'You're all right, Teddy!' " chorused Van Dorn and the Secret Service chief.

"Bully!" shouted the President. His fist beat the time on his knee and he broke into song.

" 'Oh! You are all right, Teddy!

You're the kind that we remember;
Don't you worry!
We are with you!
You are all right, Teddy!
And we'll prove it in November.'

"Stop the auto! I'm going to thank these people personally."

44

The President jumped down from the White Steamer before it stopped rolling.

Van Dorn and the corps chief flanked him instantly. Too excited to wait to join the end of the parade, the crowd surged at them from both sides.

"Did you see what that monkey's wearing?"

Van Dorn was trying to look in every direction at once. "What was that, sir?"

"The monkey's hat!" said Roosevelt. "He's wearing a Rough Rider's hat . . . Chief! Fetch that Consul General."

"I can't leave your side, sir."

"Hop to it, man. I need a translator."

Suddenly, Isaac Bell was there, saying, "I'll cover."

"Of course," whispered Antonio Branco when Isaac Bell materialized in the space vacated by the Secret Service bodyguard.

"Where else would you be?"

Then the crowd pushing forward blocked his view of the President. At the same time, it blocked Bell's view of the elderly Sicilian groom cranking the street organ. With every eye fixed on President Roosevelt, it was all the cover Branco needed. He slipped in front of the old man and took the crank in his right hand and the monkey's chain in his left. Not a note of music was lost, and a gentle tug of the chain made the animal jump on his shoulder, having learned in just a few days that its kindly new master would reward it with a segment of an orange.

"Step back, both of you," ordered the President.

"Mr. President, for your safety —"

"You're too tall. You make me look like a coward. These are hardworking men. They won't hurt me."

Roosevelt grasped hands with the nearest laborer. "Hello there. Thank you for building the aqueduct."

The laborer whipped off his hat, pressed it to his heart, and smiled.

"I know you don't understand a word I just said, but you will when you learn English." He pumped his hand harder. "The point is, building this aqueduct with the

469

sweat of your brow will benefit all of us."

Roosevelt grabbed the next man's hand. "Hello there. Thank you. You're doing a bully job."

"Bully!" echoed the laborer. *"Bully! Bully! Bully!"* And Isaac Bell saw that if Roosevelt hadn't been sure of his welcome, he was now. Beaming like a locomotive headlamp, he grabbed more hands. They were almost to the organ grinder.

"Where the devil's that translator?"

"I see him coming," said Bell.

The chief of the Secret Service protection corps was gripping Italy's Consul General for New York City like a satchel. Both were gasping for breath from their hard run.

"Mr. President, it is a great honor —"

"I want you to translate to the organ grinder that I am deeply touched that he played my campaign song and dressed his monkey in a Rough Rider hat. That takes the kind of clear-eyed gumption that makes a top-notch American . . . Boys," he shot over his shoulder at Isaac Bell and Van Dorn. "I told you to stand back. You, too, chief. Give these Eye-talians a chance to enjoy themselves."

He threw an arm around the Consul General and plowed ahead. "Tell him I had a monkey friend living next door when I was a little boy. I always wanted one, but I had to settle for Uncle Robert's. Tell him I like monkeys, always have . . . There he is! Hello, monkey."

The little animal tugged off its hat and held it out.

"Bell? Van Dorn? You have any money?"

In the midst of the tumult, Isaac Bell smelled shoe polish again and this time he knew why. It had nothing to do with an eight-day stupor and everything to do with the memory of smelling an organ grinder's monkey on Elizabeth Street while he was disguised with black shoe polish in his hair. And he knew now what set off the memory: the zoo smell in Antonio Branco's room at Raven's Eyrie.

President Roosevelt dropped Joseph Van Dorn's coin into the monkey's hat and reached out to shake the organ grinder's hand. The bent and grizzled old man sprang to his full height, whipped open a knife, and thrust.

Isaac Bell stepped in front of Theodore Roosevelt.

BOOK IV
THE GANGSTER

"Isaac Bell doesn't know this river like I do."

45

Antonio Branco's stiletto pierced Isaac Bell's coat and jacket and vest, ripped through his shirt and stopped with a shrill clink of iron and steel.

"What?" gasped Antonio Branco.

"I borrowed your partner's chain mail," said Isaac Bell and hit the gangster with all his might.

Antonio Branco flew backwards into the crowd.

His arms shot in the air, his knife tumbled from his hand, his eyes glazed. Men pounced on the stunned gangster and wrestled him back on his feet.

"Well held," shouted Roosevelt. "Bring the scoundrel here."

They yanked him deeper into the crowd.

Isaac Bell was already plunging in after them, with Van Dorn right behind him.

The Black Hand formed a protective cordon and ran like a football flying wedge, with the heaviest men in the lead and Branco safe within. Laborers scattered out of their way. Those who tried to stop them were steamrollered to the ground.

Four more gorillas blocked Bell and Van Dorn in a maneuver as strategic as the flying wedge. The detectives pounded their way out of the slugfest, but by then Antonio Branco and his rescuers were far down the hill, running toward the railroad tracks.

Bell ran full speed after them. Van Dorn fell behind. He couldn't keep the younger man's pace, and Bell shouted over his shoulder that Eddie Edwards was watching Culp's train. "Cut straight to the yards. I'll stick with Branco."

Branco appeared to have recovered from Bell's punch. He was running under his own steam now, wing-footing, yet drawing ahead of his Black Hand guard. Suddenly, he veered away from the train yards, crossed the railroad tracks, and ran directly to the river.

His men stopped, turned around, and fanned out to face Isaac Bell.

The tall detective pulled his pistol and opened fire, dropped the two closest to him, and charged through the gap in their line. He did not waste ammunition on Branco, who was out of range and running so purposefully that Bell wondered whether J. B. Culp had managed to sneak his Franklin out of the estate right under the Van Dorn noses.

He reached the track embankment and climbed to the rails. From that slight elevation, he saw Branco had planned an emergency escape even faster than an auto or a train. The ice yacht *Daphne* waited at the riverbank. At the helm, the bulky figure of J. B. Culp urged him to run faster. Antonio Branco hurtled, slipping and sliding, down the final slope, with Isaac Bell drawing close.

The gangster fell, slid, rolled to his feet, and vaulted into the car beside Culp.

Culp flipped the mooring line he had looped around a bankside piling and sheeted in his sail. The tall triangle of canvas shivered. But *Daphne* did not move. Her iron runners had frozen to the ice.

Bell put on a burst of speed. He still had his gun in hand.

Culp scrambled out of the car and kicked the rudder and the right-hand runners, yelling frantically at Branco to free the runner on his side. Bell was less than fifty feet away when they broke loose.

"Push!" Bell heard Culp shout, and the two men shoved the ice yacht away from the bank. The wind stirred her masthead pennant. Her sail fluttered. One second, Branco and Culp were pushing the ice yacht; the next, they were running for their lives, trying to jump on before she sped away from them.

Bell was on the verge of trying to stop and plant his feet on the ice to take a desperate shot with the pistol before they got away. But as her sail grabbed the wind and she took off in earnest, he saw the mooring line dragging behind her. He ran harder and dived after it with his hand outstretched.

The end of the mooring line was jumping like a cobra. He caught it. A foot of rope burned through his hand before he could clamp around it. Then a gust slammed into the sail, and the rope nearly jerked his arm out of his shoulder, and, in the next instant, the big yacht was dragging him over the ice at thirty miles an hour. He flipped onto his back and stuffed his gun in his coat and then held on with both hands. He had hoped the extra weight would slow the yacht, but as long as the wind blew, she was simply too powerful. Now his only hope was to hang on for another quarter mile. The yacht was racing downriver. So long as Culp didn't change course, it was dragging Bell toward his own ice yacht, which he had tied

478

up near Cornwall Landing.

The mooring line was less than twenty feet long, and Bell heard Culp laugh. Branco was poised to cut the line. Culp stayed him with a gesture, pointed at a clump of ridged ice, and steered for it.

"Cheese grater coming up, Bell."

Daphne's runners rang on the ridges and an instant later Bell was dragged over the rough. He held tight as it banged his ribs and knees.

"Another?"

One more, thought Bell. He could see his boat now. Almost there, and Culp inadvertently steered closer, intent on aiming for an even higher ridge to shake him off when *Daphne* slammed over it. Bell let go, freely sliding, swinging his legs in front of him to take the impact with his boots, hit hard, sprang to his feet, and staggered to his boat.

"He's coming after us," said Branco.

"Let him."

Culp slammed his yacht skillfully into a deliberate crash turn. It spun her a hundred eighty degrees and put them on a course up the river, with the west wind abeam, the lightning-quick *Daphne*'s best point of sail.

"What went wrong back there?"

"I don't know," said Branco.

"Is that all you have to say for yourself?"

Branco was eerily calm and entirely in possession of himself. "I've lost a battle, not a war."

"What about me?"

"You've lost a dream, not your life."

"They will come after me," said Culp.

"Nothing can be pinned to you that would nail you." Branco reached inside his coat, and a stiletto gleamed in his hand. "But if you are afraid and are thinking of selling me out to save yourself, then you *will* lose your life. Take the pistol out of your coat by the barrel and hand it to me, butt first."

Culp was painfully aware that they were only two feet apart in the tiny cockpit and he had one hand encumbered by the tiller. At the speed they were moving, to release the tiller for even one second to try to block the stiletto could cause a catastrophic spinout. "If you kill me, who will outrun Bell?"

"That will be between Bell and me." He gestured imperiously with the blade.

Culp said, "I'll want it back if Bell gets closer. I'm sure I'm a better shot than you."

"I'm sure you are. I never bother with a gun," said Branco. *"Give it to me!"*

Culp saw no choice but to relent. Branco shoved it in his coat.

"Tell me where you are taking me."

"Option three, as I promised, is to sail you to the Albany rail yards. I have a special standing by. Or if you don't think it's safe, you can steal a ride on a freight train."

"How far?"

"At this rate, we'll make it in two hours."

Antonio Branco glanced over his shoulder. "Bell is closer."

"It will be dark soon," said Culp. "And Isaac Bell does not know this river like I do."

Isaac Bell's ice yacht raced up the Hudson River, vibrating sharply, tearing through patches of fresh snow, flopping hard when the runners banged over ice hummocks, and jumping watery cracks where the tide had lifted the ice. She was heavier than Culp's boat — built of white ash, instead of aluminum, and carrying lead ballasts Bell had strapped to the outsides of her runner plank to hold her down in the squall winds. Using the extra pounds and her oversize sail to advantage, he veered off course to increase velocity on a favorable beam wind, then glided back on course, with her extra weight sustaining momentum.

Bell thought it was strange that an experienced racer like Culp wasn't using the same tactic when he saw him catching up. If the magnate was trying to lure him into pistol range, he would get his wish.

By the time the speeding yachts had whipped past the lights of Newburgh, Bell had drawn within a hundred yards. He could see Branco and Culp in the cockpit, their faces white blurs as they looked over their shoulders to gauge his progress in the fading light.

Culp changed course abruptly.

Half a second later, Bell saw a horse right in front of him.

46

It was a tremendous plow horse, plodding in harness, and it reared in terror as Isaac Bell's sail bore down on it. Appearing so suddenly, at sixty miles an hour, and seen from a cockpit twelve inches above the ice, it looked as big as Culp's stuffed grizzly.

Isaac Bell yanked his tiller.

Culp had led him into the middle of an ice harvest. Men and horses were plowing grooves in the ice and cutting it into cakes to be stored for next summer. They had sawed open a wide patch of open water that gleamed black as coal.

Bell's boat skidded violently. Centrifugal force nearly flicked him out of the cockpit. The boat was sliding sideways, out of control, and headed straight at the black water. Ten feet from it, Bell's runners bit the ice again, his rudder responded, and he skittered the boat along the edge, dodged another horse and plow, and hurled himself back on course, his eyes locked on the tall white triangle of *Daphne*'s sail.

Another mile flashed by.

He caught the beam wind again and gained some more. When only forty yards separated the yachts, he locked a leg over the tiller, drew his automatic, braced it with both hands, and waited until the runners were humming steadily over a smooth patch. When he opened fire, he missed, but not by much, and it had the desired effect. Antonio Branco did not even flinch, but J. B. Culp ducked from the slugs whistling past his ears. He lost control and *Daphne* spun out, whirling in circles and dropping speed. Bell's boat passed her before he could untangle his leg and steer to a stop.

Culp recovered, caught the wind, and took off like a rocket.

Bell tore after him, closer than before. *You're not as bold as you think you are,* thought Bell. He saw Branco hand something to Culp. The next instant, flame lanced as Culp fired the pistol Branco had given him. Lead thudded into Bell's mast. A bullet whined close to his face.

Daphne's runners and rudder left the ice and she was suddenly airborne. An instant later, Bell hit what had launched her — a snowdrift ramped up by the wind and frozen solid. His boat flew, soaring high and far. It felt like she would fall backwards, but the lead weights strapped to her runner plank balanced her and she landed back on the ice, upright and racing ahead.

Before she crashed back down again, Bell glimpsed in the distance another ice harvest. They were finishing for the day. The men and horses were near shore, loading the cakes into an icehouse. All that remained where they had worked in the middle of the river was the open cut. Black water stretched the length of a football field.

Bell fired a shot to distract Culp and veered his yacht to build speed. When he had, and was racing parallel to *Daphne,* he suddenly changed course and drove straight at her. The sight of Bell's enormous sail suddenly flying at him unnerved J. B. Culp and he reflexively jerked his tiller to steer away before the yachts collided. The violent turn spun his in a circle.

She pinwheeled beyond his command — sliding and spinning on the slick surface — flew off the ice, and slammed into the black water. The impact of the abrupt stop from fifty miles an hour to zero snapped both legs of her double mast. Boom, yard, and sails crashed down on her runner plank, which was sinking quickly and already half submerged.

Isaac Bell skidded his yacht to a halt twenty feet from the abyss and dropped his sail. The masterminds of a national crime organization were his at last. Only drowning could save them from justice.

He ran to the brink with a rope in one hand and his gun in the other.

The sea tide had turned. Receding swiftly downstream in tandem with the Hudson's powerful current, it seized *Daphne*'s fallen rigging. The river filled her sail, as if with a watery wind, and dashed the shattered yacht against the solid ice at the edge of the cut.

Branco and Culp battled their way out of the tangle of rigging and canvas and tried to climb off. The current forced her bowsprit under the ice. A stump of her mast caught on the edge. The wreckage hung motionless for a heartbeat, then continued sliding under as it sank.

Isaac Bell threw his rope.

J. B. Culp caught it and clambered onto the ice shelf. Antonio Branco was right behind him, heaving himself toward safety even as the boat slid under. He planted one foot on solid ice, teetered backwards, and caught his balance by grabbing Culp's coat.

Bell dug in his heels, fighting to keep from sliding as he took the weight of both men.

The rope jerked in his hands. Through it, he could feel Culp gather his full strength. Suddenly, the magnate whirled about. His leg levered up like a placekicker's. His boot smashed into Branco's gut and threw him backwards into the water.

The expressions on Branco's mobile face flickered like a nickelodeon. Disbelief. Rage. Abject terror in the split second before the river sluiced him under the ice.

Isaac Bell leveled his gun at J. B. Culp, who was still holding the line the detective had thrown to him. "John Butler Culp, you are under arrest. Get on my boat and tie that rope around your ankles."

The tall, broad-shouldered patrician glanced disdainfully at Bell's gun. Then he pointed at the black water that had swallowed Antonio Branco.

"Evidence of your vague allegations against me is scanter than ever now. Besides, everyone saw Branco try to kill the President. They'll all agree that drowning was a well-deserved death for the dago gangster."

"But now I've got you for murder," said Isaac Bell. "Saw it with my own eyes. I'll bet, ten-to-one, that the judge and jury will agree on the electric chair for the *American* gangster."

Epilogue:
The Cartel Buster

One week later

The Van Dorn Detective Agency, Joe Petrosino's NYPD Italian Squad, Captain Mike Coligney's Tenderloin Precinct plainclothesmen, and the Treasury Department's Secret Service landed on Antonio Branco's suddenly leaderless bombers, extortionists, gorillas, counterfeiters, and smugglers like an army rolling up enemy flanks.

Isaac Bell listed the names of the arrested on the bull pen blackboard, which had been so hastily erased in the weeklong rush that his illustration for the Raven's Eyrie raid shone through as if it were under tracing paper. Gorillas were superimposed on Culp's gymnasium. Smugglers covered his gatehouse. Counterfeiters grouped on the power plant.

A cheer went up when Harry Warren and Archie Abbott telephoned good news at the end of the week. Vito Rizzo, whom Bell had arrested in the confessional, had jumped bail granted by a Tammany judge. Warren and Abbott had just hauled him out of a sewer pipe, which pretty much wrapped up the remains of Branco's organization.

"Harry should have looked there in the first place," said Walter Kisley.

"O.K., Helen," said Grady Forrer. "Now's the time. Give it to him."

The detectives gathered around Isaac Bell. Helen Mills handed him a narrow box. It was wrapped in tissue paper and tied with a dainty ribbon. Bell shook it. It rattled. "Sounds like diamonds. Right size for a necklace, but I don't tend to wear them."

"Open it up, Isaac!"

"The boys at Storm King found it."

Bell untied the ribbon, tore the tissue paper, and raised the lid. He could see that it had indeed been a necklace box. But inside, nestled in velvet, was a four-inch pocket knife.

"Branco dropped it on account of being punched hard," said Eddie Edwards.

"Turn it over, Isaac. Read the inscription."

They had attached a small silver plaque engraved with the words

PROPERTY OF
CARTEL-BUSTER BELL

489

"This calls for a drink!" shouted many Van Dorns.

"Champagne!" said Helen Mills. "I'm buying in the cellar bar."

The bull pen emptied in a flash.

Bell stayed there alone, opening and closing Antonio Branco's knife.

"It's time, Isaac."

A very sad looking Marion Morgan stood in the doorway in traveling clothes.

Bell took her bag and they hurried across 42nd Street to Grand Central and found her state room on the 20th Century Limited to Chicago, the first leg on her trip back to San Francisco. "I'm going to miss you terribly," she said.

"I don't think you will."

"How can you say that? Won't you miss me?"

"Not right away."

"Why are you grinning like a baboon?"

"I had an interesting talk with Mr. Van Dorn."

"Oh, Isaac! Did he make you Chief Investigator?"

"Not yet. But the Boss fears that some Black Hand could still be hanging about. So he has assigned you Van Dorn protection all the way to San Francisco. This inside door connects to your personal bodyguard's state room. If you're ever frightened, all you have to do is knock."

Bell stepped through the door and closed it behind him. The porter had already unpacked the bag and hung his suits he had sent ahead. A bottle of Billecart-Salmon Brut Rosé sat uncorked on a table in a sterling silver bucket.

Forty minutes later, as he was taking off his shirt, the 20th pulled into Croton-Harmon to exchange its electric city locomotive for a fast steamer. Bell heard a knock at the door. He opened it with growing anticipation. Marion had changed into the silk robe she had worn for him in her San Francisco cottage.

He wasted no time with words. He pulled Marion toward him and kissed her. Then he swept her into his arms and carried her into his bedroom.

ABOUT THE AUTHORS

Clive Cussler is the author or coauthor of more than fifty previous books in five best-selling series, including Dirk Pitt®, NUMA® Files, Oregon Files, Isaac Bell, and Fargo. His most recent *New York Times*−bestselling novels are *Piranha, The Assassin, The Solomon Curse,* and *The Pharaoh's Secret.* His nonfiction works include *Built for Adventure: The Classic Automobiles of Clive Cussler and Dirk Pitt*, plus *The Sea Hunters* and *The Sea Hunters II*; these describe the true adventures of the real NUMA, which, led by Cussler, searches for lost ships of historic significance. With his crew of volunteers, Cussler has discovered more than sixty ships, including the long-lost Confederate ship *Hunley*. He lives in Arizona.

Justin Scott's novels include *The Shipkiller* and *Normandie Triangle*; the Ben Abbott detective series; and modern sea thrillers published under the pen name Paul Garrison. The coauthor with Clive Cussler of seven previous Isaac Bell novels, he lives in Connecticut.

The employees of Thorndike Press hope you have enjoyed this Large Print book. All our Thorndike, Wheeler, and Kennebec Large Print titles are designed for easy reading, and all our books are made to last. Other Thorndike Press Large Print books are available at your library, through selected bookstores, or directly from us.

For information about titles, please call:
  (800) 223-1244

or visit our Web site at:
  http://gale.cengage.com/thorndike

To share your comments, please write:
  Publisher
  Thorndike Press
  10 Water St., Suite 310
  Waterville, ME 04901